Dani
teenag
– and actually read them all. Now she writes her own characters who clamour for attention in the midst of the chaos that is her life. Residing in the southern U.S. with a husband, two kids, two dogs, and one grumpy cat, she stays busy until she can closet herself away with her characters once more.

New York Times and *USA TODAY* bestselling author **Barbara Dunlop** has written more than forty novels for Mills & Boon, including the acclaimed CHICAGO SONS series for Mills & Boon Desire. Her sexy, light-hearted stories regularly hit bestsellers lists. Barbara is a three-time finalist for the Romance Writers of America's RITA award.

A typical Piscean, USA TODAY bestselling author **Yvonne Lindsay** has always preferred her imagination to the real world. Married to her blind-date hero and with two adult children, she spends her days crafting the stories of her heart, and in her spare time she can be found with her nose in a book reliving the power of love, or knitting socks and daydreaming.

Boardroom

COLLECTION

February 2018

March 2018

April 2018

May 2018

June 2018

July 2018

Scandal in the Boardroom

DANI WADE

BARBARA DUNLOP

YVONNE LINDSAY

MILLS & BOON

Published in Great Britain 2018
by Mills & Boon, an imprint of HarperCollins*Publishers*
1 London Bridge Street, London, SE1 9GF

ISBN: 978-0-263-93584-4

09-0318

MIX
Paper from
responsible sources
FSC™ C007454

This book is produced from independently certified FSC™ paper to ensure responsible forest management.

For more information visit: www.harpercollins.co.uk/green

Printed and bound in Spain
by CPI, Barcelona

HIS BY DESIGN

DANI WADE

For my fabulous editor,
Kathryn Lye

One

This was not how her morning was supposed to play out.

Ziara Divan rushed down the hallway of Eternity Designs, her brain pounding with the knowledge that she was late. Her cheeks burned as a result of her jog from the parking garage in workday pumps, and her suit skirt rode up the panty hose strangling her legs.

She threw her purse under her desk and grabbed her tablet from the drawer, turning it on as she continued down the hall with more speed than decorum. Rounding the corner into Vivian Creighton's outer office, Ziara ground to a halt. Vivian's assistant's desk was empty.

Breathe, Ziara. Pull yourself together.

She straightened her clothes in an attempt to regain her prized professional facade. But the agitated urgency to move, to get into the office quickly, still pounded in her chest. She wasn't perfect, but she made sure she came pretty dang close as an executive assistant in training, no matter how many minutes she spent stuck on a backed-up Georgia interstate.

As she struggled to regulate her breathing, Ziara heard

voices from beyond the door to the inner sanctum. At first, she couldn't grasp the idea that someone was yelling, because this was Vivian's office. Vivian didn't yell. It went totally against the traditional Southern rules of behavior for all ladies. But Vivian's voice was definitely raised. Ziara inched closer.

The other voice was male, deep. *Oh no.*

"…will not let you ruin my father's company…"

Sloan Creighton. Vivian's stepson. He came into the office rarely, but when he did he brought a tornadic level of energy and caused an unwanted tingle of awareness at the base of Ziara's spine. Though she studiously avoided him on his rare visits, he always seemed to find her. And flirt with her. And just generally turn her sense of professionalism upside down. The best reason to avoid him.

Vivian's own voice was muffled, but parts of Sloan's words came through the solid wood.

"…our biggest buyer rejected all the designs…"

Ziara's heart sank, threatening to drop out of her chest. Her knees went weak enough to force her to grab the frame of the door.

Ziara had suspected that last week's meeting with their largest retail account hadn't gone as planned, but the few who had attended were keeping quiet. Losing that buyer could mean ruin for Eternity Designs, something Ziara didn't want to see happen. She loved her job; this place, these people had also provided the stability and acceptance that had been lacking her entire life.

"…you have no choice…"

And neither did Ziara. She had to go through that door. Vivian had said to be in her office at eight sharp; it was now 8:17 a.m. But the thought of Sloan and the way his cool, effortless good looks and flirty attitude affected her body and her psyche made her want to return to the crowded freeway.

But backing down wasn't an option. With a deep breath to fortify herself, she headed through the doorway.

Sloan stood tall over Vivian, his voice ringing clear in the room. "I *will* have more voice in Eternity Designs, starting now. I'll need the next three months. If my fall line is a hit with our buyers, you will sign over enough of your shares for me to own fifty-five percent…and relinquish complete creative control. To. Me."

Ziara paused just inside the door, her mind absorbing those incredible words, while Sloan and Vivian glared at each other across Vivian's desk. For a moment Ziara's panic overrode everything, even the tempting sight of Sloan's strong shoulders and firm backside.

As the tension crept higher and higher, Ziara finally broke. Into the silence, she said, "Would you like me to come back, Vivian?"

Like pushing Play on a paused DVD, Vivian and Sloan both turned and looked in her direction. She met Vivian's eyes first, checking in with her boss and mentor. The narrowed glare and tight mouth signified a frustration that radiated like a cracked web through Vivian's normal composure. As if she realized how she must look, Vivian straightened, smoothing her elegant close-cropped curls into place. "Good morning, Ziara. Please sit."

"Now, Sloan," she said, turning her attention back to him. "Explain to me why I would ever agree to such ridiculous demands."

Sloan was too happy to comply. "Let me guess, commissions are down, creditors are closing accounts and you don't have a clue how to get yourself out of this situation." He straightened with confidence. "But I do."

"I'm sure I can find someone else to do the same."

"In enough time to make a difference? I don't think so."

She conceded to her stepson's ultimatum by leaning back in her chair, her composure shaken enough that she fiddled with the wedding band still gracing her left hand.

At least she didn't seem to notice—or care—that Ziara was late. Sloan, on the other hand, started cataloging everything about her. His gaze traveled down the length of her body to her toes, then back up with leisurely enjoyment.

Dragging her own composure around her like a cloak that

granted her invisibility, Ziara walked with measured steps across the carpeting to a chair beside Vivian's desk. A glance from under her lashes caught Sloan's interested stare zeroing in on the V of her suit jacket, where the modest edge of a lacy camisole peaked into view. With a great struggle, she forced herself not to adjust, to hold still while his eyes wandered back up to her vulnerable neck. The knowing smirk on his contoured lips sparked arousal beneath her irritation, confusing her further.

Damn man. She could see why Vivian found him so infuriating—professional behavior seemed to be a foreign concept to him. She'd seen the spark of interest before, though never quite this blatantly. Of course, his simple presence had always created an uncomfortable heat in her core that prompted her to keep any previous meetings as short and far apart as possible.

If she'd simply passed him on the street, Ziara would never have suspected him of the professional dedication he was displaying now. His collar-length, sun-streaked hair and the slight crook of his previously broken nose said "surfer boy" more than it did "hard-hitting negotiator." But the perfectly tailored dress shirt and pants, paired with his take-no-prisoners attitude, demonstrated the real man inside. His electric-blue eyes confirmed her suspicions that his core was pure steel.

She was thankful when he turned back to his stepmother. "This is my father's legacy we're talking about, Vivian. I save other people's businesses every day. Resurrecting Eternity Designs is right up my alley," he said.

"Yes," Vivian said, letting the word draw out. "Your...fix-it-up business."

"You could call it that. I call it the very lucrative process of taking failing companies and turning them into profit-making machines. Too bad you didn't get in touch with me sooner, but then you'd have to admit that you screwed up."

The slap of Vivian's hand on her desk made Ziara jump. She watched her with wide eyes, shocked by the venom scarring Vivian's normally genteel facade.

"Your father didn't trust you to take care of his legacy enough to leave it all to you. Why should I?"

Sloan stalked back and rested his hands on the desk, so he could loom over his stepmother. "And whose fault was that? Who slipped poisonous thoughts into his mind from day one, turning him against me so he could be yours and yours alone? Hell, Vivian, if I didn't know better, I'd think you set his whole will up. You're the one who made him insist I go for my MBA instead of continuing to pursue my own plans of fashion design, aren't you?"

"I don't know what you're talking about."

"Of course you do. After all, going from Daddy's assistant to his wife meant you got to control his entire life and not just his business, didn't it?"

Oh. Dear. Ziara's lungs shut down, trapping the air inside. Vivian's early involvement with Eternity Designs had never been explicitly discussed. Ziara had simply assumed she'd started working with the company sometime after she'd married Mr. Creighton.

The knowledge left Ziara reeling. How many times had Vivian admonished her that only tramps got involved with their coworkers? Ever since her childhood, when Ziara had been bullied because of her mother's lack of morals, she'd avoided anything that would suggest she was the same. Vivian's lessons had simply reinforced Ziara's focus on professionalism and the building of a flawless reputation.

Vivian's hand shook as she pointed at her stepson. "Don't talk to me that way, Sloan. It's disrespectful. Your father would never approve of your tone."

Sloan leaned in, hard. "Well, he's not here to reprimand me. If you wanted my respect, you should have tried earning it a long time ago. Now it's too late."

"It's never too late to expect you to be a gentleman. But we just couldn't get those lessons to stick."

Sloan laughed, collapsing into the chair as his body shook with a tainted kind of humor. Ziara felt like she was watching a tennis match. Sloan clearly thought he was the winner.

Vivian conceded with less graciousness than Ziara had ever seen her display, but then again, she'd learned quite a few new things about her mentor in the past ten minutes. Vivian hadn't always been a lady. Disbelief still ricocheted throughout Ziara like the ball inside a pinball machine.

"Fine, Sloan. Do whatever it is you do," Vivian forced out through clenched teeth.

"I'll have that in writing, I think," Sloan said.

"As demanding as you are, I'm amazed anyone will work with you."

"Oh, I'll manage," he said with a cocky quirk of his shapely lips.

"Not alone, you won't. The last thing I need is you wandering around unattended."

"Aw, Vivian. I didn't know you cared. Oh wait, you don't," Sloan said with saccharin sweetness.

"I care about Eternity Designs," she said.

His gaze scanned Vivian's face as if to determine the catch. "Anyone you saddle me with better know what they're doing and how to take orders."

"Oh, I have no doubt she'll work like a charm…and be able to keep you in line."

Ziara's heart picked up speed when Vivian's elegant, bejeweled fingers waved in her direction. *No. No, no, no.* The effort to hide her sudden panic and appear in control might just give her a heart attack.

Vivian's voice trickled through her consciousness, breaking her inward focus. "Your history with assistants is well-known, Sloan. They crawl all over you like bees in honey. That won't be an issue with Ziara. I've trained her well. She knows more about how we conduct business here than anyone except my own assistant. And her behavior is impeccable—unlike yours."

What was she—a slave girl at auction? *Would the buyer prefer pretty and pliable or plain but talented?* Though dependable was exactly the look she was going for, the thought still disconcerted her.

"Well, Vivian, isn't that thoughtful of you?" he said.

Ziara glanced up to find Sloan's gaze directed her way. His earlier anger had turned his bright blue eyes icily sharp, his body rigid, his jaw tight. But now he eased back in a chair, propping his elbows on the arms. His fingers absently stroked the upper ridge of his lip, drawing her attention to the sensuous curve of his mouth. His turbulent look suddenly softened like ice thawing beneath a heat lamp.

Her emotions seesawed as his gaze traveled south, visually caressing the extra length of leg exposed by her hasty drop into her chair. She could almost feel his touch sliding along the edge of her skirt, tickling the sensitive skin on the backs of her legs.

Bit by bit, Ziara used up her willpower forcing herself to sit impassively. The twitch of her thighs urged her to shift her feet, but she resisted. That would tell him just how much he affected her. Tightening her muscles, she tried to crack down on the spreading fire, to no avail. Ignoring physical desire had never been a problem before him.

Her new boss.

Her soothingly subtle gray business suit, so comfortable in the luxurious air-conditioning only moments ago, now felt heavy, itchy. Her nipples peaked against their confinement. She felt that he peered through her professional armor to the woman she kept hidden deep inside.

How could a simple look make her so aware, too aware? As if she lacked something only he could provide.

As casually as possible, she adjusted her position and her skirt, covering her legs down past her knees.

Knowledge leaked into his eyes, as well as smug satisfaction. *He did that on purpose.* Feeling a need to defend herself, she met him with a flick of her lashes. Slowly she lifted her left brow.

He grinned, not at all intimidated by her challenge. "Be in my office and ready to work first thing tomorrow morning."

She could handle his antagonistic, dismissive tone; she welcomed it to counteract her strange reaction to him. Unlike efficient orders and professional expectations, the sensations created with that hot, hard stare set her nerves on edge.

But she could handle it. She'd pulled herself up from a sludge-pile existence and become a woman with goals and dreams and skills. She could control herself for the three months it would take to get Eternity Designs back in the spotlight and earn her stripes as an executive assistant. But how was she going to control him?

Ziara. Her classic beauty and calm demeanor distracted Sloan from Vivian's condescension. Staring his new assistant down made him hotter than he'd been in a long time. Vivian's insistence that Ziara wouldn't follow the path of his previous assistants didn't worry him. As annoying as it had been to replace three employees in less than two years because they insisted they were *in love* with him, he might have to pursue this woman. Her pretend lack of interest challenged him, but turning Ziara's head could provide plenty of ammunition in his war with Vivian.

How ironic that the very thing he'd avoided in his professional life—intimate involvement with an employee—could give him a leg up in this situation. It felt wrong even thinking that way, but winning her loyalty could give him the freedom to do whatever he wanted without Vivian's interference. He needed every advantage to fight against Vivian. His stepmother was totally immune to his charm, which drew cheeky toddlers, blue-haired dames and women of every age in between. If Vivian had been a typical trophy wife, at least Sloan could have fallen back on his practiced grin and genuine appreciation of the female species, but, instead, dear old Dad had the foresight to marry a savvy woman. One steeped in Southern tradition and brimming with a Southern belle's ingenuity to survive. Too bad her temperament had always favored Scarlett's machinations as opposed to Melanie's sweetness.

She viewed his father's memory and Eternity Designs as hers; Sloan was a threat to her reign as queen. His frustration had been building over this situation for years and he let it out for once.

"We need to shake things up," he said. "We can't afford to

lose our biggest account because we're afraid to break out of the mold. Reliance on tradition is getting you nowhere. Eternity Designs needs a modern edge, a new designer, a revamped portfolio. Pronto."

That was exactly what Vivian didn't want to hear. "Your father prided himself on the tradition inherent in this company and its designs," she said, elegantly restrained anger sharpening her tone. "This discussion demonstrates exactly why he chose me to continue the legacy of Eternity Designs."

Not you.

The wedding gown design firm had been in his family for three generations—if his current 40 percent share of it counted for anything. With Vivian, it didn't. But the words of the accountant told him now was the time to insist on the control she'd denied him for so long.

"The whole company will go under if something isn't done immediately."

"Sixty percent ownership doesn't mean you're God," he said, ignoring the burn of betrayal. "It's a good thing dear ol' Dad isn't alive to see how you've run it into the ground." Yep. Payback was a bitch.

A quick glance revealed Ziara stiffening, in surprise or defense he wasn't sure. If she knew what the posture did for her magnificent breasts, she'd hunch in on herself for eternity. He paced back and forth in front of Vivian's desk, arousal and frustration fueling his restlessness. The business expert in him was tired of talking.

The man in him begged for a totally different kind of action.

Watching Ziara's reactions to his and Vivian's little fight fascinated him more than he would have thought. Her exotic, raven-haired beauty brought to mind sensual, spice-scented nights. What would she look like with that thick bun let loose around her shoulders? With that suit jacket loosened up a few buttons? Seducing her out of her loyalty to Vivian was going to be such guilty fun.

He'd avoided getting involved with his employees like a contagious disease, to the point that he hadn't even had an assistant for six months. But his desperation called for outrageous actions—like storming into Vivian's office this morning. Finding out Ziara had given up company loyalty for carnal indulgence would probably mean a quick dismissal, but he couldn't let that stop him. For Ziara this was a job; she'd find another one soon enough.

For Sloan, Eternity Designs was a legacy.

Vivian's haughty belle persona reappeared. "You're awfully sure of yourself, Sloan. Overconfidence leads to nasty downfalls. Those unconventional methods of yours won't work in such a traditional company."

"Those unconventional methods are just what Eternity needs. Less tradition, not more." He turned to Ziara. Might as well put her to the test first thing. "What do you think? Is Eternity's current path leading to success?"

"I…I…" Her almond-shaped eyes flicked back and forth between him and her mentor, panic darkening their chocolate color. After a moment she said, "Our designers do beautiful work, enough to build a loyal following. Families come here generation after generation to commission their dresses. Our motto, our focus has built a legacy. I have no proof otherwise."

Test number one: fail.

Vivian echoed Ziara's words. "Eternity Designs is truly *where tradition and style forever align*."

Quoting the company's motto as a defense ramped up Sloan's anger. He needed to save this business. His father had worked hard to build it. He'd loved it just as Sloan did. Despite their differences at the time of his death, the 40 percent he'd gifted to Sloan in his will told him his father had wanted him to have some small part of his family's heritage. He had to believe that, had to believe Vivian hadn't poisoned every ounce of their father-son bond.

He glared at them both. "Maybe our motto needs to change."

Ziara held very still, the only movement the frantic pulse beating at the base of that silky throat. But Vivian sighed heavily, with a touch of drama. She would have called it flair. He knew he wouldn't like what came next.

"I've been thinking about options to get us through this little slump. I have a few friends who might know potential backers. That should tide us over until spring."

Shock immobilized Sloan for a moment. Then a sharp spike of panic sliced through the numbness. Then another…and another. "We're not letting an outsider buy into this company."

"I'll do what I have to in order to save Eternity."

"Except call in the one man whose skills would provide the lifeline? Did you honestly think I'd sit back, mouth shut, while you let Eternity go out of the family?" He straightened, the hardball negotiator stepping onto the court. "You know me better than that, Vivian."

With a blink, uncertainty leaked into Vivian's eyes. "I truly don't understand why you'd care."

He shook his head slowly, sorrow over the state of his relationship with his late father leaking underneath the anger. "That right there proves how little you know me…or knew my father. This place was his life—" in the end more than even his son "—I want nothing more than for his life's work to continue, to prove to his memory I'm more than you made me out to be. A hard worker, capable of contributing to the family dream, instead of a slacker who cares about nothing but myself. You're still looking at me as a grieving kid, Vivian. Not the man I've actually become, the man my father saw in me before he died."

But the tightening around her mouth told him she'd never see it that way. After years of convincing her husband that his only son was impulsive and undependable, repeatedly citing his teenage antics, his father had left *her* with the majority ownership of Eternity Designs. That's all she cared about.

"Sloan, I would prefer to keep this inside family lines, such as they are. So I'll stand by my word and give you a chance. But in the meantime, I'll be working on a backup plan."

It wasn't much of a compromise, as they went, but he'd take what he could get. He needed carte blanche over the fall line. Because if Vivian knew the plans gathering mass in his mind, she'd shut him down in a heartbeat.

Her mouth pulled into a strained smile. "Just don't go forgetting who is in charge around here."

"I won't. We'll pretend you're in charge while I become the linchpin holding everything together."

It was a low blow, but he was beyond caring. Vivian straightened, her shoulders squaring as the pinching around her mouth deepened. Then a calculating look slid across her face, warning him he was about to pay for his disrespect.

"I have a caveat of my own. If you should happen to walk away before the fall line is presented—" her tone said she could happily run him off with a shotgun "—then Eternity Designs will become solely mine."

Two

Nothing like a new challenge and a gorgeous woman to work with.

Sloan listened to Ziara's movements in the outer office as he sat at his desk. He'd wondered whether she'd postpone coming in until the last minute, but here she was thirty minutes early, moving into her new office.

Yesterday she'd both confounded and fascinated him. Her exotic, Indian beauty stirred many un-bosslike urges. Her attempts to keep that beauty under wraps teased his senses. Did she think pulling her luxurious dark hair tight into a bun and covering those shapely legs made her a better employee? It probably did in Vivian's eyes, but Sloan was a whole other matter.

Something she'd learn soon enough, and hopefully enjoy. Though he'd never seduced any of his employees—he spent more time running from than running after—he wasn't above using this mutual attraction as one more tool to secure control of Eternity Designs. He would need her help to understand how things worked around here, to facilitate his relationships with the other employees after being shut out in the cold since his father's death. If tempting her loyalty in his direction meant the reports to Vivian became fewer and further between, or even stopped, all the better.

Crossing the room with a heightened sense of anticipation, he eased through without alerting her to his entrance. She stood behind the desk, the chair pushed aside to give her room to reallocate her personal stuff. Her movements were elegant but efficient as she placed pens and papers in the desk drawers. Her careful concentration told him she had a precise way she wanted things and she'd find a way to create order in this new space.

He barely held back laughter as he sized her up. He was a red-blooded male and his body naturally heated despite her choice of clothes. She'd opted for a longer skirt and boxier jacket, as if that would hide the curvy shape of her hips and ass. But it was the scarf he found most amusing. From the back, he could see the curl of material around her neck. Did it merely cover her throat in the front, or had she gone all out to hide every single hint of bare skin, tucking the ends into her jacket?

Didn't she realize that *don't touch me* attitude set her up as his own personal challenge?

"Settling in okay?" he asked.

Her jerk of surprise should have made him feel guilty, but he suspected he had to sneak up on this one before she cut him off at the knees with her stern librarian attitude.

"Yes," she said. "I'm almost ready."

"No hurry," he murmured, tracking the glide of her fingers over a few pictures. No people that he could see, just atmospheric photographs of simple wooden bridges, each in a different season. She arranged them carefully along the top of the nearby shelf, then reached into the remaining cardboard box once more.

Pulling out an object wrapped in cotton batting, she uncovered it layer by layer. She steadily revealed a glass object inscribed with words that she rubbed over a few times with the wrapping.

Too quick for her to stop him, he lifted the object from her hands for a closer look. "What's this?" he asked.

"Be careful."

"Ziara, you wound me," he said with a cheesy helping of drama. "I promise not to drop it."

The cut-glass award was shaped in the outline of a flowing gown, inscribed with the date and Employee of the Year. Ziara Divan. "Employee of the Year, huh?"

"I've worked hard to get where I am."

"And where is that exactly?"

"If all goes well, I'll be promoted to Vivian's personal assistant when Abigail retires next spring."

"Wow, a full-fledged executive assistant at the tender age of—"

She drew a deep breath, as if he were a toddler trying her patience. "Twenty-seven."

"So young to be so buttoned-down." He aimed a pointed look at her scarf, which did indeed drape down to cover that delectable collarbone and upper chest.

"There are worse things to be."

"Like what?"

For a moment it looked like she would speak, but then those full lips pressed tight. Her hand extended, palm up, and her perfectly manicured fingertips curled in a *give it to me* gesture. "Behave, please."

He stepped closer, moving past her invisible *keep away* signs. "Let's get something straight here, Ziara. You're playing by my rules now. I'd imagine I have seriously different requirements for becoming *Employee of the Year.*"

She swallowed hard. "Excuse me?"

She reached for the award, moving her body even closer to him, and he used the opportunity to snag an edge of the scarf. Luckily for him, it was only loosely twisted and unraveled like a dream from around her neck and into his hands.

Award forgotten, her hands clamped to her bare neckline, then she glared at him. "What do you think you're doing?"

"A little employee training." He rubbed the material between his fingers but resisted the urge to lift it to his nose and find out if it smelled like her. Vanilla and cinnamon spice. "I'm not nearly as stuffy as Vivian. I don't run my office that way."

"Mr. Creighton—"

"Uh-uh. Sloan."

He was surprised she could talk through teeth that tightly clenched. "Sloan, your behavior is inappropriate in the extreme."

"Is it? Are you going to charge me with sexual harassment?"

That cool eyebrow lifted in condemnation. "If I have to."

Her response was so unexpected, he almost choked. Man, he sure enjoyed a woman with spice, but she didn't need to know that. Yet. "Oh, I don't think you will."

She opened her mouth, but he continued on. "I know Vivian gave you this job for a reason." He leaned even closer to her, watching her heartbeat speed up in the well of her collarbone. "And not just because you're organized and can turn in paperwork on time. After all, she knows something about assistants and their access to—how can I say this diplomatically—company secrets."

Not even an attempt at a response this time.

He pushed a little harder. "Isn't that right, Vivian's little spy?"

"That's insulting."

But she didn't look insulted. The waver of her gaze and uncertain look meant one thing: guilt. "There's no point in pretending, Ziara. Vivian put you here to keep an eye on me, and report back everything she needs—or doesn't need—to know. But that's okay."

Her eyes jerked back to his, widening to give him a great view of chocolate irises shot with gold sparks.

"Just remember," he said, "forewarned is forearmed."

For long seconds neither of them moved, gazes locked in either a worthy battle or forbidden attraction, he wasn't sure. All he felt was the blood pumping hard in his veins and an excitement he hadn't brought to a job in many, many years.

With shaking hands she finally pulled the award from his

grasp and turned to place it on the corner of her desk. Then, she pulled out a thick folder from a drawer of the filing cabinet. "Here is information on the current preparations for the fall line. I thought—"

He lifted the file from her unsteady hands, resentment that he had to rely on her for information mixing with the other emotions roiling through him. "What do we have here?"

She managed to maintain an outward calm. Almost. "Actually, I thought you might like me to familiarize myself with the project *you're here for.*"

Her eyes begged, a moment of peace, but he wasn't in the mood for mercy. "Let's take this discussion into my office."

A spy, he'd said. She'd never really thought about it that way.

How had she been promoted from executive assistant in training to spy in one morning? Proving herself to Vivian had been a long-held goal, but doing it now could put her in a very awkward position.

One last glance at her Employee of the Year award stilled her spinning universe. Looking at it, her uneasiness and frustration melted away and her resolve strengthened.

This is what I want. I'm almost there. Becoming executive assistant to the CEO of a major design firm had been her goal from her first day at Eternity Designs. At twenty-seven, the finish line loomed much closer than she'd dared to hope, despite the lack of money for anything other than a trade school degree.

She'd grown up with nothing—no, less than nothing. Oh, they'd technically had enough to live on, but every spare cent had gone for slutty clothes and accessories for her mother to attract the newer, better sugar daddy around the corner.

She'd dreamed of escaping from the trash that still stained her heart into her own office situated right outside of her role model Vivian Creighton's. But would the price be worth this sacrifice?

Vivian and Sloan are playing a game and I'm stuck in the middle.

Ziara was smart enough to realize it. Her firm loyalty to

Vivian notwithstanding, her choices from here on out had to be dedicated to what was best for Eternity Designs. That was her only guarantee of keeping a clear conscience.

Vivian had given her a long lecture on all things Sloan yesterday afternoon. *He's not to be trusted. Why wouldn't his father have just given him the business if he wanted him to run it? He's up to something, I know it.* Ziara had questions of her own, concerns about a man who spent his life reviving companies but completely ignored his family heritage until it was almost too late. If Sloan truly sought to ruin the company, as Vivian had also suggested…well, she wasn't about to let him put anything over on her.

She'd just watch closely and learn to deal with him. She'd always been a stellar student. If she hesitated before crossing the threshold into his office, it didn't mean anything. Drawing in a deep breath, she straightened her shoulders. A little over three months and her training period would be complete. This was simply a small bump on a long road.

She pushed the dilemmas from her mind and entered the room.

Sloan had chosen a corner office at the opposite end of the building from Vivian's, his windows overlooking the sidewalk and shops that lined the streets in this part of town. Quaint, with a touch of subdued elegance, Ziara had always thought, and easily accessible through a MARTA stop only a few blocks away.

Instead of the soothing cream carpet prevalent in the rest of the offices, the flooring here had been replaced with dark wood planks. A desk just a shade or two darker dominated one corner, facing out so that Sloan could see the entire room, from the door to the floor-to-ceiling windows. He crossed the thick blue-and-burgundy rug to stand before them now, hands in his pockets, looking down from the fifth-story view.

For long moments he remained silhouetted against the lightened windows. His strong shoulders spoke of strength and shelter. The line tapered down to his waist, where his hands in his pockets drew the material of his dress pants across the high, firm cheeks of his backside.

Ziara shook her head slightly, grateful he couldn't see her. Being close to this overwhelmingly masculine presence on a daily basis had the potential to open up a whole host of dark desires she preferred to keep locked deep inside. Choosing a leather chair a safe distance away, she sat, primly crossing her legs at the ankles. She held herself rigid as she prepared to take notes, make phone calls, whatever he wanted of her.

"Did you know this was once my father's office?"

Surprise skittered through Ziara's controlled pose. "No," she murmured.

"I used to play right here on a rug while he worked," Sloan said. "I used to watch him stare out these same windows, while he worked out problems."

His voice was easy, soft with memory. He started to pace, firm steps along the length of the windows. Two glorious views. Candy for her sweet-starved eyes.

But warning lights started flashing through her brain as she thought about his words. She'd never had any type of loving parental relationships, and had cut all ties with her mother at the age of seventeen. But Sloan seemed to feel very passionately about his father, despite Vivian's insistence that Mr. Creighton had found his son a huge disappointment. Why had Sloan—

No. Thinking about Sloan's private life—his childhood, wishes, regrets—could not lead to anything good. Personalizing him outside of their business interactions would weaken her objectivity. She had to focus on work, not skipping through fantasyland.

After a minute or two, he clasped his hands behind his back, his long fingers tapping against his palms. "First things first," he murmured. "Where to start—"

"I've got a list here from Mrs. Creighton, and—"

His laughter echoed through the room, the sound truly amused rather than the nasty version she'd heard in Vivian's office. He paused in his imaginary trek to catch his breath and clutched his chest in mock astonishment. "Surely you jest. I don't think so, sweetheart. We'll be doing this my way."

Well, that's reassuring. Ziara had a feeling she was about to get a lesson in all things Sloan—and it would turn everything she'd planned for on its ear. She pulled out her handy-dandy tablet to take notes, since that seemed to be her only function here.

"We'll need new ideas, new designs, definitely a new designer," he said, his voice so matter-of-fact that she blinked for a moment, unable to handle the transition from sexy hunk to demanding boss that quickly. But she managed to pull herself together.

Then his words truly registered. Yikes! A new designer definitely would not go over well.

Sloan continued. "Something splashy. Something to draw in big buyers, get people talking, get them curious…"

He dropped into the chair behind his desk. "Presenting the line, one buyer at a time in the studio, is standard fare. We need a fireworks show, not a firecracker…I've got it!" Sloan jerked to his feet, palms slapping on his desk with enough force to startle her. "We'll bring fashion week right here to Atlanta, Georgia. We'll put on a fashion show." He started to pace, throwing ideas out with such enthusiasm that she found herself pulled into the spirit without even realizing it. Before she knew it, he had location ideas, preshow party ideas, guest list suggestions, and on and on until he ran out of steam about an hour later.

Ziara's fingers ached from typing so fast; even she had to concede to Sloan's intelligence. Once he latched onto an idea, he thought through every angle—catch, plus and minus. Very impressive. If he truly had plans to destroy Eternity Designs, he was going about it the wrong way.

Glancing up in the sudden silence, she found Sloan staring directly at her. She should have been alarmed, afraid of what he might see, but she had sunk so deeply under the spell of his voice that she merely floated.

His eyes widened at whatever he saw in her own, then

flashed with a heat that echoed deep inside her core. The connection remained taut for long moments as the heat gained momentum like a house afire.

Only when it threatened to burst out of control did Ziara panic. She bent her head to focus on the tablet still sitting in her lap. Though she felt hot enough for her fingers to burn it, the tablet was miraculously unsinged.

A new kind of heat enveloped her—embarrassment. As Sloan approached, her teeth worried her lower lip. Would he say something? Think she'd changed her mind about him? Think that she was silently asking him to come on to her? With her limited experience, she wasn't even sure what kind of message she'd just sent. As her imagination picked up speed, Sloan paused a few steps away.

Then he continued around his desk and sat with a squeak of leather. Out of the corner of her eye, she saw his elbows settle onto the arms of the chair as if familiar with the pose, his fingers forming a peak with his fingertips. Relief swept through her, a cooling breeze, though it couldn't extinguish the fire altogether. She chose to ignore it.

"So we'll be putting on a fall fashion show this year. You'll need to book the venue and start construction on the backdrop. Some plans can't be finalized until closer to the actual date, but pick out invitations, contact the modeling agency so we can line up models, all that stuff."

He leaned forward, his gaze seeing into the distance. "My focus will be on finding the right designer to carry out my ideas."

That was a discussion she'd prefer to postpone for, oh, forever. A new designer would shake the foundations of Eternity, regardless of how wonderful he was.

"And what would those ideas be?" she asked, poised to type. How was she going to tell Vivian all of this? Ziara was excited by some of the plans, but change was definitely not Vivian's forte.

Sloan grinned, resorting to his ample sex appeal in the blink of an eye. "Uh-uh. I'm not giving it up that easily."

Their eyes met and held. In the aftermath of their earlier connection, his bright blue gaze unnerved her more than ever. Not only did it threaten her internal control, it made her want to clamp the top of her jacket closed to hide every hint of cleavage. She pressed her thighs together in a purely feminine gesture of defense.

Slowly he rose and circled the desk, leaning his hips against the front. The angle allowed him to tower over her, while inadvertently giving her a level view of—

No, she wouldn't look. Her fight-or-flight instincts kicked in with a rush. She needed a few moments away from this man's disturbing sensuality. Heck, a few hours would be better. Rising to her feet, she said, "If that's all, I'll start—"

"Ziara."

Her fingers fiddled with her tablet while her gaze examined the polished floorboards.

"I expect hard work out of all my employees. I don't think that will be a problem with you. But trust…trust has to be earned, doesn't it?"

The guilt burned deep inside, because she knew she'd have to tell what she'd learned to Vivian—sooner rather than later. But it was her strong work ethic that just might tear her in two. Her dedication demanded she do what was right for Eternity Designs; her loyalty demanded she do anything Vivian asked of her.

"Though hiring and firing is Vivian's department for now," he continued, his voice deceptively benign, "be aware you wouldn't be in this office if I didn't want you to be." He stopped an arm's length from her, bringing the icy heat of his gaze closer, stinging her conscience. "You have your own reasons for being loyal to Vivian."

She heard the implied question behind his statement. She swallowed, the urge to speak unnerving. How could she describe all Vivian had done for her, the hands-on coaching and molding of her abilities? She opted for short and sweet.

"Vivian saw my willingness to do a job right, even as a simple secretary. To uphold the ideals of this company."

"Where tradition and style forever align," Sloan murmured.

A slight smile tugged her lips. Her chin lifted. She knew her intentions here were right, no matter what anyone else thought. Pride in her hard work, in pulling herself up from the bottom rung of the ladder, refused to let him condemn her loyalties. "Yes."

Sloan stepped even closer. The urge to retreat exploded in her belly. Her muscles jumped to high alert, tightening in preparation for flight.

"I, too, value hard work, initiative and loyalty." He paused, as if choosing his words carefully. "Just don't forget who you work for now."

The pressure of his stare proved too much with Vivian's expectations still flashing neon in Ziara's brain. Her gaze fell, grazing his fit body to the tips of his Gucci dress shoes. A short nod was all she could manage.

She wasn't likely to forget anything about Sloan.

Still, the need to push back rose. "Wanting to uphold the values of this company isn't a bad thing. After all, it is the way your father wanted this business run." She ignored the twinge of her conscience. The truth hurt. This time, she leaned closer to him. "People other than you are allowed to care about this place, you know."

Something flashed across his face that she couldn't quite read, but it encouraged her to push harder. Not for Vivian. Not for her job. For Eternity Designs. "If you would just tell me what you're trying to do here instead of leaving me in the dark, then maybe I could help."

He met her halfway, crowding into her personal space with a sexy grin. "You'll have to try harder than that to access my… secrets."

Three

Sloan took a deep breath and wrestled with his libido for a moment before managing to lock it down. How could the simple sounds of Ziara at her desk turn him into a dirty old man? Well, not quite old, if the level of urgency he felt was anything to go by.

They had a long day ahead—he was pretty sure she was going to hate him by the time he was done, but as the saying went, he had to get rid of the old to make room for the new.

He would need Ziara's help to carry out his plans without permanent damage. Robert and Anthony were indeed good designers, but designers who needed a serious shake-up. Vivian had offered Ziara for her expertise and he planned to conquer a large portion of his new territory today.

After a moment of silence, Ziara peeked around the door. "Do you need me for anything this morning, Mr. Creighton?"

Oh, honey, I need you for something really bad. Even though it was totally inappropriate, he couldn't tame the thought. Once again Ziara was wrapped in a narrow skirt and suit jacket, although this one was a dark chocolate-brown that complemented her eyes, bringing out the golden flecks with a glimpse of a silky gold camisole. A little better, though seeing her abundant hair pinned to the nape of her neck just made his hands itch to let it all loose.

He shifted in his seat. "I've got a full agenda today. Where do we stand so far?"

Ziara's efficiency impressed him. Not only had she started contacting people and places yesterday, she'd made a detailed list of the facts so he could compare easily and make decisions.

Old business out of the way, he straightened his shoulders, preparing to face the hardest part of the day. "Let's take a trip down to the design floor and see what's what with the Old Brigade."

The *Old Brigade* was the employees' term for the two main designers who headed and vetted all the dress designs for the company. Though by no means original, they'd each been with the company for over fifteen years.

Ziara hesitated, frozen for a moment like a deer caught in headlights at dusk; then she gathered her tablet and smoothed down her skirt.

He let her maintain her silence as they crossed into the hall, but he couldn't afford for her to hold back. Everything might as well be out in the open.

He stopped in the middle of the deserted hallway. "Look, Ziara," he said, turning to face her. "One of the reasons you're here is to help me with intercompany relations, schedules, procedures, et cetera. Right?"

"Yes, Mr. Creighton."

The prim purse of her full mouth had his brows rising, a grin tugging at his lips. "Didn't we decide on Sloan? After all, over the next three months, we're going to be spending a helluva lot of time together."

Her lips tightened a touch more before she conceded. "Yes, Sloan."

Teasing her out of that "strictly business" attitude was way too much fun. "Now, I can't do my job if you don't do your job—"

A weighty protest formed in her eyes, though her face remained calm. This woman's responses werc seriously under wraps. He had to look very closely to catch the signals, but they told him some genuinely hot emotions hid beneath the surface. "Don't get me wrong, you've been very helpful. But I need an honest rundown of what I'm facing on the design floor today."

"I—I—"

"Honesty. Right now. Got it?"

"Why do you need my opinion? You said you'd been here often as a child."

"And as a child I noticed the person most important to me—my father, and the place I spent the most time—his office. The rest? Not so much. I haven't set foot on the design floor since I was ten."

Her gaze zeroed in on his face for a moment, then she spoke. "Anthony and Robert are very talented designers."

Keeping his irritation from showing proved a little easier beneath her disapproving glare.

"The trouble will come from Robert—he's ruled the design floor through talent and overpowering personality for years. Anthony's a sweetheart, but don't take his lack of attitude for subservience. He's soaking it all in, processing it in his own time and making his own decisions."

He grinned. "That wasn't so bad, was it?"

The low growl from her throat surprised him, sending a shock of sensation right where he didn't need it. *Keep it light. Best to just move on.* "Let's go." But he was getting a really good idea how to provoke her into an honest response.

Just irritate her beyond measure.

The elevator took them down to the third floor and they stepped out onto the observation deck. The design department occupied most of the second floor, but the large exhibition space below could be viewed and accessed from the open walkway they now occupied.

As he and Ziara made their way down the spiral staircase, Ziara's heels clicking on the metal steps, the designers appeared to be gearing up for the day.

"Ziara," Robert exclaimed as she descended the last two steps. "What brings you to our little kingdom?"

Anthony simply smiled and wrapped her in a half hug. Her smile was natural and easy, but she didn't return the touch. *Interesting.*

"I wanted to introduce y'all to Mrs. Creighton's stepson, Sloan Creighton."

The designers exchanged a look, but it didn't display as much alarm as Sloan had anticipated. Nor resignation, either. His Spidey senses started to tingle.

"Yes, yes," Robert said, leading the way by offering his hand. "I believe I remember James mentioning you to us, *Dieu ait son âme.*"

God rest his soul, indeed. Out of the corner of his eye, Sloan could see Ziara glance his way. Since it was obvious from their benign reception that neither designer had a clue what was coming down the pike, Sloan decided to play along.

"Vivian tells me you two are working on the fall line. I'd love to see the best of Eternity's upcoming designs," he said, ignoring Ziara's sudden stare.

The men were only too happy to show off. Too bad they didn't realize they were arming him to take them both down. They exchanged excited glances, then walked toward the display boards in unison.

Sloan stepped closer to Ziara as they followed. "Just relax and follow my lead," he murmured from the corner of his mouth.

After listening to Robert expound on the sketches for over half an hour, Sloan was definitely unimpressed. Just as he imagined their buyer had been.

When Robert finally wound down, Sloan's voice filled the stillness. "Did you listen to anything that buyer said?"

The men stiffened, but there wasn't anything they could say in their own defense.

Sloan pushed forward. "She said the designs were stale. She said the dresses were old-fashioned. Not classic. Not retro. Those are buzz words. Compliments. Stale is not." He gestured toward the stack of drawings. "Nothing has changed here. Nothing. I can find this same thing in any bridal magazine—from ten years ago."

"How would you know what the buyer said?" Anthony asked, his voice sounding weak after the booming quality of Robert's.

"And who do you think you are, to come in here and criticize our work?" Robert added.

"I am now the creative director of Eternity Designs's fall line. From here on out, all decisions from this department must be approved solely by me."

The silence was so absolute it rang loud in his ears. Robert's face gradually turned a shade of purple and Anthony's eyes flicked back and forth between the other people in the room as if he expected someone to tell him what was really going on here.

Finally Robert spoke, his voice coming from deep in his barreled chest. "Ziara, if this is a joke, it isn't funny."

"He isn't kidding, Robert," she said in her most soothing voice.

"Look," Sloan said, impatient with the theatrics. "We have a lot to do and a very short time to do it in. Whether you were informed of this decision previously is not my problem. Getting Eternity Designs back on track is—and I'll be doing it my way."

"Why would we need—"

"Are you truly going to pretend you don't know why I'm here?" Sloan met Robert's blustery gaze directly. "You may not pay much attention to financial statements while you're down here in fantasyland, but I know for a fact you were present when the Bridal Boutique buyer ripped your designs apart. Would you like me to go into more detail, or do you remember it for yourself?"

Anthony again joined the conversation. "No, we remember it well enough."

"Good. I am here to get Eternity back in the black and at

the forefront of the wedding apparel industry. So for the next three months you will answer to me—and only me."

"We won't do it," Robert insisted. "After thirty years as a designer, I refuse to have my ideas approved by an amateur."

"Then I'll bring in someone who will."

Harsh. But he knew from his own history that sometimes the hardest lessons were the most memorable…if you used them to your advantage. Just like he'd turned his father's rejection into professional success.

Moving swiftly across the space, Sloan lifted the entire stack of drawings and dumped them into a nearby trash can. "Start over."

Ziara and Anthony gasped at the same time. But it was Robert he continued to focus on, the leader of this little group. Bring him to heel and the rest would follow.

Robert sputtered his indignation while Anthony's face crumpled as if he was going to cry. How in the world could he get through to these yahoos?

Sloan didn't anticipate Ziara's sudden tight grip on his arm. She pulled him out of hearing range and turned to face him.

"Do you really think this is the way to gain their cooperation?"

He tried to focus on her words, but his own frustration quickly morphed into desire as she moved close enough for them to hear each other without eavesdroppers. All that solid, testosterone-induced drive melted into liquid desire that pounded in his veins with a thrumming rhythm. Lord have mercy, how had this woman gotten under his skin so quickly?

"I don't need their cooperation. If they don't do what I tell them, they're out of here."

A repressive frown marred those full lips. "Robert and Anthony have always been the stars of Eternity Designs. You should treat them with more respect."

How could those lips, pressed tight like a disapproving schoolmarm's, still come across as sexy? He was actually struggling to follow her words. Him. The king of keeping things professional.

"Don't you see, Ziara, that's the problem," he finally managed. "They've had people kissing their asses for years, with no challenges to their work. They think they can give a minimal effort and still be put on a pedestal. And Eternity suffers for it."

"They do work—"

He could almost kiss her for the concern in the dark depths of her eyes but it was misplaced. "Not enough. Where's the market research, the fresh, new ideas? They don't just happen by playing around all day. Continued success takes more effort."

Understanding made a reluctant appearance in her gorgeous brown eyes. For some reason it made all the difference in the world to him. "I know I sound harsh. But they're grown men who've been catered to for years. A polite request isn't going to even make a dent." Reaching out, he brushed his thumb along the softened curve of her jaw. "I do have a method behind my madness, I promise."

The feel of her silky skin beneath his touch was magic, along with the warmth and subtle catch of her breath. They both froze in surprise for a moment. It was all Sloan could do to resist brushing his lips over the same spot.

Whoa. This was the design floor, not a nightclub…not even the privacy of his office. And judging by the utter silence laced with antagonism behind his back, Sloan knew *Robert* wouldn't hesitate to throw around accusations of sexual misconduct. With Ziara's approval or without it.

He took a careful step back, letting his hand drop to his side. "Just remember something—I wouldn't be here if they'd been doing their jobs right in the first place. Okay?"

Her nod was firm, though her eyes were still a little dazed.

This meeting needed to get back on track. "Ziara," he snapped, but with a little less bite than he'd used on the men. "The tablet, please."

She hurried to obey, giving him a moment to regain his focus before turning back to the others. When she handed over the device, he noticed the care she took not to touch him again.

After a moment of tapping on the smooth surface, he paused, looking up at the group around him.

"Current trends favor retro designs, new twists on the old, avant-garde as well as classic." During his recent research, he'd seen some unique retro looks in the fashion and wedding magazines, and they had sparked his own creative imagination.

"In less than three months, I'll be showcasing our newest designs during a professional fashion show. We're going to bring fashion week right here to Atlanta. It'll be an exclusive, invitation-only event that I want people talking about for months."

As Sloan continued to explain the fall show, excitement crept over the anger that had tightened the designers' faces. He might have punctured their egos earlier, but now he was tempting them.

Lifting the tablet, he turned it around to face them. "Every event needs a theme, a focal point. This is ours."

"A car? Are you insane?" Robert yelled, returning to his angry disbelief.

"Not just any car, a Rolls-Royce. A classic car epitomizing the elegance, sleek design and subtle sensuality of the late 1930s. An era where women flaunted sexy curves, draped their bodies with fabrics that showcased their femininity, and set out to entice the opposite sex. Think of the actresses of the time—Marlene Dietrich, Mae West, Vivian Leigh. The dresses they wore—the draped material, exposed backs…"

He caught a glimmer of understanding in Ziara's eyes. Knowledge of where he was going with this idea.

"Ridiculous," Robert insisted. "This is the stupidest thing I've heard in my lifetime."

Sloan wasn't backing down. "We're going to do this and do it right. Get on board, or jump overboard. Your choice."

When had work started feeling like a taffy puller?

Ziara waited until Sloan left the building for lunch before heading to Vivian's office. Her stomach cramped, knowing Vivian would have already heard about the upcoming show, but also knowing she couldn't blatantly walk out of Sloan's office straight to his stepmother's.

Observing Sloan for two days had taught her one thing already—he wasn't playing. His knowledge this morning showed he had done his homework on the market, design, themes, even fashion shows. He'd been calm but firm, occasionally harsh, with Robert and Anthony. Stepping solidly into a leadership role, even if he had to do it by force.

Most disturbing of all, his ideas for the show intrigued her.

With some organization, this could be an incredibly successful event, one the upper classes of Atlanta society would flock to in droves. Eternity Designs would be on the tip of everyone's tongues and the front page in the society section. Notable brides would once again be drawn to the showroom for one-of-a-kind dresses.

But to her shame, Sloan's appeal continued to taunt her on a more physical level. Vivian had insisted she was the last woman who would be tempted by Sloan's charm, but the need that had crawled into her body at his singular touch frightened her. She'd seen her mother move from man to man, taking whatever they could give her, using her body to manipulate them. Mixing business with pleasure was the last thing Ziara wanted in her life. The level of temptation here actually scared her bone deep.

Abigail gave her a sympathetic look as she entered the room. "She's waiting on you, Ziara."

I bet she is. Her hand pausing on the doorknob, Ziara only let herself hesitate a second before going in.

"Ah, Ziara," Vivian said from behind her antique desk. "I see you have finally deigned to bring me news."

Vivian gestured for her to sit. The walk across the room distracted Ziara from the uneasiness caused by Vivian's words. "I felt it appropriate to wait until Sloan left for lunch—"

"Why? He's surely aware that one of your jobs is to keep me informed. Next time I want to hear it from you, rather than the office grapevine."

Yes, but I couldn't bring myself to rub my choices in his face.

She'd probably heard from the Old Brigade, who'd run to Vivian to tattle the minute they'd realized they were losing control.

Ziara wondered if they remembered Vivian had once been a mere secretary—and how long it had taken them to accept the new order of things when she took over. Given the evidence from this morning, Ziara didn't think acceptance had come quickly.

"I'm very excited about this new idea for the line's presentation," she started.

"Ah yes, the fashion show. I hate to admit it, but I'm seeing the merits of this plan myself. I want a full report."

"I've just started working on the details. I'm looking into venues, modeling agencies and such."

"Keep me informed as everything takes shape."

Ziara murmured, "Yes, ma'am," under her breath, but Vivian was already moving on.

"Make it good. Getting some choice buyers in here will make this the must-have ticket of the fall season. I'll have Abigail get you a list of contacts, and I want to know as soon as the RSVPs come in."

If Sloan was a train squishing her on the tracks, Vivian was a wrecking ball, destroying Ziara's calm handling of this difficult assignment. Her mentor ran through a laundry list of items she wanted Ziara to check into, almost doubling the amount of work Sloan had given her. She saw quite a few late nights in her near future.

"Since you will be in the thick of all of this, Ziara—" Vivian's spine straightened as if bracing herself for what was to come "—you should know...if our largest buyer pulls her orders, as she has threatened if the line doesn't move in a more modern, unique direction, it will put the company in a very disadvantageous financial position."

Even Vivian's attempt at genteel diplomacy couldn't hide the facts: Eternity Designs was in deep financial trouble. The confirmation of the actual problem had Ziara's stomach dropping like it would on a roller coaster, a ride she avoided getting on at all costs.

Coming to work here, helping to build some of the finest dresses and dreams, had been like finding her true home. She wasn't ready to leave.

Vivian's fingers spun her wedding band in an endless circle. "So you can see how very important it is for the fall line to be not just good, but spectacular. By putting you in his office, I can let Sloan think he's in charge until we see what he decides to do with the fall line." Vivian's heeled pump set up a twitchy rhythm. "I've known him for a long time. He's sneaky, deceptive. His mother's lower-class roots are showing, I guess."

Ziara controlled the surprise that threatened to bloom on her face. Social standing had always been important to Vivian, but Ziara had never before seen evidence of prejudice.

"I know you said he was rebellious as a teenager." Perfectly normal, in Ziara's opinion. "Why would you think he's up to something now?"

Being on the receiving end of Vivian's glare wasn't comfortable.

"Haven't you ever heard that a leopard never changes its spots?" Vivian asked. "Besides, there are rumors that he uses some rather ruthless tactics to get his way these days." Her pen tapped against her desk. One thump, then two. "He's up to something," she continued. "And I need to stay on top of it. *You* need to stay on top of it."

Ziara wasn't sure if the turmoil gaining ground in her gut was troubled conscience or the guilt of temptation, but she couldn't simply ignore it. "Vivian, I really, well, I simply think that someone else might be more suited to working with Sl—Mr. Creighton. I could easily coordinate the show details from—"

"His office. That's where I put you and that's where you will stay. Or is there some reason you would request a change?"

The last thing Ziara wanted to do was explain the ins and outs of the past two days. If only she could make Vivian understand… "Honestly, I don't feel very comfortable with the position I'm in. If you think Sloan will stop anything he's doing because of me, well, he won't. I just—"

Vivian's head tilted slightly to the side, her brown eyes studying Ziara with sudden intensity. For the first time in a long time, Ziara wanted to hide from her boss, to squirrel away the reactions she had to Sloan just as she had the secrets of her past. Vivian would never accept her if she knew either one.

"Have I not done enough for you, Ziara?"

Not expecting the attack, Ziara found herself speechless.

"Have I not taught you all that I can about running this business, about behaving professionally, about coming out ahead of those not willing to put every ounce of effort into their jobs?"

"Yes, ma'am. You've been more than generous."

"Then why do I suddenly feel like all of that effort has been wasted on the wrong person?"

Panic shot deep, mixing with the fear Ziara carried on a daily basis: that one day, everything she'd worked so hard for would crash down into a pile of rubble. She would not go back to being the uneducated girl condemned by everyone around her.

"I certainly don't want you to feel that way," Ziara said over the pounding of her heart. "I'm very grateful—

"I see plenty, Ziara," Vivian snapped, her eyes as harsh as her tone. "And what I'm seeing isn't gratitude, understand?"

Knowing she'd overstepped Vivian's invisible limit, Ziara conceded quickly. "Yes, ma'am."

"You've worked very hard to get where you are, Ziara. That's why I chose you to succeed Abigail as my executive assistant when she retires later this year."

At the praise, a glow bloomed beneath her fear. She'd yearned to be recognized for her accomplishments for as long as she could remember. First at school, then at community college, from her first job till now. Though she hadn't found validation at home, her move to Atlanta had been the start of a whole new life.

"I'm confident that you'll do what's best for Eternity Designs." Vivian stood, her posture and classically tailored business suit a picture of authority. Ziara moved quickly to join her.

"This position, though difficult, will also be excellent training for you, and I don't have to worry about the Creighton good looks turning your head like some of the less dedicated girls around here. Do I?"

Ziara realized the question was rhetorical, so she simply shook her head, keeping her growing doubts to herself. Oh, she had no intention of falling into bed with a man like Sloan Creighton. On the other hand, how did she keep his charm and obvious business smarts from influencing her away from what Vivian wanted?

Vivian moved on, unaware of Ziara's fears. "By the time we come out of this, Eternity Designs will be set for the future. I'll be in charge, and you'll have that job as my E.A."

Ziara shifted in her heels. "But what if he succeeds? How can you risk him gaining a majority's ownership if you don't trust him?"

Vivian turned away, her face hidden as she crossed to the window. "Don't worry," she said, twisting her wedding ring around her finger again. "I'll take care of that."

Knowing she'd been dismissed, Ziara retreated to the safety of the outer office, where Abigail waited with a kind smile and some lists.

"Thank you, Abigail."

"No problem, sweetie. Just let me know if you have any questions."

How about, *Will I make it through this without losing my freakin' mind?* Or, *Is everyone going to hate me before this show is over?* But she said nothing, conscious for once of exactly how alone she was.

Walking through the doorway, she found Sloan leaning against her desk. Her stomach dropped to her toes and a flush suffused her cheeks. The guilt was probably glaring out from her downcast gaze and shifting feet.

Where was this guilt coming from? A shot of surprise jolted through her at the answer. The guilt didn't stem from tattling like a four-year-old. That was the best thing for Eternity Designs…for now. She simply didn't want to face him knowing she'd tried to get out of working with him. Her feet stuttered to stillness and she swallowed, praying her voice would work at this point. “May I help you with something, Mr. Creighton?”

Those bright blue eyes, so full of life earlier today, were now cold enough to freeze the devil himself in his tracks. His mouth crooked up on one side, his boyish good looks now brittle around the edges. Oh yeah, he knew what she was up to, and there was no defense against that knowledge.

“I don’t know why I’m surprised.”

For some unknown reason, she couldn’t brush this moment aside with professionalism or tactful confusion. “I don’t know, either. You told me you understood my duties here.”

“That doesn’t mean I have to like it.”

Me, either.

Ziara struggled to return to that place where she was strictly a secretary performing an assigned task, but she couldn’t. Some kind of barrier had been breached with his touch earlier today, and she was very afraid there was no going back from it.

She had the distinct feeling he wouldn’t let her go back even if she tried. His next words confirmed her suspicions. “Too bad I can’t give you what you really deserve.”

“And what would that be?” she asked, though the naughty mischief melting the iceberg should have warned her she’d moved into dangerous territory.

“A spanking.”

Four

The next few days went by relatively smoothly as Ziara discovered the ins and outs of working for Sloan Creighton.

He liked his coffee black with just a touch of sugar for sweetness, but he only drank it in the morning. After eleven, he switched to Mountain Dew. He came into the office around nine-thirty every morning, smelling of citrus and a spicy undertone after his daily game of racquetball. He paced while he dictated letters, his long legs performing for her benefit alone. While dreaming up new show ideas, he liked to lean back in his chair with his Gucci-clad feet propped on the edge of the desk.

She often caught a glimpse of him standing at those floor-to-ceiling windows watching people walk by five stories below, deep enough in thought that she'd close the door behind her with extra force to remind him of her presence.

She was getting to know him way too well.

This new knowledge was uncomfortable, but not as uncomfortable as the suspicion that he was cataloging some things about her, as well. Those damn eyes! Not to mention the occasional spicy remark, like that spanking comment, that she pretended to ignore no matter how outrageous he got. The last thing he needed was encouragement.

Today shattered the routine when Sloan hit the outer door like a bull. She hadn't seen that controlled anger since his first day, that contained heat he'd wielded against Vivian like a fine-tuned weapon.

"I've got a lot of calls to make, Ziara. Don't bother me."

"Yes, Mr. Creighton," she said reverting to formality in her confusion. She watched those long strides carry him into his office, the door slamming behind him. Definitely a good day to keep her head down and work on clearing the clutter from her desk.

A few hours of muffled yelling and banging later, she decided now was probably a good time to escape. She made her way through the corridors to the design floor. Anthony met her a few feet in with a quick and quiet hug. He knew exactly why she was here. Leading her across the room, he showed her the new shipment of sample materials scattered across a large table.

"Robert is very upset with me," he said. "He thinks I'm a sellout."

Ziara glanced over his shoulder at the normally boisterous man now sitting quietly at a drafting table. "Why would he think that?" she asked, keeping her voice low to match Anthony's.

He gestured toward the materials. "Because I ordered these."

Ziara took in the mixtures of cream, pinks, barely there blues and an almost yellow color on a display table that was normally white, white and white. "Hmm. I can see where that would be a problem."

"I've tried to move Robert in new directions for years now, especially as grumblings surfaced from the buyers. But he just won't listen."

"I don't think Mr. Creighton will give him that option."

"Well, maybe he will succeed where I have failed." With a sad smile, he wandered back across the room, leaving Ziara alone for what he knew was her favorite pastime.

Picking up the nearby invoices, she started matching the

materials on the table with the names and prices on the sheets of paper. She studied the fresh array of colors, the textures, drape and a myriad of other things.

In an ideal world—where she would have had a supportive family, scholarships and no need to be her own sole support immediately after getting her GED—she would have been a supplier, searching out the finest materials, the best deals for the entire company in accessories, gemstones, beading, lining, everything. As it was, she could spend hours immersed in the research but allowed herself only small windows here and there. Luckily Anthony wasn't threatened by her presence or interest, so he'd spent many a minute teaching her bits and pieces. Bless his heart.

"Enjoying yourself?"

Ziara froze, her hand buried in a pile of pink-tinged satin. To her knowledge, Vivian didn't know about her little visits here. Yet it hadn't taken Sloan a week to uncover her secret.

"I'm sorry, Mr. Creigh—um, Sloan. Did you need me for something?"

When he squeezed the back of his neck as if to relieve the tension gathered there, she couldn't help but sympathize.

"I definitely need you, Ziara. Don't you know that?"

Her gaze zeroed in on his face, searching for the intention behind the words. His bright blue eyes were now tired, but a shiver of awareness still snuck down her spine. No matter how he looked, no matter what he said, she felt he was bringing her to an awareness of him as a man—and herself as a woman.

She murmured, "I'm happy to oblige." Then cringed inside at the many ways her words could be misinterpreted. She straightened as he moved closer. He reached toward her stomach, which tightened in anticipation—but his hand bypassed her to explore the materials on the table beyond.

A smoky-blue chiffon, almost gray, held his attention. "Very nice," he murmured, the sound almost seductive, as though he was encouraging…something. He lifted the material, testing the feel, weight and drape.

His hands fascinated her, the long fingers with their neatly clipped nails a sharp contrast to the fragile-looking material. But his eyes drew her, too. Those bright blues had darkened as if he were looking inward rather than at the material he handled so skillfully.

"What is this?" he asked.

"It's a light chiffon, mostly used for accents and layering," she said.

Snapping out of his thoughts, he glanced at her in surprise. "Been studying your materials, have you?"

Warmth flooded into her cheeks and chest. "Anthony has been teaching me."

Rather than the condemnation she'd expected, his eyes softened in appreciation. "Show me."

Sloan found himself entranced as Ziara explained the contrasts between silks, chiffons, satins and numerous other materials used in dressmaking. Not over the information itself, even though it was appreciated, but the unguarded spark in her eyes.

Then there was the show: her slender arms lifting each material to demonstrate its ability to drape, the thickness and what it might be used for.

"You could have been a supplier," he said, drawn in by her enthusiasm.

The stillness that invaded her body told him he'd hit a sore spot, even though her lowered lashes hid her expression from him. Not quite understanding, he asked, "Why didn't you? This stuff obviously interests you."

The muscles around her mouth tightened, then she raised her guarded gaze. "Fashion production and supply chain management degrees don't come cheap." She started sorting the material by color. "Tuition was nonexistent for me, so that type of dream wasn't even on the table. I looked at my options and chose what worked with my skills. It wasn't until I came here that I realized how interesting this side of the business could be."

"Your parents weren't able to help?"

Her mouth twisted. “Not even close. It was just my mother and me, anyway. She didn’t think school was worth much.”

“What about your guidance counselor? If your grades were good, scholarships could have helped.”

“Maybe in another life.”

The spark of curiosity that ran through his body was exciting but dangerous. He took the leap, anyway. “Why?”

Finally she stopped rearranging the material so she could glare at him. “Look. I came from a really small town, even more southern than Atlanta, with not enough money and very few options. I worked my way through secretarial school with two jobs, eating peanut butter from a spoon every night. Not everyone needs a high salary and trust fund to be successful.”

That should have stung—and it did, but not in the personal way he expected. He could see how hard she must have worked to attain her level of success at such a young age—which meant this wasn’t just a job to her.

She wasn’t just Vivian’s pet.

He couldn’t think about what that meant to his plans. So he let his mind conjure pictures of her caressing the fabric. Within seconds, he began to visualize designs: a sleek gown of pale pink satin, almost bright against her dark skin, drifting low over her naked back, accented with white diamonds and silver thread. The smoky chiffon shaped into three-dimensional flowers at the shoulders of a structured gray, almost silver, silk dress. The creamy yellow draped tight across her torso in tiny pleats that met at the curve of her hip, then released into a waterfall of softly lilting, creamy white feathers.

All of them made exclusively for the incredible body before him.

His horrible morning dissolved under the rush of creative energy.

“What are you thinking?” he heard her say, her voice echoing slightly as she pulled him from his own head, that place where he created all the things he needed, wanted, with the easy strokes of his mind.

It didn’t matter whether it was building plans, an office design, extensive renovations…or, apparently, wedding dresses. He had only to envision it and the lines appeared in the forefront of his mind. It was very helpful, incredibly productive and totally intoxicating.

Which was the only explanation he had for what he did next. Reaching around her to the desk, he snagged paper and a drawing pencil. The move brought him flush with her side, prompting a surge of heat wherever their bodies met, though he forced himself to move away quickly.

He could tell she felt it, too, by the widening of her eyes and the way she held her breath. He shoved the materials on the table aside and started to draw. Within minutes, he had a simple outline of the pink satin dress he'd imagined, though he kept the distinctive characteristics of the model vague.

"Wow," she breathed. "That's gorgeous."

"Thank you."

Her smile warmed him, intoxicating in its sincerity. He often had the feeling that she simply responded to him the way she should, the way an assistant was expected to respond to her boss. Not this time.

Fire lurked beneath the surface of this buttoned-down babe, and he desperately wanted to release it—even if he was her boss.

"I mean it," he continued, anxious to avoid the temptation of his thoughts. "You've shown me exactly what I need."

Before he could do something stupid like kiss those full red lips, he pivoted on his heel and walked away. Now that he had a direction, he knew just how to carry it out.

Eternity Designs would never be the same.

Sloan stalked down the hall toward the elevators, the adrenaline still thrumming through his veins. Pictures of Ziara racing through his mind.

"How's your new assistant working out, Sloan?"

Damn it. He'd been so close to the open doorway!

He pivoted to find Vivian standing in the shadows. Had she been waiting for him to walk by? Had she watched as he and Ziara talked?

"Great choice, Vivian. She'll serve me just fine, I think."

Vivian studied him with the same barely tolerant expression she'd used after many of his teenage escapades. "What's wrong?"

Ah, the pitfalls of working with someone who'd watched him grow up. He moved a few steps closer. Lowering his voice, he tightened his control over the high levels of excitement, frustration and arousal still surging through his veins.

"It won't work, Vivian. Whatever reason you have for planting Ziara in my office—it won't work. I'm still going to do what I think is best for Eternity."

Patronizing was the only way to describe her smile. "I know exactly where Ziara's loyalties lie. She'll do the job I gave her."

"I'm going ahead with my plans, regardless." The feel of the sketch held securely in his grasp brought a surge of certainty. He was on the right path; now he needed the one person who would help him carry it out.

"So you've talked the Old Brigade into actually carrying out your crazy theme?" she asked, concern dampening her smug demeanor. Ah, she'd be so happy if he was stuck working with her two lackeys, wouldn't she?

"Robert and Anthony will fall in line soon enough." His chest tightened as all his earlier frustration rushed forward again.

She shook her head slowly. "Not according to Robert—I believe his exact words were 'over my dead body.'"

Her smug expression shattered his control like nothing else could have. "I wouldn't get too tickled if I were you."

"And why is that?"

"I'm about to turn Eternity Designs upside down."

The *ding* of the elevator signaled his escape. Sloan strode through the doors and turned back to see Vivian's perplexed expression just as they closed.

Five

Ziara dished up her quick version of paella into an oversize, bright green bowl, pausing a moment to inhale the spicy scent of peppers, andouille sausage and shrimp. Padding across to the table, she savored the coolness of the tiled kitchen floor on her bare feet.

After a long, deep drink of sweetened tea, she picked up her book in one hand and her fork in the other. Having survived her rough day at work, her mind craved the relaxing and safe surroundings of home. An early start to her weekend.

She'd worked so hard for her house and turned it into her very own sanctuary. Most important, it was as far from the environment she'd grown up in as possible.

Only here could she let down the defenses. She could safely indulge her passion for cooking, love of reading and flair for color.

She desperately needed that in the aftermath of her confusing response to her boss. Sloan was flirty, no doubt about it, but she'd always held herself to a higher standard. To think a few smiles, some genuine listening and one hot touch could turn her sensible head made her very angry—with herself.

The first bite of paella ignited a burn on her tongue that spread like flash fire up the walls of her mouth to the roof and inner edge of her lips. Yummy, but she suspected her turbulent thoughts had made her heavy-handed with the spices.

Ziara jumped at the jangle of the doorbell. She rarely had visitors—no family, no close friends. It was only five, so it was still fairly light out. Daylight savings time wouldn't hit for another month. Maybe it was a salesman or one of the neighbors' kids fund-raising for school. She sighed.

Traversing the short hallway linking the kitchen with the living room, Ziara paused to glance through the small window that ran down the side of the door. She wasn't above pretending she wasn't home.

The silhouette on the other side didn't quite register at first except to look vaguely familiar. Then, in an instant, it felt as if the heat from the paella exploded at the base of her neck and spread along her skull. Surely that wasn't Sloan so casually posed in the shade of her front porch?

She jerked back, suddenly vulnerable in her cotton yoga pants and old T-shirt, so thin it offered little to no coverage.

Cringing when the doorbell rang again, she looked up to find Sloan blocking the view from the window. Well, he knew she was here. Good manners insisted she open the door and see what he wanted. Muttering under her breath, she decided she now had a very personal reason for being irritated.

Grasping the cool metal of the knob, she pulled the door open just enough to see his handsome face.

"Sloan," she said, her voice more a question than an acknowledgment. She didn't issue an invitation, but apparently he didn't need one. Placing his palm flat on the door, he pushed inside, walking by her as if coming in was his right. She stood dumbfounded for a moment, then closed the door and leaned back against it, her arms crossed beneath breasts that tingled in his presence—without her permission.

"To what do I owe the pleasure?"

Her tone implied that seeing him was as far from a pleasure as she could get. She'd been well on the road to relaxation, but now her back was military straight and the muscles on each side of her neck tightened in protest. Even worse, she couldn't decide if it was because she didn't want him here... or because she did.

"Hi." He flashed his usual confident smile.

Up went her brow. He studied her expression with interest before his gaze moved to his surroundings.

A sense of invasion rose from the pit of her stomach, overriding the awareness that always seemed to come with his presence. She shifted uneasily as he walked around the room, gliding a finger along her favorite fleece throw and pausing to examine the exotic lines of the dancer in the picture over the mantel.

"Sloan," she said when the tension ratcheted up to an unbearable high, "what are you doing here?"

He faced her, his calm expression mocking the tremble that had slipped into her voice.

"I'll tell you," he said, "if you give me a plate of whatever smells so good. Suddenly I'm very hungry."

No, her mind screamed. She didn't want his presence lingering in her home, but short of pushing him back out the door, she had no idea how to refuse.

Sucking in a deep breath, she led the way back to the kitchen, ultraconscious as she passed him of the air grazing her bare arms and the gentle slap of her feet on the uncarpeted floors.

Crossing to the cabinet, she decided she might as well comply and find out what was going on. With efficient movements, she fixed him a plate and drink before settling him at the opposite end of the table from her. She ignored the smirk on his face as she returned to her seat.

He lifted his fork, then sniffed appreciatively before meeting her eyes.

"I know the perfect designer."

"I wasn't aware we needed one. We already have two." His

knowing look had her admitting, "Okay, we have at least one willing to help."

"But I've figured out the one person who can bring my vision to life."

His epiphany obviously accounted for the change in his mood, but not his presence—his most unwanted presence—here. "I'm glad. Couldn't this have waited until Monday?"

He shook his head, then hefted a heaping forkful of rice and spicy meat to his mouth. It had to be a sin to watch those sculpted lips close around anything, even something as innocent as a fork.

She didn't warn him about the heat. He'd probably just blow it off with some macho line. Besides, he was part of what had led to all that spice in the first place.

Suddenly his eyes widened and he coughed, just managing to keep the food in his mouth long enough to swallow. She leaned back with a feeling of satisfaction as his hand shot out for his glass. That would teach him not to push his way in where he wasn't wanted.

"Wow," he said after a long drink of iced tea, "that packs a wallop."

Watching him dig back in without a hint of hesitation, she thought, *Yes, it does*. "I'm glad you like it," she murmured, instead.

He cleared most of his plate, all the while studying her with intent looks that burned more than the food burned her mouth. Goose bumps spread along her skin despite the heat of the food.

She pushed her long hair back behind her shoulders, licking her dry, spicy lips. "Does Vivian approve of the new designer?"

"On the contrary, she'd have a very genteel hissy fit if she knew who he was."

She hesitated. Her gaze locked on her nearly empty plate before braving another glance at him. "So you haven't discussed this with her?"

He shook his head, waves of dark blond hair caressing the masculine angles of his face. "I don't plan to clue her in anytime soon." He leaned forward. "Do you?"

She leaned forward, too. "Let's get one thing straight. Whatever actions I take are for the good of the company. Convince me of the merits of your plan, and you won't have to worry about where my loyalties lie."

He stood, prowling around the sunny kitchen. His cool good looks blended with the greens and golds, the blue accents a reflection of his eyes, the pine cabinets just a touch lighter than his hair. He looked as if he belonged in this room.

He was testing her, but instead of resentment, an excited rush sizzled inside.

"This place isn't anything like I'd imagined," he said out of the blue.

As he took in the kitchen and her in one sweep, she wished for the ability to snap her fingers and be wearing a business suit instead of her relax-and-cook gear.

In an attempt to repress more personal discussions, she said, "I can't think why you'd wonder about it at all."

He stalked across the room and reached out to touch a strand of her loose hair that had fallen forward over her shoulder. "Who knew you had so much to hide."

Her quick intake of breath was her only outward response, but inside she mentally retreated. She couldn't afford to let him in on her secrets if she wanted to remain a respectable part of his business. Knowing would change everything. It always did. The few she'd told her deepest feelings to had turned their backs on her in an instant, and then she'd learned the golden rule of silence.

Standing, she stalked back down the hall and pulled the door open, not so discreetly inviting him to leave.

He followed, the soft-soled boots he wore silent on the wood floor, his face unreadable. Pulling a card from his wallet, he scribbled on the back. "Here's my cell phone number in case you need to contact me."

She stared blankly at the card in his hand. "Aren't you coming into the office on Monday?"

"No," he said. "And neither are you."

"Why not?"

That sexy grin was back. "Pack your bags. We're going to Vegas."

Six

Sloan arrived at the airport with plenty of time to spare. He eased through security, then settled in to wait. Ziara seemed the type to arrive early, but after last night he realized he didn't know a thing about her. Not the real Ziara. Underneath that cool, businesslike exterior lurked a woman he suspected burned as hot as her paella. That intrigued him. What intrigued him more was the *why*.

Why was she so different at work? This wasn't a case of the same woman just acting on a more professional level. No, this was two totally different women.

The rich, resonant colors in the living room—burgundy, flaming oranges and yellows, deep purple accented with gold—seemed such a natural setting for her dark beauty. Why would she dress down in drab grays, browns and navies?

That hair, soft around her face, a silky waterfall draping her chest and shoulders, made him want to spread it across a pillow or, better yet, across his chest. Of course, if she was hoping to disguise her thick, satin glory, she'd failed. Pulling it up to the crown of her head as she did at work only emphasized the exotic slant of her eyes and the exquisite lines of her cheekbones.

Did she get her spicy, riveting beauty from her mother? In all the simple elegance of her home, Sloan hadn't seen one personal photograph on display—not one of Ziara or any family, which struck him as odd.

He glanced over to see her standing in line for security. Looking at his watch, he realized she'd waited until the last moment to arrive. He smiled. Now that he knew what was inside, he wouldn't let her revert back to "all business."

A familiar ache built throughout his body as he watched her progress across the waiting area. The whoosh of adrenaline was similar to the rush of creativity, only a thousand times stronger. He no longer just wanted this woman—he *had* to have her. Which was a problem, because he was technically her boss. Temporarily. Although, if she was also his lover, then he'd know exactly where her loyalties lay. He could live with that...couldn't he?

"Good morning, Sloan," she said, settling into a seat across the aisle from him.

He frowned as she pulled out her mobile phone and searched for a number. "Don't you know it's rude to ignore someone to talk on the phone?"

"Not when it's business."

"What's business?"

She motioned between the two of them. "This trip." Waving the phone for a minute, she continued, "And this call."

Oh, no she didn't. "What kind of business call could you possibly be making on a Saturday morning?"

"I'm calling Vivian. It was too late to call her last night and I should let her know where we'll be. You didn't give me nearly enough time pack and get ready and call her this morning."

And I'm not about to give you a chance now, either. He eyed her stiff shoulders and the haughty tilt to her chin as she studied the screen. She wore her defiance like a uniform—one he wanted to remove inch by inch. "Don't, Ziara."

"Why not?"

"Seriously? What good is it going to do?"

"It just might preserve my job when all this is over," she said, those chocolate eyes finally meeting his head-on. "Or did you forget that someone else has a stake in this besides you?"

Ouch. He knew it, even when he wished he didn't. *Not everyone needs a high salary and trust fund to be successful.* She needed her job. If everything didn't work out, he'd help her find a new one.

Standing, he loomed over her, hearing the call to board blast from the speakers around them. "Still, I'm in charge on this trip. Remember?"

With a quick snatch, he grabbed her phone and stored it deep in the pocket of his khakis. Still within reach…barely.

"Give that back," she demanded, her voice shaking.

"No. But you are welcome to come get it, if you want."

The anger that exploded over her face didn't hide the hint of interest that surfaced. Enjoying a touch of satisfaction, he grabbed his carry-on and strolled across the waiting area to board the flight. The whole time he could feel her glare directly between his shoulder blades.

This would be a fun flight.

On the plane, she lowered into the seat next to him with exquisite care, her tense jaw signaling extreme displeasure. He really shouldn't be enjoying this so much.

"Give back my phone."

"No," he said, giving a little jiggle of his pocket. "Look at it this way—at least you'll have an excuse when she asks why you didn't call."

If he had to guess, he'd say he was seeing his assistant go supernova. Not a sound was made, but the air almost shook around her before she closed her eyes and drew in a deep breath. As they started to taxi, she took out a paperback and began to read. Clearly all avoidance tactics were in full effect now, probably for his own safety. He grinned. Biding his time was a talent he'd long ago acquired.

He allowed her to avoid him until they'd reached cruising

altitude. Then his nimble fingers plucked the book from hers before she knew what was coming.

"Hey," she protested. "Are you planning to make stealing a habit?"

"I don't know. Haven't you learned yet it's rude to ignore the person you're traveling with?"

She angled herself toward the window, leaving him with a devastating view of her elegant nose and full lips, not to mention thick lashes that added to the mystery of her eyes. "I didn't want you to feel you had to entertain me."

He handed back the book, murmuring, "I'll just bet you did."

She shot him a sharp look but tucked the book into her purse for safekeeping. Settling back in her seat, she folded her hands in her lap like the prim woman he suspected she wasn't. If she only knew what that contradiction did to him. Actually, it was probably a good thing she didn't. Ten thousand feet up in an airplane wasn't the ideal place for arousal.

"Aren't you curious about the designer we're going to see?"

She tilted her head toward him, the sun through the window highlighting the curve of her jaw and the smooth caramel skin of her neck. He bet she'd taste just as sweet.

"Okay," she said, drawing out the word. "I'll bite. Who is it?"

Sloan accepted a drink from the flight attendant. Passing Ziara one of the small glasses, he deliberately brushed his fingers along hers. Her quick retreat confirmed his suspicions. She wasn't as immune to him as she'd like. If he played his cards right on this trip, Ziara's loyalties to him would far outweigh any hold Vivian had on her.

"Patrick was my college roommate. He was a fashion design major while I stuck it out on the business track." He paused a moment at her considering look. "I immediately thought of him when I decided to do this project, but he turned me down."

"Then why are we on a plane to Las Vegas?"

"I'm going to change his mind."

* * *

Great. She wasn't on a flight to Las Vegas to meet their new designer but to court one. A reluctant one.

She shouldn't be surprised that Sloan wouldn't take no for an answer. Keeping that in mind in her own dealings with him would be smart. After all, hadn't he just shown her in graphic detail how opposed he was to a little phone call? If he thought she was going to go diving into his pants for her phone—or tell Vivian exactly where said phone had been—he was gravely mistaken.

Maybe she could dig into his plans before he realized what she was doing and shut her out completely.

"I don't know of any big wedding dress designers based in Vegas. Who does he work for?"

Sloan's smirk didn't answer any questions; it only created more. "You won't believe it until you see it."

She sighed in frustration. "What does that mean?"

He leaned toward her, his eyes meeting hers head-on. Her stomach jumped, but she told herself it was from turbulence.

"Ziara, we're on our way to Las Vegas. Relax and enjoy a little pleasure with your business."

Alarm skittered through Ziara when her mental walls didn't go up immediately. She actually wanted to give in to the attraction tempting her, but knew doing so would cost her all she'd worked so hard for, so she pulled back.

"I'm just here to work," she said, hoping she sounded like an old, repressive aunt. "What do you think it will take to convince this friend of yours to change his mind?"

He frowned, collapsing back in his seat. She couldn't help but admire the ease he seemed to feel in his body. "Probably something I'm not going to want to give."

"Why?"

"Because he knows me too well."

She angled toward him in her small seat. "So you must have been really close and stayed in touch all this time."

He shrugged. "We have similar interests."

What did that mean? Ziara wanted to pull her hair in frustration. Or better yet, shake Sloan until all the answers she wanted just tumbled out. His secretive, *I don't trust you* attitude was getting really old, really quick. If he couldn't trust her, that was his problem. Though she should probably be happy she wasn't dealing with a flirty, sexy boss, instead.

"Is there anything you'd like to do in Vegas?" Sloan asked out of the blue. "A show? Shopping?" His gaze slid over her, heating her flesh even through her sensible pantsuit. "Dance with a sexy stranger?"

From anyone else, the question would have seemed presumptuous and sleazy, but from Sloan it was, well, presumptuous and tempting. What would it be like to dance secure in his arms, to give herself up to his lead without having to worry where he'd take her? Without having to worry how he'd feel about her in the morning?

She'd never chance it. This time she leaned forward, meeting him head-on so there would be no mistakes. This tactic had worked time and again in the past. Attitude was everything, though the lock on her bedroom door had come in handy too.

She might be physically tempted like never before, but it wouldn't show. She wouldn't allow it.

"Let's get this straight," she said in a calm, nonthreatening sort of way. "I have no interest outside of helping you find your designer and launch the fall line. I'm here to do my job. Period."

Instead of backtracking or scrambling for excuses like all the men before him under her no-nonsense glare, Sloan simply watched her lips as she formed the words, his gaze tracing every curve. The urge to moisten them with a slip of her tongue grew strong.

A satisfied expression crossed his face, as if he'd stumbled upon a secret she hid deep inside. "We'll see," he said simply, then leaned back in his chair and closed his eyes, leaving her to stew in her amazement at his audacity.

We'll see. *We'll see?* He'd see nothing more than her hand making contact with his face if he tried to pull anything on her.

She knew far too much about the ways of men and the

lengths they'd go to have a woman. She'd seen every trick before; nothing impressed her now. They all ended up looking at you like trash once you gave in. She'd vowed a long time ago that she'd never endure that. Respect meant everything to her. If she couldn't have it romantically, she'd earn it through hard work and initiative in her career.

She never let herself down. That was the only thing she could count on.

Seven

Ziara kept reminding herself of that until the plane touched down late that afternoon. The Nevada heat drained her. Just walking from the airport to the taxi sparked a thirst that for once had nothing to do with Sloan.

They checked into the hotel with relative ease. The elegant suite, thankfully complete with two bedrooms with locking doors, offered an enticing view from Ziara's balcony. Despite her resolve to focus on work, Ziara couldn't deny the little tendrils of excitement spreading through her veins. Vegas was an animal all its own and it tempted her curiosity almost as much as Sloan and his mystery designer.

As the sunset crept over the horizon and lights sparked on, she didn't care about the reputation of Sin City; she just wanted to indulge in a little color and stimulation.

She tried to dig some information out of Sloan during dinner in their sitting area. Knowing his plans would grant her more control and distract her from Sloan's good looks. He'd changed into a lightweight tan suit that brought out the blond highlights in his thick hair. The blue dress shirt, with the top buttons undone, echoed the icy blue of his eyes. He projected an aura of sophisticated relaxation. She couldn't help but envy that cool attitude.

Distraction, that's what she needed. "What is the itinerary while we're here?"

Sloan didn't even look up from his filet mignon. "I'm not sure."

She stifled a sigh. "Do we have an appointment to meet with your friend?"

"I'm afraid not." He paused to chew a bite of crunchy fried potatoes.

How did he eat like that and still maintain those lean muscles without an ounce of extra flesh?

"This trip was a spur-of-the-moment decision."

Really? She could feel her frustration tightening the muscles along her neck. Hadn't he planned any part of this little jaunt? Planning was her modus operandi. Besides, if the designer refused to meet with Sloan, this entire trip would be a complete waste of time.

"So is there at least a plan of attack?"

Realizing her frustration was beginning to ooze through the cracks in her calm facade, she cringed. Maybe she should just concentrate on the juicy chicken Alfredo on her plate. Then she quit caring altogether as she noticed the shake in Sloan's shoulders.

Tilting her head, she caught a glimpse of his laughing mouth. She barely restrained the urge to kick his shin with her pointy dress pumps. Taking a deep breath, instead, she applied herself to her food in outward silence, but inside her mind was calling him every name in the book. And she knew quite a few more than people imagined.

Sloan must have decided he'd tested her type A personality quite enough, because he broke the silence. "I bought tickets for a show here tonight. Since we won't be able to catch up with Patrick until later, we might as well enjoy ourselves."

He studied her as if expecting a protest, but she decided to ease off the hall monitor bit for a little while. Heck, everyone needed a day off. Including her. If he wanted to take her out—strictly as her boss—then who was she to complain?

After finishing their meal, Sloan cleared everything to the room service cart and rolled it outside the door. Ziara changed into the only nonbusiness outfit she'd brought. The plain summer skirt and lack of a suit jacket evoked a sense of freedom from her responsibilities. Paired with a light summer sweater, she was ready to be entertained. The assessing look in Sloan's eyes had her reluctantly standing a bit straighter.

Exiting the elevators, they crossed through the hotel lobby toward the theater. Passing the opening to the casino, various restaurants and shops, Ziara caught the excitement of tourists and let herself slowly slip into the mood, just a little.

A burgundy-uniformed usher led them to seats close to the front, slightly left of the center aisle. Sloan must have pulled strings to get such good seats at the last minute. As the lights lowered and the stage came alive, Ziara's breath caught in her throat. She felt close enough to be part of the action, yet isolated in the dark, alone, with only the warmth of Sloan's arm next to hers anchoring her.

The show was a compilation of variety acts. As Sloan's laughter rumbled in his chest at the comedian, Ziara let herself join in. She held her breath, awed over the awesome acrobatics and stunts in various sketches.

At one point Sloan stretched out his long legs, the brush of material against the bare skin of her calf setting off goose bumps. His gaze branded her like a heat-seeking missile, taking in her reactions to the various acts onstage, reminding her to temper her laughter or excitement.

She thoroughly enjoyed the evening until the next-to-last act. As a scantily clad woman gracefully crossed the stage and burst into song, Ziara cringed in her seat.

She knew the song well—it had been one of her mother's favorites. The scene was from a musical about a prostitute who'd found Mr. Right and hoped he'd look past her profession to the woman within. As fellow "call girls" made their way onto the stage to join in the chorus, Ziara shifted in her seat.

Like a neon sign right before her face, the scene reminded her of all she had to lose if she gave in to her attraction to Sloan. Her past and future colliding in one tempting, disastrous physical attraction. Each word of the song pounded at her temples, reawakening her anger and resolution.

She wasn't her mother and never would be. But she knew from experience that people, especially men, treated her differently when they found out about her childhood. Their attitudes changed. Their words changed. Above all, their eyes changed.

Vivian would definitely change if Ziara's past found the light of day.

Abruptly Sloan stood, grasping her hand to pull her to her feet, then guide her up the aisle to the muted lighting of the foyer. As he paused outside the auditorium doors, she turned to him, acutely conscious of his hand still wrapped around hers. She blinked, her vision adjusting to the faint light, bright after the darkness of the theater.

"What is it?" she asked, withdrawing slightly as he studied her with uncomfortable intensity. That gaze didn't miss much, and she felt as vulnerable as an open book right now.

"You seemed to have lost interest, so I thought it was time to go," Sloan said, a question in his voice.

She shifted, firmly drawing her hand from his grasp. "What makes you say that?"

Stupid! Her defensiveness would surely make him even more curious. Too bad she didn't have a real zipper in her mouth like she'd pretended to as a child, then she could zip her lips shut so nothing incriminating could leak out.

He stepped closer, as if to regain any ground lost by letting go of her hand. She checked the urge to retreat. "You kept wiggling. You seemed uncomfortable and weren't watching the stage despite the excellent performances."

He reached out and pushed an errant strand of hair back behind her ear. Her flesh tingled at the contact, speeding up her heartbeat.

"Was it the performance or the content?"

Now her heart pounded in her chest, drowning out any

sound around her. She made the mistake of meeting his gaze; those cool, steady eyes coaxing her to spill her secrets. But if he knew, knew what her mother had been, those eyes would change. They would glitter, hard as ice, as he condemned her just like her classmates and the townspeople of good ol' Macon, Georgia. Only this time, the life she'd built would be at stake, not just her heart.

"We've got somewhere to be," he said, turning away without waiting for an answer. Had he drawn his own conclusions?

As she followed him down several hallways, she pulled herself back into professional mode, sharp and on alert around Sloan's prying eyes.

Her first inkling that all was not as she suspected came when Sloan led her through a nondescript door that opened into a back corridor near the theater. After several minutes of walking, they came to a door marked Backstage with a doorman keeping a close eye on things. Sloan pulled something from his jacket pocket and the man waved him in.

Going through that door was like entering another dimension. Whereas earlier Ziara had been dazzled by the lights, sounds and effortless flow of the production, now she was amazed that such beauty came from such chaos.

Performers stood in groups chatting or rushing to and from who knows where. Stagehands attended to curtains, props and other mysterious tasks, sidestepping anyone or anything in their way. But it was nearly silent chaos, for the tone of the noise remained low and soft, ever aware of the audience and performance not too far away.

Sloan led her deeper into the backstage area, through rooms containing waiting performers. Here the noise level rose, protected from the stage by distance. Finally they came to a long, narrow room lined with dressing tables. Sloan didn't even blink at the number of women—very toned, well-built women—in various stages of undress, though several certainly noticed him.

He made a beeline to the far end of the room with Ziara cautiously following, awkward under the eyes tracking their progress. Finally Sloan stopped, moving slightly to one side so that Ziara came up even with him. Before them stood one of the performers, a showgirl decked out in a wisp of spandex and sequins. Ziara's gaze trailed down the outfit to catch sight of a man crouched behind the girl, one hand inside the bottom of her outfit and a needle and thread in the other. His spiky blond hair was just level with her rear end, as he leaned close to repair a seam.

"Ziara," Sloan said, "I'd like you to meet Patrick Vinalay, my roommate from college."

Ziara's heart stopped at the shock, then resumed beating again triple time.

This would definitely not go over well. Vivian would throw a true hissy fit if Sloan hired this man to design her wedding dresses. Ziara managed a sickly smile as Sloan introduced her to Patrick's assistant, who was standing nearby.

"Welcome to the drudgery behind the glamour," Patrick said, waving a hand around them at the glittering chaos.

"It's nice to meet you," she murmured, at a loss for anything else to say. Fortunately he turned to Sloan, relieving her of the need for small talk. Her brain couldn't form a coherent sentence; she was still shell-shocked by the bomb Sloan had dropped on her.

What had he been thinking, to offer a man with this background first chance to modernize their line? Patrick was probably great at what he did, but that was the problem. What bride wanted to look like a Vegas showgirl on her wedding day? Eternity Designs was known for its elegance, subtle beauty... not tacky sequins.

Patrick stood, dropping the needle and thread on a table behind him. "So what brings you to Vegas, Sloan? I guess if you brought your assistant, you aren't here for a little *wink-wink*." Patrick accompanied the words with the matching motion. Then his eyes widened. "Or are you?"

The sound of distress—all Ziara could manage—had both men turning toward her. Patrick quickly backtracked. "I'm just kidding! A little off-color college humor between buddies. I'll try to remember my audience in the future."

But the serious consideration she caught lurking in Sloan's gaze sent heat rushing to her face. And the knowledge that some physical recreation hadn't been far from her mind from the moment she'd laid eyes on Sloan Creighton.

Moving closer, he cupped a hand on Patrick's shoulder. "I'm actually here on business."

A knowing, exasperated look crossed Patrick's face. "This wouldn't be about the design position, would it?"

"Of course. Why else would I take time out of my busy schedule to come to Sin City?"

"Oh, how about the glamour? The excitement?"

"Do I look like I have time for all that?" Sloan asked without a change of expression.

Patrick prodded some more. "Sexy women and high-stakes gambling?"

As a waiting showgirl called to Patrick, Sloan laughed. "I don't need all that. I just need a designer."

Shaking his head, Patrick gestured toward the girl in front of him. "Look, I've got to get this done before she has to be onstage for the final number. We'll talk after the curtain falls. Now get out of here," he said with a stern look around the dressing room. "You're distracting the girls."

Patrick's assistant peeked around his boss's shoulder. "And the boys," he said, his tone flirty.

Ziara tensed, unsure how Sloan would feel about this turn of events, but he simply threw a look at Patrick.

"Don't bother," Patrick said. "He's not interested, much to the disappointment of many of my friends throughout the years."

He favored Ziara with another cheeky wink, then crouched behind the woman once more. Ziara pulled Sloan by his arm into a darkened, abandoned corner. "Have you totally lost your mind?" she asked, her tone surprisingly calm and steady, though she was shaking on the inside. Her controlled voice and out-of-control words prompted a laugh from Sloan.

Knowing by now that honesty was the best way to reach him, she continued, "Do you have a death wish? Because Vivian will certainly kill you if you try to bring a costume designer in to work on our wedding dress line."

Sloan's eyes narrowed, his back stiffening in a way that made her swallow, hard. "Our? If I don't step up now, before Bridal Boutique sees the fall designs, there won't be a business left to save. This isn't a game to me, Ziara."

He loomed closer, his broad shoulders inducing a feeling of claustrophobia in the dusty space, leaving her vulnerable to his size. "Since it isn't Vivian's reputation on the line, I don't give a damn what she thinks."

"I understand your urgency, just not your secrecy. This wild idea is exactly why you need someone to provide balance," Ziara said.

"For the record, I'm keeping it quiet because I don't want her shooting down a plan that has nothing to do with her. Understand?"

Ziara drew in a deep breath, choking a little on the dry, dusty air. She knew exactly what Sloan meant. Vivian would do everything in her power to stop this, even if it lost them the Bridal Boutique account. Reputation was everything to her, as Ziara well knew.

"I don't agree with this choice." Ziara waved a hand in Patrick's general direction. "I understand why you are trying so hard to fix this problem. But why him?"

"Because he knows what he's doing," Sloan said.

"That's right," Patrick said from over Sloan's right shoulder, making Ziara jump. "I do know what I'm doing. Besides a degree in fashion design, I know my way around a booty, as you can see." He quirked a grin. "That should come in handy designing lingerie."

Ziara's chest tightened, cutting off her breath for a moment. Sloan's body remained close enough that she could feel the half laugh, half groan he choked back, but when she looked up, his face was still.

Her heart knew this wasn't a joke. Vivian had sensed all

along that Sloan was holding something back, that he might try something crazy. She'd had good reason to be concerned, because this was big. A lingerie line, no matter how tastefully done, would shatter Eternity's conservative reputation forever.

"You're adding a lingerie line," she said with a soft undertone of conviction. "No wonder you've been… You certainly did have something to hide."

Sloan's chin jutted forward, his aggressive stance for once matching his personality. "Are you going to run to Vivian and tattle like a good little girl?"

"Vivian. Good God!" Patrick said with an exaggerated shiver. "If she's involved, that's just one more reason to turn you down. That woman could intimidate the Pope."

Sloan ignored him, his gaze locked with Ziara's. He reached out to once more trace her jawline, his fingers gently abrasive against her sensitive skin.

"Which will it be, Ziara? Friend or foe?"

Eight

Sloan watched as Ziara struggled not to fidget during brunch the next morning. He knew exactly what the problem was, but putting her out of her misery by laying out a plan for the day wouldn't be nearly as fun as his current torture tactics.

She bided her time through coffee, waffles, eggs, mimosas and filet mignon, until she looked like the words would burst through her locked lips at the slightest provocation. He waited just a minute more, but she beat him to it.

"Are we seeing Patrick today?"

"I'm not entirely sure of his plans. We'll have to play it by ear." He could see uncertainty roll over her like a bumpy log. Any minute now steam would come billowing out of her ears. How could it be more fun to torture this woman than it was to sleep with other women? How had he even reached the point where he would ask himself that question?

"So are you excited about the lingerie line?" Sloan asked, a grin finally breaking free.

"Look," she said, that disapproving librarian look making a reappearance. "This is not some kind of game like you seem to think it is. Start talking, or I'll be on the phone to Vivian in two minutes."

He felt his mouth drop open, unable to believe she would adopt his own overbearing approach. Yet aroused by it, just the same.

"I want to understand, Sloan. I really do. But lingerie? Please explain this to me."

He drew in a deep breath before starting. "It's all about marketability—" His hand shot up to stop her from interrupting. "Let me explain." He wiped his mouth with the cloth napkin, then tossed it onto his plate.

"Vivian is focused on making the least amount of change that she can to get by." Standing, he worked off his restless energy by pacing to the glass balcony doors. "Hell if I know why. But that's not how to run a profitable business that will remain stable for the foreseeable future."

He saw logical understanding in her eyes but not the spark of passion he hoped for. He found himself wanting her to understand, needing her to understand. "Modern designs are great. Any willing designer can make those changes." His pacing picked up speed. "But I want a whole new approach—something different, a big splash to make us stand out from the crowd."

Halting, he found himself across the room from her. She sat at the table, her hands folded loosely on the smooth black top. His mind filled with an image of her dressed in lace and pearls for her wedding day, the epitome of elegance.

He mused aloud. "Most women shopping for their weddings already associate Eternity Designs's brand with their big day. Why not expand their thinking to their wedding night, too?"

She shifted. Fear battled with a growing interest in her eyes.

Suddenly he stepped forward, approaching her at a slow stalk. Her throat worked as she swallowed hard. He circled around, pausing behind her. The sweet scent of vanilla swirled in the air. Her personal scent. His gaze branded her at the vulnerable base of her neck.

"Think about it, Ziara—" Just like he was. "There you are,

preparing to put on the dress of your dreams. What do you wear underneath it?"

Leaning forward, he caged her in with an arm on each side. The glimpse of her face lured him to push her further. "Do you want to squeeze into a too-tight piece of Lycra? Itchy lace? Ugly beige?"

Her brows drew together over her now-closed eyes. Following his body's instincts, he lowered his voice, hoping to evoke the images in her mind.

"Or would you rather stand before the mirror in something just as sexy and beautiful as your dress, confident that your husband-to-be will be just as happy when your dress comes off as when he sees you walking down that aisle?"

He shifted closer, his own mind exploding with visions of her in flaming red satin, dark purple silk and then nothing at all. He barely covered a groan.

"Think about a silky smooth body shaper trimmed in soft lace, the same cream color as the dress. No ugly stitching and oxygen-stealing constriction. A strapless bra the perfect shape for your dress's neckline, with smooth, shaped cups and peek-aboo netting."

A grimace twisted her lips.

"What was that?" he whispered, speaking very close to her right ear. Shivers raced across her skin.

"Nothing," she said, but her voice choked on its way out.

"Ah, methinks the lady has a small problem with sensual…"

Her breath paused just as he did.

"…clothes."

With a whoosh, she started to breathe again. *Dangerous territory,* his mind whispered. She wasn't just resisting because of Vivian—she shied away because something was making her uneasy. Why was a woman whose home was filled with color and spice afraid of the same when she was in his presence?

"You know what?" he asked, backing away as a plan took shape in his brain.

He circled around to stand beside her. Though what came next would probably be the last thing on her agenda, he refused to ask. Only demand. He wanted to know *why*. "We'll perform a little experiment."

"Experiment?" Her high-pitched squeak sent a hot flush through him.

"Yep, time for a field trip." He grabbed her hand, urging her to her feet when she would have resisted. "Let's go."

Oh, this situation had just escalated from bad idea to worse.

The elevator offered her no protection from his probing gaze. She shifted from foot to foot, as if she was a naughty schoolgirl on her way to the principal's office.

He took advantage of their isolation to push her a little further. "Why are you so judgmental of the lingerie idea? Is it the notion of change or the lingerie itself?"

She kept her gaze resolutely fixed on the numbers marking their downward journey. "I'm simply worried about my job," she said. "Vivian would not appreciate having Eternity Designs associated with…that…"

"Ah, so it's the lingerie itself."

"What?" she asked with a gasp, only to look at him and catch his satisfied grin. "I did not say that."

The grin widened. "You didn't have to."

He didn't speak again, but instead let the silence build until she rushed to fill it. "I think it's just, you know." Her hand gestured toward her body in an awkward jerk.

"I don't know. What?" He drew the word out.

"It just seems dirty."

"Seen a lot of it, have you?"

Ziara gave a simple shrug of her shoulders, but the red that rushed up her chest and into her cheeks told a whole different story. And had him licking his lips.

"Obviously not," he said as the elevator doors slid open on the ground floor. "It's time for your education."

Ziara struggled not to choke on her hot embarrassment as she stood beside Sloan. Not even her Indian heritage could hide this blush.

Around my mom's house, I saw it all the time. But she wasn't about to detail her mother's favorite business wear. That woman had never made a secret of what she did for a living—at home or away from it.

Ziara followed Sloan at a trot as he strode through the bustling indoor avenues that traversed the ground floor of their hotel. At first she suspected they were heading for the casino floor with its scantily clad waitresses or even another show. Instead, they silently traveled quite a distance to an indoor promenade fashioned as a replica of a high-end Parisian shopping district lined with quaint, expensive little shops.

Now they stood facing one and she was deathly afraid of what he would demand next.

A lingerie store.

If he expected her to tour a place like that with him at her side, the heat might rise to explosive temperatures. Tremors radiated from her thighs to her calves. It could have been the fast pace of the walk, but she suspected it was dread of what loomed on her horizon.

Sloan made no immediate demands. Instead, he planted his feet, crossed his arms over his chest and studied the delicate ironwork framing the front windows. "What do you see, Ziara?"

The stuff of my nightmares. She settled for, "A store."

The sound grumbling low in his throat could have been disapproval…or a threat. "Look closer. Describe it to me."

Taking a deep breath, she brought her focus to the windows.

The wince was involuntary, a force of habit as she glimpsed the barely there bra-and-panty sets, the sheer teddies, the lace-only gowns. So she turned her attention to the framework—aged wrought iron in fancy curlicues decorating the windows as if they were paintings—

"Out loud," Sloan said, breaking into her thoughts. His voice remained soft, but there was no mistaking the steel undertone. "Describe it to me, Ziara."

Swallowing anger at his high-handedness, she said, "The windows remind me of pictures, feminine and delicate. The pink-and-brown decor is also feminine, like candy and chocolate, but classy, like a sophisticated chocolatier."

"Very good. Go on."

She let her eyes slip to the lingerie, then quickly pulled back. "I don't know. It's underwear." Or outerwear, depending on the woman.

Silence engulfed them in the midst of the eddying crowd. As the seconds ticked by, Ziara's internal tension wound tighter and tighter. Whatever this test was, she was obviously failing.

"Ziara, I want you to go inside."

Yikes.

"Go inside and see for yourself. And I mean really look. Lingerie does not have to be slutty."

She scoffed. "Tell that to—" Her teeth clamped shut.

"To who?" he asked, his voice barely loud enough to be heard above the noise from the crowds.

The shake of her head was sharp, a reflection of the anger building inside of her. She had no idea where it came from or why it filled her so quickly. But it had to stop. *She* had to stop. The cracks would get too wide and then she'd never be able to repair them.

"I can't do this, Sloan." Turning on her heel, she was stopped by two strong hands with the softest of holds on her upper arms.

"Wait, Ziara," he said, his voice once more soft, speaking into her ear just as he had in the privacy of their suite. Here, it was just as intimate. "You can do this. I know you can. You simply have to trust me."

"You don't know," she whispered, not even sure he could hear her.

"Whatever it is, I want you to lock it away."

She thought she had, but not well enough.

"Lock it away and go in with fresh eyes. Use those gorgeously sensitive fingers to explore, to discover. Trust me."

If only I could... But she couldn't say that out loud, so she simply nodded her head. His hands slid down her arms, then defected to her waist, leaving tingles of awareness in their wake. Then he turned her to once again face the storefront. "Go in."

She was halfway to the door when the fear took hold of her. Glancing over her shoulder, her eyes met his. Without a word, he urged her forward. Without a word, she followed his command.

The fabrics were beautiful, tempting her to touch, to stroke, to explore the texture and feel. But each time she reached out, she could sense Sloan tracking her progress from display to display. His gaze blanketed her in warmth, strength. She could almost feel him surrounding her, pushing her, enticing her.

A nightgown, pale gray and silky smooth, slid over her fingertips. She could imagine it against her skin, caressing her hips, the sensitive tips of her breasts. Sloan's gaze had her wondering if he imagined her in the silvery fabric, too.

Somehow the nightie and a matching robe found their way into her hands. A spot of the same silvery gray color caught her eye from a nearby table. Panties had always been utilitarian for her. Waistband and shape were chosen for comfort.

But with the first stroke she imagined wearing them for Sloan's hot gaze. She couldn't begin to see herself in a thong, but the dramatic curve of the high-cut briefs would line the edges of her backside with sheer lace. The phantom feel of his fingers tracing the edges brought a shiver along her spine, daring her to look over her shoulder through the outer windows.

She couldn't, wouldn't, but she scooped several colors into her hands and moved to the register before she could think any more about it. All the while, Sloan's presence called to her from just outside the door. His tracking gaze should have induced embarrassment. Instead, every glimpse of him through those wide windows brought the warm reminder of comfort, encouragement and, yes, trust. Along with a desire to be a woman she was not.

Without him she'd have never even spared this store a glance.

Her rush out the door slowed as she noticed a corner set off from the rest of the store. A quick glance made her think, *Wedding night,* prompting her to pause, to wonder.

A younger woman held up a thigh-length confection of cream satin, lace and pearls. Her companion, who was old enough to be her mother and probably was, smiled, whispering something that encouraged a nod from the daughter. They walked toward the dressing rooms, leaving Ziara watching them with loneliness creeping into her heart.

And confusion.

At first she'd been convinced Sloan was out of his mind. But maybe, just maybe, he was on the right track.

Getting married was a precious vow. She knew that even though she'd never witnessed or wanted that happily ever after herself. What if Sloan could extend the traditions of Eternity Designs to the private celebrations of marriage and not just the public ones?

For an instant the desire to experience a love deep enough for that kind of commitment overwhelmed her, settling at the pit of her stomach in a tide of need. She'd been alone so long, depending only on herself, the only person she could trust. What would it be like to give in to those feelings of overwhelming attraction, to trust someone to understand your needs rather than judge you for them?

She shook her head. With unerring accuracy, she turned to the windows and met Sloan's bright blue gaze once more. Deliberately lowering her lashes, she forced her thoughts to the lasting image of the mother's smile. She would never experience the feminine bond of shopping for her wedding night. Even though her mother wasn't dead, shopping for lingerie with a prostitute was a whole different experience from what she'd just witnessed. She knew. She'd lived it.

Nine

Following Sloan back into the cool air-conditioning of the hotel suite, Ziara noticed the sweat coating her neck and scalp as she took her purchases to her room. A pounding headache—whether from the building tension or lingering emotions—throbbed in her temples and down along her jaw. A few minutes alone, that's all she needed. Time away from Sloan's probing gaze and questioning looks.

He'd watched her closely as she returned to him on the promenade, his eyes flicking between her face and the bag in her hands. That's when the arousal had hit her, this time piercing and sharp. Almost painful. It would be a long time before she forgot that particular sensation.

In the bathroom she pulled the pins from her hair, allowing the heavy weight to fall below her shoulders. She ran a quick brush through the mass. Sometimes just letting it down was enough to ease her tension headaches.

Walking into her bedroom, she moved to close her door so she could rest for a while, but the phone rang. Not hearing any sound in the suite outside, she crossed to the extension beside her bed, stretching her neck from side to side as she went. Taking a deep breath, she answered.

"Hello?"

"Ziara?" Vivian's voice rang in her ear, stealing her breath for a moment. A wealth of suspicion and condemnation resided in that one word.

"Yes, Vivian?"

"Would you like to explain to me what you are doing in Sloan's hotel room?"

For a moment, Ziara's head swirled. Her own concerns mixed with remembered insults and insinuations from the past. She forced herself to breathe, remembering Vivian knew nothing about her past. And never would if she had anything to say about it.

"Actually," Ziara said, grateful her voice came out calm and even, "I'm in my own room. Sloan booked us into a suite so we'd have a common area for working."

Vivian didn't answer immediately, as if pondering Ziara's explanation. This time her voice was a little less tight. "Good. I'd hate to see your reputation compromised by Sloan's charm."

Words rushed to Ziara's lips in her own defense, but she held them back. They would sound like token protests. Besides, hadn't she been tempted? Like Eve by the snake.

"Thank you for your concern," she murmured.

"Ziara, why didn't you contact me about this trip? Why didn't you keep me informed as I instructed?"

Because my phone was resting a little too close to your stepson's privates for me to comfortably make a phone call.

She could have made the phone call after getting to the hotel, but by that time she'd convinced herself that Monday was soon enough to let Vivian know.

Oh, wouldn't that go over well? She decided on a half-truth. "By the time I realized we were going, it was too late to call. I mistakenly thought I could inform you of everything when I returned."

Maybe her growing attraction for Sloan was corroding the responsible part of her brain, but she just hadn't been able to call without his consent. Her mind had justified the need for more information, more…something.

Now she had more of the facts, and she was starting to see Sloan's point of view. Scary, but holding back seemed to be the right plan. For now. Besides, Vivian would faint dead away if she knew who Sloan was here to see.

"I'm truly sorry, Vivian." She used her most placating tone, the one reserved for unhappy clients. "I had to rush to be ready for an early flight Saturday morning."

There wasn't any need to tell her Sloan had come to her house. Vivian would find that move totally unprofessional.

"I see. That does sound like a stunt he would pull. We all know he wants me kept in the dark as long as possible."

Thankfully, that statement was totally true.

"Well, on a personal level, let me warn you, if I may." Vivian's tone didn't sound like a gentle warning. More like a harsh command. "Be careful. You don't want to end up like all the rest of Sloan's assistants, now do you?"

"What do you mean?"

"He has a history of going through them like Kleenex. Oh, he says the feelings, the misconceptions are all their faults. But I know that they are drawn in by his charm, and when he's used them, he discards them with little thought."

Aren't you glad that attitude didn't run in the family? Ziara knew the thought was petty, but Vivian's comments disturbed her on many levels. She didn't want to believe, but then again, what if Vivian spoke the truth? Didn't Sloan flirt and tease her? Hadn't he just taken her to a lingerie store?

Ziara's goal for her entire adult life had been an honorable career. She wanted an employer who respected her for who she was, what she was capable of, not a series of dirty, no-meaning encounters that would put her back in the ugliness of her childhood. Especially if she did it with her boss.

"I promise to keep that in mind."

"Good. I'm only trying to look out for you," Vivian said in an overly sweet tone. "As your mentor, and someone who knows Sloan very well, I don't want to see you get hurt."

"I understand, Vivian."

Even as she spoke, Ziara could feel guilt creeping in. Vivian had done so much for her. Her loyalties toward the woman who had nurtured her career and Eternity Designs were being ripped apart, piece by piece, by her growing attraction to Sloan, reinforcing the doubt Vivian planted in her mind.

"Now," Vivian's voice intruded, "I assume you've gone to Las Vegas to court a designer, though why he'd be there I have no clue. And why we need one is lost on me."

Yet another topic fraught with minefields. "Yes, Sloan is looking into a designer here, but I don't think anything definitive has been decided."

"Hmm, does he look any good? What do you think of his work?"

Well, if you are into tassels and sequins... "Actually I haven't had the chance to see any of his work yet," she said, hiding behind another little lie. Because if Vivian knew Sloan wanted a costume designer, she'd be on the first plane headed anywhere near Las Vegas. Ziara wasn't ready for that—yet. "I've only briefly met him. I think Sloan is hoping for a more formal meeting tonight."

She could hear the *tap, tap, tap* of Vivian's gold pen against her desk. That habit always indicated she was thinking hard.

"Well, I guess it wouldn't do any good to tell him I called. Is there anything else you think I need to know?"

Ziara's stomach tightened. Her legs went shaky. This was a big step, putting her own career on the line. But some small niggle in the pit of her stomach said Sloan might be on to something with this lingerie idea. He certainly wasn't going to get a lot of cooperation from Robert. She had to know for sure before she could decide where her *company* loyalty lay.

"No. Right now there's nothing more to tell."

Another tension-filled pause. Did Vivian suspect she knew more than she was letting on? "Very well. Keep me informed."

Ziara stifled a sigh and said simply, "Yes, ma'am."

After disconnecting, Ziara sank to the bed, her wobbly knees no longer able to support her traitorous stand.

Had she just made an irrevocable decision based on her physical response to the wrong man, a man who could never be more than her boss, instead of practical career considerations? She hoped not, because if Vivian learned she'd hid something so important from her, her career with Eternity Designs would be over.

Was making the fall line a success more important than her own need for security? The answers weren't so clear-cut anymore—no matter who ended up controlling the company. Hopefully, Vivian would never know at what point Ziara discovered the truth.

Like any dangerous pilgrimage, moving forward was the only option. She had to see where Sloan was heading with what she now knew were two new lines. Rising to her feet, she straightened her clothes, then turned toward the door, all thoughts of a nap now abolished from her mind.

Sloan stood in the doorway.

Ziara froze, absorbing his powerful presence, though he leaned casually against the doorframe with his arms crossed over his chest. His face had softened into a slight smile, but his eyes tracked her every move.

The contrast threw her off once more. On the outside he appeared approachable, carefree and happy, but those intense blue eyes alerted her to the hunter within. Pushing away from the frame, he stalked toward her, the tired lines on his face becoming faintly visible. This quest was wearing on him, as well. Her fingers itched to trace the weariness with her fingertips, soothing it away like she would a wrinkle out of fabric, but she forced her hands to remain still.

Stopping so close that a deep breath would bring his chest into contact with hers, he slid his hands into her hair and covered her lips with his own.

Ziara's widened eyes closed as the explosion of sensation from her lips connected with the feel of his hands in the tumble of her hair. He kneaded her scalp as if to massage away the tension hiding there, and she melted into his embrace. Reason and logic disappeared. He could do whatever he wanted. *Just don't stop touching me.*

Never one to do things by half measures, Sloan's tongue plunged through her parted lips, sweeping across her own, igniting a flash of longing through her body. Long after the last of her intelligence had leaked from her brain, he pulled back a fraction. His hands remained anchored in her hair, his minty breath fanning across her face.

Forcing her heavy lids upward, her eyes met his. "What was that for?" she asked, embarrassed by the husky whisper of her voice.

His hands tightened against her head for a moment as if to draw her forward for another kiss but, instead, he spoke. "For keeping my secrets."

They stood immobile for long minutes, afraid to move and bring reality back into their fragile peace. Ziara had never experienced anything like their kiss. Everything before had been a simple match set to flame, but this time fireworks exploded.

She needed to back away, but she didn't.

Slowly his hands drew the silky weight of her hair forward and over her shoulders. "Beautiful," he whispered, though his eyes never left hers.

An urge unlike any she'd ever experienced swept through her. No previous desire, no previous need felt real compared to the intensity of this moment. With no thought, she leaned forward, eager to taste his kiss once more. He didn't back away.

Until a knock sounded on the door.

Sloan escaped to the outer room, leaving Ziara behind. One deep breath followed another. If he could just get his head in gear and think this through, he'd make the right choice. When he opened the door, a courier brought in a simple white box, fairly long and thick in size, tied with a deep purple bow.

Sloan closed the door and turned to catch sight of Ziara standing in her bedroom doorway. She hugged herself loosely across her middle, warning him that awkwardness had set in. Good thing he had something to break the ice.

He drew in another deep breath, willing his heart to stop racing. His response to her was unbelievably strong. "You have a delivery," he said.

"Me?"

As she walked to the table, he noted her hair swinging midway down her back. His hands itched to bury themselves in the dark, silky fullness again. He'd always suspected her hair would be extravagant when set free from the constraint of that bun thing, but the sight and feel of it surpassed his tantalizing dreams.

He watched her delicately untie the bow, her care and precision not surprising him. But her restraint had a different quality to it, something more than just her normal reserve.

He studied her movements. The contained excitement on her face, the slight parting of her lips. Did she ever receive surprises? Was there no one in her life to offer those happy moments, big or small? With an unexpected spike of jealousy, he hoped there wasn't another man. He'd seen no evidence of anyone at her house.

Was her family the reason she'd closed herself off from the sensual parts of life? Had someone hurt her, damaged her?

She lifted the lid slowly, then pushed aside the tissue covering the contents. Her eyes widened, that sweet mouth opening in a silent O. She didn't remove whatever was inside, simply caressed it with exploring fingertips just as he'd seen her do with the lingerie and design fabrics.

Before those luscious strokes could completely shatter his control, Sloan walked forward to peer into the box himself. At first all he could see were layers upon layers of sheer, brightly colored fabric before he realized an expensive dress lay inside.

Sloan's suspicions were confirmed when Ziara pulled out the card tucked among the golden tissue.

"Patrick. But why?" she asked, turning to face him, though one hand remained resting amid the folds of the dress.

He opened the note. "We're invited to a party Patrick is hosting tonight. He wants you to wear this," he said, handing the paper over for her to read. His earlier jealousy settled like a lead brick in his stomach because Sloan himself hadn't been the one to make her eyes light up like stars.

She gazed back into the box but still didn't lift the dress. "I can't believe he did that." She looked at Sloan, a frown drawing those elegantly arched brows together. "Is this appropriate? I don't want to give the wrong impression."

"You worry too much. Of course it's okay to accept a gift. I'd say it's a sign we're headed in the right direction." Reaching in, he found the straps and lifted the dress, shaking it out to its full length. "Exquisite," he murmured.

Patrick's mind must have run along similar lines as Sloan's. The vibrant, flaming colors would be a stunning complement to Ziara's dark caramel skin and black hair. The soft, handkerchief layers of the skirt echoed her femininity, as did the cut pieces attached to the form-revealing bodice. His lips pressed together as he slipped into creative mode.

"I don't think I can wear this."

Sloan surfaced from his thoughts at the sound of Ziara's shaky voice. "Of course you can. This dress was made for you."

She shook her head, those soft waves of hair framing her face. "No, I can't. I'd feel too exposed."

Exposed? The dress did have only single straps across the shoulders, though they were thicker than spaghetti straps. The scoop of the neckline would reveal a little bit of cleavage, leaving her chest and arms bare. His mouth watered at the thought of all that delectable skin on display for his starving imagination.

He eyed the jacket she was wearing—her standard office fare. He remembered the T-shirt with its three-quarter-length sleeves that she wore in the middle of a hot Southern summer. Maybe there was more to her clothing than just an overblown sense of professionalism. If she was going to be stubborn about this—a grim smile slipped out—he had the perfect ammo for fighting back.

"Don't be stupid. You're wearing it."

"No." Her arms folded around her waist as if to anchor her clothes. Did she think he would strip her naked to force her to wear it? The tightening in his groin reminded him his thoughts were moving into dangerous territory.

He pulled back immediately, but pushing *her* out of her comfort zone would be good for her. The sensuous, open woman he'd glimpsed at her house needed releasing. If he benefited at the same time, all the better.

He tossed the dress toward the box, crowding forward to tower over her. "You don't get it, do you?" He connected his gaze with hers, insuring he had her full attention. This wasn't about business for him…his descent from lofty goals was gaining speed. But business was what she understood, so that's the reasoning he'd use.

"I want Patrick as my designer, and I'll do whatever I have to for him to agree. So if he sent a garbage bag with holes for the head and arms, you would be wearing that."

Her back stiffened and those lush lips thinned. Still he drove his point home. "We'll do whatever Patrick wants. Don't forget who's the boss around here."

Her eyes narrowed to a glare, her softly pointed chin edging up a notch.

"Now," he said, before he could give in to the temptation to kiss her pretty pout away, "go hang the dress up. We've got a party to get ready for."

"What are you talking about?" she asked. "The party isn't until eight tonight, and it's just now three."

God, her anger made her that much more beautiful and awoke an urge to channel it into a more mutually beneficial emotion.

"Trust me," he said. "We'll make every minute count."

Ten

Ziara's knees developed a tremor as she stared at herself in the mirror, making her unsteady on high-heeled gold sandals.

Sloan had instructed the hairdresser to leave her hair down, though she'd tucked one side up with a comb behind Ziara's ear. The orange, red and purple swirls of the dress and glint of gold threads hinted at a gypsy look, overlaid with Moroccan belly dancer.

The movement of the dress was reminiscent of veils, which emphasized the impression, along with her muted Indian heritage. Her skin seemed darker, more exotic. Her eyes more mysterious and shadowed. Her bearing more regal, like a princess tucked away in a harem—sensual, yet above approach.

The tremors grew, taking on a life of their own. Reminding herself that as Sloan's date, she didn't have to worry about anyone harassing her, she forced herself to walk to the door. But then, Sloan couldn't protect her from her own weaknesses, could he?

When she finally found the courage to leave her room, Sloan waited near the glass balcony doors. He turned to face her, his body a long, lean silhouette against the glittering backdrop of the city, whiskey tumbler in hand. An ache bloomed within her, a desire to meet him as an equal—strong, passionate and confident instead of closed off and broken.

He moved slowly into the light as he drank from the tumbler. His tongue slid across his lips, catching the last trace of amber alcohol. She followed the movement with her eyes, wishing she could lick the same path. He watched her, his light eyes sparking with desire as his gaze devoured the length of her body. These two days with him had attuned her to a whole level of herself she'd never known.

She stepped forward, conscious of the skirt, sheer from right above her knee down to the handkerchief points. Fear or revulsion should have set in, but neither did. Just a need to feel the heat of his mouth once again covering hers, her pulse pounding throughout the secret places of her body.

He stopped only inches away, forcing her to look up to see his face. The smooth line of his jaw, the taut muscles along his neck worked as he swallowed, making her own mouth water. But he didn't dip his head to indulge; instead, his eyes narrowed as a sexy grin spread across his full lips.

"I knew Patrick was the right designer for the job. He certainly knows what he's doing. This dress makes you look like magic."

His praise prompted her to stand a little straighter, ache to move a little closer, so she pulled back.

After clearing his throat, he said, "There was something else in the box."

"More?" She gestured to herself. "This is way too generous."

Sloan shrugged, his strong shoulders rippling under the slippery thin material of his button-down shirt. The blue made his eyes even more electric. Reaching into the pocket of his usual khaki pants, he pulled out a glittering length of golden circles. "He's a designer," Sloan said. "They want the look to be complete."

Ziara's mouth drained of moisture. Anxiety pounded at the

base of her throat, even though logic told her there wasn't any need for nerves. Then Sloan moved to put the chain around her throat.

"No." The force in her voice wasn't necessary, but she couldn't control it. Moderating a little, she continued, "No, please. I don't really like jewelry. It makes me uncomfortable."

"Why?" he asked with a frown.

Knowing any protest would just give him an opportunity to argue, she turned away. Moving to the balcony door of the suite, she escaped into the hallway with quick steps.

The limousine took them to a modest estate a short distance from the Strip. Ziara stepped out into night air that carried the tinkling sound of a center courtyard fountain. Through the open veranda windows drifted a soft rock song. The melody sounded vaguely familiar.

Sloan slipped up next to her, then tucked her hand into the crook of his arm. The gesture was a bit old-fashioned, part possessive, part protective. Despite her usual "no touching" rule, this calmed her nerves as they made their way up the stone steps.

They hadn't moved ten feet from the car before Patrick appeared through one of the arched doorways. The open floor plan of the house allowed glimpses of the adjoining rooms through the repeated arches.

"Ziara, you look exquisite," Patrick said, inspecting his creation and her in it. "Of course, I knew you would." Though his gaze lingered at her bare throat, he didn't mention the jewelry.

She smiled. "Thank you. And thank you for sending the dress." She fingered the skirt with her free hand, glancing down at the flaming swirl of material. "It's so beautiful."

Having stood silent long enough, Sloan said, "I knew you had talent, but this proves it. I'm tempted to up my offer."

Patrick frowned. "Sloan, no business. This is a party. Don't you remember how to have fun?" He pulled Ziara gently into his own grasp. "Let's mingle and meet about a hundred of my closest friends."

Ziara laughed, surprised the sound floated from her so

freely. The loosening of her control was almost a physical sensation.

Then she simply let herself follow Patrick's lead. He took them from group to group, making introductions. He didn't mention Ziara's status as Sloan's assistant. Her instinct was to correct him the first time, but something stopped her at the last minute. She didn't want to be that person right now, which was both scary and exhilarating.

Would the universe fall apart if she loosened up for just this one night?

They finally settled in with a small group of Patrick's theater buddies, one or two of whom had also known Sloan since college. After a period of catching up, one of the men turned to her. "And what do you do, Ziara?"

Unsure how much she should reveal, she answered, "I'm an executive assistant in training at a wedding gown design firm."

"Hey, Sloan, doesn't your family own one of those?" one of the men asked.

"Yep."

"Which is why I'm in training—to keep him on track," she said, unable to resist teasing.

Everyone chuckled. Before Sloan could make a snappy reply, Patrick stepped into the gap between them. "Could I borrow my buddies here for a few minutes? There's something I think they'd like to see."

Ziara nodded, smiling as the men stepped away. The women around her chatted about the wedding dress industry, distracting her from a sudden sense of vulnerability. With a deep breath, she remembered she could take care of herself. She'd been doing it every day since a very early age.

After chatting for a while, she excused herself to hunt down a drink. Despite the variety of alcohol at the bar, the parched Nevada air had put Ziara in desperate need of plain old water. When the waiter gave her the bottle, she opened it gratefully. The chilly liquid soothed her dry throat.

Someone bumped into her from behind, hard. Grimacing as

cold water splashed across her bodice, she tightened her grip on her drink and spun around.

"I'm sorry," said a man in a navy suit with a loosened tie, the top three buttons of his shirt undone. His gaze wavered and he took precise care in pronouncing his words. He was obviously drunk but trying to hide it.

"No harm done," she said, brushing at the water spots darkening her dress. She replaced the lid on her bottle for good measure. "It's just water. It'll dry."

He stared at her a moment before a pseudo-charming smile tightened his loose lips. "That's nice."

Her tension mounted as he closed the gap between them. She told herself he wouldn't attempt anything in a room full of people, but she'd seen enough drunks to know they were unpredictable.

"You're really pretty," he said, only slurring the words a little. His slight adjustment to his tie and straightening of his shoulders reinforced his attempt at being suave. It wasn't working for her.

"Thank you." She moved back a few steps before forcing herself to stop. *Stand your ground.*

"I think such beauty deserves a kiss." As the man advanced, Ziara held up her hands to maintain distance between them. Her water bottle dropped to the floor.

"Stop right there," she said, remembered panic adding force to her words. "I'm not interested, so you can just back away."

He paused. "What do you mean, not interested? I bet you're just saying that. Women who look like you are always interested."

His assumption punctured her normally impenetrable armor. Her arms wavered long enough for him to slip through. Grabbing her, he dragged her body closer. "I'll just have a taste of the goods for sale."

If his earlier words were a pinprick, these were a knife to the heart. The pain that lanced through her provided the strength to slam her foot down on his toes as he leaned forward to touch his lips to hers. Then she shoved him back, straight into Patrick's chest.

Sloan's friend surveyed the situation with wide eyes behind his designer wire-rimmed glasses. Sliding an arm around the man's shoulders, he said, "Come on, Michael. Let's get you into a taxi before my friend here decides to find the nearest meat grinder."

As Patrick led the drunk away, Sloan moved close to study her but kept his hands to himself. Her contrary body protested, aching for his touch.

"Are you okay?" he asked, his face tight.

"I'm fine," she said, struggling to control the sudden shake in her voice. She reached down for her water bottle. "No big deal."

He leaned forward until his eyes were level with hers. "Really? Because I don't think that guy's foot would agree with you."

A glance in that direction showed Patrick and the drunk had disappeared. "I'm sorry I made a scene at Patrick's party. I'll certainly apologize and smooth things over when he returns."

Sloan clasped her wrist, using it to guide her to a secluded corner. "I don't give a damn about any scene. That guy's lucky I didn't coldcock him. I'm kind of jealous that you handled it without me."

Though his mouth remained serious, his eyes smiled into hers. She was never so glad to see the crinkles along the sides.

"Well, a woman has to do what a woman has to do. This is the twenty-first century, you know."

"Does that mean I can't lead while we dance?" They shared a smile, then he bent close to her ear, his breath ruffling her hair. "I have the odd compulsion to throw a blanket over you. But I doubt you need me for protection."

She shivered, afraid of her sudden yearning for connection. Her body felt as if it was attached to an electric pulse. She'd never had this reaction to the few lovers she'd previously accepted, men she'd chosen very carefully for their safe auras.

The two who'd made it to the sexual stage hadn't been worth a repeat performance.

She had an inkling being with Sloan would be the performance of her life.

"Let's dance," he said in a husky whisper.

She stiffened, trying to pull back as he led her through the crowded rooms to the patio. "I don't think that's a good idea, Sloan. I've never danced before."

He paused. "Never?"

She shook her head.

"Not on a date?"

"No."

"Not even at a school dance?"

She shook her head again, not about to tell him she'd gone extra lengths to stay away from the guys around her school. Her mother's reputation wasn't a secret in her small hometown. Ziara had been harassed on more than one occasion by boys and girls alike—boys who expected something from her, girls who judged her for the same reason.

Sloan's trademark sexy grin slid into place, softening his face and sparking in those intent eyes. "Then I'll be the first."

They stepped onto the back patio, an oasis in the desert. Framed by potted and hanging plants, the stone mosaic floor created texture and color. Soft lighting from outdoor torches combined with the stars overhead, giving the feel of vast open space despite the others dancing and talking around them.

As a slow song floated on the air, Sloan chuckled. "Great. This will be an easy start."

With trepidation, Ziara let him pull her into his arms. Her fears—of giving in, of him seeing how she reacted and completely humiliating herself—kept her stiff. But when he settled her chest against his, their bodies in complete alignment, her muscles relaxed without her permission.

Her body openly rejoiced in Sloan's nearness, letting the earlier encounter fade from memory. The nervous shivers radiating from deep inside were chased away by his proximity—heat, height and a touch of humor.

She instinctively moved in time with him. He didn't lead her into anything fancy, but he didn't just shuffle his feet, either. Other than holding her firm and close, he didn't make any other move to touch her. He didn't have to. She responded fluidly to every brush, every breath. And she didn't have to wonder if she was the only one feeling this, because the hardness of his body made it very clear he was along for the ride.

As one song blended into the next, Sloan pulled back enough to see her face illuminated in the soft glow of the torches. "Better now?" he asked.

"Of course," she said, hoping to brush aside any further references to the earlier upset.

"Those smooth moves made it look like you have experience defending yourself."

He'd never know how much. Instead, she shrugged. "Self-defense course at the Y."

He nodded but continued to watch her. At least she thought he did. Looking down, his face hovered over her in shadow, leaving her guessing. It should have been a relief to not see that intense purpose in his eyes, but instead the mysterious darkness both drew and scared her.

She knew just the way to redirect her thoughts.

"I'm starting to see what you mean. You talk a good game about company direction and expanding on buyers' demands, but…thank you for showing me."

His mouth opened as if he would speak, but then he brushed a soft kiss against her temple. "You're welcome."

As the song shifted into something a little rowdier, Sloan guided her off the dance floor to a secluded corner of the patio. The dry air was noticeably cooler, bringing gooseflesh to the surface of her skin. But the incredible view of the moon riding low in the sky over distant mountains distracted her.

"Ziara," Sloan said, his voice low and intimate. "I realize Vivian doesn't trust me—" The hand he raised to stop her words compelled her to pause. "I understand why she doesn't. Considering our history, she shouldn't. But I do actually know what I'm doing. Maybe the design part is new to me, but I've been buying companies and rebuilding them, sometimes after devastating setbacks, for more years than I care to count. I *can* do this."

His focus shifted out into the night. He leaned forward, resting his elbows on the stone balustrade. "But more than that, my father meant a lot to me. She thinks she's cornered the market on those emotions, but she hasn't."

Ziara recognized the ache in his voice from that first encounter in his father's office. "This really does mean a lot to you, doesn't it?" she asked, her voice barely above a whisper.

His head dipped as if in defeat, though she couldn't imagine him being defeated by anything—even Vivian's determined animosity.

"My childhood was wonderful until my mother died."

Ziara couldn't imagine how different her life would have been without her mother, how much better. "How old were you?"

"Fourteen."

She winced. "That's a bad age for major upheaval."

"Yes," he said with a slow nod as he looked out at the desert sky. "Her death was quick, only six weeks after she was diagnosed with a brain tumor." His pause was heavy with memories. "I had a new stepmother within a year."

What had his father been thinking? "It must have been hard for him to be alone."

"He wasn't alone. He had me." His deep sigh blew away any sounds of self-pity. "My father changed after he married Vivian," he said, the words slow but gaining speed. "Life became all about his new wife—her demands, her needs, her desires. What little was left went to his company, not to a fifteen-year-old boy in need of reassurance after losing his mother to cancer."

The picture of isolation he painted was nearly as bad as her own teenage years, living in her mother's house but not really *living* with her mother.

"She told my father I was lazy, unmotivated. But instead of wondering why, he simply condemned me. Any protests were considered a teenager's way of trying to weasel out of the consequences."

"And things never got better, even after you became an adult?"

"Not with Vivian poisoning his brain. At least, not that I could tell." He turned to her, the movement bringing them almost as close as they'd been on the dance floor. "He died from a heart attack, you know. Very unexpected."

Ziara had known, but he seemed to need to talk so she let him.

"When the lawyer read his will, I could hear Vivian screaming in frustration even though she never uttered a sound. The fact that he left me any part of Eternity Designs completely shocked her."

As if he needed some connection with Ziara, his hands reached out to rub up and down her arms, warming her from the outside in. "But that forty percent meant more to me than all the money, houses and stuff Vivian inherited. I could have sold it, resented it. But it made me think that in some small way, he had truly seen what I'd made of my life and was telling me that he believed in me."

An alien urge to wrap her arms around his waist and snuggle close swept through her. She just barely kept herself from acting. "Then why did you stay away so long?" If the company had meant so much to him, why had he left Vivian to it?

Laughter rumbled in his chest, the vibration echoing in her own and setting off all kinds of sparks under her skin. "You've seen how well Vivian works with me. For Eternity's own well-being, I stepped back from the running of it. She wanted free rein. I gave it to her."

"But you knew the time would come..."

"I knew without strong business acumen, Vivian probably couldn't keep the firm afloat. So I waited, and showed up when she didn't have a choice but to let me step in."

His cold calculation should disturb her, but what choice had he been given?

"Vivian should have known I wouldn't walk away forever," Sloan said. "Eternity is the only part of my father that I have left."

Which said all she needed to hear.

Eleven

Retracing their steps back through the house, Sloan found Patrick in the front room surrounded by people laughing. He gestured, letting his friend know he needed a moment.

Patrick approached with a casual, lanky stride. If he'd been into computers, he'd have been a geek, but he'd been designing clothes and dressing those around him for most of his life. He and Sloan had bonded as young men over the neglect of their home lives. Despite their many differences, Patrick was always the person to shake Sloan out of his anger, force him to look in a new direction or simply bust his chops until he could solve his problems. Sloan offered the same support, and they took every opportunity to dog each other about relationships, jobs and various life issues, just like the brothers they should have been.

Now Sloan needed something more than camaraderie. His thoughts must have shown, because Patrick flashed a rueful grin. "Do-or-die time, huh?" he said.

Sloan didn't disappoint. "Yep."

With a gesture Patrick directed them to his office. As Ziara moved into the space, she gasped. Sloan watched with a warm feeling in his chest as an almost childlike excitement burst over her face. He certainly understood.

The room was completely out of character with the rest of the house except for the pale walls and arches over the double windows. Otherwise, overflowing bookshelves lined every other wall, with more shelves jutting out to create aisles and hidden nooks. There were several oversize leather chairs with huge ottomans and a table-style desk supported by intertwined pieces of wood that formed the legs. It was slick, modern, but washed with an antique feel. An incredible contrast that Ziara obviously loved.

"This is so unique," she breathed.

"Patrick would live in here if everyone would leave him alone," Sloan said, earning a sucker punch in his upper arm.

"Would not."

"Would, too, you little recluse."

Ziara looked back at them in surprise, then glanced at the door separating them from the party.

"That's right, Ziara. Sloan calls me a recluse, but look at the parties I put on. He's clearly delusional. As is perfectly evident by his insistence that I join him in this crazy designing venture."

"I'm not giving up, Patrick. You have to give me an honest chance at talking you into this."

His friend waved toward the closed door, and the lavish house and glittering guests beyond it. "Why would I want to leave all this?"

"You know you get bored easily. This is just an opportunity for a new challenge." He might as well start off simple.

"You think working with fifty cast members and a demanding director isn't challenging?"

"How about—to teach an old nemesis she doesn't know what's best?"

Sloan noticed Ziara stiffen out of the corner of his eyes. Though her back was turned politely to them as she perused a nearby bookshelf, he still couldn't dismiss the connection he had to her every emotion.

His jaw tightened as he remembered seeing her fight off that drunk. Granted, the guy wouldn't get too far in a crowded party, but something about the practiced way Ziara had handled him made Sloan uneasy. What had happened to her that she needed to know how to defend herself? Classes at the Y, his ass!

He forced his attention back to Patrick. "Look, it's time to step up to the plate, buddy. We're leaving tomorrow. Are you following me or not?"

"I'd have to be crazy to sign on to pull together a show in less than three months."

Sloan grinned. "But think of the thrill."

"Vivian is not going to like this," Patrick said with a careful glance at Ziara. "The last time I did something she didn't like, she threatened to have me arrested."

Ziara gasped. "What did you do?" she asked.

Patrick had the grace to look away. "Well, we snuck into the liquor cabinet when she wasn't home and guzzled half the bottles down."

Ziara frowned.

"Give us a break," Sloan said. "We were only nineteen at the time. And how were we to know she had guests coming over for drinks the next day?"

Both men laughed, which felt good to Sloan. He missed those simpler times, when his struggles with Vivian only impacted himself and sometimes Patrick instead of the livelihood of close to a hundred people.

"It made an impression, that's for sure," Patrick said with a shudder. "Her expression..."

Sloan tried again. "So view this as the chance to show Vivian you've grown up from a spoiled little rich boy to an extremely talented designer."

"Flattery will get you everywhere," Patrick said. He rocked back on his heels, indicating to Sloan he was finally considering his offer without saying a word.

"I'm serious," Sloan said, stepping forward. "You don't need flattery. You know what you're capable of. You work on these live shows because it gives you something to do and an excuse to be here. Just give it a shot. If nothing else, just get me through this show."

This time Patrick leaned forward to meet him head-on. "I want final say on all designs."

Sloan shook his head. "Robert and Anthony would come unglued. They've been there forever. It wouldn't be right, Patrick. Besides, you would only be tweaking the main line with modern elements, not actually designing the clothes completely."

But Patrick wasn't swayed. "This isn't a power trip, Sloan. It's the only way I can have two lines finalized by fashion week." He glanced carefully around the room. "You do want the lingerie line ready for the show, too?"

Not looking at Ziara, Sloan inclined his head. He simply had to trust that this weekend had taught her all she needed to know. And that she'd stand by him—or at least near him—if Vivian went ballistic. "You would have complete control over that line. I want to open with both in two months."

Patrick stared at him for a long moment, then shook his head. "I can't believe I'm saying this, but yes—I'll do it. You are going to make it worth my while?"

"Always," Sloan agreed.

"Then I'll see you on Wednesday." Still muttering to himself, he left them to attend to his other guests.

Mission accomplished, Sloan's instincts set their sights on another prey, another conquest. As he and Ziara settled into the limo, his senses were attuned solely to her, the soft whisper of her breath, the smooth swish of her skirts as she crossed her legs, the spicy scent of her skin mixed with some illusive floral perfume.

His mind drifted back to this morning, watching her through the windows of the lingerie store. When she'd first entered, she stood almost paralyzed, looking so lost and unsure. So unlike herself. He'd almost dragged her back out rather than strip her of her usual strength.

But the point had been more important than protecting her. And now, he had the image of her explorations burned into his brain.

He was downright hooked.

Shame filled him as he remembered his casual thoughts about getting close to her in order to gain her loyalty. All it had taken was a true glimpse of her response and this game had become strictly personal.

Sloan slumped back in the seat, staring out the window of their limo. Getting Eternity Designs back on track was kicking his ass.

Ziara spoke into the darkness. "Well, you did it."

He couldn't tell from her tone whether she approved or not. Probably not. He wasn't worried. She was a walking example of what Patrick was capable of—the proof was in his design.

But Sloan didn't want to think about work. He'd rather have her in front of him so he could touch her, stroke her breasts until her nipples peaked—

"Yep," he finally got around to replying, his tone ironic but showing his fatigue.

"I hope Patrick knows what he's getting into. This time frame will mean a lot of late nights."

"He won't mind me working him like a dog," Sloan joked, chuckling when she looked askance at him. "Patrick may come from money, but he worked hard in school and at his job. He'll come through for us."

She nodded, but he still sensed her hesitation. There wasn't anything he could do about that. She'd see in time.

Her silhouette, profiled against the night, accelerated the beating of his heart. Sloan breathed deep, forcing calm to cover his growing need. He noted the slope and angles of Ziara's cheekbones. A model's face. Why did she work so hard to hide her beauty? He was more determined than ever to find out.

The conviction that she would be his surged deep in his soul.

He wanted to unravel the mystery, find what she hid beneath the surface so well. Why she hid at all.

"This is an interesting place," she said, her eyes focused on the approaching city lights.

He studied the thick dark lashes concealing her thoughts from him. "I'm glad you like it. Patrick takes a lot of pride in his work *and* play."

"It shows. But I didn't mean just tonight. More like Las Vegas in general." She absently rubbed the material of her dress between two fingers. "A combination of decadence, debauchery and the everyday. Kind of like life."

He scooted closer, gaining ground until he could touch her hair with the hand resting across the back of the seat. "How so?"

She dropped her head back so that it landed in his palm, but she didn't seem to notice. The silky weight of her hair made him want to run his hands through it, massage her scalp until she moaned, use handfuls of it to guide her mouth to all the places where he wanted to feel that wet warmth.

"Well," she went on, "maybe not everyone's life, but at least mine. My old life."

The opportunity opened before him like a lit doorway. Adrenaline aftershock, sleepiness and the shakedown of her natural barriers were lowering her inhibitions. The facade was melting away.

He told himself he should hold back, but they'd shot way past a professional relationship at this point. As he caressed her scalp, he knew deep down he would get to the bottom of the contradictions in her personality that had him tied in knots. For all the wrong reasons.

The intimacy of the limo, shrouded in gray shadows, invited him to explore the secret places, the dark desires beneath her surface. It would surely be the experience of his life.

"Rough childhood?" he asked.

Her eyes closed a moment as she shuddered. "You have no idea."

She turned toward him, those dark eyes sucking him away

from the voice of reason. "My mother…" She paused, biting her lip as if afraid to say more. "My mother was so wrapped up in her own needs, her little games, that she didn't care about what happened to me. She abandoned me."

Though he'd heard quite a few tales of childhood woe in his time, the desolation darkening Ziara's face ignited a protective streak in the pit of his stomach. "How old were you?"

Her fingers worried the fabric now. "Officially? Seventeen. Unofficially? So long before that I can't remember when."

Thoughts tumbled through his mind about what could happen to a seventeen-year-old girl who looked like Ziara without anyone to protect her.

"What about your dad?" he asked.

Her fingers jerked then went still. "I wouldn't know. I never met him." A few minutes passed before she said, "I think I could use a drink now."

Reaching out, he trailed his fingers down the back of her tense hand. "I don't think you need alcohol."

"Yes. I do."

"Why?" Sloan asked, taking the risk of looking straight into those tempting eyes. Half-mast lids were sleepy, sultry. Sexy. Man, if she decided to drink, who knew where they'd end up?

Her desire to let go had him shaking. It must be worse than he thought for her to resort to booze. "Why?" he repeated, hoping conversation would distract him from his thoughts and rapidly escalating erection.

"Because without it I'll never do this." She twisted, her lips brushing his, though she stopped short of a firm kiss.

The fire that burst through him burned away his inhibitions with one clean flare. "Ziara," he said, pulling her gaze to his. "You don't need liquid courage to do that."

Something perverse inside of him exulted in her making the first move, so he remained still. A quick lick of her lips sent a shiver of anticipation through him. Her lashes lowered as she pressed closer. Her lips barely met his before he took the reins back.

Burying both his hands in the soft fall of her hair, he stormed her mouth, sliding his tongue inside. Without further invitation, he explored the moist heat within before returning to caress her lips with his own. So soft, yet meeting him halfway, she beckoned and commanded his response without a word.

A flash of lights outside the windows eased Sloan from the cocoon of intimacy they shared. Though they were behind tinted windows and privacy glass, they were still in a public place.

And he wanted to do something they could be arrested for in public. Even in Las Vegas.

Resigning himself to a snail's pace, Sloan resumed his exploration of Ziara's mouth. He resisted the urgency surging under his skin. Their first time together shouldn't be in the back of a limo with a driver on the other side of the glass.

But he couldn't stop himself from exploring the boundaries a little. Drawing his hands down the side of her neck, he pulled her mouth closer, letting one hand travel to cup her breast. The soft weight overflowing his palm made him groan, but her electric response had him swearing.

Luckily at that moment they came to a stop in front of their hotel. Sloan opened the door himself and pulled Ziara out behind him. He rushed through the lobby and into the elevator with her a few steps behind. His hands trembled as he swept the key card through the lock, then pulled her into the suite with less finesse than demand.

The dim light of the suite was barely enough to silhouette Ziara's beautiful face. The stillness in the room as the door clicked shut only accentuated the pounding of the blood in his veins. He stalked forward, using their still-clasped hands to draw her near. He was pleased to see she didn't cower from him, from the intensity of his desire.

"Ziara, I need you."

This time it was she who anchored her hands in his hair. "And I need you," she choked out. "I really do."

Her voice shook at first but quickly firmed, though she sounded surprised. Whether at the need or the admission, he wasn't sure, but he didn't question his good fortune. Letting her pull his head down, he met her swollen lips once more, tasting the sweet burn he now associated with Ziara herself.

Allowing his hands free rein, they roamed her body, cupping those full breasts and squeezing them gently together. Her nipples hardened into peaks he could feel through the layers of fabric.

He followed the curve of her waist to the flare of her hips, finally drawing her tight against his erection.

Ziara bit lightly against his lower lip, sending Sloan's body and mind flying apart. Grabbing the zipper hidden along her side, he jerked it down, then the dress. Ziara gasped, but he didn't care. He just needed to touch her skin with his.

Instinct took over. His lips only left hers long enough to pull his shirt over his head. Drawing her against him, he groaned at the sensation of flesh against flesh, hotter than he could ever remember being. His head fell back, only to drop forward again to bury in her neck.

Her sweet, spicy scent drove him to taste her skin. Working his way down, he licked and nibbled the smooth column of her neck and the curve of her collarbone. He fell to his knees so he could savor the textures of her breasts and nipples.

Only then did he become aware of her panting breath, too jagged for passion. Releasing her sweet flesh, he looked up, catching the glint of moisture on her cheeks in the lights filtering through the far windows. "Ziara?"

"Please stop."

Twelve

Ziara stayed in her room the next morning until the last possible minute. Hiding wasn't the noblest of behaviors, but she simply couldn't face Sloan after calling a halt to…whatever last night had been.

How would she ever explain why she'd led him on, then left him hanging like that? How could she ever look herself in the eyes again and not remember her actions? Behavior that brought memories of her mother flooding to the surface. No matter how much her mind insisted she wasn't using Sloan, the fact that he was her boss couldn't be ignored. She refused to participate in anything reminiscent of her mother's life, built on sex, money and scheming for everything she could get.

Drawing in a deep breath, she smoothed her hair back into its usual bun. More aware than ever of the facade she presented in her business suit, she grabbed the handle of her rolling suitcase and opened the door. Sloan stood silent near the outer door, his own luggage not far away, remains of breakfast littering the table near the window.

Keeping her chin lifted and her eyes focused over his shoulder, she somehow crossed the room without stumbling or being sick. By the time she neared Sloan, his hand rested on the doorknob, but he made no move to leave. She could actually feel him looking at her, and her insides shivered. Part of her cowered in humiliation; the other part flared back to life with arousal.

For long moments Sloan didn't move, keeping them locked in a silent battle. The tension ate away at her composure.

"I just have one question," he finally said, his voice strained and husky. "Why?"

She spit out the words she'd rehearsed during the long, dragging hours of the night. "You're my boss. It just isn't right."

She must have managed the right level of conviction, because he opened the door and led the way outside. Watching him stride away struck her as bittersweet.

The flight home, long and silent, was punctuated by agonizingly polite phrases like "Excuse me" and "Would you like a drink?" Her body pulled in on itself, making her wish she could shrink into oblivion. But she couldn't. Not yet. Soon, though.

Unfortunately, Ziara was left with lots of time to think over what had occurred between them, as if she hadn't replayed it a hundred times in the dark of night. His kiss had been seductive in more than the obvious sense. It had made her blossom with beauty, power and wantonness. Therein lay the rub. She wanted to revel in the passion Sloan evoked, whether they were sparring or kissing. But she couldn't because it might lead to becoming the one thing she'd promised herself she never would.

As for work, she couldn't fathom how she'd ever behave normally again. Why did it have to be this particular man who affected her like this? The one man who could tear down the respectable career she'd worked so long and hard for with just a few words.

Deciding to bite the bullet as they stood at the luggage carousel, she turned and said, "Would you like me to pick up some lunch on my way to work?"

"Go home," he said.

Ziara's body froze with her emotions. She couldn't see for

a moment. Everything went blurry. When her vision cleared, Sloan was propping her suitcase in front of her. Was he so fed up, so desperate to be rid of her, he would fire her despite Vivian's insistence that they work together? Not that Vivian would oppose him once she found out what Ziara had done.

"Rest today," he said, his voice a little softer this time. His gaze inventoried her face, probably noting the swelling under her eyes and the red rims she'd been unable to cover this morning. "The real work starts tomorrow."

He turned and walked away without looking back, leaving confusion and an achy longing behind.

Desperately needing something to distract herself, Ziara tried to catch up on things she probably wouldn't have a chance to do in the weeks to come unless Sloan changed his mind about firing her before tomorrow. Deep cleaning the house and weeding the flower beds were always good for keeping her hands busy. Too bad her mind didn't want to cooperate.

But even if he didn't fire her, she knew in her heart she'd have to move on as soon as the show was over. Even if Vivian graciously extended the offer to be her executive assistant to Ziara, just knowing Sloan was right around the corner and could appear at any minute would keep her on edge.

It looked like she'd end up losing, after all. Her heart tightened, grieving as much for the loss of her beloved position within this company as it did for the necessity of keeping Sloan at arm's length. She hadn't just worked for Eternity Designs, she'd believed in its values, its purpose, and had hoped security could be found within its ranks.

As she went inside to clean up, she couldn't hold the tears back any longer. They mingled with the streaming water of the shower, invisible enough that she could dismiss her shame.

What was happening to her? All these emotions, so long buried deep inside, were erupting at every twist and turn. This was exactly why she didn't want them—because she couldn't control them. Or maybe she grieved because she did want them yet couldn't express them.

Guess she could add confusion to the messy pile.

Tears spent, she dried off, shaking away the last vestiges of depression and guilt. She dressed casually in khaki capris and a fuchsia T-shirt, then brushed out her hair in front of the bathroom vanity. Everyone was allowed one colossal mistake in their lifetime, right? This was hers. At least her conscience was clear. Her mistake wouldn't hurt anyone but herself.

Padding into the kitchen, she immersed herself in cooking dinner. Something as far from paella as she could get.

She threw together a quick southwestern chicken panini, which she coupled simply with apple and orange sections. Delicious as it was, she'd only managed to choke down half when the doorbell rang. Grateful for an excuse to give up on the pretense of eating, she straightened her T-shirt on the way to the door.

Shock sizzled through her when the door swung open to reveal Vivian. Without waiting for an invitation, her mentor glided inside. Ziara remained speechless for a moment. In the six years she'd been working for Eternity Designs, she'd never seen the Creightons outside the office. Now in the space of a week, both of them had shown up unannounced at her house.

After a thorough glance around the room, Vivian turned to face Ziara. "Is he here?"

Though Ziara understood, she still asked, "Who?"

"Sloan, of course."

Ziara easily pulled her facade into place, almost amazed at how well she could handle the accusation. But then again, she didn't have anything left to lose. "Sloan is not here, Vivian, and I resent the implication that he would be."

Vivian studied her for a moment, brows raised as if surprised Ziara would stand up for herself. Then her chin dipped in a slow nod of acknowledgment. Luckily Ziara found she could meet Vivian's eyes without a problem. A glimmer of compassion streaked through her as she noted Vivian's disarray, in contrast to her usually immaculate appearance.

"Perhaps we could sit and talk," Ziara said. She gestured Vivian into the sitting area facing the fireplace. The overstuffed chair and chaise weren't necessarily elegant, but they were comfortable and their deep burgundy hue complemented the fire-glazed tiles covering the hearth. "Can I get you something to drink? Coffee? Sweet tea?"

Vivian shook her head, a trembling sigh escaping her coppery brown lips. "That's what I so like about you, Ziara," she said. "Always cool under pressure, knowing just the right thing to say."

Ziara perched on the edge of the chaise opposite Vivian, wishing the same were true in her relationship with Sloan. *Business.* Business relationship with Sloan. They didn't have anything outside of that…anymore.

"I know my accusation was rude. But considering Sloan's history with assistants and this trip to Vegas…" She made a vague gesture with her hand, her diamond rings glittering in the soft evening light. "I assumed something I shouldn't have, knowing you. You are far too smart a girl to get mixed up with a smooth talker like my stepson."

Ziara prudently kept her mouth shut and her face impassive.

"Did Sloan procure a designer?"

Ziara now wished they'd go back to the sex issue. There were a lot less mines in that field.

Vivian grimaced. "Ziara, I'm going to find out eventually. I'd rather be informed now than surprised in front of my employees."

Ziara was too emotionally exhausted to come up with a clever sidestep. "He's hired Patrick Vinalay."

Vivian stood immediately, the *click* of her heels rapping on the wood floor. "I should have known Patrick would be the one to take him up on the offer. But it will put a kink in my plans."

Ziara frowned. "What do you mean?"

Vivian turned to face her, the pale cream of her skin contrasting with the bold colors of Ziara's home. "I thought I could get around whatever he might do by influencing Robert to cause a few delays until I could find a backer to bail me out, but having someone else on the design floor will change that."

With a jolt, Ziara realized how serious Vivian was about

this. Her mentor, the woman who had taught her the meaning of professionalism, had actually considered sabotaging her own company. Delays in production could have bogged down the rest of the process, resulting in major issues at showtime. Maybe even cancellation.

Unaware of Ziara's growing alarm, Vivian smiled and said, "I'll just have to find another way to get what I want."

Sloan paused for a moment after exiting the elevator, his pulse pounding as he stared at the door to his office suite down the hall. How ironic that after years of sidestepping persistently amorous employees, he now found himself on the other end, wondering how he could go back to acting like a normal boss. Especially when all he wanted was to lay Ziara across his desk and— He coughed to clear his throat. *This wasn't helping.*

If only he hadn't seen those red-rimmed eyes. Knowing how much he'd upset her, when she could usually be counted on as the calm one, put those boundaries firmly back into place. Determined not to cause any embarrassment, he marched forward.

"Good morning, Ziara," he said as he swept by her desk. "Could you get me the location contract, please?"

"Sure," she mumbled.

He took that for as good a sign as he was gonna get. They spent the morning focused on the push for the show, smoothing out location details and ordering fabrics Sloan already knew they needed.

Ziara left for lunch at 11:30 a.m. on the dot, but Sloan stayed behind, trying to breathe after a morning of straining to act normal and, honestly, trying to hide his erection. Once he had himself under control, he figured it might be a good idea if he headed down and gave the Old Brigade a heads-up. Patrick was due to be in sometime today, but he hadn't texted Sloan to let him know when.

Exiting on the third floor, he heard raised voices. *Oops. This visit was just a little too late.* He eased onto the overlook. Remaining back in the shadows, he studied the scene below. Patrick had arrived and no one was happy about it. Seeing

Ziara standing to one side of the fray, he made his way down the staircase and slipped up behind her.

Unable to resist, he leaned in close to her ear. "Did I miss the start of the war?"

In his chest, he felt the shivers that moved down her spine, urging him to press closer. How quickly his resolve was shaken by the temptation of almost touching that caramel skin.

His mind focused on the heat from the exposed curve of her neck and the vanilla scent drifting from the tamed confection of her hair.

"I ran into Patrick at the door," she murmured. "And made the mistake of letting him in."

Patrick was throwing out orders as if he owned the place, which didn't surprise Sloan in the least. Patrick knew how to captivate a room, but true resistance didn't bring out the best in him. No one appeared to be playing nicely.

"This is my studio and it will run the way I say," Robert bellowed.

Patrick folded his arms over his chest. "Really? When I signed on it was with the express understanding that final say would be mine."

Robert gasped, his hand clasping his heart, in contrast to Anthony, who stood silently in the background, watching the scene before him with somber eyes. "Say it isn't so!"

Patrick chuckled, prompting Robert to launch into a litany of French while Anthony's face turned red to the point of glowing. Sloan feared the way he bottled things up might cause a heart attack.

Taking control, Sloan let his voice boom out across the massive room, bringing everything to a halt. "That's enough."

Ziara jumped as he moved away from her, stepping forward from his position on the sidelines. "Patrick is here to modernize the line."

"But we don't need him," Robert insisted.

Sloan went on as if he hadn't spoken. "He will take the basic designs you put together and adjust or add to them as needed.

I have given him final say in the overall designs for the fall line to speed things up."

As Robert sputtered, Sloan pinned him with a look. "Do you want this studio to close?"

"No," Robert said, resignation in the very lines of his face.

"Then I suggest you find a way to make this work."

Not as diplomatic as he could have handled it, but effective. Sloan let his gaze sweep the whole group. "You two will put together the basic designs we've already approved, with Patrick adding what he believes is necessary. He'll have his hands full between that and his additional line."

"Additional line?" They all jumped as Vivian's voice erupted from behind them. "And what would that be?"

She walked toward the men, bypassing Ziara with barely a glance. Sloan's blood started to pound through his veins, that instinct to clash rising to the fore. But he checked himself, his curiosity starting to stir. How much had his little assistant given away already? He'd been with her most of the morning, but he couldn't account for every phone call, every second in the office. Or out of it.

"Still causing trouble, I see, Patrick," she said.

"Vivian." Patrick grinned. "As lovely and cold as ever."

She frowned but let the comment pass as her eyes swept over the men to rest on Sloan. "What do you mean, another line? We'll have a hard enough time coming up with one." She turned to examine Patrick from under raised brows. "Don't tell me he's going to do some kind of trashy, glitzy gowns. Surely taste hasn't gone that far downhill."

Why was she ignoring Ziara? He didn't want to believe that Ziara would rat him out, but Vivian was her mentor. Was Vivian testing him? Did she already know what was coming? The thought nibbled at the back of his brain. Ziara stood at the rear of the group, her brows lowered, arms crossed tightly over her stomach. Noting every curve, every shift, he still couldn't tell if she was transmitting nerves or guilt. He remembered her tortured expression as she'd asked him to stop—*please don't let it be guilt.* Deep inside, he needed her to be innocent, needed someone to be on his side.

"Actually, Vivian, it won't involve wedding dresses at all," Sloan said, going on the offensive.

Vivian stiffened. Enjoying himself, he let a smirk slip onto his lips. Even though Ziara's silent stare weighed heavy on him.

"Then what is it?" Vivian asked.

"He'll be launching our new lingerie line."

Sloan may have delivered the news with just a bit too much relish. The room became so still that from several feet away he heard Vivian's ragged intake of breath.

"Absolutely not!"

The furious look she threw Ziara definitively answered his questions—the woman he'd held in his arms, who clung so tightly to her professionalism that she would turn away from the inferno they created together, had stood her ground. Or rather, his ground. She'd kept his secret, despite the risk of losing the career Vivian held in the palm of her hand.

Now—if he didn't succeed, he wouldn't just lose the company. Ziara would lose everything she'd worked so hard to achieve.

Thirteen

Sloan and Patrick holed up in his office for most of the afternoon while Ziara practically collapsed at her desk. Work was beyond her for the first time in her life.

As if in slow motion, she relived Vivian turning until her accusing eyes met Ziara's. She knew Vivian would forever hold her responsible for not telling her about the lingerie line the day before. Her stomach clenched as the ramifications of her actions hit her. When Vivian turned and left without a word, Ziara had said her final goodbyes to the position she'd worked so hard to attain.

Vivian would never give it to someone she couldn't trust.

But would Sloan believe her now if Ziara came to him with the truth? She'd been trying all day to find the right time to tell him about Vivian's threat, but each time she'd hesitated. They'd maintained a strictly professional attitude toward each other that she'd been afraid to upset. That balance was so fragile. What would happen if she brought up such a personal subject?

"Wish me luck, sweet cheeks," Patrick said, sweeping by her toward the suite doors. "I'm off to face Mutt and Jeff."

She frowned, her strained emotions too heavy to hide. "Their names are Robert and Anthony."

He leaned against the doorframe. "It was just a joke."

"I know. But Robert and Anthony are going to have a difficult time adjusting to this. They've devoted many years to this company. Joking might not be the way to go."

A light grin tugged his lips. "I can take a hint. Just remember, I'm making the best of a situation they created."

Hoping her expression told him she understood, she nodded and watched him slip out the door. Then she dropped her head into her hands as the roller coaster of emotions of the past few days—heck, the past few hours—got the better of her.

She'd lost so much—her direction, her focus—and for what? Where would she go from here? Once Sloan got through the fall show she'd have to leave. But how could she find a job that would mean as much to her as this one?

"Ziara."

She heard Sloan's husky voice at the same moment that his heated palm cupped the back of her neck. She sensed him kneeling beside her chair, but she couldn't bring herself to raise her head, because she knew her face would be an open book at the moment.

"Ziara," he tried again. "Are you okay?"

No, she wanted to cry. Instead, she wiped the emotion from her face as she would tears, then sat up straight. She nodded shortly. "Yes. I'm just tired."

Skirting around her, he propped himself on the edge of her desk. She tried hard not to notice the sculpted muscles of his thigh, revealed by the pull of his slacks.

That husky drawl came again. "Do you need to go home?"

Like the snap of a twig, the pressure broke her prized control. She tilted her head to the side in order to face him. "Why are you being so nice to me?"

He choked on a laugh, those electric eyes widening. "Am I not supposed to be?"

"No. I mean, after..." She shook her head. "I'm not handling this very well."

"Me, either," he said, his voice deepening as he slid off the desk, then lifted her to stand before him. Using her arms to draw her against his chest, he bent to take her lips in a kiss that made no mistake as to his needs.

To Ziara's shame, she couldn't pull away, even knowing they were at the office. Her lips opened with a groan and her mind shut down. On a purely physical level, she met him pant for pant, kiss for kiss, lick for lick. Sloan's hands tightened to the point of pain on her arms, but it was one more sensation in the flood. Her control completely evaporating, she allowed him to lead her wherever he wanted to go.

Suddenly he pulled away, staring down at her, leaving her dazed and panting. "Not one word. Just go in my office."

Confused, Ziara thought he was speaking to her until she caught a glimpse of Patrick sweeping past. Her eyes snapped shut, her head dropping forward in shame. How could she have let this happen? Here of all places.

With a nudge of his fingers under her chin, Sloan raised her face. Opening her eyes, she noted his expression numbly at first, then with growing awe.

Instead of the crazed lust or judgment she'd expected, his eyes sparked with honest desire and a touch of tenderness. A reverence she'd never expected to receive from a man warmed the icy blue of his eyes. The look sent her own need into hyperdrive.

"I guess we'll have to put this discussion on hold," he said, tracing her moist lips with his thumb. His eyes narrowed in resolve. "But we will talk, Ziara, because neither of us is going to be able to ignore what's happening here."

Turning, he entered his office and shut the door behind him, leaving her to wilt into her chair. She should be worrying about Patrick—what he'd seen, what he assumed. She should be worrying about Vivian and her own future. Instead, she trembled inside, thinking only of Sloan's parting words.

Sloan and Patrick remained in conference so long that Ziara took the opportunity to slip out and head home. She desperately needed some time to herself, time to sort through her feelings.

As she concentrated on assembling lasagna for dinner, hoping the tedious layering would help her focus, she acknowledged that she'd had other reasons for calling a halt to things in Las Vegas. Reasons much deeper than Sloan being her boss.

Because, deep down, the thing she feared most was what might come the morning after. She didn't know how to do more, or whether he would want to do more…or if he would even care about the consequences. But every time he looked at her with that mixture of passion and admiration, she came a foot closer to crossing that inevitable line. She forced her mind to give it a rest as she focused on the task at hand. Sauce, noodles, sauce, ricotta cheese, mozzarella, then noodles again. Swaying slightly to the sultry jazz music playing through the house's sound system, she savored the feel of the cool tile beneath her bare feet. Breathing deep, she pulled in the smell of tomatoes and oregano enriching the air around her, blending with the darkness creeping down outside to cool the summer heat.

She'd just grated a small block of Parmesan onto the top and put the pan in the oven when the doorbell rang. An uncharacteristic expletive slipped out as she wiped her hands. The sound of her own doorbell now filled her with dread.

She barely got the lock turned when the door burst open. Sloan stalked through, slamming it shut behind him. Holding her gaze, he slipped the lock back into place, then strode across the small foyer to where she'd backed up against the love seat.

Without a word, his hands anchored in her hair, dragging her mouth to his. She had a brief moment to wonder about his obsession with her hair before surrendering to the dark current of desire.

Her body melted into his, her head automatically tilting to

the side to accommodate his mouth. When she made no protest, his hands slid from her hair over her shoulders and along her spine to cup her rear end, pulling her forward to meet his erection. With a groan, he pushed into the cradle of her hips. Her body arched, rising to meet his demands.

Before she could think, her shirt was unbuttoned. He peeled it open to reveal her breasts. Pulling back just the upper part of his body, Sloan spent moments memorizing the view. The pressure from below reassured her that he liked what he saw.

She wished she could see his hands as they cupped her through her bra, but she couldn't tear her gaze away from his face. Thoughts of losing his respect fled in the wake of the awe glowing in his expression, the utter pleasure he took in touching her.

Pride intensified her response. She wanted to revel in his reactions. Pushing herself farther into his hands, she shivered as a zing shot from her nipples to that all-important point between her thighs. The pressure there was heavenly yet growing more urgent with his every touch.

Allowing her head to fall back, she lost all strength as he sucked and licked his way along her neck. He anchored her to his body with his arm around her hips.

After pausing for a moment to savor the rapid pulse at the vulnerable base of her neck, he lifted her into his arms and carried her down the hallway. As if by instinct, he strode past several rooms with barely a glance, pausing outside only one.

"I should have known," he murmured, then strode across the room to lay her on the bed. Soft illumination from the doorway and a candle lit earlier glinted off the gold threads in the purple bedspread, the silky material caressing her bare skin when Sloan laid her down. After stripping her, he stood and tore off his own clothes, his gaze never leaving hers as he quickly slid on protection.

The sight of his body took her breath away. Long, lean muscles. Smooth, firm chest. Strong, tight thighs. Her core ached for the steely length between them. She wanted to touch him, savor every new discovery. But he was already crawling onto the bed and spreading her trembling thighs to his gaze.

The flash of vulnerability surprised her. She knew he wouldn't hurt her, wouldn't humiliate her. But the fears still lingered.

"Sloan, slow down," she gasped.

He stretched to take her mouth in a hard kiss before resting his forehead against hers. His panting breath sounded loud in the quiet. Only faint music could be heard from down the hall.

"I can't, Ziara," he said. "I've waited too long, wanted too hard. Please let me in now."

She hesitated, knowing that if she did, there would be no turning back. Already her hands and thighs shook with the effort of holding herself together, but her need was too great. She had to meet him all the way. As she'd feared, there would be no half measures.

And hopefully no regrets.

She groaned, her thighs sliding apart. Reaching down with a boldness that surprised her, she took him in her hand and guided him to her hot, wet entrance. He pushed inside with one plunge.

His body in hers sparked a tingly firestorm that burned between her thighs and spread outward to every point of her body. To the tips of her fingers, the top of her head. She could feel him imprinting on every part of her.

As he moved, the fire built higher and hotter. She'd never yearned to let go like this. Even though warnings screamed inside her brain, for once she thrust them away, so she could revel in how he made her feel.

She was drunk—not off wine, but off the sensation of having him so deep inside her, having him devour her with his gaze, having him stroke and praise her. His possession went straight to her head like tiny champagne bubbles.

With a cry, a sharp peak overcame her, but his whispered words in her ear brought her quickly to another.

The contractions were intense and powerful but not satisfying. As he levered onto his arms and pounded between her thighs, her body writhed, lifting to meet him, demanding more and more until she finally exploded in an outward expansion. Thousands of pieces flying out, a moment of nothingness, then floating back to make her whole again.

As she collapsed into the softness of the comforter, she heard Sloan shout. He buried himself hard within her body, holding stone still as he emptied himself.

A part of her, she dimly thought, then accepted him into her arms when he collapsed. Absently she stroked the slick muscles of his back, wanting only to keep this connection from fading so reality couldn't enter.

He groaned and moved against her but didn't try to leave. His mouth traveled up her neck, settling below her ear as he nuzzled close. Sensation stabbed into her nipples, and her hips lifted in response.

With an appreciative chuckle, he slowly pulled away, then disappeared into the bathroom with his pants after a quick brush of his lips over hers. Who knew when sex worked, really worked, that there were so many shocks along the way? With this man, only this one, sex had been one incredible sensation after another.

She lay in the bed, absorbing the quiet, but as she stared at the chiffon strips of material that formed her canopy, tension rapidly spilled back into her system.

What was she doing here? In the rush of sensations, thinking had been beyond her. As panic set in, she jerked to her feet, rushing through the room to grab clothes and drag them back on.

Her regular clothes didn't feel nearly secure enough, so she pulled a sweater from the closet and slid her arms inside, tightening its hold on her like a straitjacket. She stared into the dark depths of the closet, grateful for the nothingness for a moment.

Until her gaze focused in on her work clothes: suit jackets, A-line skirts, dress pants, severe button-down shirts. Work. She was a different person there. He was a different person—her boss.

The panic spread, making it hard to breathe. She didn't even hear Sloan until he was right behind her. "Ziara, are you okay?"

She didn't respond. She couldn't with her throat closing. When his arms reached around to circle her waist, she jumped, whirling toward him, then backing into the darkness of the closet in a misguided effort at hiding.

"Hey, it's all right," he said, his voice still as husky as when he'd been moaning in her bed. "What's the matter?"

Her head started to shake back and forth. "I can't do this. I really can't. We just can't do this."

She realized her eyes had closed, enfolding her in the darkness. After a deep breath, she opened them to focus on Sloan's face just inches from hers. His breath warmed her cheek.

"Talk to me, Ziara."

Sucking in air seemed a herculean task, but she managed, calling on years of maintaining a perfectly calm demeanor. When she could finally focus on Sloan in front of her, she took in his pale features without the protection of her normal walls. The thought almost started the panic again, but she shoved it away, tucking it down in a teeny tiny box to deal with later. Much later.

"I'm s-sorry..." she stuttered. "I've never had, whatever that was..."

"I think you had a panic attack," Sloan said. His shoulders dropped as he relaxed, though his hands continued to cup her face. "Are you okay?"

"I think so." *No, absolutely not.*

"Want to tell me what brought that on?"

"I...I..." Just one more deep breath. "I guess it just hit me. What happened. What—what we'd done."

He nodded as if her stream of consciousness made any sense at all. "Come here," he said.

When she started to follow him, she realized her muscles had turned into Twizzlers. She walked, but it took all her concentration to keep everything from wiggling all over the place. Wow. Since when did sex turn people completely unstable? Of course, she'd felt that way ever since she'd met Sloan, so this wasn't something new.

He led her to the overstuffed reading chair in the corner of the bedroom, where he settled and pulled her into his lap, all in one motion. Protest wasn't an option. He simply did what he wanted.

Unconsciously her fingers made short, light strokes across the top of his pecs, exploring the light smattering of hair that rested beneath them.

"I'm going to ask one more time," he said gently. "What's going on in that little worry factory in your head?"

Any other time, she would have smiled at the analogy, because it was pretty close to accurate. But right now she couldn't. "Sloan, this is completely wrong—"

"Doesn't feel that way," he said, his mouth nuzzling into the crook of her neck.

The shivers he elicited felt so good, but she gallantly reached for control. "Stop," she said, proud of her firm, no-nonsense tone, though her attempts to stand were promptly thwarted. "Sloan, you're my boss. I can't believe I lost my head long enough to forget that."

"I can." She didn't appreciate his grin. Her stern stare changed his tune. "Look. I understand this is a little unusual. But the fact is, I'm not technically your employer. Vivian is. And—" he continued a little louder when she would have argued "—I'm working with you temporarily. Once Abigail retires, you'll go back to working in Vivian's office."

Her frown drew tighter as she realized he hadn't come to the same conclusions she had. Vivian wasn't going to keep her on, no matter what. Better to change tactics. "You'll abandon the company?"

Luckily Sloan kept a hold on her when he jerked to his feet or she would have fallen. But he quickly let go to pace several feet away. He didn't give her a chance to get steady before he started speaking, his voice rough and low. "What the hell? Why would you think that?"

"I...I didn't mean..." Maybe it would be better to keep her

mouth shut. She truly wasn't sure where the question had come from, except she knew Vivian hadn't been worried about Sloan being around long-term. She chose the safe route. "I know you have other companies, other projects."

"Yes, but my father's company means a hell of a lot more to me than those."

Immediately guilt settled in Ziara's stomach. In her own panic, she'd forgotten the whole reason Sloan was even at Eternity Designs. "I'm sorry, Sloan."

For a moment he didn't move, his tall body a looming tower, his head lowered as if in grief. But when his head lifted once more, none of that emotion showed on his face. He crossed the short space between them to take her once more in his arms. "Look, this will be fine. I'm only your boss for a couple more months, at the most. Until then we'll keep this strictly out of the office."

She couldn't help but wonder if she accepted his reasoning simply to give herself permission to stay right where she was, burrowed deep in his warmth and masculine scent. But for once she was going to do what she wanted, not what the job required. "Agreed," she whispered.

After a thorough kiss, Sloan cocked his head to one side. His nostrils flared as he breathed deep.

"What's that smell?" he asked.

Sniffing, Ziara caught a whiff of Sloan's citrusy scent, followed quickly by the sharp tang of burning cheese.

"Oh, no," she said, rushing toward the hall. "The lasagna."

Fourteen

Ziara was able to salvage most of dinner because only the outer edges had burned. Sloan found this very amusing and teased her as they ate.

"You are a great cook," he finally said. "Who taught you?"

She picked up their plates and crossed to the sink, feeling a little too vulnerable still to face him. "I taught myself." Turning on the water, she rinsed the plates. "My mom…worked a lot. I had to either cook or live off cheese and crackers."

Not wanting to elaborate, she concentrated on cleaning up. Ever since her brain had come down from its mind-numbing high, she'd been struggling with conflicting emotions. She didn't want to enjoy being with Sloan, and the fact that she did—although *enjoy* was way too mild a word for how she was feeling—was something she might not be ready to face. Being with him intimately hadn't been dirty or sordid or even ordinary. And it wasn't just the sex she'd enjoyed, it was the eating and talking and laughing….

Ziara was so lost in thought that she didn't notice Sloan approaching until his warmth cradled her back. "What are you doing?" he asked, his hands resting on her hips. His moist lips nuzzled through her hair to the back of her neck.

More than anything she wanted to melt into his warmth, to experience again the joy of being a part of him.

"I—I'm cleaning up. What does it look like?"

"What if I want some more?"

Twisting in his grip, she tried to see his face. "Why didn't you say something? You can have another plate."

He closed in, his hips tight against her backside, giving her an unmistakable impression of his hardness. "I didn't mean more food."

Her breathing accelerated, currents of excitement jumping from his hands straight between her thighs. She wanted to stroke back and forth, letting every inch of her back discover every inch of his front. Then she'd turn and repeat the moves all over.

He was an addiction. A tempting treat. She could discover every texture and taste of his body, branding him as hers with her scent and touch. As his hands traveled from her hips to her breasts, she wondered if she was losing her mind.

At least she was enjoying the ride.

He turned her to face him, claiming her mouth with his. Slowly unbuttoning and unzipping her capris, he allowed them to slide down to the floor around her feet, followed quickly by her panties.

With a flex of his biceps, he lifted her onto the tile counter. A squeal rang out as her bare bottom met the chilled surface. He chuckled.

"That's sadistic," she accused.

He grinned, his dark gold hair falling softly from the crown of his head to frame his devilish good looks, reminding her of a Hollywood bad boy.

"I'm all about the sensations," he said.

The grin quickly melted into a more serious look, making her feel like prey. Her heartbeat picked up again, and she tried to pull him to her, but he didn't budge. Layers disappeared:

her sweater and cotton T-shirt, followed by the tank she'd put on in lieu of a bra.

He kissed her thoroughly, letting his hands trail down her arms, which he guided behind her and propped on the counter.

When he released her mouth, she found herself leaning back on her braced arms, her body on display for him to peruse at his leisure. Instantly awkwardness swept in. How could she let him see every little part that she'd kept hidden for so long?

When she tried to lift herself up, his hands on her shoulders held her still. After one dark look, his gaze moved down… along with his hands. She should have felt shamed, wanton in this position, especially when he pushed between her legs and propped her feet on his hips. There was absolutely nowhere to hide.

She let her head fall back and her eyes close. Therein lay her only protection from his onslaught.

Before he finally entered her, he had explored each and every part of her body with thorough intent, branding her with his touch.

She didn't recognize the moans and whimpers erupting from her mouth. She only knew if she didn't have him, she couldn't make it through the next few minutes. His body in hers was a momentary relief, but when he thrust deep, the fire returned ten times hotter. She exploded within minutes, Sloan following close behind.

With their ragged breathing echoing off the tile, she didn't even care about being put back together again.

Pulling himself out of Ziara's bed at two-thirty the next morning wasn't an easy or pleasant task for Sloan, but he forced himself to return to his own house. They needed to slow down—and certainly needed to downplay anything that smacked of a relationship, sexual or otherwise.

He'd tossed aside Ziara's concerns last night and he stood by his decision on both counts. But he knew no matter what he'd told her earlier, Vivian would kick her to the curb the minute she discovered they were sleeping together. She was only barely tolerating Ziara after learning about the lingerie line.

So he'd stay in control. They'd be careful. He could have her and protect her—somehow.

When he'd suspected a mystery lay beneath Ziara's cool exterior, he hadn't known the half of it. He felt like he'd cracked that hard surface and found the richest pool of tempting dark chocolate, so deep he could drown in her.

Willingly.

That was the scary part. Her loyalty, her integrity, her professionalism—all wrapped up in the sexiest package he'd ever touched. It made him want the very thing he was trying to hide: a chance just to be with her. He couldn't articulate the why of it. It was just Ziara.

Coming through the door to his office suite seven hours later, he barely controlled his double take. There sat Ziara, looking as calm, crisp and professional as she always did. He couldn't reconcile it with the woman who'd wrapped her silky, toned legs around his waist while he gave her multiple orgasms the night before.

Looking at her now, he wanted to kiss color into her lips and cheeks. Better yet, make her eyes glint with mischievous passion. But that was in direct violation of their agreement. He barely controlled the impulse to rip every last pin out of her hair until it fell in a black cascade down her back.

Wouldn't Vivian just love that?

As if sensing a presence, she glanced up from her desk, eyebrow raised in inquiry. A tentative smile peeked from her lips—not her normal professional greeting, but a small, secretive smile full of the knowledge of what they'd done to each other the night before.

He stalked to her desk and leaned forward onto his hands. "I want to tear your clothes off."

Her eyes widened a bit before returning to normal. Her lips pressed together as if to contain a laugh, though it didn't disguise their sensual fullness. "Shh, not in the office. Besides,

Abigail called to say Vivian wanted you on the design floor in twenty minutes. A reporter is coming to interview y'all."

He cursed under his breath. "Guess I'll have to put my plans on hold until tonight then. The least you can do is come along and protect me from the big, bad dragon lady."

He paused, giving her a moment to back out. Her subdued "Sure" swept through him like a victory dance. He wouldn't jeopardize her reputation here at work, but he had to have her again. Soon.

Fatigue hovered at the edges of Sloan's consciousness a few hours later. The reporter had been excited about something new and different to feature in an upcoming society page, and had snapped at least a hundred pictures of the design floor.

Ziara had tried a few times to head back up to the office, but Sloan or Patrick always distracted her before she could get away. Constantly conferring with her over details of the actual show and even some of the fabric choices had kept her in close range—exactly where Sloan wanted her.

But she'd definitely started to lag at the end, her normally calm tone growing short and her posture tight. The most trying thing, the one thing that seemed to tap her energy while revving up Sloan's, had been Vivian's disapproving stare. Oh, she'd managed to keep it out of range of the camera, but Sloan could feel the bad vibes emanating from her on more than one occasion. At least she seemed to be an equal opportunity dispenser of disapproval. No one but the reporter and Robert could do any right this morning.

Sloan just wanted to crawl back under the covers and sleep, right up against his naked assistant. Problem was, lunchtime had barely arrived.

"Check out the feature in the Sunday paper on the seventeenth," the reporter threw back over her shoulder as she and the cameraman swept from the room.

Sloan could see his own weariness reflected back at him in Patrick. "Is it just me," his friend asked, "or was that woman way too perky for anytime before lunch?"

A giggle slipped from Ziara's lips, but she quickly went silent under Vivian's disapproving gaze.

"Considering how quickly we're trying to pull this together, we should be grateful for all the publicity we can get," the stern matron said.

Ziara backed slowly away, disquiet leaking through the cracks of her professional facade. Patrick simply raised a brow and turned away, letting the comment slide over him like water off a raincoat.

"Ziara," Sloan said, ready to get away from the old witch himself. "Let's head back upstairs and get some work done before the whole day is gone."

They arrived at the elevators together, slipping in just as the door opened, not realizing Vivian had joined them until they turned back to face the closing door. *Damn it. Would this day never end?*

"Since I realize a written report is a bit too much to expect from you, Sloan, why don't you bring me up-to-date on where we stand at the moment?" she said.

Not seeing the point of haggling, Sloan gave her a quick rundown of the current budget and status on the design work. By the time he finished, they were in the upper hallway and Ziara was eyeing the door leading toward their office—and away from Vivian—with desperate yearning. Sloan couldn't blame her. Vivian's shoulders tightened the longer Sloan spoke, even though he presented the facts in a clear, dry manner. Any minute now she was gonna blow her top.

"And when are you planning to show me the designs for the…lingerie?" Vivian asked, making the word sound like trash to be picked up from the side of the road. *Ah, here it came.* "Or were you planning on surprising me, just as you did with Patrick?"

"I didn't realize you expected me to run every idea by you, especially since your approval isn't necessary," Sloan replied.

Ziara pressed her lips together, her tension palpable. This did have all the makings of a pissing match and for once he'd rather be anywhere else. Like in Ziara's cozy, colorful bedroom.

"I simply think that running things by me would show a little decency, since I am still the majority owner of this establishment."

Sloan kept it short, but not sweet. "Decency isn't part of our agreement."

"You mean not a part of your agreement—or hers, I'm learning."

"That's enough, Vivian."

She chose to ignore Sloan's warning, turning the full force of her ire on Ziara. "You were supposed to be keeping an eye out on him, keeping me informed."

"I did," Ziara said with quiet dignity, though Sloan read unease in her carefully guarded expression.

"About everything?"

"Ziara is doing what she thinks is right for this company," Sloan interrupted. "She loves Eternity Designs and wants to see it regain its rightful place in the market, just as I do."

Vivian shot another glare over Sloan's shoulder, so palpable it probably burned Ziara's skin. "What's best for Eternity isn't her decision to make. It's mine."

"Typical of you, Vivian. Last I remember, your decisions ran this place into the ground." Sloan's voice was laced with so much venom he was surprised any of them were left standing. Years of resentment and loneliness surged inside him, anger over losing his father breaking through the surface. "Drop it. Ziara's doing a damn good job bringing this show to life. She can't do that and be at your beck and call all the time. Or don't you remember how much work that really is?"

If anything, Vivian's gaze turned positively glacial. "What I remember is all the work I've put into keeping this company afloat. Your father's dream has kept me going since his death."

"And you've shut me out," Sloan fought back. He was in rare form today. "But that's what you wanted, wasn't it?"

"I did what I thought was best, what *your father* would have wanted."

Sloan stalked closer, the carpeting muffling his steps. "If

Father wanted me out, why would he have bothered leaving me forty percent?"

"How would it have looked if he'd left his son with nothing?"

"You know, Vivian," he said, "I don't think he cared about how things looked nearly as much as you do."

The truth hit really hard, and Vivian's face flushed a mottled red. "I will not let you ruin me."

"If I wanted to, you couldn't stop me."

Sloan turned and walked away, calling Ziara to follow him. But the memory of Vivian's face remained with him for the rest of the afternoon.

Outrage? Yes. Anger? Yes. But something else, something underneath that hinted at desperation. What would Vivian do if she felt that Sloan had backed her into a corner? If he succeeded, would Vivian rejoice in Eternity Designs's success or ruin it for the chance to keep her position as its CEO?

And did his lover have any idea what might be coming their way?

Fifteen

A few days later, Ziara stalked down the hall after a frustrating hour mediating between the two-ton egos on thc design floor downstairs. As if her emotions weren't shaky enough! She could barely restrain herself from yelling, *Behave like the adults you are or I'll send you to time-out like you deserve.*

But she'd managed to keep her prized cool. Just barely.

Since their confrontation with Vivian, the cracks in her professional facade started by Sloan's lovemaking had widened. Vivian's rejection hurt, more than the taunts of her childhood, but she'd pushed through to do whatever she could to make this show a success. She owed Eternity Designs and Vivian that much, even if Vivian didn't want it.

Deep inside she'd convinced herself that Vivian would change her mind once Eternity Designs regained stable footing. She'd understand Ziara's decisions, instead of condemning her—and somehow Ziara would be able to remain a part of this home away from home.

Somehow.

Finally reaching her desk, she sank into the seat and swiveled to face the desktop. Exhaustion lowered over her like a heavy mantle. The long days of tension and emotional turmoil—good and bad—were taking their toll. As she dropped her head into her hands, her elbow connected with something on her desk. Glancing down, she found a long, rectangular present wrapped in iridescent paper. Her mind remained blank for long moments, but slowly trickles of excitement filtered in.

Gifts were few and far between in her life. The small Christmas presents exchanged in the office and with a couple of neighbors were the extent of her experience. She almost couldn't believe someone had gotten her something special, something just for her.

Lifting the box, she found a piece of Sloan's personal stationary underneath: "Enjoy, Sloan." With delicate care, she peeled back the paper, revealing a flat, black jeweler's box with feminine gold lettering: Par Excellence, Las Vegas.

Old fears made her drop the box like she'd discovered a big, hairy tarantula was living inside it. The simple package filled her with dread despite her commonsense knowledge that it was just a box, a small gift of appreciation. Giving herself a firm talking-to, she reached out to pick it up with a fairly steady hand.

Her heart started freezing before she even had the lid open. By the time the teardrop diamond pendant, hung on a delicate gold chain, came into view, she'd gone completely numb.

"Is that from your trip to Vegas?"

The unexpected sound of Vivian's voice made Ziara jump. She almost never came to Sloan's office, preferring to send Abigail when she needed something. What sin had Ziara committed to condemn her to Vivian's presence at just this moment? The layer of distaste underlying Vivian's tone compounded her own churning emotions.

"I suppose so," Ziara said, too shaken to play defense. With a deep breath, she looked up at her former mentor.

Vivian watched her for a moment, her gaze then moving to the sparkling necklace. "You are a dedicated employee with the tact and control to excel as an executive assistant, Ziara.

I've been extremely concerned by your behavior since you took this position."

"I don't understand," Ziara said, her words more forceful than she would normally have used with her employer. She shook her head. "I thought you trusted my judgment? You are the one who put me here."

Vivian nodded. "That's because I thought you had the ability to fulfill the position where others had failed. Without becoming personally involved. Now I know I was wrong."

"I thought you wanted me to insure Eternity's success—that's what I'm trying to do."

"By worming your way into Sloan's bed?"

The words stole Ziara's breath, cutting through the cold, but Vivian wasn't through with her.

"Oh, I know how this works. I was even accused of it myself. No one understood what my husband and I had, how we felt about each other." She raked her eyes over Ziara's trembling body, encased in a perfect pink suit, with harsh judgment. "But I never stooped to using my body to get what I wanted."

If she could have doubled over in pain, Ziara would have. Instead, she felt locked in a swirling fog that mixed old accusations with new ones. Vivian turned toward the door but paused before leaving. "Ziara," she said without turning around. "Rest assured, if Sloan doesn't get rid of you when he's done, then I will. There's no place at Eternity Designs for smut like you."

Her exit was as quiet as her arrival.

With an unnatural calm, Ziara put the lid back on the box. The memories called up by the piece of jewelry had more power to hurt her than even the threat of losing her position here. Under normal circumstances, she could have buried them quickly and gone about her day, but these weren't normal circumstances.

Rising to her feet, she walked into Sloan's office without her usual knock. He looked up in surprise from the papers he'd been perusing on the desktop. "Was that Vivian I heard out there?" he asked.

He glanced from her face to the box in her hand. "I saw that in Vegas. I hope you like it."

Leaning forward, she placed the box squarely on his desk in a parody of the way she'd found it. He looked up in confusion, allowing her to meet his gaze straight on.

"Just so you know," she said, her voice calm but hollow, "I don't require payment for services rendered."

Then she turned on her heel and stalked out.

As dusk deepened to full dark several hours later, Ziara heard Sloan's Mercedes purr into her driveway. She'd been half expecting it, half dreading it. The stubbornness of his personality wouldn't let him leave her alone after their earlier scene.

And she wasn't anywhere near ready for him to be here.

Her eyes were probably still puffy from crying on the way home. She hadn't cried in a long time, but twice in a month was unheard-of. The emotional release after everything that had happened proved inescapable.

The loss of control bothered her because it wasn't *her.* She was the cool one, stable, clearheaded. But today she'd turned into a crying, hurting mess, desperate to close the door on a past that had reared its ugly head despite her attempts to get as far away as possible.

And it was All. His. Fault.

Not waiting for him to knock, she jerked the door open as he marched up the stone walkway. Pressure built inside as her anger swelled. Anger at him. At Vivian and her accusations. At the gift. At her lack of control. At her need for him, even after everything.

Catching sight of her in the doorway, he stopped short in surprise. "What do you want?" Because if he thought he was getting sex, he was sadly mistaken. No matter that her body clamored at the sight of him. The latent desire added another layer of dirt to her already soiled soul.

"Can I come in?"

Those commonplace, even words destroyed the last of her manners. Turning away, she left the door open for him to enter if he wanted to—she had no doubt that he would, even though she made it clear he wasn't welcome.

She stopped moving in the middle of the living room. Turning to face him, her arms instinctively crossed over her stomach to protect herself from any ugliness to come. She thought she'd escaped all the drama when she'd finally moved from her mother's house. But like her shadow, it had a way of catching up with her.

Sloan carefully—too carefully—closed the door, then approached her with cautious steps.

"Do you want to tell me what's going on?" He paused, and when she didn't answer, he continued. "Or am I going to have to drag it out of you?"

The anger that crept through her like lava spurred her to speak. It strengthened her backbone and lifted her chin. "I thought I made myself clear at the office."

"You think I'm paying you for sex?" His incredulous tone jarred her.

"I'm your employee. We…slept together. Then you gave me expensive jewelry. What am I supposed to think?"

That full mouth twisted. "Oh, maybe that it's a *gift?*"

"Vivian certainly didn't think that."

His eyes widened when he heard his stepmother's name. Ziara squeezed her arms tighter, hoping to hold in the tide of hurt and anger. She should have known going for a guy outside the safe zone would leave her feeling like a slut. So her self-image was a little skewed—years of bullying at home and school would do that. But Vivian's words had convinced her that she was repeating history.

Everything she'd felt for Sloan up until now—the dizzying rush of desire, need and freedom—wasn't pure at all. Just shameful. No one really needed another person that strongly. It had to be a mirage, a fantasy.

"What does Vivian have to do with this?" He stepped closer, one measured movement at a time. Ziara retreated until the back of her knees hit the side of the chaise.

"She came in while I was opening the box."

"Convenient, seeing as how she rarely comes to my office."

She glanced away. The logistics didn't matter now. Just the broken pieces left behind.

He reached out to tilt her face up, giving her no choice but to look at him. "She accused you of sleeping with me." His mouth tightened, compressing his lips and whitening the edges. "I don't care what Vivian said. She has no proof," he continued when she neither confirmed nor denied it. "Her view is a little skewed, black-and-white in a world of gray. She sees me as some kind of playboy, when the opposite is actually true."

Ziara couldn't stop her eyebrows from lifting.

Sloan chuckled. "Yes, I know it's hard to believe, but I've actually had to let three assistants go because they pursued me, not the other way around. This—" he gestured between the two of them "—is new to me, believe it or not."

He slid onto the chaise, pulling her back until her shoulders met his solid chest. "This isn't about me taking advantage of you because you are an employee, you're convenient or even because you're so damn hot. I thought..."

She leaned into his warmth, her spine too weak to keep her upright. Even though she knew it was wrong, her chest ached with her need to believe him. "So what is it about?"

"I don't know," he said, reaching around to cup her cheek in the warmth of his hand. "But I sure want to find out."

His kiss was gentle with a touch of erotic edge. She melted into him, afraid to believe, yet afraid not to. Old fears were hard to kill off. Like horror movie villains, they seemed to rise constantly from the dead.

Finally he pulled back. Standing, he picked her up, then resettled them both onto the chaise with her firmly planted on his lap. "I saw the necklace in Las Vegas," he said, his hands already burrowing into her hair to excavate the pins confining it. "I don't know why I bought it. I just knew it would look stunning nestled right here." He brushed his knuckle across the hollow at the base of her throat. "Bright against your skin."

She shifted, swallowing hard. "Then why give it to me today? We agreed to keep this out of the office."

He laughed softly, a kind of exasperated sound that rumbled against her chest. "I honestly didn't think about it. I thought it might be a nice gesture after all the hard work you've done, and, well, Vivian hasn't been easy on you. I wanted to do something nice for you."

He felt so good, so solid beneath her hands. Looking up, she let her eyes meet his, the bright blue mesmerizing in the near darkness. Would it hurt anyone but her if she believed him, just for a little while? She'd lost everything else during this debacle. Why should she have to give him up this soon? Surrendering with a sigh, she melted into the crook of his shoulder. "I'm sorry."

He shrugged. "What made you think I intended it as a payoff?"

She knew she shouldn't say it. But the words snuck out of their own volition—without her consent.

"There was an…incident when I was younger."

"What happened?"

She shouldn't tell, she couldn't. No one in the intervening ten years had ever known.

As if he were listening to her thoughts, he pressed a soft kiss to her temple and murmured, "I'll trade you. Tell me something about you, and I'll swap it for something about me."

The temptation, coupled with the darkening shadows in the room, coaxed the rest of the story from her.

"When I was a teenager, one of my mother's many…boyfriends…showed up at the house one day while she wasn't home. He said he was there to see me, to give me a present."

She snuggled closer, seeking Sloan's protection. "He gave me a beautiful ruby necklace. It was gorgeous, but even at that age I knew something wasn't right about him giving it to me." Her stomach clenched in remembered dread.

"Just then my mother came home. When she saw the necklace in my hand, she had a fit."

The accusations had been the worst—much worse than getting slapped and having the "gift" snatched from her hand. Her mother had accused her of trying to steal her client, not listening to a word Ziara said in her own defense. "Finally, he convinced her it didn't mean anything, but I stayed out of his way from then on. The way he watched me..."

Sloan's body absorbed her shudder. It felt so good not to be by herself anymore. She'd been alone, entirely alone, since that day so long ago.

Despite his promises to her mother, that man had tried to come into her bedroom one night. But she'd managed to slip out the window before he'd finished picking the simple lock.

Under cover of night, she'd watched him walk around her bedroom, touching her things. The next day she'd made a trip to a local hardware store, where a nice old man had sold her everything she'd needed to install a dead bolt. Ziara relied on herself alone after that. Until the day of her seventeenth birthday, when she'd left home without a forwarding address.

Ziara looked up at Sloan. Those memories from long ago influenced her current decisions more than she'd like to admit. "I shouldn't have jumped to conclusions."

"Just remember, not everyone thinks like Vivian does. Just look at Patrick. He's always telling me how great you are." He smiled, though his eyes didn't warm in color, and carried her to bed. "It's been a long week. Let's get some rest."

Gently, he stripped them both. Leaning over, he settled them against the pillows in a move that seemed natural to him. Ziara remained stiff for long moments before gradually relaxing into his hold. Never had she lain in another person's embrace, not even the loving hold of a parent. Until Sloan. Here with him, like this, felt like home. Warm, secure, safe... The final bit of awkwardness melted away.

"Tell me something now," she said, eager to shift the focus. "Tell me about your father."

She'd never had one, couldn't even imagine what it would be like to have a man in the house. Her mother's men had just been visitors who had brought nothing but indifference at best, anger and pain at worst.

Sloan's hands rubbed up and down her arms, lulling her into a drowsy state. "My father was always laughing, always happy, until my mother died. They were very much in love through it all." His hand started to squeeze, massaging up and around her shoulder. "I'll never forget, one time when she was really bad off with the cancer, he took me with him on a business trip."

"Where did you go?"

"I don't even remember, but I know we went to some kind of trade show. I remember following him through walls of people, listening to his voice as he talked to other men, having him introduce me like I was one of the adults, soaking it all in as he explained stuff to me."

His heartbeat thudded evenly under her cheek. "Did you learn a lot?"

"I was thirteen years old. I still remember every word."

As she drifted to sleep, the happy wistfulness in his voice brought on dreams of a family she'd never had.

Sixteen

The fast-approaching deadline for the fall show escalated the rush to complete the two lines, so the days got busy and the nights even busier.

She ran messages back and forth between Sloan and the design team and mediated a few squabbles, though the three designers had formed an uneasy truce among them. Vivian lay low as the time for the fall show approached. Ziara occasionally wondered how she felt, but no longer had an in to inquire how Vivian was doing.

She and Sloan spent most nights together, always at her place, with Sloan never staying all night. She didn't protest. What was the point of trying to force him into something he didn't want?

Only one night did they deviate from the pattern.

Sloan and Patrick had been holed up in a conference until about forty minutes past normal shutdown time. Ziara knew she could leave, but her greedy feminine nature urged her to wait. She could ask Sloan if he wanted her to cook dinner. If he'd like to unwind with a drink, a hot shower, a… She groaned, allowing her head to fall forward into her hands. Shameless. She was utterly shameless.

"Night, sweet cheeks."

She jerked upright, returning Patrick's smile as he sauntered out the door. Blushing, she turned to find Sloan leaning against the doorframe connecting their offices.

"You look tired," he said, his gaze scanning her face. "Am I driving you too hard?"

His sensual tone added deeper meaning to his words. She shook her head, her throat too tight to speak.

He reached for her arms, rubbing his hands along them in light, comforting strokes. "Why don't you go ahead home?" He nodded toward his open office door. "I still have some work that needs to be finished tonight."

She knew she should do exactly that. She should go home, rest and have a good night's sleep. Nibbling on her lower lip, she realized she didn't want to do what she *should*. That wasn't how she wanted to spend her evening. Studying the fatigue darkening Sloan's normally vibrant eyes, she realized she wanted to take care of him. Ease a little of the strain he was under. She chose not to wonder why but to just act.

"Why don't I go get something for dinner and bring it back here?"

As surprise lightened his eyes, she spoke faster. "It would save you some time. You wouldn't have to stop working as long and could get done sooner. I don't mind—"

The rush of words ended when he placed his lips over hers. She leaned into the gentle kiss for a moment. He pulled back until their lips barely brushed against each other.

"That sounds great," he breathed.

Her chest flooded with warmth as he pressed his mouth over hers once more, then returned to his office.

She tried not to be overly pleased as she raced home and changed into a gypsy skirt and tunic that she belted low on her hips. Though she never went out anywhere without her hair confined in some way, tonight she let it down and brushed it, the long strokes heightening her anticipation.

Sloan's obsession with her hair only grew. He was constantly touching it, burying his hands in it, especially as he rode her to climax. She was anxious to see how he reacted to her wearing it down at the office, even if it was after hours.

She stopped by a replica fifties diner near the office and ordered the deluxe burger and fries Sloan indulged in every so often, with a chicken salad sandwich for herself, before rushing back. When she walked through the office door, his eyes scanned her slowly from the tips of her strappy heels to the crown of her jet-colored hair. His gaze narrowed as it returned to her face.

"Oh, you so don't play fair," he said.

Her laughter floated around them as they spread the food on the small table in Sloan's sitting area. They ate in silence, staring out the floor-to-ceiling windows at the city lights. His eyes frequently rested on her hair. It felt so good to be free, to enjoy the moment.

"Why do you and Vivian fight so much?" Ziara asked, her earlier concern about the older woman still lingering in her mind. "It isn't just the business, either. You two seem at odds about most everything."

Sloan took his time chewing and swallowing. Ziara thought he wouldn't answer, though his face remained relaxed and open.

"She married my father when I was a teenager. I'm sure that rough adjustment period set some bad patterns in how we relate to each other."

He took another bite, chewing slowly, distracted by his thoughts. Her eyes strayed to the working muscles of his jaw and throat.

"My dad and I had a pretty laid-back arrangement until she came along. I don't know if she told him to take me in hand or what, but after their marriage it was rules, rules, rules and 'this is how we expect you to act.'"

"At the risk of sounding clichéd, at least someone cared," she said, forcing any self-pity from her voice.

Besides the dead bolt she'd installed on her door, she'd

stayed as far from home as possible. Often she ended up being at the public library until closing. She'd gotten a job at the local drugstore at sixteen, working her way up to assistant manager, saving every penny until she could leave town and lose herself in Atlanta. Her mother hadn't cared about her while she was home. She probably cared even less now.

His eyes snapped in her direction. "Do you know how Patrick and I met?"

"You said you met in high school."

He nodded shortly. "And he was my roommate in college. I was assigned to that room because I listed my original major as fashion design."

Ziara frowned. "I didn't realize—"

He broke in. "Vivian hated the idea. She told my father that I'd need a business degree if I wanted to run the company one day. He decided if I didn't change my major, he'd cut me off."

And he still hadn't gotten to run the company. The urge to defend his younger self rose, but she choked it back. "You and Patrick remained friends?"

"I know Vivian thought it was to spite her—and we got a kick out of rubbing her nose in it." He grinned. "But Patrick and I had become close by then. He taught me a lot about the design business that my father never did."

Just as Ziara was learning a lot more with Sloan than Vivian had ever taught her. "And he was the first person you turned to when you needed…a designer," she said, standing up to gather their trash.

"And he expects nothing more of me than to be myself and work hard to create success. I respect that."

As he came up behind her and kissed her on the neck, she wondered if he'd added the last bit for her benefit. Was he telling her what he needed out of a relationship?

No expectations? No commitment?

She frowned. She wouldn't be one of those women who turned into a clinging vine the minute a man showed any interest. As she shifted in Sloan's arms, she vowed to do the same as Patrick. She would enjoy the part of Sloan she had for as long as she had him.

She savored his hold until his guiding touch turned her toward him.

"I've waited long enough," he said.

He pulled her over next to him on the leather couch. She had a quick thought that she must have truly lost perspective to be doing this in his office before she could only focus on Sloan and his hands in her hair.

Later, much later, she woke alone on the couch. Disoriented, she sat up. Cool air caressing her skin reminded her of her nakedness. She grabbed the blanket Sloan must have covered her with and wrapped it over her shoulders.

Glancing around, she spotted Sloan hunched over his father's drafting table near the window, absorbed in the paper before him. He didn't look up as she hastily dressed, noting the clock read nearly one in the morning.

Walking to where Sloan stood, she peeked around his shoulder. To her surprise, the drawing was one of the designs for the fall show. The lingerie designs.

The table was covered with drawings in various stages of completion. They were classically beautiful—delicate, colorful and feminine—not slutty as she'd feared from the first. The designs were delicately sexy, with an exotic flavor that drew her.

"These are beautiful, Sloan," she said.

He grunted, seeming lost in thought. "What they need to be is finished."

She smiled. If she knew anyone who thrived under the pressure, it was Sloan. He might dislike—okay, hate—external expectations, but when it came to his expectations of himself, he didn't just meet them. He exceeded them.

But she was surprised by these drawings. They were his. Sloan's. Not Patrick's. Not Robert's. Not Anthony's. Sloan drew with sure strokes, bringing the design to life by catching the fluidity of the fabric, the lace detail and the fit against the body beneath. Compared to the one design sketch he'd shown her before, these were easily Picassos. And he'd kept them secret from her all this time.

She felt blown away—a bit sad that he hadn't told her before now—but blown away, nonetheless.

The scratch of pencil on paper continued a moment; then he froze. With extra care his eyes lifted to meet hers.

"Hey there," she said, residual emotions sharpening her tone just a bit. "Remember me?"

His jaw worked, allowing her to gauge the tension gripping him. Keeping her voice calm and free of accusation, she asked, "Were you ever going to tell me?"

"I don't know."

Um, ouch.

Something of her reaction must have caught his eye because he started throwing out excuses. And they actually made sense. "I've always drawn, always wanted to learn more about design, but never got the chance once I changed my major. After Dad died and Vivian forced me out of the company, I didn't see the point. But I've always wanted to try."

"Is Patrick some kind of front?"

His smile was a bit lopsided. "Hell, no. He's had to give me a crash course ever since he came home. Without him this would be a disaster. I've drawn up building plans for years." He looked over the pages before him, a kind of fascinated pride brightening his already light eyes.

"But why keep it a secret?" She struggled to keep disappointment out of her voice.

His mouth twisted. "You've seen how Vivian reacted to Patrick. Do you think she'd have signed any kind of agreement if she even remotely knew I would be in on the actual designs? Hell, my ideas for the show were shot to hell and back, but in the end she had no choice but to accept it." His naked shoulders lifted in a shrug, drawing her attention away from his sardonic grin for a moment. "It was one less battle to fight."

Which made sense, but she couldn't help wondering why he

hadn't told her. Didn't he think she'd understand after everything they'd said to each other, done with each other?

Maybe he didn't trust her as much as she'd thought he did.

Returning to the scared-rabbit mentality of her childhood had never been one of Ziara's life goals, but these days she found herself fearing the world around her like that lost, lonely child once more.

She wasn't entirely sure how to stop it. Throughout the next week, anxiety rolled over her whenever Sloan wasn't with her. Even though it was a stupid, feminine insecurity, she realized she wasn't as immune to the disease as she would have hoped.

Which was why she was awake at seven o'clock on a Sunday morning instead of curled up in the arms of the only man to ever inspire her to snuggle. He'd slipped into her bed after a really late night at the office and slept the morning away. But here she was trudging to the kitchen for some coffee, rather than waking him up.

When a knock sounded on her door, her heart jumped. *Please don't let that be Vivian.* All she needed was to confirm Vivian's already glaring accusations by having Sloan walk out from her bedroom in his favorite pajamas—his birthday suit.

When she opened the door, she stood for a moment in puzzlement. The woman's face wasn't familiar to her, but one look at her clothes and Ziara almost had a heart attack.

"Mom?" she croaked.

Her mother cracked her gum in the same way she'd been doing all her life. "I told you not to call me that, remember?"

I've done my best to forget. "Sorry. What can I do for you, Vera?"

"Aren't you going to let me in?" she asked.

Ziara didn't move, but shock kept her from shutting the door in her mother's face. She'd never prepared for this scenario, never dreamed her mother would track her here to Atlanta—or even care enough to want to find out where she was. This situation was completely alien, but anger started to seep around the edges of her confusion.

She wasn't about to taint her home with even a hint of bad memories. Pushing forward, she met her mother on the porch and closed the door firmly behind her. "What are you doing here?"

Vera knew Ziara better than to play the loving-mother card. "Well, I saw your picture in the newspaper, looking all fancy, prim and proper. Almost didn't recognize you."

Probably because she hadn't seen Ziara, truly seen her, since before she'd hit puberty. "That doesn't explain what you're doing here, at my house."

"Well, if you wanted to hide, you shouldn't put Z. Divan in the phone book. I picked up on that right off."

As her mother prowled the porch, Ziara performed her own inspection. The years hadn't been kind, by any means. Not surprising, since her mother had started binge drinking about a year before Ziara left for good. Her once-thick, shiny hair had been teased to lift its lifelessness. Wrinkles radiated from her mouth as if she'd taken up smoking, hard. But one thing remained the same: her clothes. The skintight animal prints hadn't looked good ten years ago, much less now.

"Right nice place you've got here, Ziara." She paused to peek inside the window along the side of the door. "Right nice. I always knew you would land on your feet."

I certainly did, with no help from you.

As Vera droned on about the house, Ziara found it easy to shut her out. There were no excuses, no changes her mother could make to establish a relationship between them—if that's what she was looking for here. Seventeen years had been opportunity enough. Even if it made her a bad person, she wasn't going to soften her heart for a woman who would put men and money ahead of her own child.

A child who had been haunted by those choices for her entire lifetime.

"Yep, you've done good. Better than I expected."

"I know." Anger seeped into Ziara's voice, making it hard and cold.

Vera stopped in her tracks as if just now getting the message. Her eyes homed in on Ziara, almost closing from all the mascara gooped on her lashes. "Guess you did get some of my genes, after all."

"Excuse me?"

Reaching into her cleavage, Vera pulled out a crumpled piece of newspaper to wave in front of her. With a quick snatch, Ziara was staring at the picture. In the foreground stood Vivian and Robert, discussing something with the reporter, but it was the background that caught her attention.

She and Sloan faced each other across one of the fabric tables. She looked as circumspect as she always did at work, but it was his expression that gave away the true nature of their relationship. She could just imagine the wolfish comment that would accompany that look on his face. Someone would have to be searching to notice, but she was pretty sure Vivian would look closely if given the chance.

Vera turned back toward the window. "That boss of yours looked like he could eat you up. Judging on his looks and money, I'd let him if I were you."

A shudder worked its way down Ziara's spine, the picture of Sloan even now sleeping in her bed burning in her mind. Despite the differences in their incomes, Vera and Vivian probably viewed this situation in a very similar manner. But what she felt for Sloan couldn't be reduced to a simple paycheck.

"Why are you really here, Vera?"

The other woman's back stiffened. "Well, I figure I fed and clothed you for seventeen years. Now that you're on your feet, payback would be the grateful thing to do. I've had a few setbacks lately, and I can't work—"

I just bet you can't. "Actually, Mother, the state paid for my raising. I took the checks to the bank every month, remember? I bought the groceries with the food stamps I managed to salvage from your purse. *I* raised me. Not you."

Anger sparked in the other woman's faded brown eyes. "I don't think so, you ungrateful brat. I worked on my back every day, something you never appreciated. And now you're going to make sure I never have to worry about money again."

Ziara crossed her arms over her chest. "This is ridiculous. Why would I give you money?"

"Because you want your next job to last longer than this one."

She froze. "What is that supposed to mean?"

"I could pay your boss a little visit. Put a little bee in his ear. After all, you certainly didn't earn those skills on your own. And I can do the same to your next boss, and your next, and your next. I'll follow you around like a bad penny until I get what I want."

Even though it was something she'd feared her entire adult life, she found herself saying, "They won't all hold me responsible for your actions."

"No, but they can hold you responsible for yours. After all, you did sleep with your boss, didn't you, dearie?"

And wasn't that the pickle she'd put herself in? Vera couldn't prove anything, but Sloan would know the truth. She had slept with him. Could she make him understand it was for love…not for money? Feeling sick, imagining what this woman would say to Sloan, she sank against the brick wall. "What do you want?" she mumbled.

"A salary of my own. You'll pay me every month to keep my mouth shut and stay at home. A nice home, not that nasty trailer I'm living in now."

Anger returned with the strength of a lightning bolt. "Like hell I will." She stalked closer, now the hunter rather than the hunted. "I'm not going to pay you a dime, *Vera*. I've paid enough for being your child. I'll just go to the police—you know blackmail is a federal crime, don't you?" Ziara wasn't sure whether it was or not, but her mother wouldn't know the difference.

Vera paled, backing toward the door. "You can't do that."

"Oh, I can and I will. Who do you think they'll believe, Mother? Me or you?" Securing Vera's arm with a firm grasp, Ziara led her off the porch and around to the driveway. A beat-up Chevy Cavalier rested at the curb, looking barely capable of going twenty miles, much less the eighty-five between Macon and Atlanta.

"Just remember this." Ziara turned Vera to look at her. Staring into those brown, sad eyes, Ziara felt her heart softening but forced steel into her voice. "I will not be manipulated. Neither will Sloan. So get back in your car and drive south. I don't want or need a mother anymore. I never did."

She waited until Vera pulled away before returning to the house. Once inside with the door firmly locked, she rested her head against the solid wood. She wouldn't cry—Vera had lost that hold on her a long time ago. She wouldn't worry—surely her mother wouldn't risk prosecution in order to get money from her. She wouldn't relent—Vera had made her bed a long time ago.

It would just be nice if she didn't have to stand her ground all alone.

Then a warm heat covered her back as Sloan brushed her hair aside to rain quick kisses across the base of her neck. "Good morning, gorgeous," he whispered against her skin. Her entire body came alive under his touch. "Did I hear you talking?" Ziara's heart started to pound, a dragging *thud, thud* that physically hurt in her chest. No matter how much bravery she could manage to Vera's face, telling Sloan the truth wasn't what she wanted. If he never knew her dirty, rank secrets, he would never look at her with pity or indifference or judgment. Even she wasn't that brave.

"A neighbor," she mumbled. "Just a neighbor who dropped by. Want some coffee?"

He growled, teeth scraping her skin this time. "I want something—but the coffee can wait until later."

Seventeen

"I think I'll head back to the office until you finish throwing your little temper tantrum."

Sloan winced as Ziara's words rang throughout the design floor, then turned to watch her dramatic exit, her body moving with the grace of a runway model and the irritation of a woman putting up with a difficult man. He'd snapped yet another order at her, one time too many, and apparently she'd had enough. He knew he took on bearish qualities the closer he got to a deadline. It hadn't bothered him before now.

But it wasn't simply the pressure that had him up in arms.

Ziara had been distant since their night here at the office. As he turned to Patrick to discuss the finer points of an orange flame pajama set, he remembered again the pure rightness of having her sleep in his arms before tearing himself away. A sense of inevitability colored every intimate moment they spent together. He couldn't decide if he was sinking fast or had already drowned—which only upped his grizzly bear aura of the moment.

Hell, there wasn't time to examine his life. He had a show to put on. Looking up, he found Patrick watching him. "What?" he demanded, not bothering to mitigate his irritable tone with his closest friend.

Patrick's face cleared. "Showing her the designs, huh? I thought you weren't big on anyone seeing them until they were done?"

Sloan shrugged, wishing Ziara hadn't let that little tidbit slip. "She was working late with me." He cringed at once again sounding like an uncaring ass, but he didn't have to explain himself.

"Does Vivian know?" Patrick asked, though his tone said he already knew the answer.

"Hell, no. I don't have to report my love life to her."

"Not about you, maybe," Patrick said, his tone unconvinced. "But she'd be interested in Ziara. You're poaching on her territory, professionally speaking. And she could make Ziara's life mighty uncomfortable after you leave."

"She already has, though Ziara admitted nothing."

"Please tell me you aren't going to leave her to face the old dragon alone when all this is over?"

"Who says I'm going anywhere?" he asked, then walked away without waiting for an answer. He knew he'd woven a complicated web. And he knew staying away from Ziara wasn't an option.

There would be plenty of time to fix all that *after* the show. Ziara's job was important to her, but he could always find her another one if he needed to keep them together. But he worried, deep down, that the approaching show was the reason behind Ziara's slowly rising wall. Was she afraid he would dump her after she was done being useful?

Deciding a quick exit was best for everyone involved, Sloan headed straight for the door instead of back upstairs to his office. He could get things done just as well from home and he wasn't in the mood to deal with interruptions. A brisk walk to his car would help with the thoughts crowding his brain.

The voice calling his name didn't register at first as the list of everything he needed to handle this afternoon ran through his mind. When he finally heard it, he turned back but didn't see anyone he recognized on the lightly populated sidewalk. A woman detached herself from the background to approach, but she wasn't familiar.

Her shaky smile revealed yellowed teeth from cigarette smoking if the bitter smell was any indication. Her clothes would have been indecent on a woman thirty years her junior, but on her… He kept his gaze trained on her face to spare them both any embarrassment.

"Are you *the* Sloan Creighton?"

Great. Media coverage could benefit a project, but it could also bring out the crazies. "Yes. How may I help you?"

The preening seemed instinctive for her, but it had Sloan shifting in his suede shoes. He glanced around—was he being pranked?

"My name is Vera, Vera Divan. I wanted to talk to you about my daughter."

Daughter? Surely not— "You mean—"

"Ziara? That's the one! She's turned into a right pretty thang, hasn't she?"

A part of him frowned in disbelief, though he made sure it didn't spread to his face. Judging by how she measured up against him, she was probably a couple of inches shorter than Ziara and the distinctly exotic flair was definitely missing. Maybe Ziara's father had been Indian, because it certainly hadn't come from her mother, whose thin, mousy-brown hair lacked her daughter's vibrant color. But a glance at her clothes revealed that they'd seen better days, sparking a moment of sympathy.

"Did you want to see Ziara, Mrs. Divan?"

"Oh, it's *Miss.* I'm not married, never have been—and I'm definitely available."

Sloan had been in many uncomfortable situations over the years, but this was one he doubted he'd forget.

"No, I didn't come to see Ziara. I came to see you after I found this." Reaching into a flashy, bright pink tote bag, she pulled out a newspaper clipping. Yet another article about their interview, but not from a newspaper that he recognized. He examined the photo. The look on his face as he talked to Ziara had him choking. They stood in the background, but the camera had still captured what was obviously a very intimate exchange.

"I'm pretty sure you get why I'd want to have a little chat, right?"

That caught his attention real quick. Though he had a feeling he wasn't dealing with a lady, he acted the part of the gentleman. With a sweep of his hand, he gestured for her to join him. "Would you care to walk with me? I'm heading to the parking garage."

Her grin was way too happy for his taste. Sloan wasn't fooled. Better to get down to business if this was headed where he thought. "What can I do for you, Miss Divan?" he asked, stumbling over the name.

One of her overly arched brows lifted even higher at his directness. "Well," she hedged, "I was just surprised as all get-out to see that picture in our local paper." She glanced sideways as they walked. "I'm from Macon, you know."

He didn't. Ziara rarely talked about her past, her family. The few tidbits he'd gleaned while in Vegas and since then hadn't painted a pretty picture, so he didn't push for more. He certainly couldn't imagine this creature giving birth to Ziara's exquisite perfection.

"But I know men," she was saying, "and a man only looks at a woman that way when he wants one thing."

Sloan jerked to a stop, swiveling to face her with tightly leashed aggression. "What the hell are you saying?"

"Not that I blame you," she said, her tone sweetly placating. "Ziara grew up around that kind of stuff. I'm glad to see she learned how to take care of herself and get what she needs. Guess she was paying attention after all. Too bad she has trouble with the follow-through."

Sloan's stomach went into a nosedive, swirling on the roller coaster before he could get off the ride. Please, please let her not be saying what he thought she was saying. He took another thorough look—short skirt, top unbuttoned enough to reveal more than the edges of her bra and abnormally high heels. In that instant, something in his memory clicked, and he recalled the woman he'd seen walking down Ziara's driveway last Sunday.

Ziara had said she'd been speaking with a neighbor. And he'd believed her. After all, he'd only seen the woman from the back—a quick glimpse out the bedroom window.

"Are you saying—"

One short, manicured finger scraped from one of his shirt buttons to the next, making his skin crawl. "That's right, honey. I'm good. Ziara learned from the best, all right. And now she wants you to pay up."

Anger started to build, low and deep. He'd spent the past five years since his father's death determined to take back from Vivian what he thought she'd stolen from him—the only piece of his father he had left. But Ziara proved even more ruthless than him.

Her mother was a prostitute. Had she truly followed in her footsteps?

There was no mistaking the insinuation. The woman before him lived the lifestyle, whether she simply used men for their money or actually walked a street corner. Ziara went in the opposite direction, had buttoned down every part of her personality. That would be why she'd latched onto Vivian, the exact opposite of the woman who'd raised her. Dressing to fit the part so she could catch even bigger fish.

The enormity of what she had done hit Sloan in the gut like a physical blow. He just prayed he didn't spew all over her mother's imitation designer shoes.

"Why isn't she here, asking for whatever the hell it is you want, herself?"

"Well, she's still a little soft when it comes to closing the deal. Not quite enough experience. When she asked me for help, I knew I'd have to step in. You'll do just as I ask." She waved the picture under his narrowed gaze. "This picture tells me most of what I need to know. Not to mention the words from Ziara's own mouth. That little trip to Las Vegas got things off to a right start, didn't they? I wonder how your stepmother would respond to accusations of sexual, um, what's that called?"

"Sexual harassment," he mumbled.

Though he knew she was wrong, and had defended his actions in the comfort of his own mind, there wasn't a whole lot he could say in his defense if charges were brought against him. And Ziara knew it.

"What, exactly, are you trying to exploit from me here?" he asked.

"Now, you don't have to say it like that." She glanced around the cool darkness inside the parking garage. "It's more like, you scratch her back, then well, you scratch my back. You've already gotten your scratch, I'm sure."

Her rough laughter had the bile rising in the back of his throat again. How could Ziara have viewed their time together as a business deal? As a bargaining chip? "Why not just come to me if she needed money?"

"Oh, money isn't what we want. Yet."

He waited, welcome numbness starting to creep through his limbs. For the first time in his life, he couldn't summon his hardball negotiator side.

"This little show you're working on? You're gonna walk away before it's done."

If the first demand hadn't shut him down, this one would have immobilized him. "Why would you want that?"

"Ziara knows it means a lot to you, but having Miss Vivian in charge means a whole lot more. Ziara owes her for all she's done, and with Miss Vivian as a boss, she'll have an executive assistant job locked down for years to come. Better deal than working for you until you get tired of her."

With each word, his disbelief was chipped away into nothing. Only one person could have told her those personal details—Ziara herself. As much as he didn't want to believe, it looked like he didn't have much choice.

"What difference does it make to you?" he asked.

"Well, it means a lot to me." She rubbed her fingers together in an age-old expression of greed. "With Ziara's status, I'll get myself a whole new makeover and access to an upscale client list." Her yellow toothed grin said she believed this delusion. There wasn't enough plastic surgery and cosmetic dentistry in the world.... "Then we'll both be living large." She sidled a little closer, forcing him to back up flush with his car. "A woman my age could use a little retirement fund, so to speak. Of course, if I had someone like you in my life, I wouldn't need one, would I?"

"And if I refuse?" There was always a catch.

"Well, you wouldn't want Ziara's secrets to get out, now would you? With your reputation, how many people wouldn't believe claims of you takin' advantage of the hired help? Those big-money contracts wouldn't come your way nearly as often, if people around here didn't want to be associated with you, huh?"

He wasn't going to show how unnerved that made him. If Atlanta was suddenly filled with accusations of sexual harassment at his father's company, no one would risk hiring him. Ziara and Eternity would look like the victims, thus keeping their reputations solidly intact while his crumbled.

One of her nails tapped the newspaper clipping. "So what do you say?"

He struggled to find a way out of this mess, but his brain remained stuck on the picture of Ziara, sleeping so innocently on the couch in his office. Disbelief still hung around because he did care, didn't he? He'd fought it, hid from it, pretended it wasn't there.

But it was.

Knowing she had him backed against a wall, he conceded. "Done."

Ziara took a deep breath of cool air, savoring the softening fall weather, before pushing through the revolving door into the Eternity Designs building early on a Thursday morning. She felt much lighter after a good night's sleep, although she'd missed Sloan's warm body curved around her as she drifted off. Amazing how quickly she'd gotten used to that.

Now she was ready to face the Abominable Snowman again.

A soft laugh escaped as she crossed to the elevator. Sloan's attitude had finally pushed her over her limit, but when she'd smarted off in return, she'd felt a surge of adrenaline. Matching wits with him energized her, made her feel alive like she hadn't in her entire life.

She smiled as she trekked down the hallway toward Sloan's office, remembering a similar walk several months ago. Now, instead of dreading seeing him, she couldn't wait. Instead of resenting her attraction to him, she reveled in it.

Turning a corner, she spied Patrick standing in the doorway to her office. He gestured for her to hurry.

"Ziara, get in here."

Ziara rolled her eyes. Patrick tended toward the melodramatic, but she accelerated in anticipation of seeing Sloan. Even when he acted like a bear, he was a lovable bear.

At the thought, her body froze, her heart seeming to stop, then start again twice as fast. She could almost feel the shell encasing her heart give one last crack before bursting into a million tiny pieces. Left behind was a pure red, bigger, more feeling muscle that beat with the certain knowledge of her feelings for Sloan.

How did she even know what she felt? It wasn't that she'd ever been in love before. Or loved anyone at all that she could remember. Maybe her mother at some point, but she retained few memories from her early childhood. She remembered very little before her tenth birthday. After that Ziara supposed she'd lost hope of it ever being returned, so whatever love she might have had died a painful death.

The only love she'd ever felt had been for her job.

Maybe that's how she knew this was love—she'd never felt like this before, about anyone. She'd never felt so exposed, so vulnerable. So alive.

Patrick practically vibrated with irritation. "Come. On."

Ziara jumped, then picked up speed as she moved toward him. "What?" she hissed.

Patrick started dragging her across the office before she could even finish the word. "You have to stop him—"

Her heels skidded as she halted just inside Sloan's office. He stood in what she thought of as his "thinking" position: facing the floor-to-ceiling windows, head down as he contemplated those scurrying below him, his shoulders broad and square, hands clasped loosely behind his back. The surveyor of his domain.

After a moment, she took in various boxes littered around the room, file drawers gaping, the top of his desk wiped clean.

Her head swiveled from one end of the room to the other, not comprehending the chaos before her.

"He's leaving."

Ziara turned to find Vivian, the jolt of shock racing through her brain down into her body. "What?" She heard her voice but never felt her lips move.

"He's leaving." Vivian's tiny smile smacked of smug superiority. "Even though this means he'll lose everything, he's decided 'everything' is no longer worth his time."

"That's not what I said at all, Vivian," Sloan growled, though he didn't turn from the window.

Vivian practically purred in her victory. "But it's what you meant, isn't it, dear?"

"I told you, I have another project that needs urgent attention. There's only so much of me to go around." His voice sounded tight, no hint of emotion seeping through.

What? Ziara's brain could barely process what was happening. Another project? What about his father's legacy? His connection?

Her gaze fell on the drafting table in the corner where she'd watched Sloan, his golden head bent forward in the lamplight, hair long enough to obscure his face. Those drawings weren't the work of someone who didn't care, someone who could simply walk away.

Pivoting slowly, she faced Sloan, who stood just as he had when she came into the room, completely oblivious to anything happening around him.

At first he didn't move, but his back straightened, becoming more rigid. Something she hadn't dreamed possible. His hands tightened around each other. Could he feel the weight of her stare between his shoulder blades?

She waited for some sign that the man she loved at least gave a damn about something, about the people involved here. Unlike Vivian. "Was it all just some kind of game?" Ziara asked. "Didn't it mean anything to you?"

He twisted, marching down on her like a bull, forcing her to retreat. "You don't get to ask questions, got it?"

He turned to Vivian, facing her with a mixture of anger and despair like nothing Ziara had ever seen. "You got what you wanted, Vivian. Now get out. If I see you again, I might just change my mind."

Vivian's voice rumbled in the background, but Ziara couldn't make out the actual words. It didn't matter. Only Sloan mattered. The sound of the office door shutting with harsh finality shook her composure.

She was left in the room with someone she didn't know, didn't recognize underneath the stone cold facade. Oh, she should recognize him, remembering Sloan's first confrontation with Vivian. But that harsh strength had never been used against her.

Never.

With the numbness slowly creeping over every part of her body, she remained frozen as he approached once more.

"I hope this is all worth it for you, Ziara."

She shook her head. "What?"

"All the lies and deception. Why would you pretend to be something you're not? Why would you present yourself as this—" his hand gestured down her body, encased in a conservative black suit "—professional, moral woman, when deep down, that's not who you really are at all?"

Ziara felt her head start to spin. The words coming from his mouth had an eerie similarity to thoughts that had whirled through her brain for ten years. She'd told herself that she was a better person, a stronger person, than the trash heap she'd crawled out of— But sometimes it seemed she hadn't shaken it at all.

How had he learned her secret?

Her voice a little shaky, she said, "I don't know what you're talking about, Sloan."

Reaching out, he pulled a thick strand of hair from her loose updo, twisting it around his fingers like he had hundreds of times before today. Only this time, his touch had an edge to it, a slight pull on the roots that communicated his anger. "Really? Are you sure, Ziara? Didn't you know this would get to me a lot quicker than dressing like a tramp?" he asked, stepping close enough for her to feel his breath across her forehead. Those icy blue eyes gave no mercy, showed no love. In light of her own recent revelation, his lack of emotion hurt all the more.

Why was he doing this?

"I met someone yesterday," he murmured, the usually seductive tone now hard as a rock. "I met your mother, Ziara. Are you sure you have nothing to tell me?"

She almost choked, but forced out, "My mother?"

"Oh, I understand why you wouldn't volunteer the information. After all, this is a rockin' body you've got going on. Wouldn't want me to get a clue too soon."

He thought she'd used him for—what? Sex? Hadn't all those late nights and intimate conversations, all the hard work she'd put into building her reputation and work ethic, meant anything? "It is not what you think."

"Oh, she spelled it out pretty plain for me…unless you have a different explanation?"

"My mother is—" In that moment, under his hard stare, years of shame and fear kept her from saying the word *prostitute*. His obvious disgust told her he'd already come to his own conclusions. Knowing her mother, she'd given him every reason to believe Ziara had followed in her footsteps. And living in a small town had taught her that most people enjoyed believing the worst about others. She'd hoped he'd see her differently than other men.

But he hadn't.

"Sloan, please understand—"

"Oh, I understand. I understand that you used me to get what you wanted."

What?

"Or should I say what you and Vivian wanted? I guess I can live with the fact that no matter what happens, I'm the one who actually lifted this place back onto its feet." He turned back to the drafting table, running a hand along its edge. "The only person whose recognition I've ever wanted is long gone. So why should I bother seeing this through? After all, I've gotten everything I wanted from you. And plenty of it."

"Sloan," she moaned. How could this be happening? How could her worst nightmares be coming true?

"Get. Out."

Hardly able to breathe, she backed slowly toward the outer door.

Sloan turned slightly to glance at her over his shoulder. "And don't worry. You won't have to prostitute yourself to me ever again. I'm long gone."

The words hurt, but what she saw in his eyes cemented the numbness spreading through her limbs.

She'd told herself all along, from the moment he'd seen her in the designer dress in Las Vegas, that she could do this as long as he looked at her a certain way—or any way except how men used to look at her mother. A mixture of lust, disgust and superiority. As long as that didn't show up on Sloan's face, she could put away all her insecurities and just be with him.

But now his eyes, those pale, electric blue eyes, were icy and cold, free of any emotion. His blank stare sliced through her, but she felt no pain.

She realized in that split second that as much as she wanted respectability and stability, had pushed herself to win Vivian's regard and respect, she couldn't care less about it in this moment. She didn't care that she'd lost everything.

All she cared about was Sloan.

But he didn't care about her. His willingness to walk away without a word, without listening to an explanation, told her everything she needed to know. That it had all been a lie.

Tears pushed into her eyes and she lowered her lids. She would not show vulnerability here, in this room that had seen the most sensual loving in her life. Now it was just a room. Cold and distant. She'd stay strong and protect herself, just as she'd been doing since she was a teenager.

The boxes once again caught her eye. Watching him pack up and leave, knowing he'd leave her behind without a twinge of regret, might just strip her of the stupor dulling everything—inside and out.

Ignoring him, she turned back to her own office. Luckily she hadn't put her purse away. The straps remained tightly clasped in one of her hands.

She wandered down the hallway as if in a trance. Nearing the turn, she heard Patrick's voice behind her. "Ziara, are you all right?"

She didn't acknowledge him, didn't even glance his way. For once she didn't care if it was her job to make things as easy as possible for her boss. Instinct said run, so she did—stepping into the elevator that opened before her like the doors to a haven.

Two days later Ziara lay motionless on her couch, staring up at the ceiling. The lights remained off, but she knew she would look a mess if anyone saw her. She'd managed to enter her bedroom only once and that had been to change out of her work clothes. She'd avoided it—and the memories of hours spent in her colorful bed with Sloan—since then.

She hadn't moved except to blink for two hours. Her mind whirled, reexamining the same questions over and over again. The one image that rose repeatedly was the look in Sloan's eyes when he'd glanced over his shoulder at her.

The blankness, so reminiscent of her life now.

She hurt too deeply to cry, to even move. So she held still and prayed it would all go away. She'd always been a doer, the type of person to take charge in a crisis, capable of handling most anything from her teen years on.

Now she simply endured.

Unable to face the office, she'd called the next day and spoken with Abigail, whose gentle voice had almost been her undoing. But then Vivian had come on the line.

"Though I'm disappointed, I completely understand how you could find yourself in this situation, Ziara," her mentor had said, her attitude far more subdued than in previous conversations. "Take a couple of days, but then we need you back in the office. The show is only seven days away and we can't afford for you to be absent longer than that. After the show, we'll talk."

Which probably meant: *I need you to get me through this event, but then you are fired.* Good or bad, she'd meet her obligations for the same reason she'd started working with Sloan—because she cared enough about Eternity Designs to see it succeed.

What she'd do after that, she didn't know.

Eighteen

Sloan stared at the blueprints for his newest reconstruction of an historic office building, but his thoughts turned again and again to the sketch of an imperial-style nightgown he knew was hiding underneath.

He should have moved on by now, but he couldn't. The show was tomorrow and he should be there, making sure everything ran smoothly, damn it.

His mind kept replaying Ziara's stiff back and shattered expression before she'd walked out of his office. Had he made a huge mistake? Had he let his pride mislead him from the truth?

She'd felt something for him. If he'd doubted it before that moment, he hadn't since. He didn't blame her for not saying it, for holding back. Not after seeing what she'd endured as a child.

He couldn't stop himself—he'd dug into Ziara's past the minute he'd returned to his old office. She'd come from a less than reputable family. Her mother had gotten pregnant with her very young—at seventeen. The same age at which Ziara had left home.

The father seemed to have been in the picture enough to

sign the birth certificate, but records indicated he'd left Macon not long after Ziara was born. His name hinted that he was the source of Ziara's exotic beauty—an Indian who had moved back to India five years ago after failing to make much of himself here in the U.S.

Vera's police record for prostitution started when Ziara was eight, with only a few arrests, but a quick conversation with an officer in Macon indicated she was well-known for her trade and generally left alone until some wife made a fuss. That same officer had told him Ziara left town as soon as she'd earned her GED, after years of being tormented by schoolmates who were well aware of her mother's profession.

But the information had only reinforced his decision to walk away. He didn't know where Vera Divan had gotten her information, or why she had confronted him that day—at least, not for sure. Suspicions lurked at the back of his mind, but honestly, the problem with Ziara meant more to him now than the business. He would not make Ziara pay any more than she already had for her upbringing. His physical relationship with her had given Vera the ammunition she'd needed to interfere in her daughter's life. What would stop her from doing it again? What if his suspicions were wrong?

Sloan sighed, running rough hands through his hair. It sucked when you realized you were in love with someone as you walked away from them.

Looking back, he could see that Ziara was ashamed, not just of her past, but of the things her mother did for money. So she'd run as far in the other direction as she could.

The buzz of the doorbell pulled Sloan's thoughts away from the scenarios swirling through his brain. Striding the length of the house, he jerked the door open. "Yes?"

"Don't have to be so short about it, Sloan."

Frowning at Patrick, whose incessant phone calls had about driven him crazy, he turned away without a word.

"Love you, too, jackass," his friend called out behind him. He didn't let Sloan's reticence stop him from coming in and making himself at home.

"What are you doing here?"

"Well, since you stopped answering my calls, what choice did I have?"

"You could have just stopped calling me. Or gone home. After all, you don't have a job here anymore."

"And let you throw away something you've worked damn hard for? Not a chance." Patrick just kept on coming. "And I do have a job, thanks to a certain someone whose name you forbid me to say."

"What happened?"

"If you wanted to know, you should have answered my phone calls."

Sloan glared, torn between curiosity and the pain of hearing her name. Patrick simply stood there with a smirk on his face, humming a few bars of "That's What Friends Are For." Infuriated, Sloan stomped through the house to the kitchen, jerking open the fridge to snag a Mountain Dew.

"I told you," Sloan said after returning and taking a long drink, "I have no interest in coming back. I'm certainly not wanted or needed there."

"According to who?"

"Vivian, for a start."

"Since when has her opinion ever counted for anything? In fact, it usually makes you do the opposite."

"Not this time."

"Why?" Patrick moved closer. "Sorry, bro, excuses are not gonna cut it."

"I told you what happened. She wouldn't even defend herself."

"Did you give her a chance or did you just railroad her with that overbearing attitude you get sometimes? Did you even tell her what you told me? What her mother said? I doubt she even knew what she was defending herself against. I told you that you were wrong…and this time, I can prove it."

"How?"

"Ziara went to bat for you—against Vivian."

Something tingled in Sloan's chest, but he ignored it. "What do you mean?"

"The lingerie line. Vivian wanted to cut it—and me—from the show. Ziara kept production moving until Vivian got wind of it, then she argued that it should stay. And so should I."

"How?" Sloan asked again, his throat tightening too much to get anything else out.

"The same argument you used, plus pointing out that a few choice tidbits have already been leaked to the press. Hints of a completely new direction for Eternity that has the RSVPs pouring in like water in a spring flood."

He was almost afraid of the answer. "Who alerted the press?"

"Not me. Not Robert or Anthony, who were surprisingly supportive of her arguments, by the way."

"Yeah?"

Patrick nodded. "So I'm guessing that only leaves one choice. Unless you did it yourself?"

"No way." Sloan's hands lifted in a hands-off gesture. "I want nothing to do with this show. Nothing."

Patrick leaned closer, his knowing look pinning Sloan where he stood. "You sure? You haven't been looking at any designs, thinking about fabric or drape or weight?" He wiggled his eyebrows. "It's very sexy when a woman comes to her man's defense."

"I'm not her man."

"Deep down, you know Ziara had nothing to do with her mother's blackmail threat. Time to admit you were wrong."

Sloan turned to face the bay window, staring out over his wooded backyard. "What if I'm not?"

"Don't you want to be?"

"Yes," Sloan said. It was harder to admit than he'd thought it would be, but it was the truth. He wanted Ziara to be innocent; he wanted that shattered look on her face to be real—not some kind of act that she'd learned from her conniving mother.

"Then don't worry about it. I, personally, am pinning my money on Vivian," Patrick said, his voice deepening in disgust.

"But I have no proof."

"And you'll never get it brooding around your house. Get back in the game, you coward."

Sloan would never have tolerated it from anyone else, but from Patrick, he knew those words were the honest truth. It was time to put his protective armor aside, face the fact that he loved Ziara and give her a chance to prove her innocence.

"Vivian will fire Ziara after this," Sloan said. "She's never tolerated me being a part of anything."

Patrick nodded. "With or without you, I think that's already her plan."

When Ziara arrived at the fashion show venue, it was a scene of organized chaos. Watching for one last quiet moment, an achy sadness spread through her. After tonight, her job at Eternity Designs would be done and she'd be on her own again. The loneliness had started creeping in earlier this week, an extension of Sloan's absence.

Spotting Patrick, she eagerly walked down the aisle, anxious not to be alone with her thoughts.

"It's beautiful," she breathed, staring at the simulated 1930s nightclub, elegant in its classic simplicity, sexy with silver and black details. The colors of the dresses and lingerie would look amazing against that backdrop. Peeking from a side wing, as if it had just dropped off guests at the show, was a 1930s silver Rolls-Royce classic car.

"Isn't it, doll?" Patrick said. "And the background changes colors." He paused. "But I guess you already knew that."

"Yes, I did," she said with a sad smile as she remembered the day she and Sloan had picked it out, together. Tucking away the pain, she turned all business. "Time to get ready for opening night, huh?"

By early evening she was a weird combination of tired and wired, with a long night still ahead of them. She didn't attend the preshow hors d'oeuvres, but she watched the crowd arrive for the event. Vivian was in her element, glimmering in a golden lace overlay gown as she smiled and conversed with members of Atlanta's elite.

No, not just Atlanta's, or even Georgia's. Ziara recognized a few of the surrounding states' political figures, not to mention the buyers for their usual venues and a few New York buyers, too.

Her heart fluttered, her stomach tightening like a fist. So much rode on this event for Eternity Designs and Sloan, even though he didn't seem to care anymore. Surely all the hard work and turmoil would be worthwhile.

Surely her heartache wouldn't be for nothing.

Ziara took her gown backstage to change. It was the same dress Patrick had sent her to wear for his party, topped with a sheer wrap in deference to the cooler fall nights.

Coming out of the dressing room, she had to walk through the space they'd set aside to prep the models. It was already filling up with half-naked women who had Ziara looking askance. A smile tugged at her mouth as she came across Patrick, kneeling behind a scantily clad model wearing a gorgeous burnt-orange negligee." Isn't this how we met?"

He grinned up at her before finishing the last few stitches. Then he stood. "I'm done, Jennifer. Thanks." He turned to her as the model walked away. "You look stunning in that dress, Ziara."

"Thank you. The designer did an incredible job." She leaned over to brush a kiss on his cheek, only to jump when someone said, "What's this?"

Hearing Sloan's voice was a little surreal. Turning, she was at a loss for words as she faced those bright blue eyes.

Patrick spoke from behind her. "You sure know how to make an entrance, buddy."

Sloan's grin made her heart ache, but she couldn't stop looking. The cool, calm facade she'd rebuilt over the past week cracked under his stare.

"Why…why are you here, Sloan?" she asked, clearing her throat in an attempt to get the words out.

"I'd like to know that myself." Vivian's voice drew their

gazes as she stormed through the curtain. "I was told you had arrived, but I have no idea for what purpose." Her eyes swept over their little group before resting back on her stepson. "I'm waiting, Sloan."

Ziara felt herself take a step back, afraid of the coming storm. Fights between Sloan and Vivian were notoriously intense, and she really wasn't up to enduring one at the moment.

"Then you'll be waiting a long time, Vivian," Sloan said. "I don't answer to you. Nor do I need an invite to my own show."

Vivian sputtered, "It's not your show."

"Oh, it is. Unless you'd like me to confiscate every dress, every item I had a hand in creating, carrying them to my car right through the front door. Your guests would love that, and we'd certainly make the society pages. And you'd still have a few left to show, I guess." The charming grin that got Ziara every time made an appearance. "Just not the best ones."

"You wouldn't dare." His charm was definitely lost on Vivian.

"Oh, I would. I assure you." He rubbed those incredibly skilled hands together. "I'm back in."

Nineteen

"Excuse me?" The high-pitched squeal in her voice would have mortified Vivian if she'd been more aware of it.

"You heard me," Sloan said, enjoying Vivian's distress. His eyes remained on her, but his senses were searching out Ziara's reactions to his presence. Now, just like the first time, she distracted him. Everything that made him a man told him to end this argument so he could sweep her away to a back room somewhere. But it was too soon for that.

Too much unfinished business between them.

"Oh no, Sloan. You left of your own accord," Vivian said.

"I prefer to think of it as a vacation."

The frustration reddening her face wasn't pretty. "That's simply semantics. It won't hold up in court."

"Wanna bet? Besides, I'm pretty sure Patrick will testify that I've been in touch with him over the past few days about final details. In my opinion, that counts." Thank goodness for Patrick's pestering. "This is simply a courtesy notice. I'll see you on the stage later." With a wink at his friend and Ziara, he turned toward the stage exit.

"So you decided you believed the little slut after all? What did she do, beg you to take her back?"

Sloan halted in midstride. He heard Ziara's gasp behind him, but forced himself to focus on Vivian alone. If she wanted to do this out in the open, let her hang herself with her own rope.

She kept right on talking. "I didn't count on that idealistic streak of your father's running through you as well, so the sexual harassment angle was definitely the way to go. I guess love didn't mean much in the face of prosecution."

Sloan pivoted slowly, his body tensing into standard negotiation mode. He'd thought the hardest part of regaining his father's company would be bluffing his way back into the deal. He'd never imagined Vivian would admit to having met Vera Divan first.

Ziara stood directly in his line of vision, her eyes trained on Vivian. Her olive skin now held a pale undertone and her gaze was hazy, unfocused, as she absorbed a blow he should have protected her from.

Patrick stepped in this time. "How did you even get Vera Divan to approach Sloan?"

"People like that will do anything for money, unlike us." Vivian kept speaking, digging the hole deeper and deeper. "She's just the daughter of a whore, Sloan. Or are you finally ready to sink to their level? Your mother's lower-class roots making themselves known."

That was all he needed. Stalking across the floor, he leaned in, dwarfing her with his size and his anger. His voice, when he spoke, was cool and deadly, but Vivian didn't seem to notice. "Actually I'm back here because my father's idealism runs strong through my veins. I want his dream to grow and thrive, not become some kind of shrine to the marriage you wanted but could never have. You always knew you were second-best, which is why you turned my father against me."

"You were simply a reminder of *her,* all free spirit and no responsibilities. The memories are what kept him from moving forward. He could have loved me just as much, given time."

"But there just wasn't enough time for you to mold him

into what you wanted, was there?" Sloan asked, his breath speeding up as he remembered the pain of the wedge Vivian drove between them. "As for Ziara, watch how you speak about her," he said. "She's not the daughter of a whore. She's a strong woman, who inspires me to be the person my father wanted me to be. She's worked hard to get where she is. She chose respectability when she could have given up, followed in her mother's footsteps. That's an example of refinement you'll never understand."

Vivian's eyes widened, fear creeping in at the edges.

Digging deep, Sloan remembered that last special moment with his father—his memories of following the taller man as he pushed through the crowd with sure steps. Sloan forged ahead. "I value traditions just as much as my father did, and he was right about one thing—you and I can't work together. So I think it would be best if you retire when Abigail does. I would hate for word to leak out about your shady dealings with Ziara's mother."

"You couldn't do that without telling people about Ziara's past."

"Who gives a damn? I certainly don't care what people think. She's not her mother—in any way. And anyone who dare speaks even her name wrong will have to deal with me. Personally."

This time Sloan's exit was straight and true. He walked out with a new connection to his father and a woman he still needed to seduce—this time into happily ever after.

Ziara glanced down at her hands, the slight vibration a little surprising. She wasn't sure if it was from witnessing the confrontation between Sloan and Vivian, or the sheer shock from seeing him again. In her heart, she knew he was only here for the business, for his father's memory. His surprising defense of her made her wish for something else, for something more personal, more private.

As she watched the glamorous throng being urged to their seats, she knew it wouldn't happen. Now that the truth was out, she'd never fit into this world. Vivian would make sure of that. And Sloan would never want to fit into hers.

As everyone settled and the lights dimmed, Ziara took a deep breath. This was it. The moment of truth. The reception of these lines would make or break Eternity Designs.

Things went well from the beginning. Guests oohed and aahed in all the right places as the wedding gowns graced the spotlight. The tightness coiled deep inside Ziara loosened as the first model for the transitional lingerie line made her entrance. Her dark coloring set off the white, slim-fitting gown against the now-pale pink backdrop.

As the emcee explained the nature of the material and the gown's function, Ziara heard whispers, and flashbulbs exploded. Just at that moment one of the runners stuck his head around the side door and motioned for Ziara.

As she approached, he whispered, "Miss Ziara, we need you."

Duty called.

Ziara and Patrick arrived back in the side wing just as Sloan started his speech. Tears in need of release ached in Ziara's throat. But she'd gotten through tonight, just as she would get through whatever lay ahead. Even if it meant starting over somewhere else.

Drinking in Sloan's confident, cocky grin as he addressed the crowd, she wished her future would keep her with Sloan.

Patrick left her side to join the other designers as Sloan introduced them. They looked like a melting pot of styles side by side, but the combination had been wildly successful. The standing ovation was proof positive.

Standing alone in the wings, Ziara's heart warmed with gratitude. Sloan had attained success, just as he deserved. He'd been right and she and Vivian had been wrong. In the end he'd saved the company they all loved.

Catching a change in Sloan's voice drew her focus back to him.

"There's one other person I must thank for making tonight

the success it is. Not only did she work tirelessly behind the scenes, she played mediator, organizer and even stagehand."

Ziara's heart thumped so loudly Sloan's next words were almost blocked out. "But most importantly, she served as the inspiration behind some of my new lingerie pieces. She taught me a very important lesson—the most amazing thing you can do in life is to be true to yourself. Not what people want you to be, the mold they shove you into, but to be what you want in life. That's the greatest challenge. She encouraged me to create some of the designs you saw tonight, and it's one of the most fulfilling things I've ever done. I hope my father would be proud."

He turned, staring straight at the spot where she trembled backstage. Gooseflesh prickled her bare arms as she listened.

"Please welcome Ziara Divan, my executive assistant at Eternity Designs."

When his hand extended toward her, she knew he meant for her to join him. Her mind was numb, yet she forced one leaden foot in front of another. As she stepped from the shadows out into the bright lights and applause, her mind came alive, racing with a dozen questions.

She ignored them, intent on reaching Sloan's side to slip her shaking hand into his outstretched one. Leaning down, he buried his head once again in the hair near her ear. "I love you, Ziara."

She shook her head, pulling back to stare with wonder into those glittering blue eyes. "What about—" she began in fear.

Sloan silenced her with one warm finger against her lips.

She heard the crowd erupt into applause, but she could only lose herself in Sloan's hot gaze and hope the fears would disappear like mist under the heat of his desire.

Later that night, long after the last guest was gone and the last dress packed away, Sloan found himself enjoying a very different kind of show in the privacy of his luxurious bathroom.

"Sloan, I really can't do this."

"Ziara, look at me." Sloan gently cupped her chin, guiding it up so she could watch the two of them in the full-length mirror. He knew she didn't want to see herself, but he wasn't going to let her hide. His gaze devoured her sensuous curves in the coppery silk. He probably shouldn't push her tonight, after everything she'd been through at the show, but part of him needed her to see the truth.

When he'd said she had been the inspiration for his lingerie pieces, he hadn't been lying. But this particular piece had been created for her—and him—alone. Like layered veils of transparent copper, burnt-orange, pale yellow and gold, the floor-length sheath both covered and revealed the curves of her body. Tempting him with her exotic beauty, showcasing the woman she was meant to be.

"Are you your mother?"

Her sharp intake of breath threatened to strain the zipper, but he wasn't backing down.

"Answer me."

"No, not even a little bit," she said, her assurance translating to her body. Her shoulders straightened. Her tension dissolved.

"Are you a beautiful woman who deserves to wear pretty things? Who wants to see how strong and sexy she is?"

Swallowing hard, her constrained voice came out a whisper. "Yes."

"Then wear this. For me."

Sloan let his eyes wander down her reflection. Luscious mounds of plump flesh overflowed the cups. While the effect wasn't quite pornographic, his body responded by tightening immediately, hard and throbbing. He'd fantasized about Ziara in various pieces of the lingerie he'd designed, but they hadn't gotten around to her wearing any for him. The reality was more spectacular than he'd imagined.

Unable to wait any longer, he did the one thing he'd been dying to since he'd seen her backstage earlier that evening—covered her lips with his own.

She pulled back way too soon. "Please understand, I didn't do this for any other reason—" He could almost hear her throat close, hear the fear she hid inside.

He knew of only one way to convince her of his love, to prove how much she deserved to be cherished and respected. That he wanted to be with her for an entire lifetime. Only one way to break through her barriers and convince the woman within.

He eased his hands up her back. When he buried his hands in her hair, pins clattered to the tile floor. He ran his fingers through the thick silk, searching for any remaining pins, then massaged her scalp until she relaxed, tension easing from her muscles. She melted against him. Tipping her face up to meet his, he was surprised to find silent tears trailing down her cheeks.

"Oh, baby, don't cry," he murmured.

"I'm not," she insisted. Swiping a hand at her cheeks, she stared at the moisture on her fingers in disbelief. He barely caught her whisper. "I've never cried, not since I was fourteen years old. Until I met you."

He guided her gaze up to meet his with a finger under her chin. "There's no need to, because I believe you. I believe *in* you."

A hopeful expression lit her darkened eyes just as her legs gave out. He clasped her to him, picking her up and striding down the passageway toward his bedroom.

He laid her on the bed, then explored her slowly, tracing every tantalizing curve through the soft fabric—her shoulders, neck, hips, calves, then back up to her stomach and breasts. Every hitch of her breath, every tremble in her limbs drew him closer, tightening the connection that bound them together—mind, body and soul.

"I can't believe how this feels," she whispered. "How you feel. I never want it to end."

"Me, either," he said before burying his face between her breasts. The round, soft weights tempted him, and were almost as distracting as her dark, tight nipples. Pulling the cups aside, he savored them as much as he did her silent declaration. One day she'd be ready to speak her true feelings. Though he had a reputation for pushing to get what he wanted, this time he'd wait as long as necessary.

Finally, widening her thighs with his knee, he settled over her.

"Now I know why having you is so different for me," he said, lifting his gaze to watch her in the shadowed moonlight.

"Why?"

"Because I love you." With those words, he pressed inside her, savoring the slick heat of her body, the arch of her back and the gasp from her lips.

No other words were spoken between them as they strove for release, each giving as much as taking until the world exploded around them. Long moments later, Sloan opened his eyes to find Ziara staring at him. He quirked a lazy eyebrow, savoring their still-connected bodies. "What is it?"

Her words were hushed, as if in reverence to the intimate connection between them. "I can't believe you believe me, after all she must have said to you. How can you still love me?"

He thought for a moment, choosing his words with care. "I should have remembered that Vivian has her own kind of ruthlessness. I'd already started to suspect, but never dreamed she'd lose her cool enough to admit her involvement with your mother." He looked into eyes surrounded by the thickest lashes he'd ever seen. "I never dreamed I'd be stupid enough to fall for it."

Trailing his knuckle along the curve of her cheek, he said, "My father was right."

"About what?"

"He said loving my mother was pure magic."

He felt her awe in the softening of her body, the tiny smile that visited her lips. As he settled once more within her arms, his hand stroked along her thigh. His mind soaked in her presence. "I love you, Ziara," he said.

"I love you, too, Sloan."

Joy burst under his skin. He brushed a tender kiss along her temple, pausing a moment to savor her declaration. Tonight truly was magic. He'd fought for what he believed in and won. As he whispered erotic intentions in her ear, he vowed to turn their dreams into reality.

For all eternity.

* * * * *

THE CEO'S ACCIDENTAL BRIDE

BARBARA DUNLOP

One

Zach Harper was the last person Kaitlin Saville expected to see standing in the hallway outside her apartment door. The tall, dark-haired, steel-eyed man was the reason she was packing her belongings, the reason she was giving up her rent-controlled apartment, the person who was forcing her to leave New York City.

Facing him, she folded her arms across her dusty blue Mets T-shirt, hoping her red eyes had faded from her earlier crying jag and that no tear streaks remained on her cheeks.

"We have a problem," Zach stated, his voice crisp, and his expression detached. His left hand was clasped around a black leather briefcase.

He wore a Grant Hicks suit and a pressed, white shirt. His red tie was made of fine silk, and his cuff links were solid gold. As usual, his hair was freshly cut, face freshly shaved, and his shoes were polished to within an inch of their lives.

"*We* don't have anything," she told him, curling her toes into the cushy socks that covered her feet below the frayed hem of her faded jeans.

She was casual, not frumpy, she told herself. A woman had a right to be casual in her own home. Where Zach Harper had no right to be in her home at all. She started to close the door on him. But his hand shot out to brace it.

His hand was broad and tanned, with a strong wrist and tapered fingers. No rings, but a platinum Cartier watch with a diamond face. "I'm not joking, Kaitlin."

"And I'm not laughing." She couldn't give one whit about any problem the high-and-mighty Zach Harper might encounter during his charmed life. The man not only got her fired, but he also had her blackballed from every architectural firm in New York City.

He glanced past her shoulder. "Can I come in?"

She pretended to think about it for a moment. "No."

He might be master of his domain at Harper Transportation and at every major business function in Manhattan, but he did not have the right to see her messy place, especially the collection of lacy lingerie sitting under the window.

He clenched his jaw.

She set her own, standing her ground.

"It's personal," he persisted, hand shifting on the briefcase handle.

"We're not friends," she pointed out.

They were, in fact, enemies. Because that was what happened when one person ruined another person's life. It didn't matter that the first person was attractive, successful, intelligent and one heck of a good dancer. He'd lost all rights to…well, anything.

Zach squared his shoulders, then glanced both ways down the narrow corridor of the fifty-year-old building. The light was dim, the patterned carpets worn. Ten doors opened into this particular section of the fifth floor. Kaitlin's apartment was at the end, next to a steel exit door and a fire alarm protected by a glass cover.

"Fine," he told her. "We'll do it out here."

Oh, no, they wouldn't. They wouldn't do anything anywhere, ever again. She started to step back into the safety of her apartment.

"You remember that night in Vegas?" he asked.

His question stopped her cold.

She would never forget the Harper corporate party at the Bellagio three months ago. Along with the singers, dancers, jugglers and acrobats who had entertained the five-hundred-strong crowd of Harper Transportation's high-end clients, there was a flamboyant Elvis impersonator who'd coaxed her and Zach from the dance floor to participate in a mock wedding.

At the time, it had seemed funny, in keeping with the lighthearted mood of the party. Of course, her sense of humor had been aided that night by several cranberry martinis. In hindsight, the event simply felt humiliating.

"The paper we signed?" Zach continued in the face of her silence.

"I don't know what you're talking about," she lied to him.

In fact, she'd come across their mock wedding license just this morning. It was tucked into the lone, slim photo album that lived in her bottom dresser drawer beneath several pairs of blue jeans.

It was stupid to have kept the souvenir. But the glow from her evening on Zach's arm had taken a few days to fade away. And at the time she'd put the marriage license away, those happy minutes on the dance floor had seemed somehow magical.

It was a ridiculous fantasy.

The man had destroyed her life the very next week.

Now, he drew a bracing breath. "It's valid."

She frowned at him. "Valid for what?"

"Marriage."

Kaitlin didn't respond. Was Zach actually suggesting they'd signed a real marriage license?

"Is this a joke?" she asked.

"Am I laughing?"

He wasn't. But then he rarely laughed. He rarely joked, either. That night, she'd later learned, was quite the anomaly for him.

A cold feeling invaded her stomach.

"We're married, Kaitlin," he told her, steel eyes unflinching.

They were not married. It had been a lark. They'd been playacting up there on the stage.

"Elvis was licensed by the state of Nevada," said Zach.

"We were drunk," Kaitlin countered, refusing to believe such a preposterous claim.

"He filed a certificate."

"How do you know that?" Her brain was revving into overdrive, calculating the possibilities and the potential consequences.

"Because my lawyers tell me so." He gave a meaningful glance past her shoulder, into the apartment. "Can I please come in?"

She thought about her mystery novels covering the couch, the entertainment magazines that were sitting out on the coffee table, the credit card and bank statements in piles beside them, revealing her shopping habits for the past month. She remembered the telltale, half-eaten package of Sugar Bob's doughnuts sitting out on the counter. And, of course, there was the box of sexy underwear on full display in the afternoon sunshine.

But, if he was telling the truth, it wasn't something she could ignore.

She gritted her teeth and ordered herself to forget about his opinion. Who cared if he found out she had a weakness for Sugar Bob's? In a matter of days, he'd be out of her life. She'd leave everything she'd ever known, start all over in another city, maybe Chicago or Los Angeles.

Her throat involuntarily tightened at the thought, and her tears threatened to freshen.

Kaitlin hated being uprooted. She'd started over so many times already, leaving security and normalcy behind as she moved from one childhood foster home to another. She'd been in this small apartment since she started college. And it was the only place that had ever felt remotely like home.

"Kaitlin?" he prompted.

She swallowed to clear the thick emotions from her throat. "Sure," she told him with grim determination, stepping aside. "Come on in."

As she shut the door, Zach took in the disarray of packing boxes littering the apartment. There wasn't anywhere for him to sit down, and she didn't offer to clear a chair. He wouldn't be staying very long.

Though she tried to ignore it, her glance shifted involuntarily to the underwear box. Zach tracked her gaze, his resting on the mauve-and-white silk teddy her friend Lindsay had bought her for Christmas last year.

"Do you mind?" she snapped, marching over to pull the cardboard flaps shut.

"Not at all," he muttered, and she thought she heard a trace of amusement in his tone.

He was laughing at her. Perfect.

The cardboard flaps sprang back open again, and she felt the unwelcome heat of a blush. She turned to face him, placing her body between Zach and her underwear.

Behind him, she spied the open box of Sugar Bob's. Three of the doughnuts were missing, transferred from the white cardboard and cellophane container to her hips around nine this morning.

Zach didn't appear to have an ounce of fat on his well-toned body. She'd be willing to bet his breakfast had consisted of fruit, whole grains and lean protein. It was probably whipped up by his personal chef, ingredients imported from France, or maybe Australia.

He perched his briefcase on top of a stack of DVDs on her end table and snapped open the latches. "I've had my lawyers draw up our divorce papers."

"We need lawyers?" Kaitlin was still struggling to comprehend the idea of marriage.

To Zach.

Her brain wanted to go a hundred different directions with that inconceivable fact, but she firmly reined it in. He might be gorgeous, wealthy and intelligent, but he was also cold, calculating and dangerous. A woman would have to be crazy to marry him.

He swung open the lid of the briefcase. "In this instance, lawyers are a necessary evil."

Kaitlin reflexively bristled at the stereotype. Her best friend, Lindsay, wasn't the least bit evil.

For a second, she let herself imagine Lindsay's reaction to this news. Lindsay would be shocked, obviously. Would she be worried? Angry? Would she laugh?

The whole situation was pretty absurd.

Kaitlin anchored her loose auburn hair behind her ears, reflexively tugging one beaded jade earring as a nervous humor bubbled up inside her. She cocked her head and waited until she had Zach's attention. "I guess what happens in Vegas sometimes follows you home."

A muscle twitched in his cheek, and it definitely wasn't from amusement. She felt a perverse sense of satisfaction at having put him even slightly off balance.

"It would help if you took this seriously," he told her.

"We were married by Elvis." She clamped determinedly down on a spurt of nervous laughter.

Zach's gray eyes flashed.

"Come on, Zach," she cajoled. "You have to admit—"

He retrieved a manila envelope. "Just sign the papers, Kaitlin."

But she wasn't ready to give up the joke. "I guess this means no honeymoon?"

He stopped breathing for a beat, and there was something familiar about the way his gaze flicked to her lips.

She was struck by a sudden, vivid memory, instantly sobering her.

Had they kissed that night in Vegas?

Every once in a while, she had a fleeting image of his mouth on hers, the heat, the taste, the pressure of his full lips. She imagined that she could remember his arms around her waist, pulling her tight against his hard body, the two of them molding together as if they belonged.

In the past, she'd always chalked it up to a fevered dream, but now she wondered…

"Zach, did we—"

He cleared his throat. "Let's try to stay on track."

"Right." She nodded, determinedly pushing the hazy image out of her mind. If she'd kissed him even once, it was the worst mistake of her life. She detested him now, and the sooner he disappeared, the better.

She reached out her hand and accepted the envelope. "It only took us five minutes to get married, no reason why the divorce should take any longer."

"Glad you see it that way." He gave a sharp nod, and his hand went to the inside pocket of his suit. "Of course, I'll want to cover any inconvenience." He extracted a gold pen and a brown leather checkbook, flipped open the cover and glanced at her. "A million?"

Kaitlin blinked in confusion. "A million what?"

He breathed a sigh of obvious impatience. "Dollars," he stated. "Don't play coy, Kaitlin. You and I both know this is going to cost me."

Her jaw involuntarily dropped a notch.

Was he crazy?

He waited expectantly.

Was he desperate?

Wait a minute. *Was* he desperate?

She gave her brain a little shake. She and Zach were husband and wife. At least in the eyes of the law. Clearly, she was a problem for him. She doubted the high-and-mighty Zach Harper ran into too many problems. At least, none that he couldn't solve with that checkbook.

Huh.

Interesting.

This time, Kaitlin did chuckle, and tapped the stiff envelope against the tabletop. She certainly didn't want Zach's money, but she sure wouldn't say no to a little payback. What woman would?

This divorce didn't have to happen in the next five minutes. She'd be in New York for at least another couple of weeks. For once in his life, Mr. Harper could bloody well wait on someone else's convenience.

She took a breath, focused her thoughts and tried to channel

Lindsay. Lindsay was brilliant, and she'd know exactly what to do in this circumstance.

Then, the answer came to Kaitlin. She raised her brows in mock innocence. "Isn't New York a joint property state?"

Zach looked confused, but then his eyes hardened to flints.

He was angry. Too bad.

"I don't recall signing a prenup," she added for good measure.

"You want more money," he spoke in a flat tone.

All she really wanted was her career back.

"You got me fired," she pointed out, feeling the need to voice the rationale for her obstinacy.

"All I did was cancel a contract," he corrected.

"You had to know I'd be the scapegoat. Who in New York City is going to hire me now?"

His voice went staccato. "I did not like your renovation design."

"I was trying to bring your building out of the 1930s." The Harper Transportation building had infinite potential, but nobody had done anything to it for at least five decades.

He glared at her a moment longer. "Fine. Have it your way. I got you fired. I apologize. Now how much?"

He wasn't the least bit sorry for having her fired. He didn't care a single thing about her. The only reason he'd even remembered her name was because of the accidental marriage. And he'd probably had to look that up.

She squared her shoulders beneath the dusty T-shirt, determined to take this victory. "Give me one good reason why I should make your life easier?"

"Because you don't want to be married any more than I do."

He had a fair point there. The mere thought of being Zach Harper's wife sent a distinct shiver coursing its way up her spine.

It was distaste. At least she was pretty sure the feeling was distaste. With any other man, she might mistake it for arousal.

"Mrs. Zach Harper." She pretended to ponder, warming to

her stubborn stance as she purposely slowed to note her half-packed apartment. "Don't you have a roomy penthouse on Fifth Avenue?"

He clicked the end of his pen, slowly lowering it to his side. "Are you daring me to call your bluff?"

She cracked her first genuine smile in three months. He wouldn't do it. Not in a million years. "Yeah," she taunted boldly. "Go ahead. Call my buff."

He stepped closer, and an annoying buzz of awareness tickled its way through her stomach. They stared each other down.

"Or you could leave the divorce papers," she offered with mock sweetness. "I'll have my lawyer read them over next week."

"Two million," he offered.

"Next week," she retorted, trying not to show her shock at the exorbitant figure. "Summon up some patience, Zachary."

"You don't know what you're doing, *Katie*."

"I'm protecting my own interests," she told him.

And there was something to be said for that. Seriously. Who could guess what his lawyers had hidden in the divorce documents?

They were both silent. Horns honked and trucks rumbled by five floors below.

"I don't trust you, Zach," she informed him tartly. Which was completely true.

His expression hardening by the second, he stuffed the pen into his pocket, then deliberately tucked the checkbook away. He closed and latched the briefcase, and sharply straightened the sleeves of his jacket.

Seconds later, the door slammed shut behind him.

Zach slid into the passenger seat of the black Porsche Carrera idling at the curb outside Kaitlin's Yorkville apartment building and yanked the door shut behind him.

"Did she sign?" asked Dylan Gilby, as he slipped the gearshift into First.

Zach tugged the seat belt over his shoulder and clicked the latch into place. "Nope."

He normally prided himself on his negotiating skills. But there was something about Kaitlin that put him off his rhythm, and the meeting had been a colossal failure.

He didn't remember her being so stubborn. To be fair, he hadn't known her particularly well. They'd met a few times before the party, but it was only in passing while she was working on the renovation plans for his office building. He remembered her as smart, diligent, fun-loving and beautiful.

He had to admit, the beautiful part certainly still held true. Dressed to the nines in Vegas, she was the most stunning woman in a very big ballroom. Even today, in a faded baseball T-shirt and jeans, she was off the charts. No wonder he'd gone along with Elvis and said "I do." He was pretty sure, in that moment, he did.

"You offered her the money?" asked Dylan.

"Of course I offered her money." Zach had wanted to be fair. Well, and he'd also wanted the problem solved quickly and quietly. Money could usually be counted on to accomplish that.

"No go?" asked Dylan.

"She's calling her lawyer," Zach admitted with a grimace, cursing under his breath. Somehow, he'd played it all wrong. He'd blown his chance to end this neatly, and he had nobody to blame but himself.

Dylan flipped on his signal light and checked the rearview mirror on the busy street. He zipped into a tight space between a Mercedes and an old Toyota. "So, basically, you're screwed."

"Thank you for that insightful analysis," Zach growled at his friend. Harper Transportation could well be on the line here, and Dylan was cracking jokes?

"What are friends for?" joked Dylan.

"Procuring single malt." If ever there was a time that called for a bracing drink, this was it.

"I have to fly today," said Dylan. "And I get the feeling you'll need every brain cell functioning."

Zach braced his elbow against the armrest as the car angled its way through traffic on the rain-dampened street. He reviewed the conversation with Kaitlin like a postgame tape. Where had he messed it up?

"Maybe I should have offered her more," he ventured, thinking out loud. "Five million? Do people say no to five million?"

"You might have to tell her the truth," Dylan offered.

"Are you out of your mind?"

"Clinically, no."

"Tell her that she's inherited my grandmother's entire estate?"

Hand the woman control on a silver platter? Did Dylan want to guarantee Zach was ruined?

"She did, in fact, inherit your grandmother's estate," Dylan pointed out.

Zach felt his blood pressure rise. He was living a nightmare, and Dylan of all people should appreciate the outrageousness of the situation.

"I don't care what kind of paperwork was filed by the Electric Chapel of Love," Zach growled. "Kaitlin Saville is not my wife. She is not entitled to half of Harper Transportation, and I will die before—"

"Her lawyer may well disagree with you."

"If her lawyer has half a brain, he'll tell her to take the two million and run." At least Zach hoped that was what her lawyer would say.

The two of them were married. Yes. He'd have to own that particular mistake. But it couldn't possibly be a situation his grandmother had remotely contemplated when she wrote her will. There was the letter of the law, and then there was the spirit of the law. His grandmother had never intended for a stranger to inherit her estate.

He had no idea if New York was, in fact, a joint property state. But even if it was, he and Kaitlin had never lived together. They'd never had sex. They'd never even realized they were married. The very thought that she'd get half of his corporation was preposterous.

"Did you think about getting an annulment?" asked Dylan.

Zach nodded. He'd talked to his lawyers about that, but they weren't encouraging. "We never slept together," he told Dylan. "But she could lie and say that we did."

"Would she lie?"

"What do I know? I thought she'd take the two million." Zach glanced around, orienting himself as they approached an entrance to Central Park. "We going anywhere near McDougal's?"

"I'm not getting you drunk at three in the afternoon." Dylan shook his head in disgust as he took a quick left. The Porsche gripped the pavement, and they barely beat an oncoming taxi.

"Are you my nursemaid?" asked Zach.

"You need a plan, not a drink."

In Zach's opinion, that was definitely debatable.

They slowed to a stop for a red light at another intersection. Two taxi drivers honked and exchanged hand gestures, while a throng of people swelled out from the sidewalk in the light drizzle and made their way between the stopped cars.

"She thinks I got her fired," Zach admitted.

"Did you?"

"No."

Dylan sent him a skeptical look. "Is she delusional? Or did you do something that resembled getting her fired?"

"Fine." Zach shifted his feet on the floor of the Porsche. "I canceled the Hutton Quinn contract to renovate the office building. The plans weren't even close to what I wanted."

"And they fired her," Dylan confirmed with a nod of comprehension.

Zach held up his palms in defense. "Their staffing choices are none of my business."

Kaitlin's renovation plans had been flamboyant and exotic in a zany, postmodern way. They weren't at all in keeping with the Harper corporate image.

Harper Transportation had been a fixture in New York City for a hundred years. People depended on them for solid reliability and consistency. Their clients were serious, hardworking people who got the job done through boom times and down times.

"Then why do you feel guilty?" asked Dylan as they swung into an underground parking lot off Saint Street.

"I don't feel guilty." It was business. Nothing more and nothing less. Zach knew guilt had no part in the equation.

It was not as if he should have accepted inferior work because he'd once danced with Kaitlin, held her in his arms, kissed her mouth and wondered for a split second if he'd actually gone to heaven. Decisions that were based on a man's sex drive were the quickest road to financial ruin.

Dylan scoffed an exclamation of disbelief as he came parallel with the valet's kiosk. He shut off the car and set the parking break.

"What?" Zach demanded.

Dylan pointed at Zach. "I know that expression. I stole wine with you from my dad's cellar when we were fifteen, and I remember the day you felt up Rosalyn Myers."

The attendant opened the driver's door, and Dylan dropped the keys into the man's waiting palm.

Zach exited the car, as well. "I didn't steal anything from Kaitlin Saville, and I certainly never—" He clamped his jaw shut as he rounded the polished, low-slung hood of the Porsche. The very last element he needed to introduce into this conversation was Kaitlin Saville's breasts.

"Maybe that's your problem," said Dylan.

Zach coughed out an inarticulate exclamation.

"You married her," Dylan said, taking obvious satisfaction in pointing that fact out as they crossed the crowded parking lot. "You must have liked her. You said yourself you haven't slept with her. Maybe you're not so much angry as horny."

"I'm angry. Trust me. I can tell the difference." Zach's interest in Kaitlin was in getting rid of her. Anything else was completely out of the question.

"Angry at her or at yourself?"

"At *her*," said Zach. "I'm just the guy trying to fix the problem here. If she'd sign the damn papers, or if my grandmother hadn't—"

"It's not nice to be mad at your grandmother," Dylan admonished.

Zach wasn't exactly angry with Grandma Sadie. But he was definitely puzzled by her behavior. Why on earth would she put the family fortune at risk? "What was she *thinking?*"

Dylan stepped up onto the painted yellow curb. "That she wanted your poor wife to have some kind of power balance."

An unsettling thought entered Zach's brain. "Did my grandmother talk to you about her will?"

"No. But she was logical and intelligent."

Zach didn't disagree with that statement. Sadie Harper had been a very intelligent, organized and capable woman. Which only made her decision more puzzling.

After Zach's parents were killed in a boating accident when he was twenty, she'd been his only living relative. They'd grown very close the past fourteen years. She was ninety-one when she died, and had grown increasingly frail over the past year. She'd passed away only a month ago.

Zach thought he was ready.

He definitely wasn't.

He and Dylan headed into the elevator, and Dylan inserted his key card for the helipad on top of the forty-story building.

"She probably wanted to sweeten the deal," Dylan offered, with a grin. He leaned back against the rail, bracing his hands on either side as the doors slid shut. "With that kind of money on the table, you'll have a fighting chance at getting a decent woman to marry you."

"Your faith in me is inspiring."

"I'm just sayin'…"

"That I'm a loser?"

The elevator accelerated upward.

Dylan happily elaborated. "That there are certain things about your personality that might put women off."

"Such as?"

"You're grumpy, stubborn and demanding. You want to drink scotch in the middle of the day, and your ass isn't what it used to be."

"My ass is none of your business." Zach might be approaching thirty-five, but he worked out four times a week, and he could still do ten miles in under an hour.

"What about you?" he challenged.

"What about me?" Dylan asked.

"We're the same age, so your ass is in as much danger as mine. But I don't see you in a hurry to settle into a relationship."

"I'm a pilot." Dylan grinned again. "Pilots are sexy. We can be old and gray, and we'll still get the girls."

"Hey, I'm a multimillionaire," Zach defended.

"Who isn't?"

The elevator came smoothly to a halt, and the doors slid open to the small glass foyer of the helipad. One of Dylan's distinctive yellow-and-black Astral Air choppers sat waiting on the rooftop. A pilot by training, Dylan had built Astral Air from a niche division of his family's corporation to one of the biggest flight service companies in America.

Dylan gave a mock salute to a uniformed technician as he and Zach jogged to the chopper and climbed inside.

He checked a row of switches and plugged in the headset. "You want me to drop you at the office?"

"What are your plans?" asked Zach. He wasn't in a hurry to be alone with his own frustrations. He had a lot of thinking to do, but first he wanted to sleep on it, start fresh, maybe forget that he'd screwed up so badly with Kaitlin.

"I'm going up to the island," said Dylan. "Aunt Ginny's been asking about me, and I promised I'd drop in."

"Mind if I tag along?"

Dylan shot him a look of surprise. Aunt Ginny could most charitably be described as eccentric. Her memory was fading, and for some reason she'd decided Zach was a reprobate. She also liked to torture the family's Stradivarius violin and read her own poetry aloud.

"She has two new Pekingese," Dylan warned.

Zach didn't care. The island had always been a retreat for him. He needed to clear his head and then come up with a contingency plan.

"I hope your dad still stocks the thirty-year-old Glenlivet," he told Dylan.

"I think we can count on that." Dylan started the engine, and the chopper's rotor blades whined to life.

Two

A week later, Kaitlin met her best friend, law professor Lindsay Rubin, in the park behind Seamount College in midtown. The cherry trees were in full bloom, scenting the air, their petals drifting to the walkway as the two women headed toward the lily pad–covered duck pond. It was lunchtime on a Wednesday, and the benches were filled with students from the college, along with businesspeople from the surrounding streets. Moms and preschool kids picnicked on blankets that dotted the lush grass.

"I finished reviewing your papers," Lindsay said, swiping her shoulder-length blond hair over the shoulders of her classic navy blazer while they strolled their way down the concrete path.

Kaitlin and Lindsay's friendship went back to their freshman year at college. Social Services had finally stepped out of Kaitlin's life, and Lindsay had left her family in Chicago. On the same floor of the college dorms, they'd formed an instant bond.

They'd stayed close friends ever since, so Lindsay knew that Zach had ruined Kaitlin's career, and she applauded Kaitlin's desire for payback.

"Am I safe to sign?" asked Kaitlin. The sunshine was warm against her bare legs and twinkled brightly where it reflected off the rippling pond. "And how soon do I have to let him off the hook?"

Lindsay grinned in obvious delight. She pressed the manila envelope against Kaitlin's chest, and Kaitlin automatically snagged it.

"Oh, it's better than that," she said.

"Better than what?" Kaitlin was puzzled

Lindsay chuckled deep in her chest. "I mean, you can name your own ticket."

"My ticket to what?"

Why was Lindsay talking in riddles?

"Life," Lindsay elaborated in a singsong voice. "What do you want? A mansion? A jet? A billion dollars?"

"I told you, I said no to the money." Kaitlin hadn't changed her mind about the money. She didn't want what she hadn't earned. "And what do you mean a billion? He was talking about two million."

"It's more than just two million." Lindsay shook her head in what appeared to be amazement. "It's Sadie Harper herself."

Kaitlin lifted her hands, palms up, to signal her incomprehension. She assumed Sadie Harper must have something to do with Zach Harper, but that was as far as she got with the connection. What did the woman have to do with his money?

Lindsay lowered her voice, sounding decidedly conspiratorial as she moved closer to Kaitlin, her gaze darting dramatically around them. "Sadie was the matriarch of the Harper family. She died a month ago at the Harper house on Serenity Island."

The pathway split, and Lindsay eased Kaitlin toward the route that skirted the pond. Their high heels clicked against the smooth, sun-warmed concrete.

Kaitlin still didn't understand Lindsay's point.

"I read a copy of her will," said Lindsay. "You, my girl, are in it."

"How can I be in it?" This conversation was making less sense by the minute. Kaitlin didn't know Sadie Harper. Up until this minute, she'd never even heard of Sadie Harper.

"In fact," Lindsay continued, a lilt of delight in her voice, "*you* are the sole beneficiary."

Kaitlin instantly halted, turning to peer at Lindsay with narrowed eyes. Traffic zipped past on Liberty, engines roaring, horns honking. Cyclist and pedestrian traffic parted around them, some people shooting annoyed looks their way.

Lindsay tugged on Kaitlin's arm, moving them off to the side of the pathway. "She left her entire estate to Mrs. Zachary Harper."

"Get out," Kaitlin breathed.

"I am dead serious."

Kaitlin stepped farther aside to make room for a pair of cyclists skirting the edge of the path. "How did she even know about me?"

"She didn't." Lindsay gave her head a shake. "That's the beauty of it. Well, part of the beauty of it. The whole thing is truly very beautiful."

"Lindsay," Kaitlin prompted with impatience.

"The will holds her estate in trust until Zach gets married," said Lindsay. "But he's already married so, in the eyes of the law, you own fifty percent of Harper Transportation."

Kaitlin's knees went weak.

No wonder Zach had seemed desperate.

No wonder he was in such a hurry to get rid of her.

"So, what do you want?" Lindsay asked again, a giggle at the end of the question.

Speechless, Kaitlin shoved the envelope back at Lindsay, overwhelmed by the thought of what was at stake. She took a step away and shook her head in silent refusal.

"I don't want anything," she finally managed to reply.

"Don't be ridiculous," Lindsay cajoled.

"The wedding was a joke," Kaitlin reminded her. "It was a mistake. I didn't mean to marry him. And I sure don't deserve half his company."

"Then take the money instead," Lindsay offered reasonably.

As if that made it better. "I'm not taking his money, either."

Lindsay held up her palms in exasperation. "So, what do you want? What's the payback?"

Kaitlin thought about it for a moment. "I want him to sweat."

Lindsay chuckled and linked her arm with Kaitlin's, turning her to resume their walk. "Trust me, honey." She patted her on the shoulder. "He is definitely sweating."

"And I want a job," said Kaitlin with conviction. That was what she'd lost in this debacle. She needed her career back.

"I don't want free money," she told Lindsay, voice strengthening. "I want a chance to prove myself. I'm a good…no, I'm a *great* architect. And all I want is a fair shot at proving it."

The path met up with the sidewalk, and Lindsay tipped her head and stared up at the Harper Transportation sign on the pillar-adorned, ten-story concrete building across the street. "So, ask him for one," she suggested.

Kaitlin squinted at the massive blue lettering. She glanced to Lindsay, then again at the sign. Suddenly, the possibilities of the situation bloomed in her brain.

A slow smile grew on her face. "There's a reason I love you," she said to Lindsay, giving her arm a squeeze. "*That* is a brilliant plan."

And it was exactly what she'd do. She would make Zach Harper give her a job. She'd make him give her the job that should have been hers in the first place—developing designs for the renovation of his corporate headquarters.

She'd pick up right where she'd left off. In fact, she'd come up with an even better concept. Then, once she'd proven to him and to the world that she was a talented architect, she'd sign whatever papers he needed her to sign. He'd have his company back, and she'd have her life back. And, most importantly, she wouldn't have to leave New York City.

The light turned green, and she tugged on Lindsay's arm. "You're coming with me."

Lindsay hesitated, staying on the curb. "I have a class now."

"We'll be quick," Kaitlin promised.

"But—"

"Come on. I need you to spout some legalese to scare him."

"Trust me, he's already scared." But Lindsay started across the street.

"Then it'll be easy," Kaitlin assured her, stepping up on the opposite curb then mounting the short concrete staircase.

They made their way across the small serviceable lobby of the Harper Transportation building. Kaitlin had been in the building many times, so she knew Zach's office was on the top floor.

While they took the groaning elevator ride up twenty stories, she straightened her short black skirt and adjusted her sleeveless, jade-green sweater, anchoring the strap of her small handbag. She moistened her lips as they exited the elevator. Then she determinedly paced down the narrow hallway to Zach's receptionist.

"I'm here to see Zach Harper," Kaitlin announced with as much confidence as she could muster.

Her pulse had increased, and her palms were starting to dampen. She was suddenly afraid the plan wouldn't work. Like a drowning woman who'd been tossed a life vest, she was afraid her chance would float away before she could grab on to it.

"Do you have an appointment?" the young brunette woman asked politely, glancing from Kaitlin to Lindsay and back again. Kaitlin had seen the woman from a distance while working on the project for Hutton Quinn, but they'd never been introduced.

"No," Kaitlin admitted, realizing the odds were slim that Zach was available at that particular moment.

Lindsay stepped forward, standing two inches taller than Kaitlin, her voice telegraphing professionalism and importance. "Tell him it's a legal matter," she said to the receptionist. "Kaitlin Saville."

The woman's head came up, curiosity flaring briefly in her blue eyes. "Of course. One moment, please." She rose from her wheeled desk chair.

"Thanks," Kaitlin whispered to Lindsay, as the receptionist walked down the hallway that stretched behind her desk. "I knew you'd come in handy."

"I'll send you a bill," Lindsay responded in an undertone.

"No, you won't." Kaitlin knew her friend better than that. Lindsay had never charged her for anything in her life.

"Ten minutes from now, you'll be able to afford me," Lindsay joked.

"Send Zach the bill," Kaitlin suggested, a nervous sense of excitement forming in her belly. If this worked. If it actually worked…

"Will do," Lindsay promised.

The receptionist returned, a practiced, professional smile on her face. "Right this way, please."

She led them past a few closed doors to the end of the hallway where a set of double doors stood open on a big, bright, burgundy-carpeted room.

She gestured them inside, and Kaitlin entered first.

If she thought Zach had looked impressive standing in her apartment last week, it was nothing compared to what his office did for him. The fine surroundings reeked of power, and he was obviously in his element.

His big desk was walnut with inset cherry panels. A matching credenza and hutch were accented with cherry wood drawers, and a bookcase opposite showcased leather-bound volumes and nautical carvings. The desk chair was also leather, and high-backed with carved wood arms. Two guest chairs flanked the front of his desk, while a meeting table stood in an arched window alcove.

As Kaitlin crossed the thick carpet, Zach came to his feet. As usual, he wore a perfectly pressed, incredibly well-cut suit. His usual white shirt was crisp and bright. The necktie was gold this time, with a subtle silver thread that picked up the sunlight.

"Thank you, Amy." He nodded to the receptionist, who closed the doors as she left the room.

His gaze flicked to Lindsay and he quirked a questioning brow in her direction.

"My lawyer," Kaitlin explained to him. "Lindsay Rubin."

"Please sit down." Zach gestured to the leather guest chairs.

But Kaitlin chose to remain standing. "I'll sign your papers," she told him.

Zach's glance went back to Lindsay, then returned to Kaitlin. The barest hint of a smile twitched his full lips, and there was a definite flare of relief in his gray eyes.

"But I want two things," Kaitlin continued.

Though she knew she ought to enjoy this, she was far too nervous to get any pleasure out of watching him sweat.

This had to work.

It simply *had* to.

Zach's brow furrowed, and she could almost feel him calculating dollar figures inside his head.

"One—" she counted on her fingers, struggling to keep a quaver from forming in her voice "—our marriage stays secret." If people found out she was married to Zach, the professional credential of renovating his building would mean less than nothing. The entire city would chalk it up to their personal relationship.

"Two," she continued, "you give me a job. Renovation design director, or some similar title."

His eyes narrowed. "You want a job?"

"Yes," she confirmed.

He appeared genuinely puzzled. "Why?"

"I'll need an office and some support staff while I finish planning the renovations to your building. Since you already have those things available here..."

He was silent for a full three seconds. "I'm offering you money, not a job."

"I don't want your money."

"Kaitlin—"

She squared her shoulders. "This is not negotiable, Zach. I get free rein, carte blanche. I do your renovation, my way, and—"

He leaned forward, tenting his fingers on the polished desktop. "Not a hope in hell."

"Excuse me?"

They glared at each other for a drawn-out second while a thousand emotions skittered along her nervous system.

He was intimidating. He was also undeniably arousing. He was both her problem and her solution. And she was terrified this chance would somehow slip through her fingers.

Then Lindsay spoke up, her voice haughty and authoritarian as she stepped into the conversation. "You should know, Mr. Harper, that I've provided Ms. Saville with a copy of Sadie Harper's will, as filed with the probate court."

The room went to dead silent.

Nobody moved, and nobody breathed.

Kaitlin forced herself to straighten to her full height. She crossed her arms over her chest, letting his stunned expression boost her confidence.

"I'll divorce you, Zach," she told him. "I'll sign the entire company over to you. Just as soon as I have my career back."

His furious gaze settled on Kaitlin. His tone turned incredulous. "You're *blackmailing* me?"

Sweat prickled her hairline, anxiety peaking within her. "I'm making you a deal."

Several beats ticked by in thick silence, while her stomach churned with anxiety.

His expression barely changed. But finally, he gave a single, curt nod.

Her heart clunked deep in her chest, while a wave of relief washed coolly over her skin.

She'd done it.

She'd bought herself a second chance.

She doubted Zach would ever forgive her. But she couldn't let herself care about that. All that mattered was she was back on the job.

From beneath the stained concrete porch of the Harper Transportation building, Kaitlin stared at the rain pounding down on Liberty Street. It was the end of her first full day of work, and her nerves had given way to a cautious optimism.

Zach hadn't made her feel particularly welcome, but she did have a desk, a cubbyhole of a windowless office, with a drafting table and a bent filing cabinet. And, though other staff members seemed confused by the sudden change in the renovation project, one of the administrative assistants had introduced her around and offered to help out.

Kaitlin inhaled the moist May air. Fat raindrops were splashing on the concrete steps, forming puddles and rivulets on the pavement below. She glanced at the gray sky and gauged the distance to the subway staircase in the next block. She wished she'd checked the weather report this morning and tossed an umbrella into her bag.

"I trust you found everything you need?" Zach's deep voice held a mocking edge behind her.

Kaitlin twisted, taking in his towering height and strong profile against the backdrop of his historic building. She was forced to remind herself that she was in the driver's seat in this circumstance. She should make him nervous, not the other way around.

"Could you have found me a smaller office?" she asked, attempting to go on the offensive. He was obviously making some kind of a point by relegating her to a closet. It didn't take a genius to figure out he was attempting to put her in her place.

"Haven't you heard?" His mouth flexed in a cool half smile, confirming her suspicions. "We're renovating."

"I notice *your* office is plenty roomy," she persisted, hoping to give him at least a twinge of guilt.

"That's because I own the company." His expression hinted that he also owned a decent portion of the world.

She arched a meaningful brow in his direction, feeling a little more in control when his expression wavered. "So do I," she pointed out.

Her victory was short-lived.

"You want me to evict a vice president for you?" Left unsaid was the understanding that while he could easily give her special treatment, they both knew it would raise questions amongst the staff, potentially compromising her desire to keep their personal relationship a secret.

"You have nothing between the executive floor and a closet?" Of course, the last thing she wanted to do was call attention to herself. He had to treat her no better and no worse than any other employee. Right now, it certainly appeared he was treating her worse.

"Take your pick," Zach offered with a careless shrug. "I'll kick someone out."

Kaitlin hiked up her shoulder bag. "And they'll know it's me."

"You do own the company," he drawled.

She rolled her eyes. "Just treat me like you would anyone else."

"That seems unlikely." He nodded to a shiny, black late-model town car cruising up to the curb. "Can I give you a lift?"

She slid him an incredulous glance. He had to be kidding.

"Hop into the boss's car after my first day of work?" Right. That would work well to keep her under the radar.

"You afraid people will get the wrong idea?"

"I'm afraid they'll get the right idea."

His mouth quirked again. "I have some papers you need to sign."

The rain wasn't letting up, but she took a tentative step forward, muttering under her breath. "No divorce yet, Mr. Harper."

He stepped into the rain beside her, keeping pace, his voice going low as hers. "They're not divorce papers, Mrs. Harper."

The title on his lips gave her a jolt. She'd spent the day trying to forget about their circumstances and focus on getting started at her job. But she was beginning to realize forgetting their circumstances was going to be nearly impossible.

They were married, *married.*

She tipped her head, surreptitiously taking in his profile, the dark eyes, the furrowed brow and the small scar on his right cheekbone. She tried to imagine an intimate relationship, where they joked and touched and—

"Kaitlin?"

She gave herself a firm mental shake, telling herself to get control. "What kind of papers?"

He glanced around, obviously confirming a sufficient buffer of space between them and the other Harper employees heading out the doors. "Confirmation of my positions as the president and CEO."

"What are you now?"

"President and CEO." His gunmetal eyes were as dark and impenetrable as the storm clouds. He was not a man who easily gave away his emotions. "There's been a change in the company ownership," he explained.

It took a moment for the enormity of his words to sink in. Without her signature, his position in the company was in jeopardy. He couldn't do what he'd always done, and he couldn't be who he'd always been, without her consent on paper.

Something hard and cold slid though her stomach.

It wasn't right that she had this kind of power. All she wanted was to do her job. She didn't want to have to sift through her confusing feelings for Zach. And she sure didn't want to have to analyze the circumstances and decide if they were fair.

They weren't. But then neither was the alternative.

"Get in the car, Kaitlin," he told her. "We need to get this signed and settled."

She couldn't help but note the stream of employees exiting from the building. Even as they dashed down the rainy steps, most of them glanced curiously at Zach. Climbing into his car in full view of a dozen coworkers was out of the question.

She leaned slightly closer, muffling her voice. "Pick me up on Grove, past the bus stop."

He gave a subtle but unmistakable eye roll. "You don't think that's a bit cloak-and-dagger?"

"I'm trying to blend," she reminded him. Her plan to rescue her career would come to a screeching halt if people had any inkling that she had some leverage over Zach.

"You'll get soaked," he warned her.

A little water was the least of her worries.

Well, except for what it would do to her shoes. They'd been on sale, her only pair of Strantas. She loved what they did for her legs, and they looked great with anything black.

She braced herself, mentally plotting a path around the worst of the scattered puddles.

"Have a nice evening, Mr. Harper," she called loud enough for passersby to hear as she trotted down the stairs.

She made her way along the sidewalk, surging with the crowd toward the traffic light at the corner. When it turned green, she paced across the street, avoiding numerous black umbrellas in her path and hopping over the gurgle of water flowing against the opposite curb.

On the other side, she negotiated her way to the edge of the sidewalk, raking her wet hair back from her forehead and tucking it behind her ears. She swiped a few raindrops from her nose then extracted her cell phone, pressing the speed dial as she hustled toward the bus stop shelter.

"Kaitlin?" came Lindsay's breathless voice.

"What are you doing?"

"Riding the bike."

Kaitlin pictured Lindsay on the stationary bike crammed into the small living space of her loft. "I'm going to be late for dinner."

"What's going on?" Lindsay huffed.

As she wove her way through the wet crowd, Kaitlin lowered her voice to mock doom. "I'm about to get into a big black car with Zach Harper."

"Better send me the license plate number."

Kaitlin cracked a grin, comforted by Lindsay's familiar sense of humor. The two women had known each other so long, they were almost always on the same wavelength. "I'll text it to you."

A deep, classic-rock bass resonated in the background. A fixture whenever Lindsay exercised. "Why are you getting in his car?"

"He wants me to sign something."

"Better let me read it first."

"I will if it looks complicated," Kaitlin promised. "He says it's to reconfirm him as president and CEO." Not that she trusted everything Zach said. In fact, thus far, she trusted exactly nothing of what Zach said.

"It could be a trick," Lindsay warned.

Kaitlin grinned into the phone. "There is yet another reason I love you."

"I've got your back. Seriously, Katie, if you see the words *irreconcilable* or *absolute* I want you to run the other way."

"Will do." Kaitlin caught sight of the black car. "Oops. There he is. Gotta go."

"Call me when you're done. I want details. And dinner." There was a gasp in Lindsay's voice. "I definitely still want dinner."

"I'll call," Kaitlin agreed, folding her phone and tucking it into the pocket of her purse as Zach swung open the back door of his car and hopped out onto the sidewalk next to her.

He flipped up the collar of his gray overcoat and gestured her inside. She gathered her own wet coat around her and ducked to climb in.

"Lunatic," he muttered under his breath.

"Lucky for you we're not having children," she said over her shoulder as she settled into the seat.

"Lucky for me we're not buying plants." He firmly shut the door behind her before walking around the vehicle to get in behind the driver.

She shook the rainwater from her fingertips, smoothing her soaked jacket and frowning at her soggy bag. "Green and Stafford in Yorkville," she said to the driver, getting an unwelcome glimpse of herself in the side mirror.

"The penthouse, Henry," Zach corrected.

"You're not dropping me off?" She wasn't sure why his bad manners surprised her. Zach was all about his own convenience. His minions obviously didn't factor in on his radar.

"Henry will take you home later," he said.

Later? She raised her brow in a question.

"The papers are at my penthouse."

Of course they were. Having the papers available in the car would be far too simple. Resigned, she plunked her bag into her lap and gave up on trying to repair her look. She was a mess, and that was that.

"Don't you worry about inconveniencing me," she drawled. "It's not like I have a life."

Henry pulled into the snarl of traffic heading for Liberty and Wildon, while Zach sent her a speculative, sidelong glance. "Stroke of a pen gets you out of this any old time you want."

She determinedly shook her head. Much as she'd love to sever both their marital and business ties, if she let him off the hook, the man would fire her in the blink of an eye.

He leaned back in the leather seat, angling his body so that he faced her. "What if I promised you could keep your job?"

Rain rattled harder on the car's sunroof, while the wipers slapped their way across the windshield, blurring the view of the street.

Kaitlin made a half turn in the seat, meeting Zach's dark eyes. "That would require me trusting you."

"You can trust me," he assured her.

She coughed out a laugh. "You ruined my *life*."

He frowned. "I made you a very wealthy woman."

"I don't want to be a wealthy woman."

"I say again. You can get out of this anytime you want."

She made a show of glancing around the interior of the car. "Is there some way to exit this conversation?" she asked him. "Or does it just keep circling the drain?"

Horns honked in the lanes beside them as Henry inched his way through a left-hand turn. Kaitlin swiped at her damp, tangled hair, resisting an urge to slip off her soggy shoes and wiggle her toes into the thick carpet.

"You're going to find it very inconvenient being my business partner," Zach warned.

She cocked her head, watching him as she spoke. "Because you'll go out of your way to make it hell?"

He resettled himself in the butter-soft seat. "And here I thought I was being subtle."

"This is fifty pages long." Standing in the middle of Zach's penthouse living room, Kaitlin frowned as she leafed her way through the document.

"It deals with control of a multimillion-dollar corporation," he returned with what he hoped resembled patience. "We could hardly jot it down on a cocktail napkin."

Though he'd had a few days to come to terms with this bizarre twist in his life, Zach was still chafing at the circumstance. He didn't want to have to justify anything about Harper Transportation to Kaitlin, even temporarily. His grandma Sadie had complete faith in him—at least he'd always thought she'd had complete faith in him. He'd never had to explain anything about the company to her. He'd basically been running the show for over a decade.

But now there was Kaitlin. And she was underfoot. And she had questions. And he could only imagine what kind of monstrosity he'd be left with for an office building.

Dylan had pointed out yesterday that appeasing Kaitlin was better than losing half his company. Maybe it was. But barely.

"I'll need to have my lawyer look at this," Kaitlin announced, reaching down to pull open her oversize shoulder bag in order to deposit the document inside.

"Give it a read before you decide," Zach cajoled through half-gritted teeth. "It's not Greek." He pointed. "You and I sign page three, authorizing the board of directors. The board members have already signed page twenty, confirming my positions. The rest is…well, read it. You'll see."

She hesitated, peering at him with suspicion. But after a moment, she sighed, dropping her bag onto his sofa. "Fine. I'll take a look."

He tried not to cringe as her wet purse hit the white leather cushion of his new, designer Fendi.

"Your coat?" he offered instead, holding out his hands to accept it. The coat he'd hang safely in his hall closet before she had a chance to drape it over his ironwood table.

She slipped out of the dripping rain jacket, revealing a clingy, black-and-burgundy, knee-length dress. It had capped sleeves, a scooped neck and a pencil-straight skirt that flowed down to her shapely legs, which were clad in black stockings. Damp as they were, her high heels accentuated slim ankles and gorgeous calves.

Though they'd spoken briefly at the office this morning, she'd been wearing her coat at the time. He'd had no idea what was hidden beneath. Just as well he hadn't had *that* image inside his brain all day long.

"Thank you," she acknowledged, handing him the coat.

"I'm…uh…" He pointed in the general direction of the hallway and the kitchen, making his escape before she noticed he was ogling her body with his mouth hanging open.

In the kitchen, he found that his housekeeper had left a note informing him there was salad and a chicken dish in the fridge. She'd also left a bottle of Cabernet on the breakfast bar. Zach automatically reached for the corkscrew, breathing through the dueling emotions of frustration and arousal.

Sure, Kaitlin was an attractive woman. He knew that. He'd known that from the minute he met her. But there were attractive women everywhere. He didn't have to fixate on her.

He popped the cork.

No. No reason at all for him to fixate on her.

In fact, maybe he should get himself a date. A date would distract him. He'd been working too hard lately, that was all. A date with another, equally attractive woman would nip this fascination with Kaitlin in the bud.

He reached for the crystal glasses hanging from the rack below the cabinet.

Dylan had offered to introduce him to his newest helicopter pilot. He'd said she was attractive and athletic. She was a Yankees fan, but he could probably live with that. And she had a master's degree in art history. Who didn't like art history?

Before Zach realized what he'd done, he'd filled two glasses with wine.

"Oh, hell."

Then again, he supposed the woman deserved a drink. If she signed the papers, they'd toast the accomplishment. If she refused to sign, maybe the wine would loosen her up, and he could take another stab at convincing her.

He shrugged out of his suit jacket, moving farther down the

hallway to the master bedroom. There, he hung the jacket in his closet, shed his tie and glanced in the mirror above his dresser.

He definitely needed a shave. And his white shirt was wrinkled from being worn all day.

He glanced once at the jacket and considered putting it back on. But common sense prevailed. Instead, he unbuttoned his cuffs and rolled up the sleeves of his shirt. If this was a date, he'd shave and redress. But it wasn't a date. And his looks would be the last thing on Kaitlin's mind.

More comfortable, he returned to the kitchen and retrieved the wineglasses. He moved down the hallway to the living room. Inside the doorway, he paused.

Kaitlin seemed to have made herself at home. She'd kicked off her strappy shoes and curled her legs beneath her, knees bent and pressed together, stocking-clad feet pushing up against the arm of his sofa. Her hair was drying to a wild, glossy halo that framed her smooth skin. And her face was a study in concentration, red lips pursed, green eyes slightly squinted as she read her way through the pages.

She looked good in his living room, somehow settled and at home.

Funny, he'd seen her dressed up, dressed down, dancing with laughter and crackling with anger. But he'd never caught her unaware. And somehow he had the feeling this was the real woman, halfway between Vegas glitter and Saturday casual, her energy turned inward, mind working. He sensed a calm intelligence in her that he hadn't noticed before.

He must have moved, because she finally noticed him.

"Wine?" he offered, raising one of the glasses, walking forward, pretending he hadn't been staring.

"You're right," she told him, letting the papers drop into her lap, stretching an arm across the back of the sofa in an obviously unintended, sensual gesture.

"Never thought I'd hear you say that." But there was no bite to his words. He'd meant to mock her, but it came off as a gentle joke.

She flipped the document back to the first page and set it in front of her on the coffee table. "I'll sign it."

"Really?" Too late, he realized he sounded surprised. To cover, he handed her the glass of wine.

She accepted the glass and shrugged. "It's exactly what you said it was."

"How about that," he couldn't help but tease.

"Shocked the heck out of me," she returned, doing a double take, seeming to note he'd shed the jacket and tie.

He sat down on the other end of the couch. "Then, cheers." He lifted his glass.

She allowed a small smile, which made her prettier than ever. She leaned toward him, holding out her glass to clink it against his. The motion gave him a glimpse of her cleavage, and he was forced to drag his gaze away from her soft breasts.

They each took a sip.

Then her smile grew, and an impish dimple appeared in her right cheek. "Tough day at the office, dear?" She mimicked what was obviously a wifely voice of concern.

Something inside him responded warmly to the banter. "You know—" he paused for effect "—the usual."

"Is this weird?" she asked, eyes narrowing.

"Yes."

"Because it feels weird. I mean, on a scale of one to, well, weird, it's weird."

"Did that make sense inside your head?"

She took another drink, waving a dismissive hand. "I'm sure you got the gist of it."

"I did. And I agree. It's weird."

"We're married." She said the words in a tone of wonder.

"Yes, we are." Zach took a healthy swig from his own glass. He'd never been married. And even if he had, he couldn't help but doubt anything could prepare a man for this particular situation.

She paused, and then her voice went soft. "I'm not trying to ruin your life, you know."

He didn't like it that she seemed so vulnerable. It was better when she was acting tough and feisty. Then, it was easier to view her as a combatant. And he was beginning to admit fighting with Kaitlin was much safer than joking with her.

He struggled to put a hard note back in his voice. "I guess it was the blackmail scheme that had me confused."

Her green eyes were clear, open and honest. "I'm not looking to gain anything."

He made a show of skeptically raising his brows.

"I'm looking to set things right," she assured him.

He tried to sound doubtful. "Is that how this is playing out inside your head?"

"Once I've earned my way back into the good graces of my profession, you'll be home free. I want a career, Zach, not your company."

He had to admit, he believed her. He understood she was trying to make her own life better. Her methods weren't the most noble from where he was standing. But he did accept the fact that he was collateral damage.

She leaned forward and flipped to the signature page of the document. "Do you have a pen?"

"Sure." He rose and crossed to the small rosewood desk that held a telephone and a reading lamp.

"I'm meeting Lindsay for dinner," Kaitlin explained from behind him. "I don't want to be too late."

"I have a date," he lied, extracting a pen from the small desk drawer. He'd call Dylan and get the number of the pretty helicopter pilot just as soon as Kaitlin left.

"You're *cheating* on me?"

Her outburst surprised him, but when he turned, he saw the laughter lurking in her jade-green eyes.

"Yes," he answered easily, not about to rise to the bait. "I've been cheating on you since the wedding."

"Men," she huffed in pretend disgust, folding her arms across her chest, accenting her breasts.

Focusing beyond her lovely figure, he shrugged an apology on behalf of his gender as he crossed the room. "What can I say?"

She accepted the pen, bending her head to sign the papers. "Well, *I've* been faithful."

He waited for the punch line.

It didn't come.

"Seriously?" he asked.

She finished her signature with a flourish, declining to answer.

But he couldn't let it go. "You haven't had sex with anybody since Vegas?"

"What do you mean *since* Vegas." She sat up straight, handing the pen back in his direction. "Who do you think I had sex with in Vegas?"

He accepted it, feeling a twinge of remorse. "I didn't mean it that—"

"The only person I was with in Vegas was you and we didn't—" The amusement suddenly fled her eyes, replaced by uncertainty. "We, uh, didn't, did we?"

Okay, *this* was interesting. "You don't remember?" He might not have total recall of the entire night's events. But he knew they hadn't made love.

Then the vulnerability was back, and she slowly shook her head. "I barely remember the wedding."

He was tempted to string her along, but quickly changed his mind. The cursed vulnerability again. It made him want to protect her, not mess with her mind.

"We didn't," he assured her.

She tilted her head to one side. "Are you sure? Do *you* remember every minute?"

Their gazes locked for a couple of heartbeats.

"I'd remember that."

"So, you can't say for sure…"

"Has this been bothering you?" he asked.

"No."

"Because it sounds like—"

Suddenly, she snagged her bag and hooked it over her shoulder, coming to her feet. "It's not bothering me. If we did it, we did it."

"We *didn't*." Not that he hadn't wanted to. Not that he wouldn't love to. Not that he wasn't still—

Damn it. He had to stop going there.

"Because I'm not pregnant or anything," she said, slipping into her sexy shoes and straightening her clingy dress. The action pulled it tighter against her lithe body, and it was more than he could do not to let his gaze take a tour.

He summoned his strength. "Kaitlin. I think we need to leave Vegas back in Vegas."

"We tried."

That was true.

"But it didn't work," she pointed out.

"Blame Elvis," he drawled, fixing his gaze firmly on her face and telling himself to leave it right there.

Her smile grew. "You're funnier than you let on, you know?"

He gritted his teeth against her softening expression, those lips, those eyes, that tousled hair. It would be so easy to pull her into his arms and kiss her.

But for the first time in his life, he ignored the powerful urge.

"Thanks for signing the papers," he offered gruffly.

"Thanks for giving me a job."

The specter of her previous designs appeared inside his head. He didn't know what he'd do if she insisted on resurrecting them.

Now might not be the time. Then again, now might be the perfect time. They seemed to have come to a truce. Maybe he should take advantage of it.

"You know that building has been in my family for five generations," he declared.

"That doesn't mean it can't look good."

"There are a lot of different ways to make it look good." Classic ways. Functional ways. They were a transportation company, for goodness' sake, not an art museum.

He wished he could interest her in using the Hugo Rosche plans as a jumping-off point. Hugo had taken over after he'd canceled Hutton Quinn. Zach had paid a penalty to get out of the contract. But Hugo had left on good terms with a reference and several prospective clients set up by Zach. Hugo's plans made the most of the existing layout, and they'd only take about six months to implement.

"And I'm going to find the best one," she breezily promised. Her bravado frightened him.

"It's my heritage you're playing with, you know."

Her expression faltered for a split second, something close to pain flitting through her eyes. But she recovered instantly, and the confidence returned. "Then, you're a very lucky man, Zach Harper. Because I'm going to make your heritage a whole lot better."

Three

The following week, Kaitlin and Lindsay made their way into the bright pool of sunshine on the roof of the Harper Transportation building. The cement was solid beneath Kaitlin's feet, and the building seemed to fit seamlessly into its surroundings. Modern high-rises towered over on two sides, while across Liberty, they studied a row of dignified—if chipped—lion statues, and looked farther to the river.

The roof was square, blocked on one side by the service level and staircase. It was bordered by a three-foot-high concrete wall. Years of rain had stained it, but the mottled color evoked a certain nobility. Kaitlin couldn't help wonder what it would be like to work under the same roof as five generations of your ancestors.

Her mother had died when she was born. Her father was "unknown," not even a name on a birth certificate. And if nineteen-year-old Yvette Saville had had relatives somewhere nobody ever found them. All Kaitlin had of her own heritage was a single, frayed and blurry photo of her mother, and the address of the rooming house where Yvette had been living prior to Kaitlin's birth.

While her anger and frustration toward Zach had diminished as the days went by, she couldn't seem to fight off the spurt of jealousy that bubbled up when she thought about his heritage. He'd had such a safe and privileged upbringing. While she was on the outside looking in, he'd been wrapped in the loving embrace of his wealthy family, wanting for nothing, experiencing the finest life had to offer.

"Explain to me again why we couldn't go straight to Rundall's for lunch?" called Lindsay. She'd fallen behind in her higher heels and straight skirt.

"See that?" Kaitlin turned to walk backward, banishing her negative thoughts as she swept her arm, pointing toward the deep blue Hudson River. "If I can get a permit to add three stories, the view will be amazing."

A steady hum of traffic rose up to meet them, while barges slipped by against the tree-dotted New Jersey shoreline.

"Will that be expensive?" asked Lindsay, as she picked her way across the rough surface, steadying herself against a mechanical box, then an air-conditioning unit.

"Wildly," said Kaitlin, picturing the expanse of glass and the marble floors.

Lindsay flashed a wide grin as she came abreast of Kaitlin near the edge of the roof. "That's my girl. Not that Harper will ever notice. The man has more money than God."

"It would seem," Kaitlin agreed, thinking back to the fine art and antiques that decorated his huge penthouse apartment.

"I've been checking," said Lindsay in a conspiratorial tone, swiping back her stray blond hairs in the freshening breeze. "Did you know it started with the pirates?"

"What started with pirates?" Kaitlin peered over the edge to the busy street below. She wished she had a scaffolding so she could see exactly how the view would look if they went up three stories.

"The Harper family wealth," Lindsay said. "Yo ho ho and a bottle of rum. Pirates."

Kaitlin stretched up on her toes, shading her eyes against the brilliant sun. "I'm sure that's just a rumor."

New York City was full of colorful stories of countless founding families. Most of them were concocted by the families themselves to add social cachet and impress their friends. The Harpers could just as easily have been former potato farmers who arrived in the city from Idaho in 1910. Perhaps they'd sold something as mundane as farmland and crops to buy their first boat and start Harper Transportation.

"Of course it's a rumor," Lindsay pointed out. "It happened three hundred years ago. It's not like they have videotape."

Kaitlin cracked a smile at her friend's faux outrage. "Are you suggesting I've inherited tainted money?"

"I'm suggesting the man you're blackmailing was descended from thieves and murderers."

"Does that scare you?" Zach didn't scare Kaitlin anymore.

Well, not much. She was still intimidated by his angry glare. And she was definitely unsettled by the sexual awareness that bloomed to life whenever he strode by. It was becoming a regular part of her workday: email, coffee, drafting, Zach. Then boom, buzz, all she could think about was kissing him.

"Hell, no," Lindsay assured her. "I'm just sayin' you should watch out for his sword."

Kaitlin waggled her finger at Lindsay in admonishment. "That's a terrible joke."

Lindsay peered closer. "Are you blushing?"

"No," Kaitlin answered with a shake of her head, switching her attention to the steel gray barge plodding up the river.

"I didn't mean it the way it sounded."

"Sure you did."

Lindsay leaned forward to get a better view of Kaitlin's face. "You *are* blushing. What did I miss?"

"Nothing. I've barely seen him in three days."

Okay, so she'd seen him from afar, more than a few times. And he looked good from that distance—no frowns, no scowls. Her reaction to him was becoming almost comically predictable.

Her pulse rate would jump. Her skin would heat up. And she'd lose her train of thought.

"Are you falling for him?" asked Lindsay.

Kaitlin started to speak, but then stopped, unwilling to lie to Lindsay. "I'm admiring his features from afar," she admitted. "Along with half of the city."

Zach was an undeniably attractive man. So she found him good-looking? Big deal. So she occasionally found him charming? Another big deal.

He had breeding and education, and plenty of practice at dating and small talk. If she forgot about the fact that he'd tried to ruin her life, she could almost pretend he was a decent guy.

"He does make a hot pirate," Lindsay concurred with a saucy grin.

"Hot" definitely described the way he'd looked that night at his penthouse, his tie off, sleeves rolled up, a day's growth of beard shadowing his chin. He'd looked every inch the rakish pirate of his ancestors. And it had been more than sexy.

Lindsay was watching her closely. "Promise me you'll keep your head in the game."

Kaitlin tucked her loose hair firmly behind her ears, taking a quick check of her diamond stud earring. "My head is completely in the game," she assured Lindsay.

There wouldn't be a repeat of Vegas. Kaitlin had slipped up that night. She'd let down her guard, and Zach had turned on her within the week.

Apparently satisfied, Lindsay eased forward to peer over the edge. Taxis, buses and delivery trucks cruised past. Three city workers in hard hats set barriers up around an open manhole, while a police cruiser, lights flashing blue and red, pulled halfway up on the wide sidewalk.

"So, have you started unpacking yet?" asked Lindsay.

"Nope." Kaitlin watched two uniformed cops stride into a deli. She was more than happy to leave the topic of Zach behind. "I'm going to take advantage of having everything out of the way. Clean the carpets and paint the walls."

"Nesting?" asked Lindsay.

"Yes, I am." When she gave herself time to think about staying put in New York City, Kaitlin felt a surge of relief lighten her shoulders. She'd curled up in her window seat yesterday evening with a cup of cocoa, simply staring for an hour at the bustle of the neighborhood.

"You deserve a great place to call home," said Lindsay, warmth and caring evident in her tone.

Kaitlin smiled her agreement. "I may even buy that new rocker." She'd been admiring a big, overstuffed gliding rocker in the window of a local furniture store for a few months now. Something about it said home.

"You?" Lindsay teased. "A frivolous expenditure?"

Kaitlin nodded with conviction. With no means of support other than her part-time job, she'd been forced to be frugal during her college years. The habit was hard to break. But she was gainfully employed now, and she had good prospects. And she was determined to make herself a real home.

"First the rocker," she explained to Lindsay. "And then the Prestige espresso machine."

"I love hearing you talk like that." Lindsay laughed.

"It feels pretty good," Kaitlin admitted, then her voice caught on her age-old sensation of loneliness. "I *can* make it a real home."

Lindsay linked her arm and nudged up against her. "You've already made it a real home."

It didn't feel like a real home to Kaitlin. Then again, how would she know? Over her childhood years, most of her placements had been in group facilities instead of with families. The workers were mostly kind, but they came and went in shifts, and they often moved on to other jobs, replaced by new people, who were also nice, but also employees, not a family.

Lindsay gave her a squeeze, obviously recognizing that Kaitlin was getting emotional. "You ready for lunch?"

"Sure thing." There was no point in dwelling on the past. She was staying in New York City, and that was a great thing. The rocker would make a difference, she was sure of it. Maybe she'd get a cat, a calico or a black-and-white gerbil. A pet would make things that much more homey.

With one last look around, she followed Lindsay inside. They locked the rooftop door and took the aging elevator back to the third floor and Kaitlin's small office.

"There you are." Zach's greeting from inside the office sounded vaguely like an accusation.

"What are you doing here?" Kaitlin's guard immediately went up. She suspiciously scanned the room, the deck, the bookshelf, her computer, checking to see if anything had been disturbed. She'd put a password on her laptop, and she was keeping the preliminary renovation drawings under lock and key.

She'd made Zach promise to give her carte blanche on the project. But she still feared, given half a chance, he would try to micromanage it. She wasn't planning on giving him half a chance.

"I have something to show you," he announced from where he stood behind her tilted drafting table.

She saw that he'd rolled out a set of blue line drawings. She moved forward to get a better view. "Those aren't mine."

"They're something Hugo Rosche put together," he responded.

Kaitlin slipped between the desk and drafting table, while Lindsay waited in the doorway of the cramped office. Kaitlin stopped shoulder-to-shoulder with Zach, and he moved closer up against the wall.

"What's different than how it is now?" she asked, moving through the pages, noting that a few walls had been relocated. The lobby had been slightly expanded, and new windows were sketched in on the first floor.

"We'd also repaint, recarpet and get a decorator," said Zach.

She glanced up at him, searching his expression. "Is this a joke?"

He frowned at her.

"Because, I mean, if it's a joke, ha-ha." She dropped the pages back into place.

He looked affronted. "It's not a joke."

She gestured to the sheets of paper. "You're not seriously suggesting I use these."

"We don't need to make massive changes in order to improve the building," he insisted.

"I'm not a decorator, Zach. I'm an architect."

"Being an architect doesn't mean you need to tear down walls for the sake of tearing down walls."

She turned and propped her butt against the side of the desk, folding her arms over her chest and facing him head on. "Did you seriously think I'd fall for this?" Because if he had, he was delusional.

He lifted his chin. "I thought you'd at least consider it."

"I just considered it. I don't like it."

"Thank you so much for keeping such an open mind."

"Thank you so much for bringing me a fait accompli."

"I paid good money for these plans." He snagged the bottom of the sheets and began to roll them up. His voice rose, the offense clear in his tone. "And I paid good money for your original plans. And now I'm paying a third time for the same work."

Lindsay shifted forward, stepping fully into the room. "Would you prefer to fire Kaitlin and meet us in court?"

Zach's steel gaze shot her way.

He glared at her briefly, then returned his attention to Kaitlin. "I thought you could use them as a starting point."

Kaitlin shrugged. "Okay," she said easily.

His hands stilled. He drew back, eyes narrowing in suspicion. Then he paused and asked, "You will?"

She shrugged again. "Since they're virtually identical to the existing building, I've already used them as a starting point."

Lindsay coughed a surprised laugh.

Zach came back to life, snapping an elastic band around the paper roll, while Kaitlin hopped out of his way.

"It's my backup plan," Zach said to Dylan. It was Sunday afternoon, and the two men maneuvered their way through the crowded rotunda at Citi Field toward a Mets game. If there was one thing he'd learned from both his father and from Dylan's dad, it was that your contingencies had to have contingencies. Plans failed all the time. An intelligent man was prepared for failure.

Dylan counted on his fingers. "Plan A was to buy her off. Plan B was getting her to agree to the Hugo Rosche drawings. Low percentage on that one working, by the way." He skirted a trash can. "And now Plan C is to find her a new job?"

Zach didn't disagree on the Rosche drawings. It had been a long shot that she'd agree to use them. But finding her a new job could easily work. It was a well thought out strategy.

"She said it herself," he explained. "Her long-term goal is to get a good job. She wants her career back on track. And I don't blame her. Thing is, it doesn't have to be my building. It could be any building."

"She wants to stay in New York City," Dylan confirmed.

"New York City is a very big place. There are plenty of buildings to renovate."

"So, you invited her to the game, because…?"

That was another element of Zach's plan. "Because she was wearing a Mets T-shirt that day at her apartment. It turns out, she's a fan."

"And odds are she's never watched a game from a Sterling Suite," Dylan elaborated.

"I'm betting she hasn't," said Zach as he came to a stop near the escalator, glancing around for Kaitlin and Lindsay. "It works exceedingly well on Fortune 500 execs. Besides, my project is temporary. If I can find her a solid offer with a good firm, then she's got something permanent."

"And in order to accept the offer, she'll have to quit your project."

"Exactly." Zach couldn't help but smile at his own genius.

Dylan, on the other hand, had a skeptical expression on his face. "Good luck with that."

"Here she is," Zach announced in a loud voice, sending Dylan a quick warning glance.

The plan was perfectly sound. But it would take some finesse.

He wouldn't try to sell her on the idea of a new job right away. Today, he only wanted to smooth the path, get a little closer to her. He'd let her know he was interested in a good outcome for both of them. No reason they had to be at odds.

Next week, he'd make a few calls, talk to a few associates, field offers for her.

Kaitlin broke her way through the escalator lineup and angled toward them.

His mood lifted at the sight of her, and he recognized the danger in that hormonal reaction. It didn't mean he had a hope in hell of changing it. But it did mean he needed to be careful, keep his emotions in check and hold himself at a distance.

She was wearing a snug white T-shirt, faded formfitting blue jeans, scuffed white sneakers and a blue-and-orange Mets cap with a jaunty ponytail sticking out the back. He'd never had a girl-next-door thing, preferring glitz and glamour in his dates. But it didn't seem to matter what Kaitlin wore. She'd be his fantasy girl in a bathrobe.

Damn. He had to shut that image down right now.

Her friend Lindsay was a half pace behind her. She had topped a pair of black jeans with a white sleeveless blouse.

They came to a halt.

"Dylan," Zach said, resisting the urge to reach out and touch Kaitlin, "meet Kaitlin Saville and Lindsay Rubin."

"The lovely bride," Dylan teased Kaitlin, and Zach tensed at the edgy joke.

"The pirate," Lindsay countered with a low laugh, smoothly inserting herself between Dylan and Kaitlin, then shaking his hand.

"Zach's the pirate," Dylan informed her, a practiced smile masking his annoyance at what he considered an insulting label.

"I've been studying Zach's family history," Lindsay countered. "And I also came across yours."

"Why don't we head this way." Zach gestured toward the elevator. He didn't want an argument to mar the day. Plus, the game was about to start.

Kaitlin followed his lead, and she fell into step beside him.

"A pirate?" she asked him in what sounded like a teasing voice.

That was encouraging.

"So I'm told," he admitted.

"Well, that explains a lot."

Before Zach could ask her to elaborate, Lindsay's voice interrupted from behind. "It seems Caldwell Gilby cut a swath through the Spanish Main, plundering gold, ammunition and rum."

Zach could well imagine Dylan's affronted expression. The sparks were about to fly. But he had to admit, he kind of liked Lindsay's audacity.

"You can't trust everything you read on the internet," Dylan returned dryly.

Kaitlin leaned a little closer to Zach, voice lowering. "Is this going to end badly?"

"Depends," he answered, listening for the next volley.

"I read it in the *Oxford Historic Encyclopedia* at the NYU Library," came Lindsay's tart retort.

"It could end badly," Zach acknowledged.

While he'd long since accepted the fact that his family's wealth had its roots in some pretty unsavory characters, Dylan had always chosen to pretend his ancestor fought against the pirate Lyndall Harper, and on the side of justice.

The two men had zigzagged across the Atlantic for years, lobbing cannonballs at each other. They'd fought, that much was true. But neither was on the right side of the law.

The suite level elevator doors had opened, so they walked inside.

"Caldwell had letters of authority from King George," said Dylan, turning to face the glowing red numbers.

"Forged and backdated in 1804," Lindsay retorted without missing a bead.

"Have you ever seen the originals?" Dylan asked. "Because I've seen the originals."

Kaitlin merely grinned at Zach from beneath her ball cap. "My money's on Lindsay."

He took in her fresh face, ruby lips, dark lashes and that enticing little dimple. He caught the scent of coconut, and for a split second he imagined her in a bright bikini, flowers in her hair, on a tropical beach.

"Is it a bet?" she asked, interrupting his thoughts.

"Sorry?" He shook himself back to reality.

"Ten bucks says Lindsay wins." She held out her hand to seal the deal.

Zach took her small, soft hand in his, shaking slowly, drawing out the touch, his attraction to her buzzing through ever nerve cell in his body. "You're on."

The elevator came smoothly to a stop, and they made their way along the wide, carpeted hallway to the luxury suite. For many years, the Harpers and the Gilbys had shared a corporate suite for Mets games. Dylan's father used them the most often, but they had proven a valuable corporate tool for all of them in wooing challenging clients.

"Wow." The exclamation whooshed out of Kaitlin as she crossed through the arched entrance and into the big, balconied room. It comfortably held twenty. A waiter was setting out snacks on the countertop bar, next to an ice-filled pail of imported beer and a couple of bottles of fine wine.

"Will you look at this." Like an excited kid, she beelined across to the open glass doors and out onto the breezy, tiered balcony, where two short rows of private seats awaited them.

Happy to leave Dylan and Lindsay to their escalating debate, Zach followed Kaitlin out.

"So this is how the other half lives," she said, bracing her hands on the painted metal rail, and gazing out over home plate. Rows of fan-filled seats cascaded below them, and a hum of excitement wafted through the air.

"It works well for entertaining clients." Zach heard a trace of apology in his voice, and he realized he wanted her to know it wasn't all about self-indulgence.

"At Shea Stadium, we used to sit over there." She pointed to the blue seats high behind third.

"Was that when you were a kid?"

She shook her head. "It was when we were in college." And a wistful tone came into her voice. "My first live game was sophomore year."

"So, you were a late bloomer?" He shifted to watch her profile, wondering what had prompted the sadness.

"As a kid, I watched as many as I could on TV." She abruptly turned to face the suite, and her tone went back to normal. "You got any beer in there?"

"No live games as a kid?" he persisted, seeing an opening to get to know her on a more personal level.

"Not a lot of money when I was a kid." She sounded defiant. He could tell he was being dared to probe further.

He opened his mouth to ask, but a cheer came up from the crowd as the players jogged onto the field.

Kaitlin clapped her hands. And by the time the din had abated, Zach decided to leave it alone. He patted one of the balcony chairs in the front row. "Have a seat. I'll bring you a beer." Two stairs up, he twisted back. "You want chips or something?"

"Hot dog?" she asked.

He couldn't help but grin at the simple request. "One hot dog, coming up."

Back inside the suite, while Dylan explained some of the finer points of King George's Letters of Authority, the waiter quickly organized hot dogs and beer.

In no time, Zach was settled next to Kaitlin, and the game was under way.

As the Mets went up to bat, they ate their loaded hot dogs. Between bites, she unselfconsciously cheered for the hits and groaned at the strikes. Zach found himself watching her more than he watched the players.

After the final bite of her hot dog, she licked a dab of mustard from the pad of her thumb. The gesture was both subconscious and sexy. Somehow, it looked remarkably like a kiss.

"That was delicious," she said, grinning around the tip of her thumb. "Thanks."

He tried to remember the last time he'd dated a woman who enjoyed the simple pleasure of a hot dog. Lobster, maybe, caviar, certainly, and expensive champagne was always a winner. But the finer things had mattered to his dates, his money had always mattered.

Then he remembered Kaitlin owned half his fortune. And he remembered they weren't on a date.

"So..." She adjusted her position, crossing one leg over the opposite knee, and adjusted her cap, apparently remembering the same things as him. "Why did you invite me here?"

He feigned innocence. "What do you mean?"

She gestured to the opulence behind them. "The suite. The baseball game. Imported beer. What's up?"

"We're working together."

"And..." She waited.

"And I thought we should get to know each other." Sure, he had another objective. But it was perfectly rational for the two of them to get to know each other. The renovations would take months. They'd be in each other's lives for quite some time to come.

"I'm not signing the divorce papers," she warned him.

"Did I ask?" There was no need for her to get paranoid.

"And I'm not changing the renovation designs, either."

"You could at least let me look at them."

"No way," she determinedly stated.

He tried feigning nonchalance. "Okay. Then let's talk about you."

She came alert. "What about me?"

"What are your plans? I mean long-term. Not just this single project."

The crack of a bat against the ball resonated through the stadium, and she turned to face forward while a runner sprinted to first. "That's no secret," she answered, gaze focused on the game. "A successful career in architecture. In New York City."

He took a sip of the cold beer, concentrating on getting this conversation just right. "I'd like to help you."

Her mouth quirked into a rueful smile. "You are helping. Reluctantly, we both know. But you *are* helping."

"I mean in addition to the Harper renovation project. I know people. I have contacts."

"I'm sure you do." She kept her attention fixed on the game while the opposing pitcher threw a strike, retiring the batter, and the Mets headed out to the field.

"Let me use them," Zach offered.

She turned then to paste him with a skeptical stare. "Use your contacts? To help *me?*"

"Yes," he assured her with a nod.

She thought about it for a few minutes while the pitcher warmed up. Zach was tempted to prompt her, but he'd messed up so many conversations with her already, he decided silence was the safer route.

"I read where you're going to the chamber of commerce dinner next Friday," she finally ventured, turning to watch him.

"The resurgence of global trade in northern Europe," he confirmed. They'd asked him to speak. He'd prefer to sit in the back and enjoy the single malt, but having a profile at these things was always good for business.

"Are you taking anyone?" she asked, gaze darting back to the action on the field.

"You mean a date?"

She nodded. "It's a dinner. I assume it would be partly social. It seems to me it would be acceptable to bring a date."

"Yes, it's acceptable. And no, I don't have one."

Another batter cracked a high fly ball. They watched the trajectory until it was caught out in center field.

"Will you take me?"

Zach rocked back and turned. A reflexive rush of excitement hit his body as he studied her profile. "You're asking me for a date?"

But she rolled her eyes and adjusted her cap. "I'm asking you to get me in the door, Zach, not dance with me. You said you wanted to help. And there will be people there who are good for my career."

"Right." He shifted in his seat, assuring himself he wasn't disappointed. It was a lie, of course. But he definitely wasn't stupid.

Dating Kaitlin would be a huge mistake. Dancing with her was out of the question. What if it was as great as he'd remembered? What then?

She drew a satisfied sigh, her shoulders relaxing. "And, before Friday, if you wouldn't mind telling at least five people that you've hired me back. Influential people. It would be great for me if word got around."

He had no right to be disappointed. This was business for her. It was business for him, too. Introducing her around at the chamber dinner played right into Plan C. She was right. There would be influential people there, a myriad of corporate executives, many of whom would have contacts in the architectural world. If he was lucky, really lucky, she'd find a job right there at the dinner.

Still, he struggled to keep his voice neutral as he told her, "Sure. No problem."

"You did offer to help," she pointed out.

"I said sure."

"Are you annoyed?" she asked.

"I'm being blackmailed," he reminded her. Was he supposed to be thrilled about it?

"Every marriage has its complications," she returned on an irreverent grin.

Just then, the Mets pitcher struck out the third batter with the bases loaded, and Kaitlin jumped from her seat to cheer.

Zach watched her in the sunlight and struggled very hard to feel annoyed. But then she punched a fist in the air, and her T-shirt rode up, revealing a strip of smooth skin above her waistband. And annoyance was the last thing he was feeling toward his accidental wife.

The chamber dinner was a dream come true for Kaitlin. The people she met were friendly and professional, and she came away feeling as if she'd met the who's who of the Manhattan business world. Zach had certainly stuck to his pledge of helping her. He'd introduced her to dozens of potential contacts, left her in interesting conversations, but seemed to magically appear whenever she felt alone or out of place.

It was nearly midnight when they finally climbed aboard his thirty-foot yacht for the return trip to Manhattan. Like the suite at the baseball game, the yacht clearly showed Zach had the means and the desire to enjoy the finer things in life. Lindsay was right, Kaitlin could spend as much as she needed on the renovations, and he'd barely notice.

The chamber dinner had been held at an island marina just off the coast of southern Manhattan. Most people had traveled by water taxi but a few, like Zach, had brought their own transportation.

"This is a nice ride," she acknowledged one more time, as they settled into a grouping of comfortable, white, cushioned furniture. The sitting area, on a teak wood deck, was positioned next to a covered hot tub near the stern of the boat, protected from the wind by a glass wall at midship, but providing an incredible view over the aft rail.

Kaitlin chose a soft armchair, while Zach took a love seat at a right angle to her, facing the stern. The pilot powered up the engine, and they glided smoothly out into the bay.

"It's slower than a helicopter," said Zach. "But I like it out here at night."

Kaitlin tipped her head and gazed at the twinkling skyline. A three-quarter moon was rising, and a few stars were visible beyond the city's glow. "You have a helicopter?"

"Dylan has the helicopters. My company owns ships."

Kaitlin had liked Dylan, even if Lindsay hadn't seemed to warm up to him. Then again, there were few things Lindsay enjoyed more than a rollicking debate, and Dylan had played right into her hand. Kaitlin was convinced Lindsay missed being in a courtroom. Lindsay had worked for a year as a litigator, and Kaitlin had always wondered about her choice to take the teaching position.

"Tell me more about the pirates," she said to Zach. She'd never met anyone with such a colorful family history.

"You want a drink or anything?" he asked.

She shook her head, slipping off her shoes and bending her knees to tuck her feet beneath her in the shimmering black cocktail dress. "One more glass of champagne, and I'll start singing karaoke."

"Champagne it is." He started to rise, his devilish smile showing straight white teeth in the muted deck light.

"Don't you dare," she warned, with a waggle of her finger. "Trust me. You do not want me to sing."

He rocked back into his seat and loosened his tie. He ran a hand, spread-fingered, through his thick hair and crossed one ankle over the opposite knee. In the buffeting breeze, with the faint traces of fatigue around his dark eyes, he looked disheveled and compellingly sexy.

"Back to the pirates," she prompted in an effort to distract herself from her burgeoning desire. "Is it all true?"

He shrugged easily. "Depends on what you've heard."

"I heard that your ancestor was a pirate, arch enemy of Dylan's ancestor, and the two of them formed a truce nearly three hundred years ago on what is now Serenity Island. I heard the nexus of your fortune is stolen treasure."

Criminal or not, she still found herself envious of his detailed family history. Zach would know details of his parents, his grandparents, his aunts and uncles, and every ancestor back three hundred years. Kaitlin would give anything to be able to go back even one generation.

"Well, it's all true," said Zach. "At least as far as we can tell. Dylan's in denial."

Kaitlin laughed lightly, remembering the argument at the baseball game. "It sure sounded like it."

Zach removed his tie and tossed it on the love-seat cushion beside him. "Dylan wants to pretend his family was pure of heart. I think he must have more scruples than me."

"You're unscrupulous?" she couldn't resist asking.

"Some would say."

"Would they be right?"

He looked her square in the eyes. "Like I'm going to answer that."

She couldn't tell if he was still teasing. And maybe that was deliberate. "Are you trying to keep me off balance?" she asked, watching his expression closely.

"You're not exactly on my side."

"I thought we'd formed a truce." She certainly felt as if they'd formed a truce tonight.

"I'm appeasing you," he told her. His tone and dark eyes were soft, but the words revealed his continued caution.

"And I'm trying to build you a masterpiece," she responded tartly.

He sighed, and seemed to relax ever so slightly. "You're trying to build yourself a masterpiece."

She had to concede that one. Her primary motivation in this was her own reputation. Of course, it was all his fault she was forced into this position.

"You make a fair point," she admitted.

"So, who's unscrupulous now?"

"I'm not unscrupulous. Just practical." She had no one in this world to depend on but herself.

Orphans learned that fact very quickly in life. If she didn't have a career, if she couldn't provide for herself, nobody would do it for her. Since she was old enough to understand, she'd feared poverty and loneliness.

She was sure the view was quite different from where Zach was sitting on millions of dollars worth of New York real estate. He had a successful company, money to burn and a lineage that went back to the dawn of statehood.

"So, what have you decided?" he asked.

"About what?" Was there anything left outstanding on their deal? She thought they were both quite clear at this point.

"My building. You've been working at it for a couple of weeks now. Tell me what you have in mind."

Kaitlin instantly saw through his ploy. No wonder he'd

behaved so well this evening. He'd been lulling her into a false send of security.

She came to her feet, keeping a close eye on him, backing toward the rail. The teak deck was cool and smooth beneath her bare feet. "Oh, no, you don't. I'm not opening myself up for a fight over the details."

He rose with her. "You'll need my input at some point. It might as well be—"

"Uh-uh." The breeze brushed the filmy, scalloped-hem dress against her legs and whipped the strands of hair that had worked their way loose from her updo. "No input. *My* project."

He widened his stance. "I'll have to approve the final designs."

The waves rolled higher, and she braced herself against the rail. "What part of carte blanche didn't you understand?"

He took a few steps forward. "The part where I sign the check."

"*We* sign the check."

He came even closer, all pretense of geniality gone from his expression. He was all business, all intimidation. "Right. And 'we' had best be happy with both the plans and the price tag."

"There is no limit on this project's budget."

He came to a halt, putting a hand on the rail, half trapping her. "I won't let you bankrupt my company."

She struggled not to react to his nearness. "Like I could possibly bankrupt Harper Transportation. You give me too much credit."

The boat lunged into a trough, and he swayed closer. "You want to see the balance sheets?"

"I want to see a new Manhattan skyline."

"It's talk like that that scares me, Kaitlin."

Her scare him?

He was the one unsettling her.

His intense expression brought her heart rate up. His lips were full, chin determined, eyes intense, and his hard, rangy body was far too close for her comfort. Sweat prickled at her hairline, formed between her breasts, gathered behind her knees, and was then cooled by the evening breeze.

His arms were only inches away. He could capture her at any moment, kiss her, ravage her.

She swallowed against her out-of-control arousal.

Any second now, she'd be throwing herself in his arms. Maybe talking about the renovation was the lesser of all evils.

"I was planning more light." Her voice came out sexy, husky, and she couldn't seem to do a thing about it. "More glass. A higher lobby. Bigger offices."

Had he moved closer?

"Bigger offices mean fewer offices," he pointed out.

She didn't disagree.

"Do you know the cost of space in midtown Manhattan?" His rebuke sounded like a caress.

"Do you know the soft value of impressing your future clients?" she returned, her brain struggling hard to grasp every coherent thought.

Had *she* moved closer? Her nose picked up his scent, and it was sensually compelling. She swore she could feel the heat of his body through his dress shirt.

"Do you think the makers of tractor parts and kitchen appliances care what my lobby looks like?" His breath puffed against her lips.

"Yes."

They stared at each other in silence, inhaling and exhaling for long seconds. The rumble of the yacht's motor filled the space around them.

Something dangerous flared in Zach's intense gray eyes. It was darkly sensual and completely compelling.

Her body answered with a rush of heat and a flare of longing that sent a throbbing message to every corner of her being.

She struggled through the muddle of emotions clouding her brain. "The people who make tractor parts also have tickets to Lincoln Center. They do care about your lobby."

"It's a building, not a piece of art." The yacht lurched, and his hand brushed against hers. She nearly groaned out loud.

"It can be both," she rasped.

Things could do double duty.

Look at Zach. He was both an adversary and a—

What? What was she saying?

He could be her lover?

"Kaitlin?" His voice was strangled, while his gaze flared with certain desire. His full lips parted, his head tipping toward hers.

The boat rolled on a fresh set of waves, and she gripped the rail, transfixed by the sight of his body closing in on hers.

She flashed back to Vegas.

He'd kissed her there.

How could she have ever doubted it?

Elvis had pronounced them husband and wife, and Zach had thrown his arms around her, kissing her thoroughly and endlessly. It was only the cheers from the crowd that had finally penetrated their haze and forced them to pull apart. It was a miracle they hadn't slept together that night.

Why hadn't they slept together that night?

She remembered getting into the elevator with a couple of her female coworkers, then stumbling into her room and dropping, fully dressed, onto the plush, king-size bed.

No Zach.

But he was here now.

And they were alone.

And she remembered. She wished she didn't. But she remembered his lips on hers, his arms around her, the strength of his embrace, the taste of his mouth, the sensual explosions that burst along her skin.

She wanted it again, wanted it so very, very much.

She gave in to her desire and leaned ever so slightly forward. His mouth instantly rushed to hers. His free arm snaked around her, pressing against the small of her back, pulling her tight as the deck surged beneath them.

She pressed forward, arms twining around his neck. Her lips softened, parted. He murmured her name, and his hand splayed farther down her spine. His tongue invaded, and the taste of him combined with the scent of the salt air, the undulation of the boat and heat of his hands brought a moan from her very core.

He shifted so that his back was to the rail. His free hand caressed her cheek, brushed through her hair, moved down to her neck, her shoulder. He pushed off the strap of her dress, then his lips followed, tasting their way along her bare, sensitized skin.

His kisses, his passion, made her gasp. She tangled her fingers through his hair, pushing her body tightly against his, shifting her thighs as his leg slipped between them. His hand cupped her breast through the flimsy fabric of her dress, while his lips found hers again, and she bent backward with the exquisite pressure of his hot kiss.

The boat lurched again, and they lost their balance, stumbling a few steps sideways.

Zach was quick to steady her, clasping her tightly to him, lips next to her ear.

"You okay?" His voice was hollow.

"I'm—" She drew a shaky breath.

Was she okay? What on earth had she just done? One minute they were arguing over office sizes, the next they were practically attacking each other.

He held her tight. Neither spoke as they drew deep breaths.

Finally, he stroked her messy hair. "Are you thinking what I'm thinking?"

"That we've both gone completely insane?"

He chuckled low. "That's pretty close."

"We can't do this."

"No kidding."

"You need to let go of me."

"I know." He didn't move.

"I'm blackmailing you. You're trying to outflank, outmaneuver and outthink me along the way. And then we're getting divorced."

"As long as we're both clear on the process."

The flutter in her stomach told her there was way more to it than that. But she had to fight it. She couldn't let herself be attracted to this man. She certainly couldn't let herself kiss him, or worse.

They were adversaries. And this was her one chance to get her life back. And she couldn't let any lingering sexual desire mess that up.

"You need to let me go, Zach."

Four

After a long, sleepless night, and a lengthy heart-to-heart with Lindsay as they drove up the coast of Long Island, Kaitlin watched her friend browse through a tray of misshapen silver coins in a small beachfront antique shop.

"I never thought I'd hear myself say this." Lindsay selected one plastic-wrapped item and read the provenance typed neatly on the attached card. "But, as your lawyer, I must strongly advise you not to sleep with your husband."

"I am *not* sleeping with my husband," Kaitlin reminded her. And she had absolutely no intention of going there. Desire and action were two completely different things.

Two women checking out a painting in the next aisle slid their curious gazes to Kaitlin, and their expressions shifted from smirks to bemusement.

Kaitlin leaned a little closer to Lindsay and whispered, "Okay, that just sounds stupid when I say it out loud."

"He's playing you," said Lindsay, dropping the first coin and switching to another, turning it over to read.

"Neither of us meant for it to happen," Kaitlin pointed out. Zach's shock and regret had seemed as genuine as hers.

Lindsay glanced up from the coin, arching her a skeptical look. "Are you sure about that?"

"I'm sure," Kaitlin returned with conviction. They'd both sworn not to let it happen again. It was as much her fault as his.

"And what were you doing right before you kissed him?" Lindsay gave up on the coin rack and meandered her way across the shop floor.

Kaitlin followed, only half paying attention to the merchandise. Lindsay was the one who'd suggested driving up the coast to visit antique stores. They'd never done it before, but Kaitlin was game for anything that would distract her.

"We were on deck," she told Lindsay. "Fantastic boat, by the way."

"You mentioned that. So, were you eating? Drinking? Stargazing?"

"Arguing art versus architecture." Kaitlin took her mind back to the first minutes of the return trip. "He wanted to see my designs."

"I rest my case." Lindsay lingered in front of a glass case displaying some more gold coins. "Aha. This is what I was looking for."

"What case?" asked Kaitlin. What was Lindsay resting?

Lindsay fluttered a dismissive hand, attention on the coins. "The case against Zach." Then she tapped her index finger against the glass in answer to a clerk's unspoken question. "I'd like to see that one."

"I don't follow," said Kaitlin.

"The coin is from the *Blue Glacier.*"

"Yes, it is," the clerk confirmed with an enthusiastic smile, unlocking the case and extracting a plastic-covered, gold, oblong coin.

"You were resting your case," Kaitlin prompted.

Lindsay inspected the coin, holding it up to the sunlight and turning it one way, then the other. "You were arguing with Zach about art versus architecture. Which side were you on, by the way?"

"Zach's afraid my renovation plans will be impractical," explained Kaitlin. "I told him architecture could be both beautiful and functional. He's stone-cold on the side of function."

"Not hard to tell that from his building." Lindsay put down her purse and slipped the coin under a big magnifying glass on a stand on the countertop.

"When did you become interested in coins?" asked Kaitlin. Lindsay was going through quite a procedure here.

"The two of you were fighting," Lindsay continued while she peered critically at the coin. "I'm assuming you were winning since, aside from holding all the trump cards, you were right." She straightened. "Then suddenly, poof, he's kissing you."

The clerk eyed Kaitlin with obvious interest, while Lindsay gave Kaitlin a knowing look. "Do you think there's a slim possibility it was a distraction? Do you think, maybe, out of desperation to seize control of the project, your *husband* might be trying to emotionally manipulate you?"

Kaitlin blinked. Manipulate her?

"You know," Lindsay continued, "if you gave away the fact you thought he was hot—"

"I never told him he was hot."

"There are other ways to give yourself away besides talking. And you *do* think he's hot."

The clerk's attention was ping-ponging between the two women.

Kaitlin realized she probably *had* given herself away. On numerous occasions. And while they were arguing on the boat, her attraction to Zach must have been written all over her face.

But what about Zach? Had he felt nothing? Could he actually be that good an actor? Had he pounced on an opportunity?

Humiliation washed over her. Lindsay was right.

"Darn it," Kaitlin hissed under her breath. "He was *faking?*"

Lindsay patted her arm in sympathy, her tone going gentle. "That'd be my guess."

Kaitlin scrunched her eyes shut.

"I'll take this one," Lindsay told the clerk. Then she wrapped a bracing arm around Kaitlin's shoulders. "Seriously, Katie. I hate to be the one to say this. But what are the odds he's falling for you?"

Lindsay was right. She was so, so right. Kaitlin had been taken in by a smooth-talking man with an agenda. He didn't want her. He wanted her architectural designs, so he could shoot holes in them, talk her out of them, save himself a bundle of money. His interests were definitely not Kaitlin's interests.

How could she have been so naive?

She clamped her jaw and took a bracing breath.

Then she opened her eyes. "You're right."

"Sorry."

"Don't sweat it. I'm fine," Kaitlin huffed. She caught a glimpse of the hefty price tag on the coin and seized the opportunity to turn the attention from herself. "You know that's two thousand dollars?"

"It's a bargain," said the clerk, punching keys on the cash register.

But Lindsay wasn't so easily distracted. "I think he's trapped. I think he's panicking. And I think *he* thinks you'll be more malleable if you fall for him."

"How long have you been interested in antique coins?" Kaitlin repeated. Notwithstanding her desire to change the subject, it really *was* a lot of money.

"I'm not interested in coins," Lindsay replied. "I'm interested in pirates."

Oh, this was priceless. "You're fixating on Dylan Gilby?"

"Wrong. I'm fixating on *Caldwell* Gilby. I'm proving that smug, superior Dylan does, indeed, owe his wealth to the ill-gotten gains of his pirate ancestor."

"The *Blue Glacier was* sunk by pirates," the clerk offered as she accepted Lindsay's credit card to pay for the purchase.

"By the *Black Fern,*" Lindsay confirmed in a knowledgeable and meaningful tone. "Captained by dear ol' Caldwell Gilby."

The clerk carefully slid the coin in a velvet pouch embossed with the store's logo. "The captain of the *Blue Glacier* tried to scuttle the ship against a reef rather than give up his cargo. But the pirates got most of it anyway. A few of the coins were recovered from the wreck in 1976." The clerk handed Lindsay the pouch. "You've made a good purchase."

As they turned for the door to exit the pretty little shop, Lindsay held up the pouch in front of Kaitlin's face. "Exhibit A."

Kaitlin searched her friend's expression. "You have got to get back in the courtroom."

"Weren't we talking about you?" asked Lindsay. "Kissing your husband?"

"I don't think so." Kaitlin was going to wallow through that one in private.

Lindsay dropped the coin into her purse and sobered. "I don't want you getting hurt in all this."

Kaitlin refused to accept that. "I'm not about to get hurt. I kissed him. Nothing more." That was, of course, the understatement of the century.

Still, they'd come to their senses before anything serious had happened. Or maybe Kaitlin was the one who'd come to her senses. Zach hadn't been emotionally involved on any level. Even now, he was probably biding his time, waiting for the next opportunity to manipulate her all over again.

"He's only after one thing," Lindsay declared with authority.

Kaitlin struggled to find the black humor. "And it's not even the usual thing."

Lindsay gave Kaitlin's shoulder another squeeze. "Just don't let your heart get caught in the crossfire."

"My heart is perfectly safe. I'm fighting for my career." Kaitlin wouldn't get tripped up again. She couldn't afford it. She was fighting against someone who was even less principled than she'd ever imagined.

Dylan showed his disagreement, backing away from Zach's office desk. "I am *not* stealing corporate secrets for you."

Zach exhaled his frustration. "They're my corporate secrets. You're not stealing them, because I *own* them."

"That's the Harper family style," Dylan sniffed in disdain. "Not the Gilbys'."

"Will you get off your moral high horse." It was all well and good for Dylan to protect his family name, but it had gotten completely out of hand the past few weeks.

"I have principles. So, sue me."

"I give you the key to my car." Zach ignored Dylan's protests and began to lay out a simple, straightforward plan.

Dylan folded his arms belligerently across the front of his business suit. "So I can break in to it."

"So you can *unlock* it. There is no breaking required."

"And steal Kaitlin's laptop."

"Her briefcase is probably a better bet," Zach suggested. "I suspect the laptop has a password. You photocopy the drawings. You put them back. You lock my trunk, and you're done."

"It's stealing, Zach. Plain and simple."

"It's photocopying, Dylan. Even Kaitlin's pit bull of a lawyer—"

"Lindsay."

Zach rapped his knuckles on his desktop. "Even Lindsay would have to admit that intellectual property created by Kaitlin while she was on the Harper Transportation payroll belongs to the company. And the company belongs to me."

"And to her."

Zach, exasperated, threw up his hands. "Whose side are you on?"

"This doesn't feel right."

Zach glared at his lifelong friend, searching for the argument that would bring Dylan around to logic. He couldn't help but wish a few of Caldwell's more disreputable genes had trickled down through the generations.

It wasn't as if they were knocking over a bank. It was nothing more than a frat prank. And he owned the damn designs. And while they might technically be half hers, they were also half his—morally, they were all his—and he had a corporation to protect. A corporation that employed thousands of people, all of them depending on Zach to make good decisions for Harper Transportation.

"I need to know she won't ruin me," he said to Dylan. "We know she's out for revenge. And think about it, Dylan. If she was only worried we'd disagree on the aesthetics of the renovation, she'd flaunt the drawings in my face. She's up to something."

Dylan stared in silence for a long minute, and Zach could almost feel him working through the elements of the situation.

"Up to what?" he finally asked, and Zach knew he had him.

"Up to spending Harper Transportation into a hole we can't climb out of then walking away and letting me sink."

"You think she'd—"

"I *don't know* what she'd do. That's my point. I don't know anything about this woman except that she blames me for everything that's wrong in her life."

Even as he said the words to Dylan, Zach was forced to silently acknowledge they weren't strictly true. He knew more than that about Kaitlin. He knew she was beautiful, feisty and funny. He knew her kisses made him forget they were enemies. And he knew he wanted her more than he'd ever wanted any woman in his life.

But that only meant he had to be tougher, even more determined to win. His feelings for her were a handicap, and he had to get past them.

"If it was you," Zach told Dylan in complete honesty, "if someone was after you, I'd lie, cheat and steal to save you."

Dylan hesitated. "That's not fair."

"How is it not fair?"

"You'd lie, cheat and steal at the drop of a hat."

Zach couldn't help but grin. It was a joke. Dylan had no basis for the accusation, and they both knew it.

Zach rounded the desk, knowing Dylan was on board. "That's because I'm a pirate at heart."

"And I am not."

Zach clapped Dylan on the shoulder. "But I'm working on you."

"That's what scares me."

"You may be a lot of things," said Zach, "but scared isn't one of them."

Dylan shook his head in both disgust and capitulation. "Give me your damn car keys," he grumbled. "And you owe me one."

Zach extracted his spare key from his pocket and handed them to Dylan. "I'll pay it back anytime you want. We'll be at Boondocks in an hour. The valet parking is off Forty-fourth."

Dylan glanced down at the silver key in his palm. "How did it come to this?"

"Lately, I ask myself that every morning."

Dylan quirked a half smile. "Maybe if you'd get yourself back on the straight and narrow."

"I am on the straight and narrow. Now get out there and steal for me."

Dylan on side, Zach cleared his evening's schedule and exited his office, making his way to the third floor. He had been making a point by putting Kaitlin in such a cramped space. It occurred to him that Dylan might be right. His moral compass could, in fact, be slipping.

He wasn't particularly proud of this next plan. But he didn't see any other way to get the information. And the situation was getting critical. Finding Kaitlin a new job wasn't going as smoothly as he'd expected. There was the real possibility he'd have to implement her renovation plans, and he couldn't afford to be blindsided by whatever extravagant and ungainly design she'd dreamed up.

He arrived at her office as she was locking the door at the end of the workday. She had both her laptop and a burgundy leather briefcase in her hands.

"You busy for dinner?" he asked without preamble.

She turned in surprise, her gaze darting up and down the hall, obviously worried about who might see them talking.

"Why?" Suspicion was clear in her tone.

"I'm attending a business event," he offered levelly.

"On your yacht?"

He tried to interpret her expression. Were her words a rebuke or a joke? Was she nervous at the thought of being alone with him again? If so, could it be because she was still attracted to him?

They'd pledged to keep their hands off each other, but she could be wavering. He was definitely wavering. He'd been wavering as soon as the words were out of his mouth.

"At Boondocks," he answered, shelving his physical desire for the moment. "I thought you might like to meet Ray Lambert."

Her green eyes widened. Ah, now he had her attention.

Ray Lambert was president of the New York Architectural Association. Zach had done his homework on this. He'd planned an introduction so valuable, it would be impossible for Kaitlin to say no to dinner.

"You're meeting Ray Lambert?" she asked cautiously.

"For dinner. Him and his wife."

Now her tone was definitely wary as she tried to gauge his motives. "And you're willing to take me along?"

Zach gave a careless shrug. "If you don't want to—"

"No, I want to." Her brow furrowed. "I'm just trying to figure out your angle."

He couldn't help but admire the way her brain was working through this. She was smart. But he was smarter. At least in this instance. With anybody but Ray Lambert, the plan would likely have failed.

"My angle is meeting your conditions for returning my company to me," Zach told her. It was true. It wasn't the whole truth, but it was part of the truth. "You want a career in this town, Ray's a good guy to meet."

She tilted her head to an unconsciously sexy angle. "No strings attached?"

His gaze automatically dropped to her luscious lips and his primal brain engaged. He didn't intend to lower his voice to a sexy timbre, nor did he plan to ease his body forward, but it all happened anyway. "What kind of strings did you have in mind?"

"You promised," she reminded him, looking trapped and worried.

"So did you."

"I'm not doing anything."

"I'm not doing anything, either," he lied. He was thinking plenty, and his body was telegraphing his desire. "Your imagination's filling in the blanks."

"You're looking at me," she accused.

"You're looking back," he countered.

"Zach."

"Katie." It was a stupid move, and not at all in keeping with his grand plan for tonight, but he reached forward and brushed his knuckles up against hers. It was a subtle touch, but it had the impact of a lightning bolt.

It obviously hit her, too. And he couldn't stop the surge of male satisfaction that overtook his body.

Her cheeks flushed, her irises deepened to emeralds. Her voice went sultry. "This isn't a date."

"Don't trust yourself?" he dared.

"I don't trust *you*."

"Smart move," he conceded, admiring her intelligence all over again as he pulled back from his brinkmanship.

He knew Harper Transportation had to be his primary concern. And he needed to get his hands on her drawings by fair means or foul. His company, his employees, his family legacy, all depended on it.

"Are you trying to make me say no?" she asked him.

"I honestly don't know what I'm trying to do." The confession was out of him before he could censor it.

Complicated didn't begin to describe his feelings for Kaitlin. He desperately wanted to kiss her. He craved the feel of her body against his. Given half a chance, he knew he'd tear off her clothes and make love to her until neither of them could move.

And then the power balance would be completely in her favor, and Harper Transportation wouldn't stand a chance.

He forced himself to back off farther, putting a buffer of space between them.

"Ray Lambert?" she confirmed, apparently willing to put up with Zach for the introduction.

He gave her a nod. Despite the detour into their inconvenient attraction to one another, his plan had worked. As he'd known it would. The intellectual evaluation of another person's emotions was an astonishingly effective tool for manipulation. And, apparently, it was a gift he had.

Her expression relaxed ever so slightly, causing a stab of guilt in his gut.

"You know, you're either nicer than I thought," she told him, "or more devious than I can understand."

"I'm much nicer than you think," Zach lied.

"Can you pick me up at home?"

He knew if he let her go home, she'd ditch the briefcase. That wasn't part of the plan. So, he made a show of glancing at his watch. "No time for that. We'll have to leave from here."

Her hesitation showed in the purse of her lips.

"I can pick you up at the bus stop again," he offered, knowing that would eliminate one of her hesitations.

It was her turn to glance at her watch. "Five minutes?"

He agreed. Then he watched until she got on the elevator. He wasn't going to risk her stowing the briefcase back in her office either.

At the opulent Boondocks restaurant, Kaitlin and Zach settled into a curved booth with Ray Lambert and his wife, Susan. The restaurant was on two levels, the upper overlooking the atrium that served as both an entrance and a lounge. Palm trees and exotic plants blooming from both floor and wall pots added to the fresh ambiance that included high ceilings, huge windows overlooking the park and natural wood and rattan screens to provide privacy between the tables.

Kaitlin had used the walk to the bus stop to call Lindsay and regain her equilibrium. Thank goodness some semblance of sanity had kept her from kissing Zach right there in the Harper building hallway.

She'd been inches, mere seconds, from throwing herself in his arms all over again and falling completely under his sensual spell. She was a fool, an undisciplined fool.

In desperation, she'd confessed to Lindsay and begged for a pep talk, needing to put some emotional armor around herself before the dinner started. As usual, Lindsay had shocked her back to reality, then used humor to put her on an even keel.

"Have we by any chance met in the past?" Ray asked Kaitlin as the two shook hands over a table set with silver, crystal and crisp white linen. Zach had slid partway around the booth seat and settled next to Susan, while Ray was directly across from Kaitlin.

"Once," she answered Ray. "Three years ago, at the NYAA conference. I was one of probably six hundred people who came through the receiving line."

He smiled at her. "That must have been it. I'm pretty good with faces."

Lindsay just hoped he wasn't remembering her ignominious firing from Hutton Quinn. Though, if he was, he didn't give anything away.

"Anyone else interested in the '97 Esme Cabernet?" Susan pointed to the wine list that was open in front of her.

Kaitlin was grateful for the change in topic.

"One of her favorites," Ray explained with a benevolent smile toward his wife. "You won't be disappointed."

Zach glanced to Kaitlin, obviously looking for her reaction.

She nodded agreeably, proud of the way her hormones were staying under control. This was a business dinner, nothing more. And it was going to stay that way. "I'd love to try it," she told Susan.

Susan smiled and closed the wine list.

A waiter immediately appeared beside their table.

While Ray ordered the wine, Kaitlin's attention caught on a couple crossing the foyer below. They were heading for the curved staircase, and even from this distance she could recognize Lindsay and Dylan.

She straightened to get a better view as they started up the stairs. What could they possibly be doing here?

Kaitlin couldn't miss Lindsay's red face. Her friend was furious.

"What the—" Though Kaitlin clamped her jaw on the unladylike exclamation, Zach swiveled to stare at her confusion. Then he followed the direction of her gaze.

Lindsay and Dylan had made it to the top of the stairs and bore down on the table. As they did, Zach sat bolt upright, obviously observing the fury on Lindsay's face.

The waiter left with the wine order just as Lindsay and Dylan arrived. They presented themselves, and Lindsay's quick gaze noted Ray and Susan. She schooled her features.

"I'm so sorry to interrupt." She smiled at Kaitlin, and her glance went meaningfully to the briefcase she held in her hand, moving it into clear view.

Burgundy.

It was Kaitlin's.

What was she doing with Kaitlin's briefcase?

"We just wanted to say hi," Lindsay continued, her voice full of forced cheer. "I met up with Dylan in the *garage*."

Kaitlin felt Zach stiffen beside her, while Dylan blushed.

Dylan? The garage? Her briefcase?

She felt her jaw drop open.

"We're going to get a table now," Lindsay announced smoothly, giving Kaitlin a soft squeeze on the shoulder. "Enjoy your dinner. But maybe we could talk later?" She hooked her arm into Dylan's and pasted him to her side.

Kaitlin couldn't help herself. She turned to gape at Zach in astonishment. Her briefcase had been in his trunk. How did Lindsay end up with it? And what was Dylan's connection?

Zach's face remained impassive as he focused beyond Kaitlin to Dylan. "We'll talk to you *later*."

Lindsay made a half turn to address Ray and Susan. "I'm really sorry to have interrupted. I hope you all enjoy your dinner."

Then she gave Kaitlin one ominous glance before propelling Dylan farther into the restaurant.

Kaitlin's immediate reaction was to follow them. But before she could rise from her seat, Zach's hand clamped down on her thigh, holding her firmly in place.

The action was shocking, the sensation electric.

"That was Dylan Gilby," he smoothly informed Ray and Susan. "Astral Air."

Kaitlin reached down to surreptitiously remove Zach's hand, but her strength was no match for his.

"I've met his father," Ray acknowledged. If he'd noticed anything strange in the conversation, he was too professional to let on.

"Dylan and I grew up together," Zach elaborated, filling the silence even while Kaitlin tried to work her leg free.

"Ah, here's the wine," Susan announced, looking pleased by the arrival of the steward.

As soon as Ray's and Susan's attention was distracted by the uncorking process, Zach leaned over. "Stay still," he hissed into Kaitlin's ear.

"What did you *do?*" Kaitlin demanded in an undertone.

"We'll talk later," he huffed.

"Bet on it."

"Stop struggling."

"Let go of me."

"Not until I'm sure you'll stay put."

"We first discovered this one in Marseille," said Ray, lifting his glass with a flourish for the ceremonial tasting.

Kaitlin quickly redirected her attention. She tried not to squirm against Zach's grip. His hand was dry and warm, slightly callused, definitely not painful, but absolutely impossible to ignore.

She wasn't wearing stockings today, and his hand was on her bare leg. His pinky finger had come to rest slightly north of her midthigh hemline. And his fingertips had curled into her sensitive inner thigh.

Now that her anger had settled to a hum, a new sensation pulsed its way through her system.

The touch of Zach's hand was turning her on.

Ray nodded his approval on the wine, and the steward filled the other three glasses before topping up Ray's.

When the wine was ready, Ray raised his glass for a toast. "A pleasure to meet you, Kaitlin. And congratulations on your contract with Harper Transportation. It's an important building."

"We're lucky to have her," Zach responded courteously.

Kaitlin thanked them both, clinked her glass against each of theirs, avoiding eye contact with Zach, then took a healthy swallow. The wine was incredibly delicious. More importantly, it contained a measure of alcohol to take the edge off her frustration.

Another waiter arrived with four large, leather-bound dinner menus, which he handed around to the table's occupants.

Zach accepted his with one hand, still not relinquishing his hold on Kaitlin.

She opened hers, trying to concentrate on the dishes and descriptions in front of her, but the neat script blurred on the page.

Had his hand moved?

Was it higher now?

Ever so slightly, and ever so slowly, but completely unmistakably his fingertips were brushing their way up the inside of her thigh.

Her muscles contracted in reaction. She could feel her skin heat, and her breathing deepened.

"The pumpkin soup to start?" he asked her, voice low and completely casual in her ear.

She opened her mouth, but she couldn't seem to form any words. She could barely sit still. Her toes curled and her fingers gripped tightly around the leather menu.

"Maybe the arugula salad?" he continued.

How could he do that? How could he sit there and behave as

if everything was normal, when she was practically jumping out of her skin?

"I'm going with the yellowfin tuna," Susan chirped.

Ray and Susan both looked to Kaitlin with questions on their faces.

Zach's hand slipped higher, and she very nearly moaned.

"Kaitlin?" he prompted.

She knew she should slap his hand away. She should call him right here, right now, on his unacceptable behavior. It would serve him right.

He'd be embarrassed in front of Ray Lambert. But then so would she. She'd be mortified if Ray—if *anyone*—knew what Zach was doing under the tablecloth.

"Arugula," she blurted out.

"The risotto is delicious," Susan offered helpfully.

Kaitlin tried to smile her thanks. But she wasn't sure if it quite came off, since she was gritting her teeth against Zach's sensual onslaught.

She balanced the heavy menu against the tabletop, holding it with one hand. Then she dropped the other to her lap, covering Zach's. "Stop," she hissed under her breath. "Please." The word came out on a desperate squeak.

His hand stilled. But then he turned it, meeting hers, and his thumb began a slow caress of her palm.

A new wave of desire flowed through her.

She could pull away anytime she wanted. But she didn't want to pull away. Lord help her, she wanted to savor the sensation, feel the raw energy pulse through her body. And when his hand turned back, and the caress resumed on her thigh, she didn't complain.

"The salmon," he said decisively, closing his menu and setting it aside.

Susan pulled her menu against her chest, speaking over the top. "The dill sauce is to die for."

Ray gave his wife's shoulder a quick, friendly caress. "It's beyond me why she doesn't weigh three hundred pounds."

"I have a great metabolism," Susan said, adding a self-deprecating laugh. "I don't do nearly enough exercise to deserve all those desserts."

Zach turned to Kaitlin, his fingertips still working magic as he spoke. "And what do you want?"

The double entendre boomed around them both.

Her gaze was drawn to the depths of his eyes, knowing there was no disguising her naked longing. "Risotto," she managed to say.

"And for dessert?" He pressed more firmly against her inner thigh, his palm sliding boldly against her sensitized skin.

"I'll decide later."

He gave a slow, satisfied smile, and a gleam of attraction turned his gray eyes to silver.

Just as she was tumbling completely and hopelessly under his spell, Lindsay's words came back to haunt her. *Do you think there's a slim possibility it was a distraction?*

Oh, no.

He was doing it, again.

And she was falling for it, willingly, and *all over again.*

Humiliation was like ice water to her hormones. She steeled her wayward desire, letting anger replace her lust.

"No dessert," she told him sternly, dropping her hand to her thigh and firmly removing his.

"Crème brûlée," said Susan. "Definitely crème brûlée for me."

Zach's gaze slid to Kaitlin for a split second. But then he obviously decided to give up. Distraction was not going to work for him this time. His behavior was reprehensible, and her lapse in judgment was thoroughly unprofessional. What would it take for her to learn?

Thankfully, Susan launched into a story about a recent business trip to Greece.

Kaitlin forced herself to listen, responding with what she hoped were friendly and intelligent answers to Ray's and Susan's questions, then asking about their trip to London and their new ski chalet in Banff, as appetizers, dinner and then dessert were served.

Zach didn't touch her again, luckily for him. Because by the time the crème brûlée was finished, the check arrived, and Ray and Susan said their good-nights, Kaitlin's mood had migrated to full-on rage.

As the waiter cleared the last of the dishes, smoothing the white linen tablecloth, Lindsay and Dylan appeared.

Lindsay plunked herself next to Zach, the briefcase between them, while Dylan sat much more reluctantly across from Kaitlin.

"They stole your briefcase," Lindsay said without preamble. "They *stole* your briefcase."

Kaitlin had presumed that was what happened. She immediately turned an accusing glare on Zach. There was no need to voice the question, so she waited silently for his explanation.

"It was in my trunk," he pointed out in his own defense. "*My* trunk."

Lindsay opened her mouth, but Dylan jumped in before she could speak. His blue eyes glittered at Zach. "Seems there are some finer points of the law you may not have taken into account here."

"They're *my* drawings," Zach stated.

The waiter reappeared, and conversation ceased. "May I offer anyone some coffee?"

"A shot of cognac in mine," said Lindsay.

"All around," Zach added gruffly, making a circle motion with his index finger.

Kaitlin wasn't inclined to argue.

"They are *my* drawings." Her words to Zach were stern as the man walked away.

"I paid you to make them," he countered.

"You *both* paid her to make them," Lindsay pointed out in an imperious tone.

"I wouldn't argue with her," Dylan muttered darkly.

Lindsay shot him a warning look.

He didn't seem the least bit intimidated by her professorial demeanor as he stared levelly back. "I had a math teacher like you once."

"Didn't seem to do you any good," she retorted.

"You stole my briefcase!" Kaitlin felt compelled to bring everyone back to the main point. "Was this entire dinner a ruse?"

She shook her head to clear it. "Of *course* it was a ruse. You're despicable, Zach. If I hadn't told Lindsay you'd invited me here. And if she didn't have a very suspicious nature—"

"A *correctly* suspicious nature," Lindsay pointed out to both men.

"—you'd have gotten away with it."

"I was planning to put it back," Dylan defended.

"I need to see the designs," said Zach, not a trace of apology in his tone. "My company, your company, pretend all you like but I'm the guy signing the check. And I'm the guy left picking up the pieces once your game is over."

"That *game* happens to be my life." She wasn't playing around here. If she didn't fix her career, she didn't have a job. If she didn't have a job, there was nobody to pay rent, nobody to buy food.

He brought his hand down on the table. "And whatever's left when the dust clears happens to be mine."

Sick to death of the contest of wills, Kaitlin capitulated.

She waved a hand toward her briefcase. "Fine. Go ahead. There's nothing you can do to change them anyway. You don't like 'em, complain all you want. I will ignore you."

Zach wasted no time in snagging the briefcase from the bench seat between him and Lindsay. He snapped open the clasps, lifted the lid and extracted the folded plans. He awkwardly spread them out on the round table.

Just then, the waiter arrived and glanced around for a place to set the coffee.

Zach ignored him, and the man signaled for a folding tray stand.

Kaitlin accepted a coffee. She took her cup in her hand, sipping it while she sat back to wait for Zach's reaction.

She suspected he'd be angry. Her designs called for some

pretty fundamental and expensive changes to his building. But a small part of her couldn't help but hope he'd surprise her.

Maybe he had better taste than she thought. Maybe he'd recognize her genius. Maybe he'd—

"Are you out of your ever-lovin' mind?" His gray eyes all but glowed in anger.

Five

In the restaurant's parking garage, Lindsay twisted the key in the ignition of her silver Audi Coupe and pushed the shifter into Reverse. They peeled out of the narrow parking spot and into the driving lane.

"I suppose that could have been worse," Kaitlin admitted as they zipped toward the exit from the underground.

Zach had hated the renovation designs. No big surprise there. But since they were in a public place, he couldn't very well yell at her. So, that was a plus. And she wouldn't change them. He could gripe as much as he liked about a modern lobby not being in keeping with his corporate image, but they both knew it was about money.

Lindsay pressed a folded bill into the parking lot attendant's hand. "He *stole* your briefcase."

"I knew not seeing them was making him crazy," said Kaitlin, still getting over the shock at this turn of events. "But I sure didn't think he'd go that far."

Lindsay flipped on her signal, watching the traffic on the

busy street. "All that righteous indignation, the insistence on principles."

"I know," Kaitlin added rapidly in agreement. "The lectures, the protestations, and then wham." She smacked her hands together. "He steals the drawings right out from under my nose."

"I'm not a pirate," Lindsay mocked as she quickly took the corner, into a small space in traffic. "Nobody in my family was ever a pirate."

Kaitlin turned to stare at her friend. "What?"

"*We* have morals and principles."

"Are you talking about Zach?"

"Zach didn't steal your drawings."

"He sure did," said Kaitlin.

"Dylan was the guy with the briefcase in his hands."

"Only because Zach asked him to get it. Dylan's just being loyal."

"Ha!" Lindsay coughed out a laugh.

"Linds?" Kaitlin searched her friend's profile.

Lindsay changed lanes on the brightly lit street, setting up for a left turn. "What?"

"I say again. Do you think you're getting a little obsessed with Dylan Gilby?"

"The man's a thief and a reprobate."

"Maybe. But Zach's our problem."

Lindsay didn't answer. She adjusted her rearview mirror then changed the radio station.

"I think Zach'll leave it alone now," she said. "I mean, he's seen the drawings. He gave it his best—"

"You're changing the subject."

"Hmm?"

Kaitlin gaped at her friend in astonishment. All this fighting was a ruse. "You've got a thing for Dylan."

"I've got a thing for proving he's a pirate," Lindsay stated primly, sitting up straight in the driver's seat, flipping on the windshield wipers. "It's an intellectual exercise."

"Intellectual, my ass."

"It's a matter of principle. Plus, the semester just ended, and I'm a little bored."

Despite all the angst of the evening, Kaitlin couldn't help but laugh. "I think it's a matter of libido."

"He's incredibly annoying," said Lindsay.

"But he is kind of cute." Kaitlin rotated her neck, trying to relieve the stress.

"Maybe," Lindsay allowed, braking as a bus pulled onto the street. "In a squeaky-clean-veneer, bad-boy-underneath kind of way."

"Is that a bad kind of way?" The few times Kaitlin had met Dylan at the office, she'd mostly found him charming. He had a twinkle in his blue eyes, could make a joke of almost anything and, if it hadn't been her briefcase in question, she might have admired his loyalty to Zach for stealing it.

Lindsay gave a self-conscious grin, rubbing her palms briskly along the curve of the steering wheel. "Fine. You caught me. I confess."

Grinning at the irony, Kaitlin continued. "His best friend's locked in an epic struggle with your best friend. You've called into question the integrity of his entire family. And you practically arrested him for stealing my briefcase. But other than that, I can see the two of you really going somewhere with this."

Lindsay shook back her hair. "I'm only window-shopping. Besides, there's nothing wrong with a little libido mixed in with an intellectual exercise."

Kaitlin couldn't help laughing. It was a relief to let the anger go. "Zach groped me under the table during dinner. How's that for libido?"

Lindsay sobered, glancing swiftly at Kaitlin before returning her attention to the road. "Seriously?"

"I guess he's still trying to distract me."

They pulled into a parking spot in front of Kaitlin's apartment building, and Lindsay set the parking brake, shifting in her seat. "Tell me that's not why you showed him the plans."

"It wasn't *that* distracting." Well, in fact he was entirely *that* distracting. But the distraction was irrelevant to her decision. "I showed him the plans to shut him up."

"You're sure?"

"I'm sure." *Mostly.*

Lindsay gave a wry grin. "Poor Zach. Part of me can't wait to see what he tries next."

And part of Kaitlin couldn't help hoping it involved seduction.

In his office Monday morning, Zach was forced to struggle to keep from fantasizing about Kaitlin. He was angry with her over the lavish designs, and he needed to stay that way in order to keep his priorities straight. Thinking about her smooth legs, her lithe body and those sensuous, kissable lips was only asking for trouble. Well, more trouble. More trouble than he'd ever had in his life.

"—to the tune of ten million dollars," Esmond Carson was saying from one of the burgundy guest chairs across from Zach's office desk.

At the mention of the number, Zach's brain rocked back to attention. "What?" he asked bluntly.

Esmond flipped through the thick file folder on his lap. The gray-haired man was nearing sixty-five. He'd been a trusted lawyer and advisor of Zach's grandmother Sadie for over thirty years. "Rent, food, teacher salaries, transportation. All of the costs are overstated in the financial reports. The foundation has a huge stack of bills in arrears. The bank account has maxed out its overdraft. That's how the mess came to my attention."

Zach couldn't believe what he was hearing. How had things gotten so out of hand? "Who *did* this?"

"Near as we can tell, it was a man named Lawrence Wellington. He was the regional manager for the city. And he disappeared the day after Sadie passed away. My guess is that he knew the embezzlement would come to light as soon as you took over."

"He stole ten million dollars?"

"That's what it looks like."

"You've called the police?"

Esmond closed the file folder, his demeanor calm, expression impassive. "We could report it."

"Damn right we're reporting it." Zach's hand went to his desk phone. Someone had stolen from his grandmother. Worse, they'd stolen from his grandmother's charitable trust. Sadie was passionate about helping inner-city kids.

"We're having him arrested and charged," Zach finished, lifting the receiver and raising it to his ear.

"That might not be your best option."

Zach paused, hand over the telephone buttons. He lifted his brows in a silent question.

"It would generate a lot of publicity," said Esmond.

"And?" Who cared? It wasn't as if they had any obligation to protect the reputation of a criminal.

"It'll be a media circus. The charity, your grandmother's name, all potentially dragged through the mud. Donors will get nervous, revenue could drop, projects might be canceled. No one and no company wants their name linked with criminal behavior, no matter how noble the charity."

"You think it would go that way?" asked Zach, weighing the possibilities in his mind, realizing Esmond had a valid point.

"I know a good private investigative firm," said Esmond. "We'll look for the guy, of course. And if there's any benefit in pressing charges, we'll press them. But my guess is we won't find him. From the records I've reviewed, Lawrence Wellington was a very shrewd operator. He'll be long gone. Sadie's money's long gone."

Zach hissed out a swearword, dropping the receiver and sliding back in his tall chair.

The two men sat in silence, midmorning sunshine streaming in the big windows, muted office sounds coming through the door, the familiar hum of traffic on Liberty Street below.

"What would Sadie want?" Esmond mused quietly.

That one was easy. "Sadie would want us to help the kids." Zach's grandmother would want them to swiftly and quietly help the kids.

Esmond agreed. "Are you in a position to write a check? I can pull this out of the fire if you can cover the losses."

What a question.

Like every other transportation company in the world, Harper's cash flow had been brutalized these past few years. He had ships sitting idle in port, others in dry dock racking up huge repair bills, customers delaying payment because of their own downturns, creditors tightening terms, and Kaitlin out there designing the Taj Mahal instead of a functional office building.

"Sure," he told Esmond. "I'll write you a check."

He put Esmond in touch with his finance director, asked Amy to have Kaitlin come to his office, then swiveled his chair to stare out at the cityscape, hoping against hope his grandmother wasn't watching over him at this particular moment. In the three short months since her death, it felt as if the entire company was coming off the rails.

Not entirely his fault, of course. But the measure of a business manager wasn't how he performed when things were going well, it was how he performed under stress. And the biggest stress of his present world was on her way up to see him right now.

A few minutes later, he heard the door open and knew it had to be Kaitlin. Amy would have announced anyone else.

"You can close it behind you," he told her without turning.

"That's okay," she said, her footsteps crossing the carpet toward his desk.

He turned his chair, coming to his feet, in no mood to be ignored. He strode around the end of the big desk. "You can close the door behind you," he repeated with emphasis.

"Zach, we—"

He breezed past her and firmly closed it himself.

"I'd prefer you didn't do that." Her voice faded off as he turned and met her head-on.

She wore a slim, charcoal-gray skirt, topped with a white-and-gold silk blouse. The skirt accented her slender waist, and was short enough to show off her shapely legs, while the blouse clung softly to her firm breasts. The top buttons were undone, showing a hint of cleavage and framing her slender neck. A twisted gold necklace dangled between her breasts, while matching earrings swung from her small ears beneath a casual updo.

His gut tightened predictably at the sight of her, and he took the few steps back to the middle of the room.

Did she have to look like a goddess every day in the office? Had the woman never heard of business suits or, better yet, sweatpants? Could she not show up in loafers instead of three-inch, strappy heels that would haunt his dreams?

"I would prefer..." She started for the door.

He snagged her arm.

She glanced pointedly down to his grip. "Are you going to manhandle me again?"

Manhandling her did begin to describe what he wanted to do. He'd gone home Friday night with his muscles stretched taut as steel. He'd tossed and turned, prayed for anger, got arousal, and when he finally slept, there she was, sexy, beckoning, but always out of reach.

He searched her expression. "Am I frightening you?"

"No."

"I'm making you angry?"

"Yes."

"Deal with it." He wouldn't scare her, but he truly didn't care if she got mad.

She set her jaw. "I am."

"Because you're making me angry, too." That wasn't the only thing she was making him. But it was the only one he'd own up to—both out loud and inside his head.

"Poor baby," she cooed.

"You're taunting me?" *That* was what she wanted to do here? He could barely believe it.

"I'm keeping the upper hand," she corrected him, crossing her arms, accentuating her breasts, increasing his view of her cleavage.

He coughed out a laugh of surprise, covering up the surge of arousal. "You think you have the upper hand?"

"I *know* I have the upper hand. And there's nothing you can say or do to make me—"

He took a step forward. He was at the end of his rope here. The woman needed to wake up to reality.

Her eyes went wide, and her lips parted ever so slightly.

"Make you what?" he breathed.

"Zach." Her tone held a warning, even as her expression turned to confusion and vulnerability.

His attention locked in on her, and her alone.

"Make you what?" he persisted.

She didn't answer. But the tip of her tongue flicked out, moistening her lips.

He closed his throat on an involuntary groan, and his world shrank further.

He shifted closer, fixated on her lips.

His thigh brushed hers.

Her lips softened, and her breathing deepened.

He inhaled the exotic perfume, daring to lift his hand, stroking the back of his knuckles against her soft cheek.

She didn't stop him. Instead, her eyelids fluttered closed, and she leaned into his caress. His desire kicked into action. And he tipped his head, leaning in without conscious thought to press his lips against hers.

They were soft, pliable, hot and delicious. Sensation instantaneously exploded inside his brain. He was back on the yacht, the ocean breeze surrounding them, her taste overpowering his senses, the stars a backdrop to their midnight passion.

His arms went around her, and hers around him. Their bodies came flush, the sensation achingly familiar. She molded to him, fitting tight in all the right places.

He moved her backward, pressing her against the office wall. His hands slipped down, cupping her tight little bottom, resisting an urge to drag her sharply against his hardening body. He was on fire for her.

His hands went to her hair, stroking through the softness, cradling her gorgeous face while he peppered kisses, tracing a line over her tiny ear, down the curve of her neck, along her shoulders, to the edge of her soft silk blouse.

Her fingers twined in his hairline. Her lips parted farther, her tongue finding his, her perfect breasts pushing tightly against his chest, beading so that he could feel them. She stretched up, coming onto her toes, fusing her mouth with his, and slid her hands beneath his jacket.

Those small hands were hot through the cotton of his shirt. He wanted to rip it off, strip her bare, hold her naked body against his own and finish what they kept starting.

But a jangling phone penetrated his brain. Sounds from the outer office came back into focus. He heard Amy's voice. Someone answered, and he came to the abrupt realization of where they were.

He forced himself to stop, cradled Kaitlin's head against his shoulder, breathing deeply, all anger toward her having evaporated.

"We did it again," he breathed.

She stiffened, pulling away. "This is why I didn't want the door closed."

He let her go, pretending it wasn't the hardest thing he'd ever done. Then he forced a note of sarcasm into his voice, refusing to let her see just how badly she made him lose control. "You don't trust yourself?"

"I don't trust *you*," she told him for at least the third time.

Fair enough. He didn't trust himself, either.

But it wasn't all him. It definitely hadn't all been him.

She straightened her blouse and smoothed her hair. "What is it you needed to see me about?"

Zach forced himself to turn away. Looking at her was only asking for more trouble.

"Can we sit?" He gestured to two padded chairs at angles to each other in front of his floor-to-ceiling windows.

Without a word, she crossed to one of them and sat down, fixing her focus on a point on the skyline outside, folding her hands primly in front of her.

Zach's hormones were still raging, but he inhaled a couple

of bracing breaths, taking a seat and focusing his own attention on a seascape painting on the wall past Kaitlin's right ear.

"I just spoke to my grandmother's lawyer," he explained, composing and discarding a number of approaches on the fly. He had to convince her to pull back on the renovations. It was more important than ever, and he couldn't afford to screw this conversation up.

Kaitlin's attention moved to his face, her lips pursing, green eyes narrowing. "What do you mean by that?"

He gave up and met her gaze. She was so damn gorgeous, feisty, challenging. Even now, he wanted to take her back into his arms and change the mood between them. "Just what I said."

"What happened?" She jerked forward in her chair. "Am I out of the will? Did you find a loophole? Are you firing me?" Then she jumped to her feet. "If you're firing me, you should have said something before..." She gestured with a sweeping arm, across the office to the spot where they'd kissed. "Before..."

Zach stood with her. "I am *not* firing you. Now, will you sit back down."

She watched him warily. "Then what's this about?"

"Sit down, and I'll tell you." He gestured to her chair and waited.

She glared at him but finally sat.

He followed suit, refocusing. This wasn't going well. It was not going well at all. "A problem has come to light with my grandmother's charitable trust."

Kaitlin's features remained schooled and neutral.

"There's been some money—a lot of money—embezzled from the bank account by a former employee."

He paused to see if she'd react, but she waited in silence.

Zach leaned slightly forward, his feet braced apart on the carpet in front of him, choosing his words carefully. "Therefore, I am going to have to shift some cash from Harper Transportation to the trust fund, or some of her projects will collapse, like the after-school tutoring programs and hot lunches."

Kaitlin finally spoke. "Do you need me to sign something?"

Zach shook his head.

"Then what?"

"Harper Transportation's cash flow will be tight for the next year or so." He mentally braced himself. "So we may need to talk seriously about scaling back on the renovation—"

"Oh, no, you don't." She emphatically crossed her arms.

"Let me—"

"You mess with my emotions."

"I'm not messing with anything," he protested.

"Try to put me off balance," she accused.

"I'm offering you honesty and reason." He was. He was giving her the bald truth of the matter.

"One minute we're kissing—" she snapped her fingers in the air "—next, you're asking for concessions."

His anger trickled back. "The two were *not* related."

"Well, it won't work this time, Mr. Zachary Harper." She tossed her pretty hair, tone going to a scoff. "Embezzlement from dear ol' granny's charitable fund, my ass."

"You think I'm *lying?*"

"Yes."

What was the matter with her? He had documentation. It was the easiest thing in the world to prove.

"I'll show you the account statements," he offered. "The bank records."

"You can show me anything you want, Zach. Any high-school kid with a laptop and a printer in his basement can fake financial statements."

"You doubt the integrity of my accountants?"

"I doubt the integrity of *you.*" She came to her feet again, color high, chin raised, shoulders squared, looking entirely ready for battle.

Once again, he rose with her.

Though her hair was in an updo, she swiped her hands behind her ears, tugging at both gold earrings. "You've tried evasion, coercion, outright threats, theft, seduction and now emotional manipulation."

He clenched his jaw, biting back an angry retort.

"Good grief, Zach. Granny, a charity and hungry kids? I'm surprised you didn't add a dying puppy to the mix." She tapped her index finger against her chest. "I am renovating, and I am doing it my way. And for that, you get half a corporation and a divorce decree. It's a bargain, and you should quit trying to change the terms."

Zach fumed, but bit back his words. He knew that anything he said would make things worse. A contingency strategy was his only hope. And he was all out of frickin' contingency strategies.

Having apparently said her piece, Kaitlin squared her shoulders. She put her sculpted nose in the air and turned on her heel to leave.

As the door shut firmly behind her, Zach unclenched his fists. He closed his eyes for a long second. Then he dropped into his chair.

The woman was past impossible.

She was suspicious. She was determined. And she was oh, so sexy.

She was going to bring down a three-hundred-year-old dynasty, and he had no idea how to stop her.

"Plan C is a bust," he informed Dylan, spinning the near empty glass of single malt on the polished, corner table at McDougals.

Dylan dropped into the padded leather chair opposite, nodding to Zach's drink. "Well, at least you waited until five."

"I'm lucky I made it past noon." How could one woman be so frustrating? Her renovation plans went way beyond repairing her reputation. What she was planning to do to his building was just plain punitive.

Dylan signaled a waiter.

"I talked to a couple dozen more people today," said Zach. "Nothing's changed. I can get her an entry-level job, easy. But nothing that comes close to the opportunity she has at Harper Transportation."

The waiter quickly took Dylan's order and left.

Dylan shrugged in capitulation. "So, give it up. Let her go for it. You'll have a weird, incredibly expensive building. And you'll live with it."

"She's adding three stories," Zach reminded Dylan. "Knocking out nearly five floors for the lobby. Did you see the marble pillars? The saltwater fish tank?"

Dylan gave a shrug. "I thought they were a nice touch."

"I bailed out Sadie's charity today."

"Why?"

"Some jackass embezzled ten million dollars. My cash flow just tanked completely. So, tell me, Dylan, do I sell off a ship or slow down repairs?"

Dylan's expression and tone immediately turned serious. "You need a loan?"

"No." Zach gave a firm shake of his head. "More debt is not the answer."

"Another partner? You want to sell me some shares?"

"And be a minor partner in my own company? I don't think so. Anyway, I'm not mixing business with friendship." Zach appreciated the offer. But this problem was his to solve.

"Fair enough," Dylan agreed. "What are your options?"

"Nothing." Zach took a drink. He needed Kaitlin to scale back on the renovation. Short of that, his options were very limited.

Selling a ship was a stupid idea. So was slowing down repairs. He'd need the entire fleet up and running so they could capitalize on any rise in demand. A company the size of Harper Transportation had to have serious cash flow to keep going. More ships, more cash flow. Fewer ships would result in a downward spiral that could prove fatal.

"Always the optimist," said Dylan, accepting his own glass of Glenlivet from the waiter.

Zach tossed back a swallow. "Kaitlin is going to bankrupt me, and there's absolutely nothing I can do to stop her."

Dylan's voice went serious again. "What exactly do you need her to do?"

Zach spun the glass again. "Come to her senses."

"Zach. Seriously. Quit wallowing in self-pity."

Zach took a bracing breath. "Okay. Right. I need her to scale back. Build me a reasonable quality, standard office building. No marble pillars. No fountains. No palm trees. And no mahogany arch. And especially no two-thousand-gallon saltwater aquarium."

Dylan thought about it for a moment. "So, make her want to do just that."

"How?" Zach demanded. "I've tried everything from bribery to reason. It's like trying to use a rowboat to turn the *Queen Mary* around."

Dylan was quiet for a few more minutes. Zach tried to focus his thoughts. He tried to get past the emotions clouding his brain and think rationally. But it didn't seem to be working.

"What about Sadie?" asked Dylan.

"What about her?" Zach didn't follow.

"Sadie left Kaitlin the company."

"And?" How was that a plus in Zach's present circumstances?

"And Kaitlin would have to be downright callous not to care about what Sadie would want."

"You think I should convince Kaitlin to respect Sadie's wishes?" That would be an awful lot easier if Sadie had actually left wishes. But her only wish seemed to be for Zach's wife to control him.

Dylan lifted his glass in a toast, ice cube clinking against the crystal. "That's exactly what I think you should do."

"What wishes? Where wishes? Sadie left no wishes, Dylan."

"Would she want a flashy, avant-garde showpiece?"

"Of course not." Zach's grandmother Sadie was all about heritage and tradition. She had been the guardian of the Harper family history Zach's entire life, and she had an abiding respect for everyone that went before her.

"Then help Kaitlin learn that," Dylan suggested.

Zach couldn't see that happening. "She's already accused me of emotionally manipulating her."

"Did you?"

"No." Zach paused. "Well, I made a couple of passes at her. But it wasn't manipulation. It was plain old lust."

"Better stop doing that." Dylan drank.

"No kidding." Though, if Zach was realistic, it was probably a whole lot easier said than done.

Zach still couldn't see Dylan's plan working. "I doubt she'll listen to me long enough to learn about Sadie. And, even if she does, she'll assume I'm lying." At this point, there was no way Kaitlin would believe anything Zach said.

"Don't tell her about Sadie."

"Then how..." Zach tapped his index finger impatiently against the table.

Dylan gave a secretive little smile and polished off his drink. "Show her Sadie."

Zach gave his head a shake of incomprehension, holding his hands palms up.

"Take her to the island," said Dylan. "Show her Sadie's handiwork. Then ask her to design something for the office building that respects your grandmother. Kaitlin seems pretty smart. She'll get it."

Zach stilled. It wasn't a half-bad idea. In fact, it was a brilliant idea.

He let out a chopped laugh. "And you claim to be honest and principled."

"I'm not suggesting you lie to her."

"But you are frighteningly devious."

"Yeah," Dylan agreed. "And I've got your back."

Six

"He's after something," Kaitlin said as Lindsay plunked a large take-out pizza from Agapitos on Kaitlin's small, dining room table. "A guy doesn't make an offer like that for no reason."

Lindsay returned to the foyer, kicked off her shoes and dropped her purse, refastening her ponytail.

It was Sunday afternoon. The Mets game was starting on the sports channel, and both women were dressed in casual sweatpants, loose T-shirts and cozy socks.

"No argument from me," she said as she followed Kaitlin into the compact kitchen area of the apartment. "My point is only that you should say yes."

Kaitlin pulled open the door to her freezer and extracted a bag of ice cubes. "And play into his hands?"

Lindsay's voice turned dreamy. "A private island? Mansions? All that delicious pirate history? I don't care what he's up to, we're going to have one hell of a weekend."

Kaitlin paused, blender lid in her hand, and stared at Lindsay. "We?"

The announcer's voice called a long fly ball, and both

women turned to watch the television in the living room. The hit was caught deep in center field, and they both groaned their disappointment before turning back to the drink making.

Lindsay hopped up on one of the two wooden stools in front of the small breakfast bar, pushed aside the weekend newspaper and leaned on her elbows. "You're not going to Serenity Island without me."

"I'm not going to Serenity Island at all." Kaitlin dumped a dozen ice cubes into the blender. There was no way in the world she'd spend an entire weekend with Zach.

"It's the chance of a lifetime," Lindsay insisted.

"Only for those of us with a pirate fetish." Kaitlin added mango, pineapple, iced tea, mint and vodka to the ice cubes, mixing up their secret recipe for mango madness. It was a Sunday tradition, along with the take-out pizza and a baseball game.

"It's not a fetish," Lindsay informed her tartly. "It's more of an obsession."

Kaitlin hit the button on the blender, filling the apartment with the grinding noise. "You want to sleep with a pirate," she called above the din. "That's a fetish. Look it up."

Lindsay's grin was unrepentant. "First off, I have to prove he's a pirate."

With the mixture blended, Kaitlin hit the off switch and poured it into two tall glasses. Lindsay shifted back to her feet, headed for a cupboard and grabbed a couple of stoneware plates and put a slice of pizza on each of them.

"Here's something," Kaitlin began as they made their way back to the living room. "Put on that red-and-gold dress, and the Vishashi shoes, then tell him you'll sleep with him if he admits he's a pirate." She stepped to one side so that Lindsay could go around and take her usual spot on the couch beside the window.

"That's not ethical," said Lindsay with a note of censure.

Kaitlin scoffed out a laugh. "As opposed to arriving on his island to gather evidence against him?"

"It's not like I'm going to break into his house," Lindsay offered reasonably.

"You're definitely not going to break into his house, since we're *not going*."

"Spoilsport."

Kaitlin settled on the couch and snagged one of the plates of pizza, gaze resting on the baseball game while she took a bite of the hot pepperoni and gooey cheese. She sighed as the comfort food hit her psyche. "I don't want to think about it anymore."

"Going to Serenity Island?"

"Zach. The renovation. The arguments. The kisses. Everything. I'm tired. I just want to sit here, watch the game and dull my senses with fat and carbs."

"That seems like a big waste of time." But Lindsay took a bite of the Agapitos, extrathick, stuffed-crust pizza and stared at the action on the television screen in silence.

Though Kaitlin tried to concentrate on the players, her mind kept switching back to Zach and his possible motives for the invitation. "I wish I had your capacity for mental chess games," she ventured out loud.

"How exactly did he ask you?" asked Lindsay, shifting at her end of the couch so she was facing Kaitlin, obviously warming up for a good discussion.

Kaitlin thought back to the moment in her office. "He was polite—excruciatingly polite—and I think a little nervous. He said he wanted me to learn about his family, get a better understanding of his grandmother."

"Any kisses, caresses, groping…?"

Kaitlin made a gesture that threatened to toss her pizza at Lindsay. "Just words."

"Were you disappointed?"

"No."

"Are you lying?"

"Only a little." Zach was one incredibly sexy man and, for better or worse, he turned Kaitlin on like there was no tomorrow. She couldn't stop it. She could barely fight the urge to act on it. Which was why visiting Serenity Island was one very, very bad idea.

There was a full count on the batter, and they both turned to watch Campbell swing and miss.

Kaitlin took a generous gulp of the mango madness. Then she gestured with her glass. "I know he's trying to outsmart me."

"Good thing we're onto him," Lindsay said.

"He gets me alone, he'll try seducing me. I know he thinks it's to his advantage." And it probably was. She couldn't think straight when he kissed her. Heck, she couldn't think straight when he looked at her.

"So turn the tables on him."

"Huh?"

"Seduce him back."

Kaitlin nearly choked on her pizza. Seduce Zach? *Seduce* Zach? Why not just jump off the top of his building and be done with it? "Are you kidding me?"

"Two can play at that game, baby." Lindsay gave a sage nod. "Women have been getting their own way through sex for thousands of years."

"You want me to *sleep* with him?"

Zach was every woman's fantasy. He was rich, great-looking, smart and funny. He'd had women fawning over him since he was a teenager. He'd likely seen and done it all. It was laughable to think Kaitlin could hold her own in bed with Zach.

"He is your husband," Lindsay pointed out.

"He's not that kind of a husband."

"Okay. Forget that," said Lindsay. "But look at it this way. If we don't go to the island, he'll try something else. If we go, he thinks he's winning. But we're onto him, and we'll be waiting for his next move."

Kaitlin had to admit, Lindsay's logic had some merit. Trouble was, the thought of Zach's next move triggered a flare of desire that curled her toes.

They flew to Serenity Island in one of Dylan's Astral Air helicopters. It was the first time Kaitlin had flown anywhere. Vacations weren't part of her foster care upbringing, and airplane tickets were not something she considered one of the necessities of life.

Their first stop after landing on the island was Dylan's parents' house. It was adjacent to the private helipad. The Gilby garage was home to a small fleet of golf carts that Kaitlin and Lindsay were informed were the only motor vehicles on the island.

David and Darcie Gilby were away in Chicago on business, but their various housekeepers and caretakers were in residence, along with Dylan's aunt Ginny, who greeted the four of them in the foyer in a bright red, 1950s swing dress with a multistrand pearl necklace and clip-on earrings.

"Young people," she cried, taking both of Dylan's hands in her own. "So nice of you to bring company."

Ginny was a very attractive woman for what must have been her age. Her face was wrinkled, but her short white hair was perfectly styled with flip curls at the ends, and her makeup was flawless. Two little white puff-ball dogs trotted across the floor, nails clicking on the hardwood until they stopped beside her.

"Hello, Auntie," said Dylan, giving the woman a kiss on her powdered cheek. "How are you?"

"And which one of these lovely young ladies is yours?" asked Ginny, sizing up both Kaitlin and Lindsay, taking in their faces, hair and clothing as if they were in a pageant and she was the judge.

"We're just friends," said Dylan.

One of the dogs gave a sharp bark.

"Nonsense." Ginny winked at Kaitlin. "This young man's a catch." She moved closer, voice lowering as if she was confiding a secret. "He has money, you know."

Kaitlin couldn't help but grin.

"Now this one—" Ginny made a half turn and shook a wrinkled finger in Zach's direction "—he's always been a hoodlum."

"Hello, Aunt Ginny," said Zach, with what was obvious patience.

"Caught him in the linen closet with Patty Kostalnik."

"Ginny," Zach protested.

"Did you now?" Kaitlin asked the older woman, her inflection making her interest obvious.

"Or was it that Pansy girl?" Ginny screwed up her wrinkled face. "Never liked that one. She used to steal my crème de menthe. It was May, because the apple trees were blooming."

Kaitlin slid a glance to Zach, enjoying his embarrassment.

He shook his head as if to deny the accusation.

"Kaitlin and Lindsay are staying at Zach's for a few days," Dylan told his aunt Ginny.

"Nonsense," Ginny retorted. "You need a wife, young man." She moved between Kaitlin and Lindsay and took each of them by an arm. "They need to stay here so you can woo them. Which one do you want?"

"They're staying with Zach," Dylan repeated.

Ginny clicked her tongue in admonishment. "You've got to learn to stand up for yourself. Don't let Zachary take them both." She looked to Kaitlin. "You want him?"

Kaitlin felt herself blush. "I'm afraid I'm already—"

She turned to Lindsay, her voice a bark of demand. "What about you?"

"Sure," said Lindsay with a mischievous grin. "Like you say, Dylan's a good catch."

Ginny beamed, while Zach chuckled, and a look of horror came over Dylan's face.

Ginny drew Lindsay off to one side. "Right this way to the kitchen, young lady. You can help me with the pie."

Dylan watched as they left the foyer and proceeded down a long hallway.

"You're not going with them?" asked Zach, still obviously controlling his laughter.

"She got herself into it," said Dylan with a fatalistic shake of his head. "The woman's on her own."

"That Pansy girl?" Kaitlin asked Zach, not ready to let him off the hook for that one.

"I was fifteen, and she was two years older."

"Uh-huh?" Kaitlin waited for more details.

"She taught me how to kiss," Zach admitted.

"And…?"

"And nothing. You jealous?"

Kaitlin frowned, sensing he was about to turn the tables. "Not me."

"Right this way," Dylan interrupted, pointing through an archway and ushering them from the foyer farther into house.

Kaitlin was happy to leave the conversation behind, and she was more than impressed by the house.

Only a few years old, the large and luxurious Gilby home was perched on a cliff overlooking the ocean and the distant coast of Connecticut. The west wall of the great room was two stories high and made completely of glass. Hardwood floors gleamed beneath open-beam ceilings, and a sweeping staircase curled toward a second-story overtop of the kitchen area where Lindsay had disappeared.

After Kaitlin had a chance to look around, they moved out onto a huge deck dotted with tables and comfortable furniture groupings. Large potted plants were placed around the perimeter, and a retractable roof was halfway shut, providing shade on half the deck and sunshine on the other.

"You must entertain a lot," Kaitlin said to Dylan, taking in the wet bar and two huge gas barbecues.

He nodded in answer to her question. "There's a great big party room downstairs. Plenty of extra bedrooms. And do you see those green roofs below the ridge?"

Kaitlin moved to the rail, leaning out to gaze along the steep side of a mountain. "I see them."

"Those are guest cottages. There's a service road that loops around the back. My mom loves to have guests here."

Kaitlin glanced straight down to see a kidney-shaped swimming pool with a couple of hot tubs beside it on a terra-cotta patio. The swimming area was surrounded by an emerald lawn. And, beyond the Gilbys' place, farther toward what looked like a sandy beach, and in the opposite direction of the cottages, she spied a stone spire and a jagged roofline that stuck up above the trees.

She pointed. "What's that down there?"

"That's Zach's place," Dylan replied.

Kaitlin glanced back at Zach in surprise. "You live in a castle?"

"It's made of stone," he replied, walking closer to the rail to join her. "And it's drafty and cavernous. I guess you could call it a castle. You know, if you wanted to sound pompous and have people laugh at you."

"It's a castle," she cooed, delighted at the thought of exploring it. "When was it built?"

"It's been around for a few generations," Zach offered without elaboration.

"Early 1700s," said Dylan. "The Harpers believe in honoring their roots."

Kaitlin's delight was replaced by an unexpected pang of jealousy deep in her chest. How many generations was that? Was there nothing not perfect about Zach's charmed life?

"I can't wait to see it," she said in what came out as a small voice.

Zach glanced sharply at her expression.

"The Harpers restore and preserve," Dylan explained. "The Gilbys prefer to bulldoze and start fresh."

"Philistines," Lindsay proclaimed as she breezed out onto the deck. In blue jeans and a green blouse, she somehow looked completely relaxed and at home.

Kaitlin, on the other hand, was now feeling awkward and jumpy. "How's the pie coming?" she asked, turning away from Zach's scrutiny.

Though she couldn't control her reflexive reactions, she had long since learned not to wallow in self-pity about her upbringing. It was what it was. She couldn't change it. She could only make the best of here and now. Well, maybe not exactly here and now. She only wanted to make it through the weekend.

"We're all invited, or should I say 'commanded' to stay for dinner," said Lindsay.

"That's Auntie," said Dylan, with a stern look for Lindsay. "You know she'll be fitting you for a wedding dress over dessert."

Lindsay fought with her unruly blond hair in the swirling wind, making a show of glancing around the deck and into the great room. "No problem," she informed him. "I could easily live here."

Dylan rolled his eyes at her irreverence.

"I've got nothing against living off the avails of pirating," she added with a jaunty waggle of her head. Then she tugged at the gold chain around her neck and pulled a gold medallion from below her blouse, swinging it in front of Dylan.

With a start, Kaitlin recognized it as the coin her friend had purchased from the antique shop. Lindsay was wearing it around her *neck?*

"What's that?" he demanded.

"Booty from your ancestor's plundering."

"It is not." But Dylan took a closer look.

"From the *Blue Glacier,*" she informed him in triumph.

"Okay. That's it." Dylan captured her arm and tugged her back across the deck. "Come here."

Kaitlin watched Dylan hustle Lindsay through the open doors into the great room. "Where's he taking her?" she asked Zach with curiosity.

"My guess is that he's showing her the Letters of Authority."

Kaitlin shook her head in amazement over their willingness to engage in this particular contest. "Lindsay spent two thousand dollars on that coin from the *Blue Glacier,*" Kaitlin told Zach. "Apparently, it was sunk by the *Black Fern* and Captain Caldwell Gilby."

"I know the story," said Zach.

"So, when do I get my ten bucks?"

He gave her a look of confusion.

"The bet at the baseball game," she reminded him. "Lindsay has unrefutable evidence that Dylan is descended from pirates. I believe that means she'll win the argument. And I believe that means you owe me ten dollars."

"Signed by King George..." Dylan's voice wafted through the open doors.

"Here we go," Zach muttered in a dire tone.

"It's still not legal," Lindsay retorted.

"Maybe not today."

Curiosity getting the better of her, Kaitlin settled to watch the debate through the open doorway.

Lindsay and Dylan were turned in profile. They were both obviously focused on something hanging on the wall.

"Forget the fact that Caldwell Gilby plundered in international waters," said Lindsay. "Just because a corrupt regime gives you permission to commit a crime—"

"One point to me," Kaitlin murmured to Zach.

"You're calling the British monarchy a corrupt regime?" Dylan demanded.

"That one's mine," said Zach, leaning back on the deck rail and crossing one ankle over the other.

"Your great, great, great, however many grandfathers held people at gunpoint—"

"Go, Lindsay," Kaitlin muttered, holding out her hand for the ten.

"I suspect it was swordpoint, maybe musketpoint," said Dylan.

"*Held* them at gunpoint," Lindsay stressed. "And took things that didn't belong to him."

Kaitlin gave Zach a smirk and tapped her index finger against her chest. Dylan didn't know who he was up against.

But Lindsay wasn't finished yet. "He sank their ships. He killed people. You don't need to be a lawyer to know he was a thief and a murderer."

"Oh, hand it over," Kaitlin demanded.

Dylan suddenly smacked Lindsay smartly on the rear.

She jumped. "Hey!"

"You crossed the line," he told her.

Kaitlin's jaw dropped. She sucked in a breath, waiting for Lindsay to react.

This was going to be bad.

Oh, it was going to be very, very bad.

Dylan said something else, but Kaitlin didn't hear the words.

In response, Lindsay leaned closer. It looked as if she was answering.

Kaitlin stayed still and waited. But the shouting didn't start, and the insults didn't fly.

Instead, Dylan reached out and stroked Lindsay's cheek. Then he butted his shoulder against hers and left it resting there.

For some reason, she didn't pull away.

Suddenly, Zach grasped Kaitlin's arm and turned her away.

"Huh?" was all she could manage to say.

"They don't need an audience," said Zach.

"But..." She couldn't help but glance once more over her shoulder. "I don't..." She turned back to stare at Zach. "Why didn't she kill him?"

"Because they're flirting, not fighting." Zach leaned on the rail, gazing into the setting sun. "Just like you and me."

The breath whooshed out of Kaitlin's chest. "We are not—"

"Oh, we so are."

"So far, so good?" asked Dylan, parking himself next to Zach at the rail of the deck after dinner. Lights shone from the windows of the Gilby house. The pool was illuminated in the yard below. And the twinkle of lights from Zach's house was visible in the distance.

"I think so." Zach motioned to the three women inside, where Ginny was playing right into his plan. "She's showing them photographs from when she and Sadie were girls."

"I dropped a hint to Lindsay," said Dylan, taking credit. "She immediately asked Ginny if there were any pictures."

"Good thought," Zach acknowledged. Ginny and Sadie had grown up together on Serenity Island. And though Ginny's short-term memory was spotty, she seemed to remember plenty of stories from decades back. She was in a perfect position to give Kaitlin some insight into his grandmother. And it had the added advantage of coming from a third party. Kaitlin couldn't accuse Zach of trying to manipulate her.

The thought that Zach could execute a master plan through the eccentric Aunt Ginny was laughable. Though, he supposed, that was exactly what they were doing.

"Lindsay's a fairly easy mark," Dylan added. "Mention a pirate, and off she goes like a heat-seeking missile."

"I notice you're protesting a bit too much about the pirates," Zach pointed out. Sure, Dylan was sensitive about his background, but Zach had never seen him pushed to anger over it.

"It sure makes her mad," Dylan mused.

"Our ancestors were not Boy Scouts," Zach felt compelled to restate.

"And the British monarchy was not a corrupt regime."

"There were a lot of beheadings."

Dylan shrugged. "Different time, different place."

"Yeah? Well, good luck getting Lindsay into bed with that argument."

Dylan's expression turned thoughtful. "Don't you worry about me. Lindsay likes a challenge. And I'm a challenge."

"That's your grand scheme?"

Dylan quirked his brows in self-confidence. "That's my grand scheme."

Zach had to admit, it was ingenious.

"Now let's talk about yours."

"Zachary?" came Ginny's imperious voice as she appeared in the doorway.

Zach glanced up.

"Over here," she commanded.

Dylan snickered as Zach pushed back to cross the deck.

Ginny beckoned him closer with a crooked finger.

"I need your help," she whispered, glancing into the great room.

"Sure." He bent his head to listen.

"We're going downstairs for some dancing." Ginny had always been a huge music fan, particularly of the big bands. And dancing had always been an important part of social functions on the island.

"No problem." He nodded.

"You ask the redhead, Miss Kaitlin." She gave Zach a conspiratorial nod. "I have a good feeling about the other one and Dylan."

"Lindsay," Zach prompted.

"He seems to have a particular interest in her rear end."

"Ginny."

She gave a short cackle. "I'm not naive."

"I never thought you were."

"You young people didn't invent premarital sex, you know."

Okay, Zach wasn't going anywhere near that conversation. "Dancing," he responded decisively and carried on into the house.

"Kaitlin," he called as he approached the two women huddled together on one of the sofas, their noses in one album and another dozen stacked on a table in front of them.

She glanced up.

"Downstairs," he instructed, pointing the way. "We're going to dance."

She blinked back at him in incomprehension.

He grinned at her surprise and strode closer, linking her arm and swooping her to her feet.

"Ginny's matchmaking," he whispered as they made their way to the wide, curved staircase. "I've been instructed to snag you as a partner so Dylan will ask Lindsay."

"She's very sweet," Kaitlin disclosed, sorting her feet out underneath herself.

"They're a family of plotters," said Zach.

"Yeah? Well, you're a fine one to talk."

Zach couldn't disagree.

They reached the bottom of the stairs, and the huge party room widened out in front of them.

"Wow," said Kaitlin, stepping across the polished, hardwood floor, moving between the pillars to gaze at the bank of glass doors that opened to the patio, the pool and the manicured lawn.

She tipped her head back to take in the high ceiling with its twinkling star lights. She put her arms out, twirled around and grinned like a six-year-old.

Not that she looked anything remotely like a child.

She wore sexy, high-heeled sandals and a pair of snug black pants. They were topped with a metallic thread tank that shimmered under the lights. While she moved, she reached up, raking her loose hair back with her fingers. It shone, and she shone, and he couldn't wait to hold her in his arms.

A member of the staff was working the sound system, and strains of "Stardust" came up to flow around them from a dozen speakers.

Ginny, Dylan and Lindsay arrived, laughing and joking as they spilled onto the polished floor.

"You need a partner, Auntie," Dylan declared, snagging her hand. It was obvious to Zach that Dylan knew exactly what his aunt was up to.

"Oh, don't you be silly," a blushing Ginny said, then slapped his hand away. "I'm far too old to dance."

Zach moved toward Kaitlin. She was definitely the one he'd be dancing with tonight. He took her easily into his arms, and moved them both to the music, swirling them away from the others.

"It's been a while since we did this," he murmured, as her body settled tentatively against his.

"And the last time didn't end so well," she pointed out. But she picked up the rhythm and ever so slowly relaxed into his lead as he stepped them toward the bank of windows.

"It could have ended better," he agreed. It could have ended with her in his bed. It should have ended that way.

He pulled back and glanced down at her beautiful face. Why hadn't it ended that way?

"Ginny said she was your grandmother's best friend when they were girls."

Zach nodded his concurrence. "Back then, my grandmother Sadie was the caretaker's daughter."

Kaitlin relaxed a little more. "Ginny said Sadie grew up here, married here and died here. All on this island."

Zach chuckled at the misleading description of Sadie's life. "They did let her off once in a while."

"Those are some really deep roots."

"I guess they are."

"Yours are even deeper."

"I suppose," he told her absently, more interested in paying attention to the way she molded against him than in talking about his family history.

She'd relaxed completely now. Her head was tucked against his shoulder, one arm around his back, their hands clasped and drawn inward, while her legs brushed his with every step.

As the song moved on, she eased closer. Their thighs met snugly together, her smooth belly and soft breasts plastered against him. Her heat seeped into his body, and he could smell the subtle scent of her perfume. It had to be her regular brand, because he remembered it from Vegas, from the yacht, from his office.

The song ended, but the sound of Count Basie immediately came up. "It Could Happen to You." Ginny obviously wasn't giving Dylan any opportunity to escape her planned romantic web with Lindsay.

Fine with Zach. Wild horses couldn't pull him away from Kaitlin.

"I was thinking—" he began.

"Shh," she interrupted.

"What?"

"Can you please not talk for a minute?"

"Sure?" But curiosity quickly got the better of him. "Why not?"

Her voice was low and sweet. "I'm pretending you're someone else."

"Ouch," he said gently, ignoring the sting of her words. Because she had pressed even closer, closing her eyes and giving herself up to his motion.

"I'm pretending I'm someone else, too." She sighed. "Just for a minute, Zach. Just for this song? I want to shut out the world and make believe I belong here."

His chest tightened.

He gathered her closer still and brushed a gentle kiss on the top of her head.

You do belong here, he silently thought.

Seven

Kaitlin had never in her life seen anything quite so magnificent as the Harper castle. And it truly was a castle. Made of weathered limestone, it had had both chimneys and turrets. It was three full stories. And there looked to be what she could only imagine was an extensive attic network beneath the steep-pitched roofs.

Inside, wood panels gleamed, while ornate, suspended chandeliers bounced light into every nook and cranny. It was furnished throughout with antiques. Rich draperies hung from high valences and thick carpets muted footfalls and gave a welcoming warmth to the cavernous rooms.

Each of three wings had a showpiece staircase that wound up through the three stories and beyond. The biggest staircase began on the main floor in the entry rotunda. From the rotunda, Zach had shown them through the great hall, a beautiful library, plus drawing and dining rooms. The kitchen was fitted with modern appliances, but stayed true to its roots through wood and stonework and the gleaming array of antique copper pots and implements hanging from ceiling racks.

Last night, Kaitlin and Lindsay had each been appointed a

guest suite on the second floor. Zach's suite was on the third, while Sadie had converted the old servants' quarters to a private bedroom, bath and sitting room on the main floor. Zach told them that the bathrooms had been added in the early 1900s and updated every few decades since.

Five staff members lived in the castle year-round: a groundskeeper, maintenance man, a cook and two personal maids to Sadie. Although the workload had obviously eased since Sadie's death, Kaitlin learned Zach kept them all on. They seemed very welcoming of company.

"Did you ever get lost in here?" Kaitlin asked Zach in the morning, as he showed her through a passageway that led to the north wing. Lindsay had left right after breakfast to swim in the pool at the Gilby house and, Kaitlin suspected, to flirt with Dylan.

"I must have as a little kid," he told her, pushing open the door that led to the pale blue sitting room that had belonged to Sadie. "But I don't ever remember being lost."

Kaitlin stepped inside the pretty room and gazed around with interest. "Can I get your cell phone number in case I have to call for help?"

"Sure," he answered easily from the doorway. "But you can orient yourself by the staircases. The carpets are blue in the main wing, burgundy in the north and gold in the east."

Sadie's sitting room housed a pale purple settee, several ornately carved tables and armchairs and a china cabinet with an amazing array of figurines, while a grand piano stood on a raised dais in the corner.

The morning sunshine streamed in through many narrow windows. Some were made of stained glass, and Kaitlin felt as if she should tiptoe through the hush.

She ran her fingers across the rich fabric coverings and the smooth wood surfaces, wandering toward the piano. "How old are these things?"

"I haven't a clue," said Zach.

She touched middle C, and the tone reverberated through the room.

"Sadie used to play," he told her. "Ginny still does sometimes."

"I learned 'Ode to Joy' on the clarinet in high school." That about summed up Kaitlin's musical experience.

She made her way to a china cabinet, peering through the glass to see figurines of cats and horses and several dozen exquisitely painted teacups. "Do you think she'd mind me looking around like this?"

"She's the reason you're here," he replied.

Kaitlin suddenly realized Zach was still standing in the doorway. She turned in time to catch a strange expression on his face.

"Something wrong?" she asked, glancing behind her, suddenly self-conscious. Perhaps he didn't want her snooping through this room after all.

"Nothing." His response was definitely short.

"Zach?" She moved closer, confused.

He blinked a couple of times, drew a deep breath. Then he braced his hand on the door frame.

"What is it?" she asked.

"I haven't come in here." He paused. "Not since..."

Kaitlin's chest squeezed around her heart. "Since your grandmother died?"

He nodded in answer.

"We can leave." She moved briskly toward the door, feeling guilty for having done something that obviously upset him.

He shaped his lips in a smile and stepped decisively into the room, stopping her forward progress. "No. Sadie put my wife in her will. It's right that you should learn about her."

For the first time, it occurred to Kaitlin that in addition to being blindsided by the news of their Vegas marriage, Zach had likely been blindsided by the will itself.

"You didn't expect your wife to inherit, did you?" she asked, watching him closely.

He paused, gazing frankly into Kaitlin's eyes. "That would be an understatement."

"Was Sadie angry with you?"

"No."

"Are you sure?"

"I'm sure."

"Maybe you didn't visit her enough."

He shook his head and moved farther into the room.

Kaitlin pivoted to watch as he walked toward the windows. "Seriously. Would she have liked you to come home more often?"

"I'm sure she would have."

"Well, maybe that's—"

"She left you a few hundred million because I didn't show up here enough?" He turned back to face her, folding his arms over his chest.

Kaitlin took a step back, blinking in shock. "Dollars?"

"It wasn't like I never came home," Zach defended.

"Okay, I'm going to forget you said that." Kaitlin knew Harper International was a very big company, but hundreds of millions? All those zeros were going to make her hyperventilate.

"She did want me to get married," Zach admitted, half musing to himself.

But Kaitlin's mind was still on the hundreds of millions of dollars. It was a massive, overwhelming responsibility. How on earth did Zach handle it?

He swept his arm, gesturing around the room. "As you can probably tell, the Harper family history was important to Sadie."

"The responsibility would freak me out," Kaitlin confessed.

"The family history?"

"The millions, billions, whatever, corporation."

"I thought we were talking about my grandmother."

Right. Kaitlin pushed the company's value to the back of her mind. It was a moot point anyway. Her involvement would be short-lived.

"What did you do to make her mad?" she asked again, knowing there had to be more than he was letting on. Zach was right, Sadie wouldn't have cut him out of her will because he didn't visit often enough.

His lips thinned as he drew an exasperated sigh. "She wasn't mad."

Kaitlin crossed her arms over her own chest, cocking her head and peering dubiously up at him.

"Fine," he finally conceded. "She was impatient for me to have children. My best guess is that she was trying to speed things up by bribing potential wives."

"That would do it," said Kaitlin with conviction, admiring Sadie's moxie. She could only imagine the lineup that would have formed around the block if Zach had been single and word got out about the will.

"I'm not sure I want the kind of woman who's attracted by money," he stated.

"She was obviously trying," Kaitlin said, defending Sadie's actions. "It was *you* who wasn't cooperating."

He rolled his eyes heavenward.

"Seriously, Zach." Kaitlin couldn't help but tease him. "I think you should step up and give your grandmother her dying wish. Get married and have a new generation of little Harper pirates."

He didn't miss a beat. "Are you volunteering for the job?"

Nice try. But he wasn't putting her on the defensive.

She smoothly tucked her hair behind her ears and took a half step in his direction, bringing them less than a foot apart. "You want me to call your bluff?"

"Go ahead."

"Sure, Zach. I'm your wife, so let's have children."

He stepped in, bring them even closer. "And you claim you're not flirting."

"I'm not flirting," she denied.

"We're talking about sex." His deep voice hummed along her nervous system, messing with her concentration.

"We're talking about babies," she corrected.

"My mistake. I thought you were making a pass at me."

She inched farther forward, stretching up to face him. "If I make a pass at you, Zachary, you'll know it."

He leaned in. "This feels like a pass, Katie."

"You wish."

"I do." He didn't laugh. Didn't back off. Didn't even flinch.

They breathed in unison for a long minute. His gaze dropped to her mouth, and the urge to surrender became more powerful with each passing second.

He seemed to guess what she was thinking. "We won't stop this time," he warned.

She knew that.

If he kissed her, they'd tear off their clothes right here in Sadie's sitting room.

Sadie's sitting room.

Kaitlin cringed and drew away.

Zach's expression faltered, but she forced herself to ignore it, pretending to be absorbed in the furniture and the decorations, moving farther from him to peer through the door into Sadie's bedroom.

It took her a minute before she thought she could speak. "Sadie seems like she was an incredible person."

"She was," said Zach, his tone giving away nothing.

Maybe Kaitlin had imagined the power of the moment. "Do you miss her?"

"Every day." There was a vacant sound to his voice that made Kaitlin turn.

She caught his unguarded expression, and a lump formed in her throat.

For all his flaws, Zach had obviously loved his grandmother.

"Back then," Ginny informed Kaitlin and Lindsay from where she lay on a deck lounger, head propped up, beside the Gilbys' pool, "Sadie was a pistol."

While Lindsay was chuckling at Ginny's stories of growing up on Serenity Island, Kaitlin had been struggling to match the seemingly meticulous, traditional Sadie who'd been in charge of the Harper castle for so many years, with the lively young girl who'd apparently run wild with Ginny.

Both Kaitlin and Lindsay were swimming in the pool. Right now, their arms were folded over the painted edge, kicking to keep their balance while Ginny shared entertaining stories. The water was refreshing in the late afternoon heat. A breeze had come up off the ocean, and dozens of birds flitted in the surrounding trees and flower gardens.

Kaitlin was beginning to think Serenity Island was paradise.

"It wasn't like it is now," Ginny continued, gesturing widely with her half-full glass of iced tea. "None of these helicopters and the like. When you were on the island, you were here until the next supply ship."

"Did you like living here?" asked Lindsay, stretching out and scissor-kicking through the water.

"We constantly plotted ways to get off," said Ginny, with a conspiratorial chuckle. "Probably ten kids in all back then, what with the families and the staff. We were seventeen. Sadie convinced my daddy that I needed to learn French. *Mais oui.* Then I convinced him I couldn't possibly go to Paris without Sadie."

"You went to Paris?" Lindsay sighed, then pushed off the pool wall and floated backward in her magenta bikini. "I love Paris."

Kaitlin had never been to Paris. Truth was, she'd never left New York State. Shelter, food and education were the top of her priority list. Anything else would have to come after that. Though, someday, she'd like to see Europe, or maybe California, even Florida.

"We took one year of our high school in France," said Ginny, draining the glass of iced tea. "Came home very sophisticated, you know."

One of the staff members immediately arrived with another pitcher of iced tea, refilling Ginny's glass. She offered some to Kaitlin and Lindsay, filling up a fresh glass for each of them. They thanked the woman and set their glasses on the pool deck in easy reach.

Kaitlin had spent several hot hours today prowling through the castle. The dusty attic rooms were particularly hot and stuffy.

Now she was grateful for the cool water of the pool and the refreshing glass of iced tea.

Ginny waited until the young woman left the pool deck and exited back into the main house.

Then she sat up straighter, leaning toward Kaitlin and Lindsay. "Zachary's grandfather, Milton Harper, took one look at Sadie in those diaphanous Parisian dresses and, boom, she was pregnant."

Kaitlin tried to hide her surprise at learning such an intimate detail. Back in the 1950s, it must have caused quite a scandal.

Lindsay quickly returned to the pool edge next to Kaitlin. "They had to get married?" she asked.

Ginny pointed a finger at Lindsay. "I'm not recommending it to you," she cautioned. "You girls want to know how to catch a man nowadays?"

"Not necessar—"

Lindsay elbowed Kaitlin in the ribs. "How?"

"Withhold sex," Ginny told them with a sage nod. "They can get it any old place they want out there—" she waved a hand toward the ocean, apparently including the world in general in her statement "—but you say no, and he'll keep coming back, sniffing around."

"Auntie," came Dylan's warning voice. But it held more than a trace of humor as he strode across the deck in a pair of blue jeans and a plain T-shirt. "I don't think that's the advice I want you giving our lady guests."

Ginny harrumphed as he leaned down to give her a kiss on the cheek.

"You're cramping my style," he admonished her with good humor.

Ginny looked to Lindsay again, gesturing to her grandnephew. "This one's a catch."

"I'll try not to sleep with him," Lindsay promised. Then she covered her chuckle with a sip from her glass.

"You'll do more than try, young lady." Ginny, on the other hand, seemed completely serious. "I like you. Don't mess this up."

Lindsay sobered. "Yes, ma'am." But as she spoke, Kaitlin caught the smoldering look that passed between her and Dylan.

For all her plain-spoken, sage wisdom, Ginny had just made a fatal error with those two. She might as well have dared them to sleep together.

"Help me up, dear." Ginny reached for Dylan, and he grasped her hand, supporting her elbow, and gently brought her to her feet.

It took her a moment to get stabilized, and Dylan kept hold of her.

"Now that you're here," she said to him, "I thought I might call Sadie—" Then she stopped herself, a fleeting look of confusion entering her aging eyes. "Silly me. I meant the rose garden. I think I'd like to visit Sadie's rose garden."

Dylan slid a look of regret in Lindsay's direction. But there was no impatience in his voice when he spoke. "I'd be happy to drive you down," he told Ginny.

Kaitlin hopped out of the pool, adjusting her mint-green bikini bottom and making sure the straps had stayed in place. "I'll do it," she offered to both Ginny and Dylan.

She'd love to tour Sadie's rose garden. There was a picture of it in its heyday on the wall of one of the drawing rooms in the castle. She'd driven one of the little golf carts between the houses that afternoon, and it was very easy.

"Thank you, dear," said Ginny as Kaitlin scrubbed the towel over her wet hair. "You're a good girl. You should go ahead and sleep with Zachary."

Kaitlin stopped drying and blinked at the old woman in shock.

"Those Harper men aren't the marrying kind," Ginny elaborated.

"Zach already married Kaitlin," Lindsay offered. Then she froze halfway out of the pool. "I mean..."

"Are you pregnant?" asked Ginny, her gaze taking a critical look at Kaitlin's flat stomach.

Kaitlin quickly shook her head. "I'm not pregnant."

"I'm sorry," Lindsay squeaked in horror.

"Well, I don't know how you trapped him," said Ginny matter-of-factly. "Sadie and I have despaired that he'd even give any woman a second glance."

Kaitlin looked to Dylan for assistance. Did the situation require further explanation? Would Ginny forget the entire conversation by morning?

But he was too busy struggling to control his laughter to be of any help.

"We're, uh, not sure it's going to work out," Kaitlin explained, feeling as though she needed to say something.

"Well, how long have you been married?" asked Ginny, slipping a thin wrap over her shoulders, obviously oblivious to the undercurrents rippling through the conversation.

Kaitlin hesitated. "Um, a few months."

"Then you've already had sex," Ginny cackled with salacious delight.

"Who's had sex?" Zach's voice startled Kaitlin as he appeared from between two of the pool cabanas and came to join the group. His curious gaze darted from one person to another.

"You and Kaitlin," said Dylan.

"*What?*" He took in Kaitlin's bathing suit–clad body, his intense gaze making goose bumps rise on her skin and heating her to the core.

"Ginny and I are going to the rose garden," she announced, swiftly wrapping the big towel around her body. There was no reason she had to remain here. Dylan could bring Zach up to speed.

She and Ginny headed for the cabana that held her clothes.

Sadie's rose garden had obviously been a spectacular showpiece in its day. Some sections of the formal gardens had been kept up over the years by the castle staff, but it was obviously too much work to keep it all from overgrowing.

As Kaitlin and Ginny had made their way through the connected stone patios, beside gazebos, along stone trails and past the family's beautifully preserved chapel, Ginny shared stories of fabulous weekend-long garden parties, and of the dignitaries that had visited the island over the years.

Kaitlin got a picture of a carefree young Sadie growing into a serious, responsible young woman, with an abiding respect for the heritage of the family she'd married into. All signs pointed to Sadie and Milton being very much in love, despite the pregnancy and their hurried wedding.

Ginny clipped flowers as she talked, and Kaitlin ended up carrying a huge armful of the roses—yellow, white, red and pink. They were fragrant and gorgeous.

At the end of their walk, Ginny pleaded exhaustion and asked Kaitlin to take the roses up to the family cemetery and lay them on Sadie's grave.

Kaitlin had easily agreed. She'd delivered Ginny to the Gilby house and into the care of the staff there. Then she'd followed Ginny's directions and driven one of the golf carts up the hill to the family cemetery.

Visiting the graveyard was a surreal experience.

Isolated and windswept, it was perched on the highest point of the island, at the end of a rocky goat track that was almost more than the cart could navigate. She had stopped at the end of the trail to discover a small, rolling meadow dotted with Harper and Gilby headstones, and some that she guessed were for other island residents, maybe the ships' crews or staff dating all the way back to the pirates Lyndall and Caldwell.

Wandering her way through the tall, blowing grass, reading the inscriptions on the headstones, she could almost hear the voices of the past generations.

Both of the pirates had married, and they'd had several children between them. Kaitlin tried to imagine what it must have been like for Emma Cinder to marry Lyndall Harper in the 1700s. Did her family know he was a pirate when they agreed to let her marry him? Had he kidnapped her, snatched her away from a loving family? Did she love him, and was she happy here in what must have been an unbelievably isolated outpost? The castle wouldn't have existed, never mind the pool, the golf carts or the indoor plumbing.

While she read the dates on the old stones, Kaitlin couldn't help but picture Zach in pirate regalia, sword in his hand, treasure chest at his feet. Had Lyndall been anything like him—stubborn, loyal, protective? Had Emma fallen in love with Lyndall and followed him here? Perhaps against her family's wishes?

As she wandered from headstone to headstone, Kaitlin tried to piece together the family histories. Some of the lives were long, while some were tragically short. Clipped messages of love and loss were etched into each stone.

A mother and an infant had died on the same day in 1857. A tragic number of the children hadn't even made it to ten years old. There were few names other than Harper and Gilby, leading Kaitlin to speculate the daughters had married and moved off the island.

Most of the young women who'd married the Harper and Gilby men had given them children, then died as grandmothers and were buried here. In one case, Claudia Harper married Jonathan Gilby. But they didn't have any children. And that seemed as close as the families came to intermingling.

Then Kaitlin came to two new headstones—clean, polished, white marble set at the edge of the cemetery. They were Drake and Annabelle Harper. Both had died June 17, 1998. They could only be Zach's parents.

Though the roses were for Sadie, Kaitlin placed a white rose on each of Zach's parents' graves. Then she lowered herself onto the rough grass, gazing across the tombstones to the faraway ocean, trying to imagine how it would feel to belong in a place like this.

She turned her memory to the single picture of her mother, and to the sad rooming house where Yvette had ended up. Kaitlin drew up her knees, wrapping her arms around them, telling herself it was all going to be okay. She *would* nail the perfect renovation for the Harper building. Then she'd find herself a permanent job. She'd stay in New York, and Lindsay would be there with her.

She'd finally build herself a home, and things would be better than ever. Starting right now. She might not have roots. But she had prospects. She had ideas. And she wasn't afraid to work hard.

A raindrop splashed on her hand.

She blinked, raised her head and glanced over her shoulder to find that billowing, dark storm clouds had moved in behind her, changing the daylight to a kind of funny twilight.

She reluctantly came to her feet and dusted off the rear end of her shorts, smoothing her white blouse as droplets sprinkled on her hair and her clothes. With one last, longing look at the family cemetery, she made her way back to the electric golf cart at the head of the trail.

Her clothes damp now, she climbed onto the narrow, vinyl bench seat, pressed her foot down on the brake, turned the key to the on position and pushed on the gas pedal.

She pushed down harder, then harder still, but nothing happened. The cart didn't move forward like it should have.

She rechecked the key, turned it to off then back to on again. Then she went through the entire procedure a second time. Still, nothing happened. She didn't move.

Rain was coming down harder now, and the clouds had blocked the last vestige of the blue sky. The wind was picking up, whipping the fat raindrops sideways through the open cart.

Kaitlin whacked her palm against the steering wheel in frustration. The timing could not have been worse.

It might be a dead battery, or it might be a malfunction. Either way, she was well and truly stuck. She retrieved her cell phone, speed dialing Lindsay's number.

The call went immediately to voice mail.

Kaitlin left a message, hoping Lindsay wasn't holed up somewhere in Dylan's arms.

Okay, so she really didn't hope that. If Lindsay truly wanted to fulfill her pirate fantasy, then Kaitlin hoped that was exactly where she was. But she hoped it wasn't a long fantasy. And she truly wished she'd jotted down Zach's cell phone number when they'd joked about it this morning. She might not be lost in his castle, but she could certainly use his help.

She glanced around the wind- and rain-swept meadow, the tombstones jutting shadows in the gloom. She told herself there were still a couple of hours until dark, so there was plenty time for Lindsay to get her message. And how long could a person possibly frolic in bed with a pirate?

Okay. Bad question.

Thunder rumbled above Kaitlin, and a burst of wind gusted sideways, splattering the raindrops against her face.

Then again, maybe Ginny would wake up from her nap and tell them Kaitlin had gone to the cemetery. Assuming Ginny remembered that Kaitlin had gone to the cemetery. Would Ginny recall that?

Kaitlin peered once again at the tombstones on the horizon. She wasn't wild about sitting here in a graveyard in the middle of a thunderstorm. Not that she was afraid of ghosts. And if any of Zach's ancestors were ghosts, she had a feeling they'd be friendly. Still, there was a horror-movie aspect to the situation that made her jumpy.

The rain beat down harder, gusting in from all sides, and soaking everything inside the cart. Her shorts grew wet. Her bare legs became streaked with rivulets of water through the dust from the meadow. And her socks and running shoes were soaking up raindrops at an alarming rate.

She rubbed the goose bumps on her bare arms, wishing she'd put on something more than a sleeveless blouse. Too bad she hadn't tossed a sweater in the backseat.

Lightning flashed directly above her, and a clap of thunder rumbled ominously through the dark sky. It occurred to her that the golf cart was made of metal, and that she was sitting on the highest point on the island.

She wasn't exactly a Boy Scout, but she did know that that particular combination could be dangerous. Fine, she'd walk already.

There was still plenty of light to see the trail. It was all downhill, and it couldn't be more than forty-five minutes, an hour tops, to get back to Dylan's house.

* * *

"What do you mean, she's not here?" Zach studied a disheveled Dylan, then Lindsay. He didn't need to know what they'd been doing. Though it was completely obvious to anyone what they'd been doing. "Where would she be?" he demanded.

He'd checked the rose garden over an hour ago. He'd also combed through the entire castle, including the attic rooms and the staff quarters. And he'd just confirmed that Aunt Ginny was napping in her room. So the two of them weren't together.

"Maybe she went to the beach?" Lindsay ventured, ineffectually smoothing her messy hair.

"When was the last time you saw her?" asked Zach.

Dylan and Lindsay exchanged guilty looks.

"Never mind." What they'd been doing for the past three hours was none of his business. And they certainly weren't Kaitlin's babysitters.

"She can't be far," Dylan said. "We're on an island."

Zach agreed. There were only so many places she could be without having flown away on a chopper or taken a boat. And she didn't do either of those things.

There was the chance that she'd fallen off a cliff.

He instantly shut that thought down. Kaitlin wasn't foolish. He was sure she was fine. He watched the rain pounding against the dark window. It seemed unlikely she'd stay outside in this. So maybe she was already back at the castle. He could call—

Wait a minute.

"You've got her cell number," he said to Lindsay.

"Right." Lindsay reached for her pockets. Then she glanced around, looking puzzled.

After a few seconds, Dylan stepped in. "I'll check the pool house."

Zach shook his head in disgust. He did not want to know the details of their tryst. He pulled out his own phone. "Just tell me her number."

Lindsay rattled it off, and Zach programmed it into his phone then dialed.

It rang several times before Kaitlin came on the line. "Hello?"

Her voice was shaky, and the wind was obviously blowing across the mouthpiece.

She was still out in the storm.

"You okay?" he found himself shouting, telling himself not to worry.

"Zach?"

"Where are you?"

"Uh..."

"Kaitlin?" Not worrying was going to be a whole lot easier once he figured out what was going on.

"I think I'm about halfway down the cemetery trail," she said.

"You're *driving* in this?" What was the matter with her?

"Not driving, I'm walking."

"What?" He couldn't help the shock in his exclamation.

"I think the cart's battery died," she explained.

Okay. That made sense. "Are you okay?"

"Mostly. Yeah, I think so. I fell."

Zach immediately headed for the garage. "I'm on my way."

Dylan and Lindsay came at his heels.

"Thanks," said Kaitlin, relief obvious in her voice.

"What were you doing up there?" he couldn't help but ask.

"Where is she?" Lindsay blustered, but Zach ignored the question, keeping his focus on Kaitlin.

"The roses," said Kaitlin, sounding breathless. "Ginny asked me to put the roses on Sadie's grave."

"Are you sure you're not hurt badly?" Adrenaline was humming through his system, heart rate automatically increasing as he moved into action.

The wind howled across the phone.

"Kaitlin?"

"I might be bleeding a little."

Zach's heart sank.

"I tripped," she continued. "I'm pretty wet, and it's dark. I can't exactly see, but my leg stings."

Zach hit the garage door button, while Dylan pulled the cover off a golf cart.

"I want you to stop walking," Zach instructed. "Wherever you are, stay put and wait for me. What can you see?"

"Trees." Was there a trace of laughter in her voice?

"How far do you think you've come?" He tried to zero in. "Is the trail rocky or dirt?"

"It's mud now."

"Good." That meant she was past the halfway point. "You want me to stay on the line with you?" he asked as he climbed onto the cart.

"I should save my battery."

"Makes sense. Give me ten minutes."

"I'll be right here."

Zach signed off and turned on the cart.

"Where is she?" Lindsay repeated.

"She was at the cemetery. Cart battery died. She's walking back."

Lindsay asked something else, but Zach was already pulling out of the garage, zipping past the helipad and turning up the mountain road. The mud was slick on the road, and the rain gusted in from all sides.

He knew he shouldn't worry. She was fine. She'd be wet and cold, but they could fix those problems in no time. But he'd feel a whole lot better once she was safe in his—

He stopped himself.

In his arms?

What the hell did that mean?

Safe *inside* was what he'd meant. Obviously. He wanted her warm and dry, just like he'd want any other human being inside and warm and dry on a night like this.

Still, it was a long ten minutes before his headlights found her.

She was soaked to the skin. Her legs were splattered in mud, her hair was dripping and her white blouse was plastered to her body.

As the cart came to a skidding stop, he could see she was shivering. He wished he'd thought to bring a blanket to wrap around her for the ride home.

Before he could jump out to help her, she climbed gingerly into the cart. So instead, he stripped off his shirt, draping it around her wet shoulders and tugging it closed at the front.

"Thanks," she breathed, settling on the seat next to him, wrapping her arms around her body.

He grabbed a flashlight from its holder behind the seat and shone it on her bare legs. "Where are you hurt?" He inspected methodically up and down.

She turned her ankle, and he saw a gash on the inside of her calf, blood mixing with the mud and rainwater.

"It doesn't look too bad," she ventured bravely.

But Zach's gut clenched at the sight, knowing it had to be painful. The sooner they got her home and cleaned up, the better.

He ditched the flashlight, turned the cart on and wrapped his arm around her shoulders, pulling her against his body in an attempt to warm her up.

"What happened?" he asked as they straightened onto the road, going back downhill.

"Ginny wanted to put the roses on Sadie's grave. But she was too tired after the tour of the garden." Kaitlin paused. "It's really nice up there at the cemetery."

"I guess." Though the last thing Zach cared about at the moment was the aesthetics of the cemetery.

Then again, Kaitlin was fine. She was cold, and she needed a bandage. But she was with him now, and she was fine. He reflexively squeezed her shoulders.

"I'm soaking your shirt," she told him.

"Don't worry about it."

"I feel stupid."

"You're not stupid. It was nice of you to help Aunt Ginny." It really was. It was very nice of her to traipse up to the cemetery to place the roses for Ginny.

"The other cart's still back there," she told him in a worried voice. "It wouldn't start. Did I do something wrong?"

"The battery life's not that long on these things."

She shivered. "Will it be hard to go and bring it back?"

"Not hard at all," he assured her. "But we'll wait until the rain stops before we do that."

The rain was pounding down harder now, the lightning strikes and thunder claps coming closer together. The cart bounced over ruts and rocks, the illumination from the headlights mostly absorbed by the pitch-dark.

"Thanks for rescuing me," she said.

Something tightened in Zach's chest, but he ignored the sensation. She was his guest. And there were real dangers on the island. The cliffs for instance. He was relieved that she was safe. It was perfectly natural.

"It was nothing," he told her.

"I was getting scared," she confessed.

"Of what?"

"I'm here on a mysterious pirate island, in a graveyard, in the dark, in a storm." Her tone went melodramatic. "The whole thing was starting to feel like a horror movie."

Zach couldn't help but smile at her joke. "In that case, I guess I did rescue you." He maneuvered around a tight curve, picking up her lightening mood. "And you probably owe me. Maybe you could be my slave for life?"

"Ha!" She knocked her head sideways against his shoulder, her teeth chattering around her words. "Nice try, Harper. First you'd command I stop blackmailing you. Then you'd make me divorce you. Then you'd fire me and kick me out of your life."

Zach didn't respond. That wasn't even close to what he'd had in mind.

Eight

In Kaitlin's guest bathroom, the claw-footed bathtub and homemade lilac candles were completely nineteenth century. While the limitless hot water and thick terry robe were pure twenty-first.

She was finally warm again.

Zach had brought Kaitlin straight to her room in the castle, where someone had laid out a tray of fruit and scones. He'd called Dylan on the way to let them know everything was fine. Half a scone and a few grapes were all she could manage before climbing directly into the tub, while Zach had disappeared into some other part of the castle.

Now the second floor was shrouded in silence. One of the staff members had obviously been in her room while she bathed, because the bed was turned down, her nightgown laid out and the heavy, ornate drapes were drawn across the boxed windows. She guessed they expected her to sleep, but Kaitlin was more curious than tired.

On her initial tour of the castle, she'd discovered the family portrait gallery that ran between the guest bedrooms and the main staircase on the second floor. She'd glanced briefly this morning at the paintings hanging there. But now that she'd read the family tombstones, she couldn't wait to put faces to the names of Zach's ancestors.

She opened her bedroom door a crack, peeping into the high-ceilinged, rectangular room. There was no one around, so she retightened the belt on the thick, white robe and tiptoed barefoot over the richly patterned carpet.

Chandeliers shone brightly, suspended from the arched, stone ceiling at intervals along the gallery. Smaller lights illuminated individual paintings, beginning with Lyndall Harper himself at one end. He looked maybe forty-five, a jeweled sword hilt in his hand, blade pointing to the floor. She couldn't help but wonder how many battles the sword had seen. Had he used it to vanquish enemies, maybe kill innocent people before stealing their treasure and taking their ships?

Of course he had.

He was a pirate.

She returned her attention to his face, shocked when she realized how much he looked like Zach. A few years older, a few pounds heavier, and there were a few more scars to his name. But the family resemblance was strong, eerily strong.

She left the painting and moved along the wall, counting down the generations to the portrait of Zach's father at the opposite end. She guessed Zach had yet to be immortalized. Maybe he'd refused to sit still long enough for his image to be painted.

She smiled at the thought.

She'd counted twelve generations between Lyndall and Zach. The paintings on this wall were all men. But she'd noticed the ladies' portraits were hung on the opposite side of the room.

She walked her way back, studying Lyndall all over again. The main staircase of the grand hall was behind him in the painting, so he'd definitely been the one to build the castle. It was strange to stand on a spot in a room, then see that same place depicted nearly three hundred years earlier. She shivered at the notion of the pirate Lyndall walking this same floor.

"Scary, isn't it?" came Zach's voice, his footfalls muted against the carpet.

For some reason, his voice didn't startle her.

"He looks just like you." She twisted, squinting from one man to the other.

"Want to see something even stranger?" He cocked his head and moved toward the wall of ladies' portraits.

Kaitlin followed him across the room.

"Emma Cinder." He nodded to the painting. "She was Lyndall's wife."

The woman sat prim and straight at a scarred wooden table, her long red hair twisted into a crown of braids. She was sewing a sampler, wearing green robes over a thin, champagne-colored, low-cut blouse with a lace fringe that barely covered her nipples. Her red lips were pursed above a delicate chin. Her cheeks were flushed. And her deep green eyes were surrounded by thick, dark lashes.

"Wow," said Kaitlin. "You don't think ten-times great-grandma when you see her."

Zach chuckled. "Look closer."

Kaitlin squinted. "What am I looking for?"

"The auburn hair, the green eyes, those full, bow-shaped lips, the curve of her chin."

Kaitlin glanced up at him in confusion.

He smoothed his hand over her damp hair. "She looks a lot like you."

"She does not." But Kaitlin's gaze moved back to the painting, peering closer.

"She sure does."

"Okay, maybe a little bit," she admitted. Their eyes were approximately the same shape, and the hair color was the same. But there were probably thousands of women in New York with green eyes and long, auburn hair.

"Maybe a lot," said Zach.

"Where was she from?" Kaitlin's curiosity was even stronger now than it had been in the cemetery. What could have brought Emma to Serenity Island with Lyndall?

"She was from London," said Zach. "A seamstress I was told. The daughter of a tavern owner."

"And she married a pirate?" Kaitlin had to admit, Lyndall was a pretty good-looking pirate. But still…

"He kidnapped her."

"No way."

Zach leaned down to Kaitlin's ear, lowering his voice to an ominous tone. "Tossed her on board his ship and, I'm assuming, had his way with her all the way across the Atlantic."

Kaitlin itched to reach up and touch the portrait. "And then they got married?"

"Then they got married."

"Do you think she was happy here? With him?" For some reason, it was important to Kaitlin to believe Emma had been happy.

"It's hard to say. I've read a few letters that she got from her family back in England. They're chatty, newsy, but they're not offering to come rescue her. So I guess she must have been okay."

"Poor thing," said Kaitlin.

"He built her a castle. And they had four children. Look here." Zach gently grasped Kaitlin's shoulders and turned her to guide her back to the men's portrait wall.

She liked it that he was touching her. There was something comforting about his broad hands firmly holding her shoulders. He'd kept his arm around her the whole ride back from the cemetery, his body offering what warmth he could in the whipping wind. And that had been comforting, too.

"Their eldest son, Nelson," said Zach, gesturing to the portrait with one hand, leaving the other gently resting on her shoulder.

"What about the rest of the children?"

"Sadie has their portraits scattered in different rooms. The other two sons died while they were still children, and the daughter went back to a convent in London."

"I saw the boys' tombstones," said Kaitlin. "Harold and William?"

"Good memory." Zach brushed her damp hair back from her face, and for some reason, she was suddenly reminded of what she was wearing.

She was naked under the white robe, her skin glowing warm, getting warmer by the minute. She realized the lapels had gaped open, and she realized the opening had Zach's attention.

Their silence charged itself with electricity.

She knew she should pull the robe closed again, but her hands stayed fast by her sides.

Zach made a half turn toward her.

His hand slowly moved from her shoulder to her neck, his fingertips brushing against her sensitive skin.

"Sometimes I think they had it easy." Zach's voice was a deep, powerful hum.

"Who?" she managed to breathe. Every fiber of her attention was on the insubstantial brush of his hand.

His other hand came up to close on the lapel of her robe. "The pirates," he answered. "They ravage first, and ask questions later."

He tugged on the robe, pulling her to him, and his mouth came down on hers. It was hot, firm, open and determined.

She swayed from the intense sensation, but his arm went around her waist to hold her steady as the kiss went on and on.

He tugged the sash of the robe, releasing the knot, so it fell open. His free hand slipped inside, encircling her waist again, pulling her bare breasts against the texture of his shirt.

Her arms were lost in the big sleeves, too tangled to be of any use. But she breathed his name, parted her lips, welcomed his tongue into the depths of her mouth.

His wide hand braced her rib cage, thumb brushing the tender skin beneath her breast. Her nipples peaked, a tingle rushing to their delicate skin. Her thighs relaxed, reflexively easing apart, and he moved between them, the denim of his pants sending shock waves through her body.

He deftly avoided the portrait as he pressed her against the smooth stone of the wall. His hand cupped her breast. His lips found her ear, her neck, the tip of her shoulder, as he pushed the robe off. It pooled at her feet, and she was completely naked.

He drew back for a split second, gazing down, drinking in the picture of her body.

"Gorgeous," he breathed, lips back to hers, hands stroking her spine, down over her buttocks, to the back of her thighs. Then up over her hips, her belly, her breasts. She gasped as he stroked his fingertips across her nipples, the sensation near painful, yet exquisite.

His hands traced her arms, twining his fingers with hers, then holding them up, braced against the wall while his mouth made its moves on her body. He pressed hot, openmouthed kisses from her lips to her neck, found her breasts, drawing each nipple into the heat, suckling until she thought her legs would give way beneath her.

She groaned his name in a plea.

He was back to her mouth, his hands moving down, covering her breasts, taking over from his lips, thumbs stroking across her wet nipples.

She tangled her hands in his hair, pushing his mouth harder against hers, kissing deeper, mind blank to everything but his taste and touch. One of his hands moved lower, stroking over her belly, toying with her silky hair, sliding forward.

She wrapped her arms around him, anchoring her body more tightly against him, saving her failing legs, burying her face in the crook of his neck and tonguing the salt taste from his skin.

His fingers slipped inside her, and a lightning bolt electrified her brain. She cried out his name, an urgency blinding her. She fumbled with the button on his jeans, dragging down the zipper.

He cupped her bottom, lifting her, spreading her legs, bracing her against the cool wall.

A small semblance of sanity remained.

"Protection?" she gasped.

"Got it."

One arm braced her bottom, while his hand cupped her chin.

He kissed her deeply, their bodies pressed together, her nerves screaming almost unbearably for completion.

"Now," she moaned. "Please, now."

It took him a second, and then he was inside her, his heat sliding home in a satisfying rush that made her bones turn to liquid and the air whoosh out of her lungs.

Her hands fisted and her toes curled as she surrendered herself to the rhythm of his urgent lovemaking. Her head tipped back, the high ceiling spinning above her. Lightning lit up the high windows, while thunder vibrated the stone walls of the castle.

She arched against him, struggling to get closer. Her breaths came in gasps, while the pulsating buzz that started at her center radiated out to overwhelm her entire body.

She cried his name again, and he answered with a guttural groan. Then the storm, the castle and their bodies throbbed together as one.

When the universe righted itself, Kaitlin slowly realized what they'd just done.

Bad enough that they'd made love with each other. But they weren't locked up in some safe, private bedroom. She was naked, in an open room of the castle, where five other people worked and lived. Any one of them could have walked up the staircase at any moment.

She let out a pained groan.

"You okay?" Zach gasped, glancing between them and around them.

"Somebody could have seen us," she whispered.

He tightened his hold on her. "Nobody would do that."

"Not on *purpose*."

"The staff are very discreet."

"Well, apparently we're not."

"God, you feel good."

She couldn't help stealing another glance toward the staircase. "I'm completely naked."

He chuckled low. "We just gave in, broke all our promises, consummated our marriage, and you're worried because somebody *might* have seen us?"

"Yes," she admitted in a small voice. She hadn't really had time to think about the consummation angle. More that they had, foolishly, given in to their physical attraction.

"You're delightful," he told her.

"That sounded patronizing."

"Did it?" His voice dropped to a sensual hush, and his mouth moved in on hers. "Because patronizing is the last thing I'm feeling right now."

His kiss was long and deep and thorough. And by the time he drew back, the pulse of arousal was starting all over in her body. She wanted him. Still.

"Again?" he asked, nibbling at her ear, his palm sliding up her rib cage toward her breast.

"Not here." She didn't want to risk it again.

"Okay by me." He gently eased himself from her body, flicked the button to close his pants, then lifted her solidly into the cradle of his arms and headed for the staircase to his bedroom.

"My robe," she protested.

"You won't need it."

Zach held Kaitlin naked in his arms, inhaling the coconut scent of her hair, reveling in the silk of her smooth skin beneath his fingertips. A sheet half covered them, but his quilts had long since been shoved off the king-size bed.

"This is gorgeous," she breathed, one hand wrapped around the ornately carved bedpost, as she gazed up at the scrollwork on his high ceiling.

"*This* is gorgeous," he corrected, stroking his way across her smooth belly to the curve of her hip bone.

She looked great in his bed, her shimmering, auburn hair splayed across his pillowcase, her ivory skin glowing against his gold silk sheets.

"I never knew people lived like this." She captured his hand that had wandered to her thigh, giving his palm a lingering kiss.

"It took me a while to figure out some people didn't," he admitted.

She released his hand and came up on one elbow. "Were you by any chance a spoiled child?"

"I wouldn't call it spoiled." He couldn't stop touching her, so he ran his palm over the curve of her hip, tracing down her shapely thigh to the tender skin behind her knee. "But I was about five before I realized everybody didn't have their own castle."

Kaitlin's eyes clouded, and she went silent.

He wanted to prompt her, but he forced himself to stay silent.

She finally spoke in a small voice. "I was about five when I realized most people had parents."

Her words shocked him to the core, and his hand stilled in its exploration. "You grew up without parents?"

She nodded, rolling to her back, a slow blink camouflaging the emotion in her eyes.

"What happened?" he asked, watching her closely.

"My mom died when I was born. She had no relatives that I ever found."

"Katie," he breathed, not knowing what else to say, his heart instantly going out to her.

She'd never mentioned her family. So he'd assumed they weren't close. He thought maybe they lived in another part of the country, Chicago perhaps, or maybe California.

"She either didn't know, or didn't say who my father was." Kaitlin made a square shape in the air with both hands. "Unknown. That's what it says on my birth certificate. Father—unknown."

Zach's hand clenched convulsively where it rested on her hip.

"I never knew," he said. Though he realized the statement was meaningless. Of course he never knew. Then again, he'd never asked. Because he hadn't wanted to know anything about her personal life. He simply wanted to finish off their business and have her gone.

Now, he felt like a heel.

"I used to wonder who she was," Kaitlin mused softly, half to herself. "A runaway princess. An orphan. Maybe a prostitute." Then her voice grew stronger, a trace of wry humor in its depths.

"Perhaps I'm descended from a hooker and her customer. What do you suppose that means?"

Zach brushed a lock of her hair back from her forehead. "I think it means you have a vivid imagination."

"It could be true," Kaitlin insisted.

"I suppose." Since the idea didn't seem to upset her, his fingertips went back to tracing a pattern on her stomach. "I guess I'm the rouge pirate, and you're the soiled dove." He brushed his knuckles against the skin beneath her bare breast. "Just so you know. That's working for me."

She lifted a pillow and halfheartedly thwacked him in the side of the head. "Everything seems to work for you."

"Only when it comes to you." He tossed the pillow out of the way, acknowledging the words were completely true. He leaned up and gently stroked her face. "Were you adopted?"

She was silent for a long moment, while her clouded jade eyes put a hundred lonely images into his brain. He regretted the question, but he couldn't call it back.

"Foster homes," she finally told him.

The simple words made his chest thump with regret. He thought back to all the heirlooms he'd shown her. The family history. The portraits, the cemetery.

"I'm so sorry," he told her. "I can't believe I threw my castle up in your face."

"You didn't know," she repeated.

"I wish I had."

"Well, *I* wish I'd grown up in a castle." Her spunk was back, and the strength of character surprised and impressed him. "But that's the way it goes," she concluded.

"We had extra rooms and everything," he teased in an attempt to keep things light.

"Could you not have come and found me sooner?"

He sobered, completely serious. "I wish I had."

Her grin slowly faded, but not to sadness.

His own want growing, he shifted forward and kissed her lips, drawing her tenderly but fully into his arms again, feeling aroused and protective all at the same time. "Was it awful?" he had to risk asking.

"It was lonely," she whispered into the crook of his neck. Then she coughed out a laugh and arched away. "I can't believe I'm telling this to you…*you* of all people."

"What about me?" He couldn't help feeling vaguely hurt.

"You're the guy who's ruining my life."

"Huh?"

She glanced around his room and spread her arms wide. "What the hell have we done?"

"We're married," he responded.

"By *Elvis*." She suddenly clambered out of bed.

He didn't want her to go, couldn't let her go.

"My robe?" she asked.

"Downstairs."

She swore.

"You don't have to leave," he pointed out. She could stay here, sleep here, lay here in his arms all night long.

She turned to face him, still naked, still glorious, still the most amazing person he'd ever met.

"This was a mistake," she told him in no uncertain terms.

He climbed out the opposite side of the bed to face her. "It may have made things a little more complicated," he conceded.

"A *little* more complicated?"

"Nothing needs to change."

"Everything just changed." She spotted his shirt, discarded on the floor, and scooped it up. "We never should have given into chemistry, Zach. Just so you know, this doesn't mean you have an advantage over me."

"What?" He wasn't following her logic.

"I have to call Lindsay." She glanced around the room. "She's probably downstairs. She's probably wondering where the heck I've gone."

"Lindsay's not downstairs," Zach announced with certainty.

Kaitlin pulled his big shirt over her head. "How would you know that?"

Zach made his way around the foot of the bed. "Lindsay's not coming back here tonight."

"But—" Kaitlin stilled. After a second, she seemed to correctly interpret the meaningful look in his eyes. "Really?"

"Really."

"You sure they did?"

"Oh, I'm sure." Zach had known Dylan his entire life. He'd seen the way Dylan looked at Lindsay. He'd also seen the way Lindsay looked back.

Kaitlin still seemed skeptical. "She said she wouldn't sleep with him until he admitted he was a pirate."

Zach barked out a laugh at an absurd memory. "I guess that explains it."

"Explains what?"

"The Jolly Roger flying over the pool house."

Kaitlin fought a grin and lost. "I want my ten bucks."

He moved closer, desperate to take her back into his arms. "Katie, you can have anything you want."

She gazed up at him. "I want to renovate your building. My way." Then she paused, tilting her head. "This has been a recorded message."

"I guess adding the condition that you sleep with me to seal the deal would be inappropriate?"

"And illegal."

"I'm a pirate, what the hell do I care about legal?"

She didn't answer him, but she didn't move away, either.

He curled his hands into fists to keep from touching her. "Sleep with me, Katie."

She hesitated, and he held his breath.

Her gaze darted in all directions, while her teeth trapped her bottom lip.

He was afraid to push, afraid not to.

Finally, he tossed caution to the wind, reaching out, snagging a handful of his shirt, drawing her to him and wrapping her deep in his arms. "I can't let you go yet."

Maybe tomorrow. Maybe never.

* * *

"It was the best pie I have *ever* tasted," Lindsay said to Kaitlin, her voice bubbling through the Gilby kitchen while Ginny scooped flour into a big steel bowl.

"My grandmother taught me that recipe," said Ginny, wiping her hands on a voluminous white apron that covered her red-and-white polka-dot dress. She had red-heeled pumps to match, and a spray of lace and plastic cherries was pinned into her hair as a small hat.

Kaitlin was fairly certain Ginny thought it was 1952.

"It's the chill on the lard, you know," Ginny continued her instructions, seeming to be in her element with the two younger women as baking students. "You need the temperature, the cutting, the mixing. Half in first. Like this."

"Do you refrigerate it?" asked Kaitlin, glancing from the stained recipe card to the bowl, watching Ginny's hands closely as they mixed the ingredients. She and Lindsay had been given the task of cutting and peeling apples and floating them in a bowl of cold water.

Ginny giggled. "That's the secret, girls." She lowered her voice, glancing around as if to make sure they were alone in the big Gilby kitchen. "We keep it in the wine cellar."

Lindsay grinned at Kaitlin, and Kaitlin grinned right back, thoroughly enjoying herself. Nobody had ever taught her to bake before. She'd watched a few cooking shows, and sometimes made cupcakes from a mix, but mostly she bought Sugar Bob's and she sure never had a sweet old lady walk her through a traditional family recipe.

"Best way to trap a man," said Ginny. "Feed him a good pie."

"Were you ever married?" asked Kaitlin. Ginny used the Gilby last name, but that might not mean anything. And she certainly seemed obsessed with getting men.

"Me?" Ginny scoffed. "No. Never."

"But you make such a great pie," Lindsay joked. "I would think you'd have to fight them off with a stick."

"Keep peeling," Ginny admonished her. "There's also the sex, you know."

Lindsay looked confused. "But yesterday you said we weren't supposed to—"

Ginny's sharp glare cut her off. "You didn't have sex with him, did you?"

"No, ma'am."

Kaitlin shot Lindsay an expression of disbelief.

Lindsay returned a warning squint.

"Good girl," said Ginny, smiling all over again. "That was my problem. Always slept with them, never married them."

"You had lovers?" The question jumped out of Kaitlin before she could censor it. When Ginny was young, lovers must have been something scandalous.

"Dustin Cartwell," said Ginny on a sigh, getting a faraway look in her eyes as she dreamily cut the lard and shortening into the flour mixture inside the bowl. "And Michael O'Conner. Phillip Magneson. Oh, and that Anderson boy, Charlie."

"Go, Ginny," sang Lindsay.

"Never met one I wanted to keep," said Ginny with a shake of her white-haired head. "They fart, you know. Drop their underwear on the floor. And the snoring? Don't get me started on the snoring." She added another scoop of lard. "Now, we'll be making this half into chunks the size of peas. Keeps it flaky."

Kaitlin met Lindsay's gaze again, her body shaking with suppressed laughter. Ginny was an absolute blast.

Her attention abruptly off men and sex, and back onto the baking, she let each of them cut in some of the lard, then she showed them how to sprinkle on the water, keeping everything chilled. They rolled out the dough, cut it into pie pans, mixed the apples with cinnamon, sugar and corn starch, then made a latticework top.

In the end, both Kaitlin and Lindsay slid decent-looking pies into the oven.

"You don't want to be sharing that with Zachary," Ginny warned Kaitlin. Then she paused, a flash of confusion crossing her face. "Oh, my. You married him, didn't you?"

"I did," Kaitlin admitted. And after last night, the marriage was feeling frighteningly real.

Ginny patted her on the arm. "Wish you'd come and talked with me first."

"Is there something wrong with Zach?" Kaitlin couldn't help but ask. Ginny had been alluding to Zach's lack of desirability since they arrived.

"Those Harper boys are heartbreakers," said Ginny with a disapproving click of her tongue. "Always have been, always will be."

Kaitlin had to admit, she could easily see Zach breaking hearts. He'd been darn near perfect last night. He'd driven through the dark to rescue her from a storm, then made exquisite love to her, teased her and sympathized with her. If a woman were to let herself fall for a man like that, heartbreak might well be the inevitable outcome.

Ginny turned to Lindsay. "Now, my Dylan. That one's a catch. He's wealthy, you know."

"I do have my own money," said Lindsay.

Ginny chuckled and gave a coquettish smile. "A girl can never have too much money."

Lindsay was obviously puzzled. "You don't mind me marrying your great-nephew for his money?"

Ginny looked askance. "What other reason is there?"

Lindsay's brows went up. "Love?"

"Oh, pooh, pooh." Ginny waved a dismissive hand. "Love comes and goes. A bank balance, now there's something a gal can count on."

"Your lovers didn't have money?" Kaitlin asked, fascinated by Ginny's experiences and opinions.

A sly look entered Ginny's eyes, and once again she glanced around the kitchen as if checking for eavesdroppers. "They had youth and enthusiasm. I think they wanted *my* money."

"Do you have any pictures?" asked Lindsay, obviously as interested as Kaitlin in the older woman's love life.

"Indeed, I do." Ginny wiped her hands on the big apron,

untying it from the back. Then she beckoned both women to follow her as she made her way toward the kitchen door.

In the stairwell, Kaitlin asked, "Did the other Harper men break women's hearts?"

"Every single one," Ginny confirmed with a decisive nod.

"But not their wives." Kaitlin's tone turned the statement into a question.

"Sometimes their wives, too."

"What about Sadie? Wasn't Sadie happy with Milton?"

"Milton was a fine man. He'd have made a good lover. But once they were married, Sadie, she worried all the time."

"That he was unfaithful?" asked Kaitlin.

Ginny stopped midstair and turned on her. "Oh, no. A Harper man would never be unfaithful." She turned and began climbing again.

"Then why did Sadie worry?"

"She was the groundskeeper's daughter. Oh, she pretended all right. But at her heart, she was never the mistress of the castle. That's why she wouldn't make any changes."

They came to the second floor, and Ginny led them down a wide hallway. Overhead skylights let in the sunshine, while art objects lined the shelves along the way.

"The castle is really beautiful," said Kaitlin. She wasn't sure she'd have changed anything, either.

"So was Sadie," said Ginny in a wistful voice. "Before Milton, we swam naked in the ocean and ran across the sand under the full moon."

"Do you really think he broke her heart?" Kaitlin persisted. Like Emma, Kaitlin really wanted to believe Sadie had been happy here.

"No. Not really. But sometimes she felt trapped, and sometimes she worried." Ginny swept open the double doors of a closet. She moved aside a fluffy quilt and extracted a battered shoebox, opening it to reveal a stack of photographs. "Ah, here we are. Come meet my lovers."

Nine

Zach found Kaitlin in the portrait gallery, gazing at a painting of his grandmother when she had been in her twenties.

"Hey," he said, coming up behind her. He didn't ask and didn't wait for permission before wrapping his arms around her waist, nestling her into the cradle of his body.

"Do you think she was happy?" Kaitlin asked.

"Yes."

"Did she love your grandfather?"

"As far as I could tell." He hadn't spent much time looking at the portraits over the past years, and his memory of his grandmother was that of an old woman. He'd forgotten how lovely she was. No wonder his grandfather had married her so young.

"Ginny says she felt trapped sometimes."

"I love Ginny dearly," Zach began, a warning in his tone.

There was a thread of laughter in Kaitlin's voice when she interrupted him. "She doesn't seem too crazy about you."

"But you know she's not all there, right?"

"She's a blast," Kaitlin responded. "And her memory seems very sharp."

"Well, it had to be a pretty big cage. They went to Europe at least twice a year, and spent half their time in Manhattan. You should have seen the garden parties. The governor, theatre stars, foreign diplomats."

"Okay, so it was a big cage," Kaitlin conceded.

"Come here. Let me show you something." Zach shifted his arm around her shoulders, guiding her down the gallery toward the staircase.

"Your room?" she asked.

"No. But I like the way you're thinking." He steered her down to the first floor then back through the hallways to Sadie's parlor.

"What are we doing?"

"I want to show you that she was happy."

He sat Kaitlin on the settee and retrieved an old photo album from Sadie's bookcase. Sitting next to her, he flipped through the pages until he came to one of the Harpers' famous garden parties. The pictures were black and white, slightly faded, but they showed the gardens in their glory, and the sharp-dressed upper crust of New York nibbling finger sandwiches and chatting away the afternoon.

"That's her." Zach pointed to his grandmother in a flowing dress and a silk flower-brimmed hat. Her smile was bright, and Zach's grandfather Milton had a hand tucked against the small of her back.

"She does look happy," Kaitlin was forced to admit.

"And that's a hedge, not prison bars," said Zach.

Kaitlin elbowed him in the ribs. "The bars are metaphorical."

"The hedge is real. So were the trips to Europe."

Kaitlin flipped the page, coming to more party photos, people laughing, drinking punch, playing croquet and wandering through the rose garden. There was a band in the gazebo, and a few couples were dancing on the patio. Some of the pictures showed children playing.

"That's my father," said Zack, smiling to himself as he pointed out the five-year-old boy in shorts, a white shirt and suspenders standing next to the duck pond. He had a rock in his hand, and one of his shoes was missing. He looked as if he was seconds away from wading after the ducks.

Kaitlin chuckled softly. "Were you anything like that as a child?"

Zach rose to retrieve another album.

"Here." He let her open it and page her way through the pictures of him as a young child.

"You were adorable," she cooed, moving from his toddler pictures to preschool to Zach at five years old, digging up flower bulbs, dirt smeared across his face and clothes.

"Yeah, let's go with adorable."

"Did you get into trouble for that?"

"I would guess I did. Probably from Grandma Sadie. Those gardens were her pride and joy."

"I never had a garden," said Kaitlin, and Zach immediately felt guilty for showing her the album. He'd done it again, parading out his past and his relatives without giving a thought to the contrast with her life.

"I bet you stayed cleaner than I did," he said, making a weak attempt at a joke.

"Once I realized—" She paused, gripping the edge of the album. "Hoo. I'm not going to do that." She turned another page.

"Do what?"

"Nothing." Her attention was focused on a series of shots of the beach and a picnic.

"Katie?"

"Nothing."

He gently removed the album from her hands. "I upset you."

"No, you didn't."

"Liar."

She straightened her shoulders. "It was hard, okay."

"I know."

"No, you don't."

"You're right. I don't." He folded the book closed and set it on the table beside him. "I'm sorry I showed you the photos. It was thoughtless."

"Don't worry about it."

"What were you going to say?"

She pasted him with a look of impatience.

"I've got all night to wait," he warned her, sitting back and making a show of getting comfortable.

She clenched her jaw, looking mulish, and he prepared himself for a contest of wills.

But then her toughness disappeared, and she swallowed. Then she closed her eyes for a second. "I was going to say…"

Part of him wanted to retract the question. But another part of him wanted to know, *needed* to know what she'd gone through as a child.

"I was going to say," she repeated, sounding small and fragile, "once I realized people could give me away." Her voice cracked. "I tried to be very, very good."

Zach honestly thought his heart was going to break.

He wrapped an arm around her and drew her close. She felt so tiny in his arms, so vulnerable. He hated that she'd been alone as a child.

"I'm sorry, Katie," he whispered against her hair.

She shook her head back and forth. "It's not your fault."

He drew a deep breath. "You've been alone for a very long time."

"I'm used to it."

But she wasn't. She couldn't be. Nobody should have to get used to not having a family. Zach had lost his parents when he was twenty, and that had been devastating enough. He'd still had his grandmother, and he'd always had the Gilbys. And he'd had Aunt Ginny, who usually liked him very much.

"Look," said Kaitlin, pulling back and wiping a single tear from her cheek. "There's a full moon outside."

He twisted his head to look out the window. "Yeah?"

"You want to go skinny-dipping?" she asked.

"Yes," he answered without hesitation.

* * *

The salt water was chilly against Kaitlin's skin, but Zach's body felt deliciously warm. He held her flush against himself, her feet dangling just above the sandy bottom. Over his left shoulder, she could see the distant lights of the Gilby house. And when she turned her head the other way, she could see the Harper castle in all its glory.

The gardens were smaller than they were in the pictures, but they were still lit up at night. And an illuminated path wound its way from the edge of the garden to the sandy beach, where she and Zach had stripped off their clothes before plunging into the surf.

"Lindsay is talking about staying a few more days," Zach offered.

Kaitlin drew back to look at him. "With Dylan?" Lindsay hadn't said anything to her. Then again, she had spent most of her time at the Gilby house.

Zach's teeth flashed white under the moonlight. "I think they have worked out their differences."

"You mean Lindsay won," Kaitlin corrected. "Where's my ten dollars, by the way?"

"Dylan thinks he's the one who won."

"He totally caved."

"I don't think he cares."

"By the way, if Ginny asks, they're not having sex."

"Ohhh-kay," Zach slowly agreed.

"She'll probably ask," Kaitlin warned. "She's obsessed with Dylan's love life."

"I won't answer," Zach pledged.

"Good."

Neither Kaitlin nor Zach spoke for a few minutes. The cool waves bobbed their bodies, while the sound of the surf rushed up on the sand, punctuating the breeze that whispered through the bushes along the shoreline.

"You want to stay, too?" Zach asked softly, rocking her back and forth in his arms.

Kaitlin stilled against him, not sure what he was asking.

"With Lindsay?" he elaborated. "For a few days? You could work right from here?"

"What about you?" she asked, still wondering what he meant by the invitation. Was he asking her to stay on the island, or to stay with him?

"If you're staying?" A slow, sultry smiled curved his mouth, darkening his eyes to slate. "I'm sure not leaving."

Kaitlin's smile grew in return. "Okay."

"Yeah?"

"Yes."

He spun her in a circle, and she wrapped her legs around his waist, her hands gripping his shoulders for balance. His hold was tight under her bottom as she knifed through the water.

The moon glistened high in the sky, surrounded by layers of stars. They were the same stars that Lyndall had used to navigate his way to the island hundreds of years ago. The same stars that Sadie had gazed at as a girl and as a woman, a mother.

Zach slowed and stopped, the waves now the only motion around them. Kaitlin gazed at the lighted gardens that Sadie had so clearly loved. The woman had been the guardian of the castle, the keeper of the family's heritage. And because of her decisions, Kaitlin had been trusted with the Harper office building.

Zach nuzzled her neck.

The office building was much newer, of course. But Kaitlin couldn't help but believe the renovations would matter to Sadie. Maybe Zach was right. Maybe wholesale change wasn't such a great thing. Maybe Kaitlin had some kind of responsibility to his family.

Maybe she needed to rethink her approach.

"Zach?" she ventured.

"Hmm?" he asked, the vibration of his lips tickling the sensitized skin of her neck.

"Could you get me a copy of the Hugo Rosche plans?"

He drew back, brows going up. "Really?"

"Yes."

"Sure." He nodded, the nod growing faster. "Of course I could."

"I'm not making any promises," she warned him.

"I understand."

"I'm just going to look." She had no idea what she was going to do now. She still needed her career, which meant she needed a fantastic project for the Harper building. But maybe there was a compromise of some kind. She just didn't know.

A smile curved Zach's mouth. "No problem."

"I don't want you to get your hopes up."

"Oh, Katie." He planted a long, warm kiss on her damp mouth. He drew back, his grin wide as he smoothed her hair. "My hopes have been up for quite some time now."

She gave in to her desire for him, tipping her head and giving her lashes a few flirtatious blinks. "And what exactly are you hoping for?"

"You. Naked."

She made a show of glancing at their bodies. "I'm liking your chances."

"In my pirate's lair." He kissed her neck once more, then her jawline, her cheek, working his way to the corner of her mouth.

"Piece of advice, Zach?"

"Speed things up?" he asked hopefully, and she couldn't help but laugh.

"For future reference, that line will probably be a lot more successful if you refer to it as a castle instead of a lair."

His hand closed over her breast, peaked and sensitized in the cool, damp air.

She gasped at the sensation.

"Lair," he repeated on a growl.

"Fine. Yes. Whatever."

Three days later, Dylan's parents arrived, back from their business meetings in Chicago. And, as usual, they brought company.

Zach was happy to see them. David and Darcie were two of his favorite people in the world. After his parents died, they'd become even more important in his life. David was a brilliant businessman, while Darcie was the most loving and compassionate honorary aunt Zach could have wished for.

Still, he knew this meant the end of his interlude with Kaitlin. Dylan would never have a woman stay at the house with his parents there, and it was past time for Zach to get back to Manhattan.

"You weren't kidding about them having a few friends over," Kaitlin observed as they drove the golf cart the last quarter mile to the Gilbys' house. Music wafted from the open windows, and it was easy to see groups of people circulating on the deck.

"What are the Gilbys like?"

"David's savvy, hardworking, a great guy to go to for advice. Darcie's friendly, gregarious. You'll like her."

"What will she think of me…?" Kaitlin's voice trailed off on the half-finished question.

He put his hand over hers. "We can let her think whatever you like." He paused, but Kaitlin didn't step in and offer a suggestion. "How about a business associate and a friend?" he asked.

Kaitlin accepted with a smile.

Zach fought a shot of disappointment, but he let it slide. He didn't want people to think Kaitlin was his business associate. He wanted them to think… He paused. What? That she was his lover? His girlfriend? His wife? His hands gripped tighter on the steering wheel. He was going to have to figure it out. Not right this minute, of course. But soon.

"Lindsay will probably stay at my place for the night," he told Kaitlin. "When it's only Ginny, well, she'd never notice. But with his parents, Dylan doesn't…"

"I understand," Kaitlin said, nodding easily.

Zach hoped Lindsay would react the same way.

Then again, that was Dylan's problem. Zach's problem was figuring out where things were left with him and Kaitlin.

Would they continue seeing each other in Manhattan? He had quickly grown used to waking up with her every morning. He liked having her around for breakfast, reconnecting over dinner. Hell, he wasn't even sure he wanted to sign the damn divorce papers anymore.

Of course, that was ridiculous.

Luckily, that decision was months away.

He glanced at Kaitlin's profile, taking in her pert nose, those gorgeous green eyes, the spray of freckles that had come out in the sun. And, of course, her wild, coconut-scented auburn hair that he buried his face into every chance he got.

At the top of the driveway, he pressed the button to open the garage door, pulling the golf cart inside, unable to shake the feeling that something precious had just ended.

He stepped out and rounded the vehicle. Then he took Kaitlin's hand, leading her to the three steps and the doorway that would take them into the house and the party.

Unable to help himself, he stopped her there, cradled her face in his hands and kissed her thoroughly.

She responded, like she always did, soft lips parted, a light touch of her tongue meshing with his. Her breasts pressed up against his chest, and she came up on her toes to meet him partway. He loved that about her.

His arms tightened around her slender waist.

This wasn't goodbye, he told himself. She worked for him, with him. They'd both be in Manhattan. They would see each other at the office every day.

Hell, they were *married*. She couldn't just run off and disappear from his life. He'd find a way to keep her with him for a long time to come.

She pulled back. "You keep this up, and they're never going to believe we're business colleagues."

"We're husband and wife," he said gruffly.

She grinned and playfully swiped her index finger across the tip of his nose. "We're pretty much faking everything here, aren't we, Zach?"

He opened his mouth to protest, but she turned away, skipping up the stairs, opening the door and ending the moment.

He quickly trapped the door with his hand before it could swing shut. Music chimed from the sound system, while chattering voices spilled from the deck into the great room. All the staff members were working, impeccably dressed and serving drinks or circulating with appetizers.

Zach knew the kitchen would be a hive of activity. He also knew Ginny would be in her element, visiting with guests into the evening until she gave in to exhaustion. He saw Kaitlin heading toward Lindsay on the deck and started after her.

"Zach," came David's booming voice. "Great to see you at home, son."

"Welcome back, sir." Zach shook his hand.

"You remember Kevin O'Connor." David gestured to a fiftyish gentleman with a three-olive martini in his hand.

"Swiss International Bank," Zach acknowledged, shaking again, checking for Kaitlin out the corner of his eye.

"Kevin has a client," David began. "He's out of Hong Kong, and he's got mining interests in Canada and South America."

"I see," Zach said, dutifully focusing his attention. Mining companies were massive shippers; ore was both heavy and voluminous. And a Hong Kong client likely had access to the mainland China market. Zach's personal life would have to go on hold for a moment.

The moment turned into half an hour. A drink was put into Zach's hand, and a third man joined them, a friend of Kevin's with an interest in manufacturing.

By the time the conversation wound down, Kaitlin was nowhere to be found. Neither was Lindsay.

He managed to track down Dylan, who was with Ginny, then he was rewarded when he heard Kaitlin's voice from behind him.

"You must be enjoying the party," she offered breezily to Ginny, who was decked out in chiffon and diamonds, a folded, lace fan in her hand and her dogs at her feet in rhinestone collars.

"And who is this young lady?" Ginny asked in an imperious tone. She leaned toward Kaitlin. "Are you here with my grandson? He's a catch, you know."

Zach turned in time to see Kaitlin's surprise morph into obvious disappointment.

"I'd stay away from this one," said Ginny, tapping Zach's arm with the fan. "He's a reprobate and a heartbreaker."

Kaitlin's eyes clouded to jade.

"Auntie—" Dylan stepped in "—this is Kaitlin Saville and Lindsay Rubin."

"Pretty," Ginny acknowledged with a gracious sweep of her fan.

"Kaitlin is my architect," said Zach.

Ginny looked at him, eyes clouding with puzzlement. "Are you changing the castle? Does Sadie know?"

There was an instant and awkward silence.

Zack had been through this before, about a dozen times so far, but it never got any easier.

He gently took Ginny's hand and lowered his tone. "Aunt Ginny, do you remember that Sadie passed away?"

Ginny drew back warily. Then she gave herself a little shake. "Of *course* I remember. I meant…" Her voice trailed off.

Dylan stepped in again. "Auntie, would you like to dance?"

Ginny snapped him with her fan, seeming to recover. "I'm too old to dance. People my age are dropping like flies." Her attention turned to Lindsay. "You should dance with my grandson. He has a lot of money."

Darcie joined the circle, and Zach took the opportunity to whisk Kaitlin away.

"You okay?" he asked as they made their way out onto the deck. The sun had set, and the lights were coming on all over the grounds. The music seemed to swell louder, and the conversation grew more animated as the guests consumed martinis, wine and single malt.

"She didn't remember me at all." Sadness was clear in Kaitlin's tone as they came to the rail.

"She will," Zach promised, not sure if he was lying or not. Ginny's early memories were her best. Recent events often escaped her.

"She taught me to bake pie." Kaitlin's voice was stilted. She leaned her arms on the railing and stared out at the ocean. "Nobody ever taught me to bake before. I was starting to think…"

She paused, then tried a lukewarm smile. "I'm being silly. She's old. Of course she forgets things. You were great."

"I didn't do anything."

"How many times have you had to tell her about your grandmother?"

"A few," Zach admitted. And he was sure that previous one wouldn't be the last. He stared at the lights at his place, wishing they were down there right now.

"Kaitlin?" Ginny's voice surprised Zach. "There you are, dear." She sidled up to Kaitlin, glancing warily around them, her voice becoming conspiratorial. "I've changed my mind."

Kaitlin's smile was bright as she blinked away the telltale sheen in her eyes. "You have?"

"That nice girl, Lindsay?"

Kaitlin nodded, and Zach smiled in relief.

"I think she should sleep with Dylan."

"What?"

Ginny placed a hand on Kaitlin's arm. "Hear me out." Then she turned and gave Zach a censorious look. "Excuse us please, Zachary. The women would like to talk."

Zach held his palms up in surrender and backed away.

He circulated through the party a little, and then Dylan caught up with him outside David's study and herded him inside to where they were alone.

Dylan seemed agitated. He crossed to the small bar and poured himself a scotch. "You okay to take Lindsay down with you tonight?"

"No problem."

Dylan waggled a second, empty glass, raising his brow to Zach in question.

"Sure," Zach answered, walking farther into the room, the noise of the party fading behind him through the open door.

"I haven't told her yet," Dylan confessed, handing Zach a crystal tumbler of single malt then taking a sip from his own.

"You need my help?"

Dylan shook his head, moving to the bay window. "She'll be disappointed. At least, I hope she'll be disappointed. But she's a trouper. She really is, Zach. She's quite the little trouper." He took another sip.

Zach moved closer. "Are you okay?"

"Sure. Fine. Why?"

Zach had never seen Dylan act this way, not over a woman, not over anything. "Something going on between you and Lindsay? I mean, other than the obvious?"

"What's the obvious?"

Treading on unfamiliar ground, Zach chose his words carefully. "A physical…connection?"

"Oh, yeah. That."

"But there's more," Zach guessed.

Dylan shot him a look that questioned his sanity, but Zach had no idea how to interpret it. Was there something serious going on between Dylan and Lindsay? Had he made her angry again?

"I should warn you," said Zach, stepping into the silence. "Aunt Ginny is out there advising Lindsay to sleep with you."

Dylan stilled. *"What?"*

"I assume it's to trap you into marriage. You might want to watch your back."

"I don't think it's my back that needs watching," Dylan muttered.

"You don't seem too worried."

Dylan shrugged.

Zach watched his friend's expression carefully. "Seriously, Dylan. Is there something going on between you two?"

Dylan frowned. "I'm not saying there is."

"Are you saying there's not?"

Dylan compressed his lips. "What about you and Kaitlin?" he asked, turning the tables.

"Nothing," Zach lied, perching on the arm of an overstuffed leather chair. He wasn't ready to talk to anybody about his relationship with Kaitlin. He didn't even have it straight in his own mind yet.

"You're sleeping with her," said Dylan.

Zach shot him a pointed look. "That's just…" In fact, Zach wasn't sure exactly what it was. Somehow his physical attraction to Kaitlin, their renovation battle and their mock marriage had all meshed together in a way that was well past confusing.

"Sex?" Dylan asked bluntly.

"It's not relevant," said Zach.

"What about the renovation? Is that relevant? You haven't forgotten why she's here, have you?"

"No, I haven't forgotten why she's here."

Dylan took another drink. "So, the plan's working?"

"It's going great," Zach admitted, trying to inject some enthusiasm for how well things were working out for him on that front. "She asked for the Hugo Rosche plans. She's been using them for the past few days. And, well, I think she's getting that Grandma Sadie wasn't progressive and flamboyant. And she's figuring it out for herself, which is exactly what we wanted."

"So, your devious little scheme is coming together in spades," Dylan summed up.

"It was *your* devious little scheme."

"You approved it," Dylan noted. "You implemented it. And it looks like you'll save yourself a bundle."

"I did," Zach agreed. Too bad saving a bundle didn't seem so important anymore. Too bad he'd started to wish he *could* give Kaitlin her dream project, unlimited funds, unfettered imagination.

"I think we've heard just about enough," Lindsay's lawyer voice cut in.

Zach whirled, nearly spilling his drink.

In the study's open doorway stood Kaitlin, her face completely pale.

Lindsay's face was beet-red.

Dylan had turned to a statue.

"You—" Lindsay pointed to Dylan, anger quaking deep in her voice "—scheming little pirate-boy. You take us back to Manhattan, right this minute."

Ten

The next afternoon, Kaitlin struggled to forget the entire weekend. If she chalked up her experience on Serenity Island to yet another childish fantasy where she found a family and lived happily ever after, she could cope with the way Zach had systematically and deliberately ripped her heart out.

It wasn't real.

It had never been real.

Working from her apartment, she'd gone back to her original renovation designs, ignoring the twinges of guilt when she thought about Ginny and Sadie and what they might think of what she was doing to the Harpers' Manhattan building.

This wasn't about Sadie, nor was it about the Harper and Gilby families. This was about Kaitlin, and her career, and her ability to stand on her own two feet and take care of herself every second of every day for the rest of her life.

So despite the knowledge that Sadie was unlikely to approve of the three extra floors, the five-story lobby, the saltwater aquarium and the palm trees, those features were staying, every single one of them. And she'd added a helipad. Who knew when Dylan would want to drop in?

She'd even thought about replacing the fountains in the lobby with a two-story waterfall. In fact, she was still considering it.

It was halfway through the afternoon, and her legs were starting to cramp. She rose from her computer, crossing the living room to the kitchen, snagging her second Sugar Bob's doughnut. She knew they were becoming an addiction. But she promised herself she'd add an extra half hour at the gym every day, and she'd kick the habit completely just as soon as the Harper building renovation was complete.

A woman could only handle so many things at once. She took a big bite.

There was a rap on her door, so she ditched the doughnut in the box and tossed the box back into her cupboard, wiping the powdered sugar from her lips.

For a split second she wondered if it might be Zach. Then, just as quickly, she promised herself she wouldn't open the door if it was.

She wouldn't.

She had absolutely nothing left to say to the man.

But when she checked through the peephole, it was Lindsay standing in the hallway. Kaitlin opened the door to find her friend balancing a large Agapitos pizza box on one hand and holding a bottle of tequila in the other.

"Pepperoni and sausage," Lindsay said without preamble, walking forward as Kaitlin opened the door up wide and shifted out of the way. "I hope you have limes."

It was only three-thirty. Somewhat early to start in on margaritas, but the day was already a nutritional bust, so what the hell?

"How are you holding up?" asked Lindsay as she crossed to the small kitchen table while Kaitlin shut and latched the apartment door.

"I am absolutely fine," said Kaitlin, her determination putting a spring in her step as she squared her shoulders.

"You are a terrible liar," Lindsay countered.

That was true enough. But Kaitlin also knew that if she said something loud enough and often enough, sometimes it started to feel true.

Kaitlin headed for the fridge, reciting the words she'd rehearsed in her mind. "So it turned out to be a con. It wasn't like we didn't expect it to be one. Zach was fighting to save money. I was fighting for my career. Our positions were incompatible from the get-go." She paused, taking a moment to regroup her emotions. "Though I have to admit, I didn't expect him to be quite so good."

She tugged open the fridge door, fighting to keep her voice even, but not doing a particularly good job. "Still, I was colossally stupid to have fallen for his act. I mean, didn't you and I call it almost to the detail before we left?"

"I never thought he'd take it as far as he did," Lindsay ventured from behind her.

"I did," said Kaitlin with a decisive nod as she bent to scoop a couple of limes from the crisper drawer. "He was trying to use sex as an advantage all along."

She'd known that. And she had no idea why she'd let herself sink so far into a ridiculous fantasy. She'd figured it out, yet in four short days he had her convinced to do exactly what he'd wanted with the renovations, and she was romping wantonly in his bed every night to boot.

Stupid move.

She snagged the limes.

Yesterday she'd been angry.

This morning she'd been heartbroken.

Right now, she was more embarrassed than anything.

"What about you?" she asked Lindsay, making up her mind to quit talking about it as she closed the fridge.

"What about me?" Lindsay had perched herself on one of the stools at the small breakfast bar with the pizza box in front of her.

Kaitlin set the limes down on the countertop and pulled a long, sharp knife out of the wooden block. "What about you and Dylan?"

"There is no me and Dylan."

"There was yesterday."

Lindsay gave her blond hair a quick toss. "He's dead to me."

"I like that," Kaitlin said defiantly, slicing into a lime. It sounded so unemotional and final.

"Have you heard anything from Zach?" Lindsay asked.

Kaitlin squeezed half a lime into the blender as she shook her head. "If I see his number, I'll hang up. And if he drops by, I won't answer the door."

"What about the renovation?"

Kaitlin emphasized her words by pointing the knife tip to her computer on the dining table. "I am doing my full-blown design. I'm adding a helipad and a waterfall. It'll be fabulous. I'll probably win an award."

Lindsay flipped open the cardboard box, folding it back to reveal the gooey, fragrant pizza. "I can't believe they turned out to be such rats."

"Dead-to-us rats," Kaitlin stated, fighting to keep her emotions in check over the thought of never seeing Zach again.

Why had she let herself trust him? Did she think he'd love her, really marry her, have babies with her and turn her life into some fantasy?

She was Kaitlin Saville, penniless orphan. Things like that didn't happen to her.

Lindsay tore a bite from one of the pizza slices and popped it into her mouth. "You thought he was the one?" she ventured softly.

Suddenly exhausted, Kaitlin set down the knife. "Stupid of me, I know."

"It's not your fault."

"It's all my fault."

"He played you."

"And I let him. I encouraged him. I helped him. And now all I have left is revenge."

"Revenge can be satisfying," said Lindsay. "Especially when it's going to save your career."

"I don't want revenge," Kaitlin responded with blunt honesty, turning to squeeze the other half of the lime into the blender. "I hate revenge. I feel like I'm getting revenge against Sadie instead of Zach." She dropped the lime peel and braced herself against the countertop.

She knew she couldn't do it.

She couldn't spend Harper money on a design she knew Sadie would hate. Her laugh sounded more like a cry.

"Katie?" Lindsay was up and rounding the breakfast bar.

"I'm fine," Kaitlin sniffed. But she wasn't fine. She was about to give up her career and her future for a family that wasn't even hers.

"Don't you love it when you know you've been a jerk?" Dylan asked, cupping his hands behind his head and stretching back in the padded chair next to Zach's office window.

Zach was standing, too restless to sit down while his mind struggled to settle on a course of action.

"I mean," Dylan continued, "sometimes you're not sure. But other times, like this, you're positive you've been a complete ass."

Zach folded his arms across his chest, watching the clouds streak across the sky far away over the Jersey shore. "Are you talking about me or you?"

"I'm talking about both of us."

Zach turned. He didn't know about Dylan's behavior, but he maintained that he'd been put in an untenable position. He never set out to hurt anyone. He was only trying to do right by his company and his family.

"And what should I have done differently?" he demanded.

Dylan grinned at Zach's upset. "I don't know. Maybe you shouldn't have pretended you were married."

"I *am* married."

"I'm guessing not for long."

Zach shook his head. "She's not going to divorce me. It's her leverage."

At least he hoped Kaitlin wasn't going to divorce him yet. He wasn't ready for that.

Dylan crossed an ankle over one knee. "Conning her into scaling back the renovation was one thing. But you're not a heartless bastard, Zach. Why'd you mess with her emotions like that?"

Zach felt his anger rise. What he'd done with Kaitlin was none of Dylan's business. It was between him and Kaitlin. It was... They were...

"And what about you?" he queried, deflecting the question. "You slept with Lindsay."

"That was a simple fling."

"And what do you think I had?"

Dylan sat up straight. "I don't know, Zach. You tell me." His gaze moved meaningfully to the package of papers on the table between them.

"That's nothing," Zach denied. That was simply him being a decent human being, something which Dylan didn't seem to believe was possible.

"You put nine private investigators on the case."

"So?" Zach had wanted something fast. More men, better speed.

"So how did that benefit you?"

"It wasn't supposed to benefit me." It was meant to benefit Kaitlin, to put a smile on her face, to banish the haunted look that came into her eyes every time the subject of his family came up, which was nearly every second they were on Serenity Island.

But the effort had pretty much been a failure. Despite the high-end manpower, all he'd found of Kaitlin's heritage was a grainy old newspaper photo showing her grandparents and her mother as a young girl. The family home had burned down, killing the grandparents and destroying all of the family possessions when Kaitlin's mother was sixteen, two years before Kaitlin was born.

The picture, two names and a gravesite were all Zach had turned up.

"You still going to give them to her?" asked Dylan.

"Sure," said Zach, with a shrug, pretending it was no big deal. "Maybe I'll mail them over."

"Mail them?"

"Mail them."

"You don't want to see her in person?"

Zach bristled. "To do what? To say what? To let her yell at me again?" Truth was, he'd give anything to see Kaitlin again, even if it was only to hear her yell. But what was the point? He'd chewed up her trust and spit it out, over and over again.

"You could tell her you sold the ship."

"Big deal." So Zach had come up with seventy-five million dollars. It wasn't as if he had a choice. Kaitlin would be full steam ahead on the renovation again, and the only way he was going to get his company back was to give her the carte blanche she'd demanded. The only way to do that was to sell an asset. So he'd sold an asset. She wouldn't give him brownie points for doing that. "You think an old newspaper photo and money I had to give her all along are going to make a difference?"

"You gotta try, Zach."

"No, I don't."

"You're in love with her."

"No, I'm not."

Dylan coughed out a cold laugh and came to his feet. "You sorry son-of-a—"

"I am not in love with Kaitlin."

He liked Kaitlin. Sure, he liked Kaitlin. What was not to like?

And, yeah, he'd have stayed with her for the foreseeable future. He'd have woken up next to her for as long as she'd let him. And maybe for a few days there he'd entertained fantasies about what could happen between them long term.

But those were just fantasies. They had nothing to do with the real world.

In the real world, he and Kaitlin were adversaries. She'd wanted to save her career, and he'd wanted to keep his company intact. She'd won. He'd lost. Nothing to be done about it now but mop up after the fallout.

"I saw your face when she walked out," Dylan offered. "I've known you your whole life, Zach."

Zach turned on him. "You know *nothing.*"

"You're going to lie to me? That's your next big plan?"

"I don't have a next big plan."

"Well, you'd better come up with one. Or you're going to lose Kaitlin forever."

The words felt like a stake in Zach's heart.

He didn't love Kaitlin. He couldn't love Kaitlin. It would be a disaster to love Kaitlin.

He swallowed.

"What about you?" he asked Dylan.

"I already have a plan," Dylan stated with smug satisfaction. "And I don't even love Lindsay. I'm just not ready to let her go yet."

"That's how it starts," said Zach.

Dylan's brows shot up. "And you know this because…?"

"What's your plan?" Zach countered.

Okay, maybe he did love Kaitlin just a little bit. But he'd get over it.

"I'm kidnapping Lindsay. She wanted a pirate, she's getting a pirate. Can I borrow your yacht?"

"You can't kidnap her."

"Watch me."

Zach took in the determination in Dylan's eyes. And for a second there, he wished he could simply kidnap Kaitlin. If he could get her on board his yacht, he could probably keep her there for a few days, maybe even a few weeks. By the end of it, like Lyndall, he might be able to win her over.

On the other hand, she might have him arrested. Or she might throw him overboard. Or she might decide the Harper building needed to be a hundred stories high and truly bankrupt him.

Kidnapping was not a real option.

Instead, he'd give her the money. He'd give her the news clipping and the photo. Then, like the gentleman he'd once been, he'd step out of her life forever.

* * *

Three margaritas later, Kaitlin splashed cold water on her face in the small bathroom of her apartment. She and Lindsay had started to giggle about half an hour back, but now she found herself fighting tears.

It didn't seem to matter that Zach had played her for a fool. She'd fallen in love with him, and no matter how many times she told herself it was all a lie, she couldn't stop wanting the man she'd known on Serenity Island.

She dried her face and ran a comb through her hair, gathering her frayed emotions. Much as she wished she could drink herself into oblivion today, it was time to stop wallowing in self-pity and get her equilibrium back.

Her career in New York was over. Truthfully, she might as well walk away from the Harper project altogether. What Sadie and Zach would want wouldn't do a thing to save Kaitlin's career.

At least most of her boxes were still packed.

Another tear leaked out, and she impatiently swiped it away. She told herself she was tough, and she was strong, and she was independent. And she would salvage her life or die trying.

She left the bathroom at a determined pace, rounding the bedroom door into the living room. There, her steps staggered to a stop.

Zach stood in the middle of her apartment, large as life and twice as sexy.

She was too stunned to shriek, too stunned to cry, too stunned to do anything, but let her jaw drop open.

"Hello, Kaitlin."

She still didn't have her bearings. "Huh?"

"I came to apologize."

She glanced swiftly around the apartment. "Where's Lindsay? How did you—?"

"Lindsay left with Dylan."

Kaitlin gave her head a little shake, but she wasn't delusional. That really was Zach standing there. "Why would she do that?"

"He kidnapped her," said Zach. "I wouldn't expect to see her for a few days."

"He can't do that."

"That's what I said," Zach agreed. "But I don't think those two have ever cared much about the rules."

"Lindsay's a lawyer." Of course she cared about the rules. She was passionate about the rules.

Zach seemed to ponder that fact for a few moments. "Yeah," he conceded. "Dylan may have a bit of a problem with that when he brings her back."

"Is that a joke?" Was Lindsay about to jump out of the closet?

Instead of answering, Zach took a few steps forward. Her heart rate increased. Her chest went tight. And a low buzz started in the base of her belly.

She knew she should fight the reaction, but she had no idea how to turn it off.

"He took my yacht," said Zach, moving closer still, his gaze locked with hers every step of the way.

"So you're an accessory to kidnapping?" Her shock at the sight of him was starting to wear off, replaced by amazement that he was actually standing here in front of her. She could feel herself sink reluctantly back into the fantasy.

"Dylan told me she wanted a pirate, so she was getting a pirate."

"Is that why you're here?" she asked. "To help Dylan?"

"No."

"Then why?"

"Because I have something for you."

She forced herself to go cold and demanding. "I hope it's a big check." She knew she'd given up, abandoned the renovation, but Zach didn't need to know that yet.

"As a matter of fact, it is."

"Good." She gave a decisive nod, marveling at her own ability to hold her composure. The urge to throw herself into Zach's arms grew more powerful by the second.

"Seventy-five million dollars," he told her.

It took a few seconds for his words to sink in.

"What?" She took a reflexive step back.

"I sold a ship."

"What?"

"I'm giving you seventy-five million dollars for the renovation."

Kaitlin blinked at him.

"But that's not the real reason I'm here."

For a split second, hope flared within her. But she squelched it. Zach couldn't be trusted. She'd learned that the hard way half a dozen times over.

He handed her an envelope. "I'm here to give you this. It's not much."

Watching him warily, Kaitlin lifted the flap. She slid out a laminated picture. It showed a twentysomething couple with a young, blonde girl at the beach. The caption was *Holiday Travelers Enjoy Fourth of July Celebrations.*

She didn't understand.

"Phillipe and Aimee Saville," Zach said softly, and it felt as if Kaitlin's heart stopped.

"It was the best I could do," he continued. "There was a house fire in 1983. None of their possessions were saved. But the private investigators found this in the archives of a New Jersey newspaper. The little girl is your mother."

Kaitlin was completely speechless.

Her grandparents?

Zach had found grandparents?

Zach had *looked* for her grandparents?

Her fingers reflexively tightened on the photograph, and she felt herself sway to one side.

Zach's hand closed around her shoulder, steadying her.

"I've had three margaritas," she told him, embarrassed. She ought to be completely sober for a moment like this.

"That explains why Lindsay went so quietly."

Kaitlin fought against the sensation of his touch, even as she struggled to make sense of his gesture. "How? Where?" *Why* had he done this?

"I had some people start looking last week. After you told me." His hand tightened on her shoulder. "And I couldn't stand to see the pain in your eyes."

Her throat closed tighter, and her chest burned with emotion. She had to blink back tears at his thoughtfulness. Her voice dropped to a pained whisper. "How am I supposed to hate you?"

He drew a deep breath. Then he closed his eyes for a long second. He reached out and gently smoothed her hair back from her forehead. "You're not."

His hand stayed there, resting against her hair. Her nerves tingled where he touched. Her body begged her to sway forward against him, even as her mind ordered her to hold still.

She couldn't trust him. She didn't trust him. Oh, my, how she wanted to trust him.

He stroked his way to her cheek, cupping her face, tilting his head at an angle she'd come to recognize, to love.

He was going to kiss her, just like he'd done a hundred times, maybe a thousand. His lips dipped closer, and she moistened her own. She inhaled his scent, and her body relaxed into the exquisite moment.

"You're not supposed to hate me," he repeated on a whisper. "You're supposed to love me."

Then, he paused with his lips just barely brushing hers. "Because I love you, Katie. I love you so much."

His mouth captured hers, sending joy cascading through her body. His kiss was deep, sweet and long. His arms wrapped fully around her, hauling her close, pulling her safely into the circle of his embrace.

She clung to him, molding against him, passion and joy making her feel weightless.

After long minutes, he finally drew back. "Renovate anything you want," he rasped. "I'll sell half the damn fleet if I have to. Just don't leave me again. Not ever."

"I gave up the new design," she told him.

He drew back. "What? Why?"

"Sadie wouldn't like it."

Zach stilled. "Sadie doesn't matter. The past doesn't matter. Only the future, Kaitlin. And you're the future. You're *my* future."

Kaitlin's heart soared at the thought of a future with Zach—such a loving, thoughtful man.

Her voice quavered as she spoke. "You found my grandparents."

"I did," he acknowledged. "I know they were buried in New Jersey."

"You know where they're buried?"

"Yes."

Twin tears rolled from Kaitlin's eyes at that. "Have I mentioned that I love you?"

"No." He shook his head. "You hadn't. And I was getting worried."

"Well, I do."

"Thank goodness." He drew a deep breath, tightening his arms around her. "I told Dylan to give me an hour. Otherwise, you were getting kidnapped, too."

"You would not."

"Hell, yes, I would. One way or another, you and I are starting on a whole new generation of Harper pirates."

Kaitlin smiled at his joke, her body sighing in contentment. "Sadie would be pleased."

"Yes, she would," Zach agreed. "She'd also be gloating over the success of her scheme. In fact, I can almost hear her chuckling from here."

Kaitlin moved her hand to take another look at the picture of her grandparents. Her grandfather was tall. Her grandmother slightly rounded with light, curly hair. And her mother looked bright-eyed and happy with a shovel and pail in her hands. "I can't believe you did this."

"We can go visit their graves." He paused. "I swapped Dylan the yacht for a helicopter. It's standing by."

Kaitlin was overwhelmed by this thoughtfulness. But she wasn't anywhere near ready to leave his arms.

She molded her body to his. "Or maybe we could go in an hour or so?"

He sucked in a breath, lifting the picture from her hand and setting it safely on an end table. Then his eyes darkened, and he bent forward to kiss her thoroughly.

"Maybe in an hour or so," he agreed and scooped her up to head for her bedroom.

Epilogue

Following a month-long kidnapping, Lindsay and Dylan's wedding was held on Serenity Island, on the emerald-green lawn at the Gilby house, next to the pool. The bride was radiant, the groom ecstatic and the guests a who's who of New York City. According to Ginny, it was the biggest party the island had held since the heyday of the 1940s.

Dylan had insisted on flying the Jolly Roger, while Ginny confided gleefully to Kaitlin that since the wedding was so rushed, she wondered if Lindsay might be pregnant.

After the toasts were made, the five-tiered cake was cut and the dancing had started in the late afternoon, Zach drew Kaitlin to one side.

"There's something I need to show you," he told her quietly, tugging her inside the house and down the hallway toward the garage.

"We can't leave now," she protested, trotting on her high heels, the glossy, champagne-colored bridesmaid dress flowing around her knees.

"We'll be back in a few minutes," he assured her, opening the garage door.

"Zach," she protested.

"What?"

"Are you crazy?"

He turned and playfully kissed the tip of her nose. "Crazy for you."

"This isn't a joke." She tried to sound stern, but she didn't seem capable of getting angry with him. Since the afternoon in her apartment, and their helicopter trip to the cemetery to put roses on her grandparents' graves, she'd been almost giddy with love.

He braced his hand against the passenger side of a golf cart. "And I'm not laughing. Hop in."

"I will not hop in." She crossed her arms stubbornly over her chest. She wasn't abandoning Lindsay on her wedding day.

"Have it your way." He gently but firmly deposited her on the narrow bench seat.

"Hey!" She scrambled to get her dress organized around herself.

"There's something I really have to show you." He jumped into the driver's side and turned on the key.

Before she could escape, the cart pulled smoothly out of the garage onto the gravel driveway and the road that led down to the castle.

"I can't believe you're kidnapping me," she harrumphed.

"It is the pirate way."

"You are *not* allowed to ravish me in the middle of a wedding reception." She smoothed her dress over her knees and put her nose primly in the air.

Zach gave her a wolfish grin, and she was forced to wonder which one of them would prevail if push came to shove, and he did decide he wanted to ravish her.

They drove all the way down to the Harper property.

As they entered the castle gardens, she felt herself relax. This had quickly become one of her favorite places in the world. It was filled with such history and such happy memories.

Zach pulled to a halt in front of the family chapel, then he hopped out and came around to assist her.

She shook her head in confusion as she clambered around the awkward dress. It was made for fashion, not mobility. The bodice was tight, coming to a drop waist, while the satin skirt billowed out with crinolines, ending at knee length. "This is what you wanted to show me?" She'd been in the gardens a thousand times.

"Have patience," he told her.

"I'll have patience after the reception. Seriously, Zach. We have to get back."

But he led her by the hand to the bottom of the chapel steps.

"What are we doing?" she breathed in frustration.

A secretive smile growing on his lips, he reached into his tux jacket pocket and drew something out, holding his palm flat so that she could focus on a small heirloom ring.

It was a delicately swirled gold band, with a sapphire center, flanked by diamonds.

"I don't know how old it is," said Zach. "But I think it might have belonged to Lyndall."

"Stolen?" Kaitlin asked, glancing up.

"Let's assume not." Zach's silver eyes sparkled. He held her hand in his, stepping forward, voice going soft. "Will you marry, Katie?"

She was still confused. "I am. I did."

"I know." He smiled. "But I don't think we got it quite right the first time." Then he nodded to the old chapel. "It's traditional for Harper brides to be married right here."

Kaitlin understood, and her chest tightened with emotion. "You want to..."

"Absolutely. Marry me, Kaitlin. Do it here. Do it now. Love me when you say the vows, and promise my family you'll stay with me forever."

She blinked back the sting of tears. "Oh, Zach."

The ancient door swung open with a groan, and a preacher appeared in the doorway.

"This way," he told them softly, turning, robes rustling as he made his way to the front of the ancient church.

Zach squeezed her hand as they mounted the steps, leading her over the uneven stone floor, past worn wooden pews, to the altar that Lyndall had built for his own wedding, the very first wedding on the island.

Kaitlin swayed sideways against Zach, absorbing the feel of his strong body.

Footsteps sounded behind them, and she glanced back to see Lindsay and Dylan, still dressed for their own wedding.

"Oh, no," she moaned under her breath.

"They insisted," Zach whispered, tucking her arm into the crook of his.

As they stopped at the front of the church, one of the staff members stepped out and handed Kaitlin a bouquet.

White roses.

From Sadie's garden.

It was beyond perfect, and Kaitlin had to blink against the sting of tears.

Lindsay and Dylan took their places, and Zach wrapped an arm around Kaitlin, gathering her close for a private word. "I love you very much, Katie," he whispered.

"And I love you," she whispered back, feeling as though her heart might burst wide open.

His tone went husky as he tenderly stroked her cheek, wiping her tears with the pad of his thumb. "Then, let's take our vows and put this ring on your finger."

* * * * *

SECRET BABY, PUBLIC AFFAIR

YVONNE LINDSAY

To my Mum and my (late) Dad,
thank you both for always letting me pursue
my imagination, my dreams and my goals
and for always encouraging me to believe
I could achieve or be whatever I wanted.

One

"You were comfort sex. Nothing more."

At least that was all she'd ever let him be. Blair maintained eye contact with Draco Sandrelli and prayed he'd leave before she did something stupid—like faint or throw up all over his highly polished handmade boots. Her stomach, which had been unsettled since breakfast, clenched in a completely different way as he flashed a smile at her, the one he'd used just before they'd tumbled into bed together for the first time.

"*Cara mia,* you know I am so much more than that."

His voice dripped sensuality, its sound sending a shimmer of heat through her. She still woke in the night remembering the sound of him, as rich as the rolling timbre of distant thunder on an electrically charged, storm-tossed evening. And worse, remembering the feel of him, the sensation of his body against hers—inside hers. She fought back the small sound that rose in her throat—a sound driven by the heat that suffused her body and insinuated itself along her nerve endings in curling tendrils of desire.

The gold flecks in Draco's green eyes glinted as he watched her reaction. For someone she'd barely met, he seemed able to read her like a book. A tiny smile played around the sensual curve of his lips. He hadn't even forgone his usual designer stubble for today's memorial service, although he'd slicked back his glossy dark hair off his almost too perfect face, its length finishing in a ducktail at his nape. On any other man the style would look ridiculous, but on Draco… Blair swallowed against the sudden dryness in her mouth.

Really, for a man he was too beautiful to be classed as handsome, but despite her reasoning her pulse still raced to a tribal beat.

"Have dinner with me tonight," he coaxed.

"No. No way. I mean it, Draco. Call what we had a holiday fling, whatever. It's not happening again. I'm home now and back at work. Which reminds me, I have things to attend to and I'm sure you do too."

No matter what, she wasn't going to ask him what he was doing here. After all, what were the odds that her uncharacteristic holiday indulgence would turn up at Ashurst Collegiate today? Especially at the memorial reception she'd agreed to do as a favor for one of her dad's oldest friends. As tempting as it was to indulge in another forbidden delight with the sole heir to the Sandrelli empire, Blair had more important things on her mind.

She summoned every ounce of self-control in her arsenal and, tipping her nose ever so slightly in the air, spun on her heel and stalked away.

She sensed, rather than heard, the moment he decided to follow her—the fine hairs on the back of her neck prickling to attention. Blair increased her pace, turned a corner in the corridor and slipped through the doorway leading into the voluminous kitchen off Jubilee Hall, where the reception was being held. She flattened herself against the wall and fought to control her hammering heartbeat, hoping like mad he hadn't seen her duck in here.

Even her hands were trembling, she realized. She hadn't been this upset since she'd caught her fiancé, Rhys, and her best friend, Alicia, in the wine cellar of the converted villa that housed Carson's, her restaurant. The pain of losing the man she'd planned her future with to the friend who was supposed to have stood beside her in the church only a few days later had been unspeakable. Their joint betrayal still stung with the sharpness of a stingray's barb.

It was what had led her to her flight to Italy and tour of Tuscany, and ultimately to Draco Sandrelli, where she'd promptly fallen under his seductive spell.

Yes, he was comfort sex all right. Totally addictive, mind-blowingly generous comfort sex. And just what she'd needed to rebuild her flagging self-esteem. Nothing more.

She shoved herself off the wall and carried on through the kitchen, mentally checking off what she needed to do before returning to Carson's and preparing for her night's clientele. She was relieved to see her personal tools of the trade had been neatly packed back into the case she'd brought them in—a quick check ensured everything was where it should be. There was nothing further for her to do. The casual crew she'd hired to work the reception would complete the cleanup and return the crockery to the restaurant in a couple of hours' time.

Blair smoothed her hands over her uniform, the tailored, crisp short-sleeved white blouse and black skirt which neatly hugged her slim hips, drawing strength from the familiarity of its texture.

She hitched the box against her hip and carried it through the kitchen to the back door and walked around on the graveled drive to where she'd parked her station wagon. She eyed the paint work on her old workhorse with a critical eye. If she hadn't taken the trip to Tuscany she could have replaced old Gertie here with a new vehicle. But if she'd done that she would have remained a victim to Rhys and Alicia's perfidy, instead of learning more about the woman she could be. About the woman she had been.

And it had been that very discovery that had taught Blair she couldn't have it all. She wasn't the kind of person who could develop an award-winning business and be a devoted life partner to anyone. No. She was happy with her decision. Work would be her life for now. And as for Draco, well, everyone was entitled to a "Draco" in their life at one time or another, she rationalized. The intensity of their affair had burned so bright and fierce, it would have totally consumed her had she stayed any longer with him. That one certain truth had made her put everything into perspective. She'd seen it happen to her father over and over, each time destroying his inner self a little more, and she'd sworn she would never succumb to such obsession.

Her wake-up call had come one morning as she'd stirred in Draco's arms, their sheets in a tangle about their naked, sated bodies, and she realized that she hadn't so much as thought about Carson's in three whole days. The realization was sobering. She'd embraced her affair with Draco with the level of passion she usually reserved solely for her work.

No, there definitely wasn't room for both a grand love and a career in her life. Her work was everything. Its success was what defined her, not something as ephemeral as physical attraction between consenting adults.

Blair had risen from their bed and packed immediately, turning a deaf ear to Draco's enticement to stay longer. As sinfully delightful as her time with Draco had been, it wasn't the kind of temptation one could build a future on. There was no security in incendiary attraction. She knew that from both her father's painful past and her own.

There was only one thing she wanted right now, and that was to see Carson's make the five-star review page of *Fine Dining* magazine. It had been her father's dream, until ill health had forced him to hand the reins of the restaurant over to Blair as he reluctantly settled into early retirement. Now it was her dream. One she thought she'd achieve with Rhys and Alicia by her side. But she could do it on her own. Carson's would become Auckland's leading restaurant. And she'd forget all about Draco Sandrelli.

Draco hesitated outside the door to the kitchen. He'd prowled the corridor in frustration, after finding no sign of Blair. She had to be in here. Unconsciously, he straightened his shoulders. They needed to talk and he wasn't taking no for an answer. When Blair had left his bed that morning he had been prepared to move mountains to get her to stay. It had only been the urgent call to his parents' home, situated a few kilometers away within the Sandrelli estate, that had stopped him. Of course, by the time he'd returned from his father's sickbed, Blair had left the palazzo, leaving no forwarding address.

Seeing her here today had taken him by surprise, but he wasn't the kind of man who looked a gift horse in the mouth. This was a second chance. The magnetism between them had been instant, and he knew better than most that that kind of draw did not happen between couples every lifetime. Too many people settled for what was expected of them—for second best. He'd done that very thing once, out of honor and respect for his family and his dead brother, but the result had been catastrophic. He would not do that again.

The attraction was too fierce.

He settled his hand on the swing door into the kitchen and entered just in time to see Blair exiting at the far end of the room. Draco's strides ate up the distance between them and he burst through the back entrance just as

Blair loaded a case into the back of the barely roadworthy vehicle in front of her.

"Blair."

"I've said all I have to say, Draco," she sighed, as she unlocked the driver's door and slid in behind the wheel.

Draco stopped her as she tried to swing her door shut.

"Ah yes, but you haven't listened yet to what I have to say."

"To be frank, I'm really not interested in what you have to say."

She tried to wrestle the door closed, and gave up with an angry huff of air when that proved impossible. She crossed her arms defensively over her stomach and stared fixedly out the windshield.

"What's the matter, Draco, can't you tolerate someone turning you down? Granted, I'm sure it probably hasn't happened often in your lifetime, but surely you can get used to it just this once," she snapped.

He smiled in response to her rancor. She sounded like a spitting kitten all in a temper.

"I just want to talk. You left so suddenly. We never had a chance to say good-bye properly."

Draco noticed that that elicited a response. Through the thin cotton of her blouse he saw the instant her nipples peaked against the sheer fabric of her bra. A bra he knew she wore more as a concession to her position at work than out of necessity. He loved her small, high breasts. Loved the way he could elicit a screaming response from her just by nipping ever so gently at their rose-pink tips. He'd never known a woman so sensitive in that area. Never enjoyed one as much as he had Blair. And he wanted to do it all again. And again.

Blair looked up, catching his gaze that was firmly riveted on her breasts.

"Oh, for goodness' sake." She reached forward to twist her keys in the ignition. "We've said all we have to say. Or at least I have. Like I said before, you were a holiday fling. Good in bed and good for my ego. But that's it. What we had is finished. Now please, let go of my car door before I have to call security."

"Now that's where I disagree, *delizia,* we are far from finished. I will let you go now, but rest assured, Blair, I will see you again and we will finish this conversation properly."

He stood back from the car and watched as she slammed the door shut without saying another word. She crashed the car into gear, and he winced at the ancient motor's protest as she floored the accelerator and spun up a rooster tail of gravel from beneath her tires.

He watched as she drove away, a grim smile of satisfaction on his face, now that the registration details of her vehicle were firmly emblazoned in his mind. She might think she'd gotten away. But his reach far exceeded his grasp and he'd find her, and have her in his bed again. Soon.

Movement over by the car park caught his attention. His best friends—Brent Colby and Adam Palmer—stood by the Moto Guzzi bikes he'd arranged to have exported to New Zealand so they could enjoy a taste of their misspent youth whenever they managed to all be in the country at the same time. They'd come a long way from the teenage maniacs who'd spent the night of their graduation dinner demon riding on the back roads near their prestigious private school, but there was nothing that beat the sensation of mastering the power of the motorbike and flying along the road.

Brent was a self-made millionaire, and if Draco hadn't already loved and respected him as much as he did, Brent would have earned that respect twice over when he'd made and then lost his fortune, only to rebuild it twenty times stronger than before. Brent's cousin, Adam, came from different stock. New Zealand old money, which, although it didn't go back as far as the Sandrelli bloodlines, could hardly be sneered at. The Palmer family was a mover and shaker in New Zealand industry, with interests spread far and wide across the globe.

Thinking about the Sandrelli bloodlines brought solemn awareness, settling like a dark cloak around his shoulders. The Sandrellis ended, or continued, with Draco, as his ailing father had pointed out to him on more than one recent occasion. The responsibility to his family history sat firmly and heavily on his shoulders alone. Which made prospects with Blair all the more interesting—if he could only get her to agree to see him again.

He jogged over to meet his friends. It was time to head back to Brent's for drinks and a few hands of cards, and on the ride back to Auckland, Draco could formulate his plan.

Blair might think she'd gotten away from him, but all she'd done was entice him all the more. Let her think she had the upper hand for now, but he knew she was no more capable of resisting him than he was of walking away from her. A man didn't get this lucky twice in his life and walk away.

The problem was, would he be able to bring his father his heart's desire before it was too late? His last stroke had been mild, but the doctors had warned that he could suffer a debilitating or fatal stroke at any time.

Draco would just have to make certain he wasn't too late. Sandrellis had dominated the countryside around the palazzo for centuries. And even though the mantle of succession had fallen by default onto his shoulders with the death of his brother ten years ago, he would not be the one who saw to their end. His union with Blair Carson would provide the grandchildren demanded by his parents—and if their incendiary attraction was anything to go by, it would be no hardship to do so.

Neither Brent nor Adam spoke as he came to a halt beside his motorbike, but the curiosity on their faces spoke volumes.

"Don't even ask," he warned as he reached for his glossy black helmet and jammed it onto his head, flipping the dark visor down over his face.

He'd tell them about Blair eventually. When he had her firmly where he wanted her.

Two

"He's here again. That makes it seven nights in a row, sweetie." Gustav, Blair's blatantly gay headwaiter smiled and raised one brow as he brought the new order to the kitchen.

Blair's knife slipped and clattered on the chopping board, narrowly missing her fingertip. She drew in a leveling breath. Draco had turned up to take a single table each night since the memorial service. He was later than usual tonight, and the anticipation of waiting and wondering whether he'd arrive, or whether he'd returned to Tuscany, had tied her stomach in knots. Her scattered attention, combined with one of her kitchen hands being off sick, had put them uncharacteristically behind schedule.

Certainly not the behavior of an award-winning chef

in an award-winning restaurant. Blair dragged her recalcitrant thoughts together. There was only one objective that could take priority in her mind, and Draco Sandrelli was not that objective.

"What did he order?"

She mentally crossed her fingers and hoped it was something she could get out quickly. Anything that would see him leave again. Soon.

"The Scaloppine alla Boscaiola, with sautéed mixed vegetables. For a big guy he sure eats light, maybe he saves his appetite for other things," Gustav responded with a slightly salacious wink before collecting an order from under the heat lamps and swinging back through the doors to the restaurant.

Blair allowed herself a brief sigh of relief. The mushroom with pork escalopes dish was simple and easy to prepare, the sautéed vegetables equally so. They were among the many dishes she'd learned to prepare during her culinary tour of Tuscany, the tour that had taken an unexpected detour from the markets and kitchens and into Draco's bed.

As Blair warmed the olive oil in a heavy pan on the stove top she tried not to think about that detour. About the overwhelming pull of attraction she'd felt the instant her eyes had met his across the courtyard, as she'd stepped off the tour bus at Palazzo Sandrelli. Nor did she want to remember the near painful urge to belong in a place like the palazzo, with its generation-worn steps leading to the front entrance and its permanence and longevity.

She and her father had lived a nomadic lifestyle after

her mother had left them. Traveling from one city to another, usually following the tourist beat of traffic in holiday seasons, to find work. Carson's had been the only thing in her life that had been a constant. It was her home, her base. And if she was to ensure its continued popularity she needed to pull her head out of the clouds and get to work, she reminded herself dourly as she added the pork slices to the pan and turned to attend to the sautéed vegetables.

It was only as she plated up the scaloppine that Blair allowed her thoughts to drift back to Draco. Each night he'd sent back compliments to the kitchen. Normally, she would have gone out into the restaurant to speak personally with her diners, but she was afraid to face him again. Afraid of her own feelings.

What if he persisted, as he'd begun to at the memorial service? What if he wanted more? Just knowing he was here under the same roof had her nerve endings singing, her skin feeling too tight for her body. Every sense within her was attuned to him, to the knowledge that, just through the swinging doors, he dined alone. And she knew he was just biding his time. Men like Draco liked to win. She'd had firsthand experience of that.

Yet still, for some strange reason she remained on tenterhooks for Draco's opinion of his meal. Like it even mattered, she scorned herself, as she carried on through the motions of completing the finishing touches on the desserts heading out to the late table of six that had just arrived.

"Blair?"

Gustav had come back through to the kitchen, mischief written all over his features.

"Please don't tell me a busload of tourists have arrived and they're all demanding the Ossibuchi," Blair countered, naming the dish that had sold out an hour ago.

"No, nothing so simple. It's Mr. Handsome. He wants to speak to you *personally*."

Blair's heart stuttered in her chest. "And you've given him my apologies, haven't you."

"No, actually. I said you'd be right out."

"Gustav!"

"Look, it's eleven-thirty, the restaurant is nearly empty, bar the dessert and coffees on table ten. You know the kitchen is under control. There's no reason why you can't go and enjoy a port with him before we close up. Go on, live a little. It's about time you had some fun."

Blair groaned inwardly. Ever since she'd broken her engagement to Rhys and summarily dismissed him and Alicia from their duties at Carson's—a dismissal that had cost her dearly afterwards when their employment lawyer had pointed out she hadn't followed due process—Gustav had been after her to lighten up and socialize.

If only he knew, she thought. She'd already had about all the fun she could handle. It was why she had thrown herself back into work as soon as she'd stepped off the plane a few weeks ago.

Gustav yanked on her apron strings and snatched the heavy linen swathe from her narrow hips, then handed her the lipstick she kept in a drawer near the swinging doors for those moments she went out to circulate amongst diners.

"Go on. It won't kill you. Look, honey, if I thought I stood a chance I'd be at that table pronto, but he's made it clear he wants you."

Reluctantly, Blair took the lipstick and swiped it across her lips.

"There, satisfied?" she said, challenging him.

"Not hardly, sweetie." He reached up and swiped the net she wore over her hair off her head and tousled her hair into a fluffy mess. "Now I'm satisfied."

Gustav took her by the shoulders, spun her around and pushed her in the direction of the restaurant.

"Don't worry about the kitchen. We'll take care of everything. You just enjoy yourself."

As the door swung closed behind her, Blair could swear she heard the faint sound of applause from her staff. A swift glance over her shoulder through the porthole-shaped window showed Gustav taking a bow. Blair fought back a smile as she turned her attention back to the man waiting on the secluded table set in the deep bay window of the old villa.

Draco rose as Blair walked toward him. For a while, he'd wondered if his waiter had been leading him on, saying that Blair would join him for an after-dinner drink, but here she was. Finally.

He raked his gaze over her, taking in the weariness that tightened the lines of her angular face. Not classically beautiful, certainly, but the sweeping arc of her slender, dark brows over eyes the color of dark chocolate, and the long straight line of her nose, lent character to a face that might otherwise be ordinary.

She walked with the grace of the naturally slender, the bulky chef's jacket over baggy checkered pants—the standard kitchen uniform here in New Zealand—hiding the long, lean strength of her body and the perfectly shaped breasts he'd bet even now were tipped with rose peaks. A sudden flush spread across her high cheekbones and her eyes glowed with the flame of heat that he knew answered his own.

Deep inside him he felt the thrum of anticipation begin to build. By the end of the night she'd be in his bed. He knew it as well as he knew the contours of her body. And he could barely wait to feel her beneath him again. They had unfinished business to resolve between them. Blair Carson would learn she couldn't run away from him and not expect him to follow.

His feral instincts wanted nothing more than to take her by the hand and lead her straight out the front door to his waiting car. To whisk her away to his Viaduct Basin apartment in the city and bare her to his gaze, to his hunger. And then to sate them both.

A fine tremor ran through his body as he fought back the urge to do just that. As she neared his table she displayed all the characteristics of a gazelle poised for flight. The last thing he wanted to do right now was scare her off. She'd run from him once before; it was up to him to ensure she wouldn't do so again.

She lifted her hand to him as she drew to a halt beside the table.

"I trust you enjoyed your meal, Mr. Sandrelli."

Draco let his lips relax into a smile, watching her pupils dilate in reaction, and her lips firm, as she read his humor at her attempt to keep things between them strictly on a business footing.

He took her hand and pulled her toward him, kissing her briefly on each cheek in traditional European style before releasing her hand and gesturing for her to take the seat adjacent to his.

"I always enjoy the fruits of your toil, Blair. Your cleverness in the kitchen is only surpassed by your—"

"Perhaps I can get you a drink. Gustav mentioned port. Is that your preference?" She wheeled away from the table but he reached out and snagged her hand.

"Stay, Gustav will bring us our drinks shortly. I wanted a little time with you first, just to talk."

"If that's what you want," Blair answered begrudgingly.

"You learned well during your time in Tuscany. The dish you served tonight, that was from your stay in Lucca, *si?*"

"Yes, I've incorporated a few of the recipes from the region into our menu. They've been popular."

"And you've been busy. You look tired." He reached across the table and brushed the pad of his thumb gently across the bluish tint to the skin beneath her eyes.

She flinched, breaking the tenuous contact almost as soon as it had begun.

"It's all good. It's what I want."

Ah, here it came. Her not-so-subtle wall of defense.

"But everyone needs some respite in their life from time to time. Tell me, *cara mia,* what do you do to unwind—to relax?"

"I've just come back from holiday, Draco. I don't need to relax."

He snorted inelegantly. "Holiday? Blair, you worked your way through that culinary tour. You can hardly call that a holiday. Except for—"

"Ah, here's our port." Blair interrupted him again, taking the two cut-crystal glasses from the silver tray Gustav held in one hand and dismissing him with a look. "Here, *salute!*"

Draco accepted the glass from her and set it down on the table in front of him. He could see straight through her. She thought if she could get him to drink his port, their conversation would be over, and he'd be gone. How wrong she was. When he left here tonight, she would be with him. Willingly.

He played with the stem of the glass, admiring the quality of the crystal. She didn't stint on anything here in the restaurant. From the fittings and furnishings to the tableware and service—it was all of the highest quality. Yes, Blair Carson took her passions seriously. And he liked that about her. A lot.

She took a sip of her port, the fortified liquid leaving a sheen on her lips. His fingers tightened reflexively as the tip of her tongue swept across her lips to remove the residual alcohol. He ached for her to take another sip, so he could lean forward and taste the port on her lips, on her tongue.

Her next words came as a surprise.

"What do you want from me Draco? What will it take to make you go away?"

He leaned back in his seat, shifting his hips slightly to ease the ache that had built low in his groin.

“What makes you think I will go away?”

She shook her head. “We both know your business demands will take you home soon. Already you’ve been here, what, a week? I imagine you’ll need to be leaving soon, I just want to know what I can do to make it sooner.”

“Come home with me.”

“To the palazzo? You have to be joking.”

Ultimately, yes, that was his goal. To have her back where she belonged, with him. But in the meantime he would be satisfied with small victories.

“Tonight. To my apartment.”

He leaned forward again and lifted her hand with his, dragging her fingertips gently across his lips. He felt the shudder of awareness course through her. The fire between them still burned bright and fierce.

“Just tonight?” her voice shook ever so slightly. “And then you’ll leave me alone?”

It was a start. He inclined his head. “I’ve missed you, Blair. Let me show you how much.”

“I—I don’t know.”

“I’m not a man to beg, *cara mia,* but I beg of you now. You cannot fight this thing between us. Even you have to admit what we have is something rare, something special. Not even with your Rhys did you share this, no?”

Her fingers flexed in his and he knew he had her. For tonight at least.

“All right. Tonight only. I’ll need to get a few things.”

“Certainly. Bring as much as you want. Stay longer.”

She withdrew her hand from his clasp. "No. It will only be tonight. Give me your address and I'll bring my car."

"That won't be necessary. I have a car and driver at my disposal. Where do we go to pick up your things."

Draco was on his feet and helping Blair to hers before she could rethink things and change her mind.

"Upstairs, I have a couple of rooms upstairs. The stairs are around the back through the kitchen."

"Then I shall wait for you here."

He leaned forward and brushed the lightest touch of his lips against hers. He knew he shouldn't have done it the second he felt her breath against his lips. What was supposed to have been a simple caress sent a flare of heat through his body, and instead of withdrawing from her, as he'd planned, his hand snaked up the slender column of her neck, his fingers tangling in the short strands of her hair so he could angle her head better to plunder the softness of her mouth. Her lips parted with a soft moan, her tongue darting to meet his. The taste of her was intoxicating, sending his blood to thrum through his body with a pagan beat.

It had been like this the first time he'd touched her. This all-consuming need to have more of her. To take what she had to offer and give back threefold in return. He'd never known such consuming passion, not even with Marcella. The thought was both sobering and enticing at the same time.

Blair's uninhibited response gave him all the answer he needed. He'd been right to pursue her, right to bide his time before making his move. She was as affected by their magnetism as he. Being here each night and not contacting her, not touching her, had been a master plan. As calculated as it sounded, it had been the only way to show her that this thing between them couldn't be ignored, but was there to be indulged in.

Dio! He couldn't get enough of her. He nipped lightly at her lower lip, suckling against the pliant tissue, absorbing the tiny sound of pleasure that emanated from deep in her throat.

The clatter of cutlery on bowls brought him suddenly to his senses and he pulled back, his fingers stroking the satin softness of her neck one last time before he forced himself to let her go.

"Hurry. I don't want to waste a moment," he said, his voice pitched low so only Blair could hear him.

For a second she wavered, as if slightly off balance. Truth be told, he felt much the same way. But then, with a slight nod, she walked away from him, her steps brisk and to the point.

Three

"Is it getting hot in here, or is it just you?" Gustav remarked, fanning himself theatrically, as Blair pushed through the kitchen doors and headed straight toward the back door.

"Can it, Gus. You got what you wanted."

"Well, technically, no. But it sure looks like you're going to. Way to go, Blair. It's about time. And don't worry about the restaurant. I'll lock up."

Blair hesitated, her hand on the back door. "What do you mean, it's about time?"

"Well, you know. Since that whole business with Rhys and Alicia, it's like all your enthusiasm for the place got sucked out of you."

Had she really been so transparent? Granted, the breakup with Rhys over his betrayal with Alicia and the subsequent legal battle over severing their employment had been draining, but she hadn't for a minute thought she'd let that impact on her work, or the workplace.

Gustav carried on. "Since you came back from Italy, it's as if you have a new vibrancy about you, and it shows in your food and everything. Everyone here is much happier. It's good. And quite frankly, if this guy is the one that made you like this, then all kudos to him. He is the one, isn't he? The one you met while you were away?"

"Yeah, he is. You don't think I'm making a mistake, do you?"

"Mistake? You have to be kidding me! Get yourself out of here before I take him off you."

"Thanks, I owe you." Blair pushed open the back door and shot up the back staircase to the compact flat she called home when she wasn't working.

She grabbed a backpack from the tiny hall closet and shoved toiletries and a change of clothes inside, then quickly divested herself of her work gear. She wrinkled her nose as she dragged on a long-sleeved T-shirt and a soft cotton skirt with an asymmetrical hemline. Then she shoved her feet into pretty, low-heeled sandals. She would have appreciated time to grab a quick shower, to rid herself of the lingering aromas of the kitchen, but she had the feeling that Draco would be dragging her still wet into the car if she kept him waiting too much longer.

A pang of need arrowed through her center. One kiss. That was all it had taken and she'd been lost to him. Lost to the sensual delight he promised with every touch of his skillful fingers, every taste of his practiced tongue.

She quickly switched off the lights and locked the

door behind her, her sandals clattering on the wooden stairs as she returned to the restaurant. To Draco.

He pushed back from the table and stood the second she entered the dining room. Butterflies danced to a crazy beat in her stomach. Was she doing the right thing? Gus seemed to think so. Draco definitely thought so. But wasn't she just setting herself up for failure? She knew how hot the flame between her and Draco had burned back in Italy. She'd left before there could be any lasting damage. By agreeing to spend this night with him, would she end up scorched and regretful? Worse, would she be able to walk away from him come morning?

He didn't give her time to think. In one instant he had taken her arm to guide her outside, in the next they were seated on the leather backseat of the limousine that had edged forward at the curbside the instant he'd set foot outside Carson's. Every nerve ending in Blair's body was on full alert, attuned to the leashed power and strength of the man seated beside her.

Draco uttered a clipped command in Italian. The limousine driver closed the smoked glass divider between them and pulled smoothly away, gliding into the late-night traffic on Ponsonby Road.

Blair reached across the space between them, and trailed her fingertips across the expensive woven fabric encasing Draco's legs. The muscles in his thigh tensed beneath her feather-light touch.

"Don't." His voice was strangled, tight. The single word forced between rigid lips. "If you touch me now I won't be able to hold myself back, and I promised myself I would wait until we reached my apartment."

Blair's breath caught in her chest and a coil of anticipation tightened low in her belly. She lifted her hand and laid it back in her lap, her eyes seeking his in the darkened compartment of the car. The knowledge that she could affect him so deeply was empowering. While it was true that the strength of her feelings for him had terrified her, had driven her from his bed and his home and sent her on the arduous and long plane journey home from Europe, right now she was afraid of nothing.

The trip from Carson's to the Viaduct Basin took only ten minutes, and as they pulled into the parking area of the apartment building Blair acknowledged she couldn't wait another moment to be alone with Draco.

His driver came around to her door and held it open for her. As she alighted she heard the two men hold a brief discussion in Italian before the driver cruised away into the night.

A trickle of unease shimmered down her spine as she stood in the portico to the high-rise waterfront apartment complex. What the hell was she thinking? A week ago she'd told Draco he'd been nothing more than comfort sex, a couple of weeks before that she'd walked away from him, determined not to succumb to his seductive spell—and yet, here she was on the point of going to bed with him again. A shiver of something else coursed through her. Something that had nothing to do with nerves and everything to do with the visceral look of intent on the face of the man walking toward her.

Still, he didn't touch her. Instead, he picked up her pack from where the driver had deposited it and headed for the door. Blair followed, slightly cowed by his silence. Was he having second thoughts?

All the way up to his penthouse apartment she sensed the heat of his gaze. Briefly, she lifted her eyes to meet his, only to swallow convulsively when faced with the naked desire reflected in their emerald depths.

The doors swooshed open and Blair followed Draco down the heavily carpeted corridor, to the set of double doors at the end. With the swipe of a key card he opened the doors and stood aside, motioning for her to enter.

Her heels clicked on the parquet floor of the entrance, their sound masking Draco's footsteps as he closed in behind her. The muffled sound of her pack landing on the floor was all the warning she had before she was consumed by a broad band of heat at her back. Strong arms wrapped around her. Draco's mouth, hot and wet, descended onto the curve of her neck, his tongue tracing a sensual line up to her ear. The hard swell of his erection pressed against her buttocks and she squirmed, her action wringing a harsh groan from his throat.

He spun her around to face him, his thigh wedging between her legs with delicious friction, to rub against that part of her that flamed, begging for his touch. Blair's back flattened against the paneled wall behind her and she lifted her arms to Draco's shoulders before tangling her fingers in his hair and dragging his mouth down to hers.

Suddenly all the hunger she'd held at bay for the past few weeks erupted beneath the onslaught of his lips, the rasp of his tongue against hers. Time and place held no consequence, every molecule in her body focused solely on this moment, this man. One night—it would be their last but it would be the best.

Her skirt hitched up under the push of Draco's hands as he stroked up her legs, his broad palms caressing the backs of her thighs before clasping the roundness of her buttocks and pulling her hard against the demanding line of his arousal. A spiral of pleasure feathered out from her core, a promise of things to come.

It was insane, what they were doing, but Blair was incapable of sane thought or behavior any more. Draco invaded her senses, her every thought, her every desire. She shuddered anew as he dragged her panties away and cupped her, his fingers slick on her body, on the evidence of her need for him. He ground the heel of his palm against her and she cried out as the tiny rockets of pleasure sparked through her.

"Please," she begged, "please, Draco. More."

She heard her words—shamelessly wanton—as they hung in the air, and knew she could wait no longer. She fumbled for his belt, sliding the leather loose from its clasp, and then unsnapped the button before ripping down his fly. She was greedy for him now, reaching past the waistband of his silk briefs, hungry to feel his satin heat against her skin.

In the instant she loosed him from the confines of his briefs he hitched her higher against the wall and hooked her legs high over his hips. He pulled a condom from his pocket before his pants slid down his legs and quickly sheathed himself. Blair reached between them to guide his hardness to her entrance and then with one deep thrust they were one. She gripped his shoulders as he surged within her, driving her closer and closer to her peak. And then, in a mad rush of sensation, she was there. Her body clenching and convulsing around him, her hands digging into his shoulders, her thighs tight bands around his waist. With a raw cry of triumph he joined her on the raft of pleasure that soared through them both, his body imprisoning her against the wall, his breath hard and fast, his heartbeat hammering in his chest.

Slowly Blair became aware of where they were. God, they hadn't even made it more than a few feet inside the door. At least he'd had the presence of mind to close it behind them. Her whole body trembled with aftershocks of delight, her breathing came in ragged gasps.

"It seems I'm somewhat lacking in finesse tonight," Draco said close to her ear, his voice uneven but carrying an unmistakable note of humor.

"So it would seem," Blair agreed, grazing her lips along the column of his throat and being rewarded as he flexed against her, sending yet another aftershock of pleasure to ripple through her body.

"I'll make it up to you. I promise."

"I don't know if I can take any more. That was so…so…" Words failed her.

"So cathartic?"

He was right. It had been cathartic. Despite the late hour, despite the fact she'd already been on her feet all night in a busy kitchen, she felt energized, invigorated. Suddenly, she looked forward to Draco's idea of making it up to her.

He lifted her slightly and withdrew from her body, letting her unhook her legs from his waist and slide them down to the ground. She was amazed she could even stand. Her skirt fluttered down around her thighs as she moved off the wall. Draco rearranged his clothing.

"Come, I think we both need to shower after that. Let me take care of you."

Blair picked up her backpack and let him take her by the hand as he led her through the apartment. Floor-to-ceiling glass faced the inner harbor and Viaduct Basin. Light glittered off a myriad of buildings and luxury super-yachts and cruisers moored in the basin to reflect on the inky surface of the ocean. The vista was surreal. About as surreal as the fact she'd just allowed herself to be swept away by a sensual hunger she'd only barely begun to acknowledge.

The master suite led off the living room, and beyond that, the master bathroom. Soft dove-gray walls softened the black-and-gray marble vanity tops and black-tiled floor. Blair placed her pack on the vast spread of marble as Draco reached inside the massive shower stall to turn on the water. His task complete, he turned back to face Blair. Even without the evidence of his arousal against his trousers she could tell by the look on his face that he wanted her again. He framed her face with his large hands and kissed her, softly this time, taking his time to play the soft tissue of her lips against his before breaking contact.

His hands went to the hem of her T-shirt and he lifted it up and over her head. He traced one finger along the line of the rose-pink lace of her bra, where it met the gentle swell of her breast, before bending his head to press soft warm kisses where his finger had just been.

With an expert hand he unsnapped the clasp at the back, and the fabric, which had so ably cupped her, slid away to reveal her to his avaricious gaze.

"So beautiful, so perfect," he murmured, rolling the tips of her nipples between his fingertips before bending his dark head to lave first one taut bud, then the other, with the tip of his tongue.

He reached behind her to unzip her skirt and let it fall to the floor, leaving her standing only in her sandals. He knelt before her and placed her hands on his shoulders before lifting one foot to unbuckle the strap at her ankle. Each movement was so measured, so deliberate—in total contrast to the uncontrolled passion that had consumed them both only minutes ago—and deep inside her Blair recognized the building fire and knew Draco's idea of making things up to her would be monumental.

Once she was completely naked, he swiftly divested himself of his shoes and socks before pulling his shirt off and sending his trousers and briefs to the floor.

He guided her into the shower stall, angling the multiple shower heads to course over her body before he closed the door behind them.

"Oh, that feels so good," Blair moaned as the pulsing spray jets massaged her back.

Draco just smiled as he filled his hands with shower gel then began to smooth the slick liquid over her shoulders and down her arms, then stroke his hands back up again. He repeated the movement several times before gently running his hands over her chest then down to cup and gently knead her breasts.

She'd never felt "enough" before Draco. Each of the

other men she'd been with before she'd met him had teased her about her breast size. Not in a cruel way, but enough to ensure that the taunts of her teenage years rose large and ugly in her mind. Enough to make her feel less than feminine, less than a woman. But beneath Draco's touch she had no doubt she was everything he wanted, the attention he paid to her breasts, to her tight, puckered nipples, left her in no doubt whatsoever.

He filled his hands again with the shower gel and continued his ministrations, sliding one hand down to cup her and spread her legs gently. He cleaned her with an intimacy she had never experienced with anyone else, but then Draco Sandrelli was like no other man Blair knew. And that was precisely why he both scintillated and terrified her. It would be too easy to succumb to his spell, to his lovemaking. To lose herself. No, no matter what delights he brought her—and she knew there would be many—she had to remain strong. To take what he offered tonight and then go back to the life she'd chosen.

A ripple of pleasure spread from her core, just a hint of what his touch promised, she knew. His hands slid around to her buttocks, softly squeezing them before running down the backs of her thighs. He dropped to his knees, his hands still running up and down the length of her legs, and she marveled she could even stand when he brought his mouth to the apex of her thighs and pressed his lips to the sensitive bundle of nerve endings there.

His tongue flicked over the nub, at first soft then more insistent. Blair knotted her fingers in his hair, holding him to her as he increased pressure, then teasingly slowed again. Her legs were trembling, barely able to hold her slight weight when he began to suckle at her. She let her head drop back as the scream of pleasure ejected from her in tune to the orgasm that nearly rent her apart.

Draco stood, supporting Blair's quaking body with the strength of his, relishing that he could bring her so much pleasure, so much passion. For a woman who kept herself locked down so tight emotionally, he'd been ecstatic to discover the deeply hidden sensuality inside her. It was a waste for her to pour all that passion purely into her work, when she could have so much more if she would only embrace it.

He turned off the shower faucets and scooped Blair into his arms. She was so slender it was as if he lifted a child—she'd lost weight since her return to New Zealand. Weight, in his opinion, she could ill afford to lose. If he'd gauged her correctly, she'd no doubt been running herself ragged since leaving him. And if he didn't miss his mark, she was already on the point of exhaustion—her physical reaction to their lovemaking already leaving her limp, shattered in his arms.

He wrapped her in a thick, dove-gray towel and dried her with painstaking care.

"Draco?"

Her voice made him look up from his ministrations.

"Hmm?" he answered, reaching for a fresh towel to dry her hair before skimming his own body dry.

"What about you?"

He smiled. "Later. For now, you rest, *si?*"

"I'm sorry, I—"

He put a fingertip to her lips. "Don't. Don't tell me you're sorry."

He guided her to the master bedroom and pulled back the voluminous, down-filled duvet and the crisp cotton sheet before gently pushing her down onto the mattress. She was asleep in moments, confirming his belief she'd been pushing herself too hard. It was certainly more than the languor of the aftermath of love-making that dragged her into somnolence. He tossed her damp towel to one corner of the room and climbed into the bed next to her, propping himself up slightly so he could watch her as she settled into a deeper sleep. Eventually, he flipped the control that dimmed the bedroom lights into darkness and settled down onto his pillow, scooping Blair against his body and pulling the sheet over them both before letting sleep claim him also.

It was her feather-light touch that woke him only a couple of hours later. Somewhere in the night she'd slid from his hold and he'd rolled onto his stomach, a position that was becoming increasingly uncomfortable as awareness flooded his body.

Blair knelt over him. Her fingers touching, yet almost not, as they traced a line up from his ankles to the backs of his knees and then higher. Blood surged to his groin as her touch coasted up the inside of his thighs. Up and down and back again, each time moving a little higher, until goose bumps raised all over his skin anticipating her next move.

He felt the mattress shift, ever so slightly, as she moved, straddling his legs, keeping him captive, prone.

He could feel her firm buttocks on the backs of his thighs, feel the heat of her core against his bare skin. It was both a torment and a pleasure.

Her touch strengthened now, deepened as she stroked the long line of muscles on either side of his spine, stopping every now and then to change her touch to that feather-soft caress that threatened to drive him crazy with want. His hands, shoved deep under his pillow, clenched into fists as he fought not to reach for her, to spin her beneath him and torture her as she now did him.

"Are you awake yet?"

The teasing note in her voice made his lips pull into a smile.

"Yes, I am awake," he ground out through clenched teeth as her fingers tracked his spine—down, down, until she skimmed the crease of his buttocks.

He felt her weight lift from his legs.

"You'd better turn over then," she instructed.

Draco rolled over, hissing in a breath as she wrapped her fingers around his hardened length and caressed him, her other hand reaching for the packet she'd already removed from the bedside cabinet. He nearly lost it as he watched her tear the foil open with her teeth and slide the condom from its wrapper, then meticulously slide it over him.

He reached for her hips as she rose above him, poised at his tip.

"Let me," she whispered, placing her hands over his. "Let me look after you this time."

He was unused to surrendering control, whether it was in the boardroom or the bedroom, but for Blair he would do this. Her heat threatened to consume him as she lowered herself to take only his tip within her body. Every instinct within him demanded he take charge, insisted he drive into her and bring them both to the shattering pleasure he knew lay in store, but he beat back the urge and forced himself to concede.

A groan broke from his throat as she tilted her hips, taking a little more of him, then more, until finally he was exactly where he wanted to be, needed to be. She clenched her inner muscles around him, holding him tight then releasing him, shifting her hips back and forth ever so slightly with each clench and release, increasing in tempo until a sheen of sweat broke out on his body and hers.

He could keep his hands from her no longer. He reached for her, his fingers closing over the small globes of her breasts, squeezing them as she thrust forward, flicking her nipples with his thumbs. And then he was lost, pleasure unleashed in waves through his body. Beyond control, he thrust upwards and was rewarded with her cry as he felt her spasm around him, again and again, her body shaking.

He supported her against his hands as she climaxed, eventually lowering her to lie over his body. Lazily he rubbed one hand up and down her back, savoring the boneless sense of completion that permeated every part of his body.

Eventually, Blair lifted herself off him and took care of the condom. A simple thing, but one no woman had ever done for him before. When she came back into the bedroom she climbed back into bed beside him and curled up against his body and Draco allowed himself to sink into sleep, secure in the knowledge she wanted him now as much as he wanted her.

Four

Blair woke to the sound of Draco moving about the room. She kept her eyes closed and focused on keeping her breathing even. She didn't want to face him. Not now. Not in the cold light of day. She'd agreed to one night, but, if she knew him, he'd want more. And he wouldn't take no for an answer.

She listened to the gentle slide of a drawer closing and then the soft sound of his bare feet on the thickly carpeted floor. She waited until the door to the bathroom was closed before opening her eyes. She wanted out of here, right now.

Yes, they'd had the most spectacular night of love-making of her life, but Draco would never let it stop there. Men like him wanted more. Needed more. With his position back at home he was expected to marry, to raise a family. He could never do that with someone like Blair, and she didn't want to be that someone anyway. She didn't have that kind of person inside her to give.

The failure with Rhys was categorical proof of that, and with her family track history—no, best not to go down that route. Besides, where would a girl like her fit in with the centuries-old traditions of Draco's life? No, it was far, far better that she make a silent retreat here and now, before he could tempt her into wanting more—wanting *him*—again.

She swept her legs off the bed, relishing the sensation of her bare feet sinking into the plush pile of the carpet. A far cry from the polished wooden floors in her small apartment, and yet another example of the differences in their lives. Blair rose from the bed, acknowledging the minor aches in her muscles. Aches which sent a flush of desire across her body as she remembered how she'd earned them.

She looked around the room for her clothing, scowling silently as she remembered that Draco had undressed her in the bathroom and she'd left her pack in there. Would she be able to slip inside and gather her things without him noticing? She doubted it. So, what did that leave? Going home wrapped in a sheet? Hardly likely, although a sense of urgency gripped her. How much longer would Draco be in the bathroom, she wondered?

She darted across the room and listened at the door, the sound of water cascading in the shower reassuring her for a moment.

There was nothing else to do but borrow something of his, she decided. She could always courier it back to him, if he even noticed it missing. She quickly rummaged through the dark cherrywood tallboy, grabbing a T-shirt and a pair of lightweight drawstring track pants. Draco was taller than she, but not by so much that the track pants would drag on the ground. She swiftly pulled the clothes on, regretting for a moment that she hadn't had a chance to grab her shoes. *Okay,* she acknowledged, *there might not be much between them in height but there certainly was in body size.* Draco's shirt hung on her like a rag, and the pants would trip her in a minute, no matter how high she hitched them to her waist. She bent to quickly roll up the legs a couple of twists and then tied the T-shirt in a knot at her lower back. *There, that was a bit better.*

But what about her feet? A quick glance in the walk-in wardrobe confirmed there was no way her narrow feet would carry off wearing a pair of Draco's running shoes or anything else in there. She'd have to forget about footwear for now and just pray she didn't have to walk too far before finding a taxi.

She stiffened as she registered the sudden silence in the bathroom behind her. Damn, he was out of the shower. She didn't have much time.

Blair shot through the apartment and let herself out the front door. She ran lightly down the corridor to the elevator and leaned on the button to call the car to the top floor, her eyes fixed on the door to Draco's apartment the whole time. When the door whooshed open behind her she jumped, and then laughed at herself for her ridiculousness. What had she been expecting? That he'd jump out from behind the elevator doors and drag her back to the apartment, hold her there as his love slave forevermore?

She rolled her eyes at her mirrored reflection in the closing doors, taking a minute to push her fingers through her hair.

One night he'd asked for. One night he'd had. It had to be enough—for both of them.

Some people might call it running away—others, well, "tactical withdrawal" were the words that immediately came to Blair's mind. If she wasn't at the apartment or the restaurant, then Draco couldn't find her, and that's just the way she wanted it. The instant Blair got back home she showered and changed into her own clothes, grateful to put on fresh underwear and to rid herself of the tingling sensation of Draco's clothing against her bare skin. All her bare skin.

She threw the clothes in a bag for dry cleaning and added them to the laundry to be picked up by their linen supply company. Then she quickly put together a few things, enough to last her a couple of days, and headed out the door.

She hadn't been to visit her father since she'd returned from Tuscany. Now seemed as good a time as any. Monday and Tuesday were supposed to be her days off, not that she usually took them, so it wasn't as if she was running away. Not really, she told herself as she threw her bag into the passenger seat of her station wagon and put the vehicle in gear. A couple of days at the beach would do her good.

As she drove down the rutted driveway toward the

house her father rented by the beach at Kaiaua, on the Seabird Coast southeast of Auckland city, she knew she'd made the right decision. Already, the soothing sounds of the sea, the cries of wheeling gulls and the soft onshore breeze began to invigorate her in a way being back at work hadn't in a long time.

She thrust open her door and loped over to the house. She ignored the two shallow stairs that led to the weathered wraparound deck and jumped the short distance, her feet landing with a muffled thud before she ran around to where she knew her father would have his French doors open to the ocean.

"Dad?" she called as she stepped inside.

A tantalizing aroma filtered through the air to tweak at her nose, and Blair instinctively followed the scent through to the compact kitchen, just beyond the airy, open living area that faced the sea.

"I thought you might turn up today," Blair Carson, Sr. commented without turning his back as Blair entered the kitchen.

"Hello to you too, Dad."

Blair smiled at his usual, taciturn nature. Not even a surprise visit could wrest a smile from his careworn features. But then she hesitated.

"What made you expect me today?"

Her dad gestured to the laptop computer open on the small kitchen table. "That."

Blair sat down at the table and focused on the screen. Even though her dad was an hour from the city now, he liked to keep a finger on the pulse of what was happening, especially in the restaurant and entertainment industries. Her heart plummeted when she identified herself and Draco in the photo. The picture showed Draco holding her fingertips to his mouth, and more damningly, showed the expression of longing on her face.

The editorial accompanying the photo was full of conjecture and innuendo about what "something new and exciting" loomed on Blair's menu. It made her feel sick to her stomach. Worse, the reporter had gone to great lengths to emphasize the title and estates that Draco would inherit on his ailing father's death, giving him a celebrity she knew he would loathe.

"I thought you'd sworn off men," her father commented dryly after she'd read the e-zine page through to its end.

"I have."

"Then what was that all about?"

"It was him."

"The one you met in Tuscany, at the palazzo? Isn't his family some kind of royalty over there?"

"Ancestral nobility, but they haven't used their title in years. But yeah," she sighed. "The very same."

"Did he follow you here?"

"No. He was at the memorial service for Mrs. Woodley. Believe me, I tried to put him off trying to see me again."

"Obviously not all that effectively." Her father turned back to the stove. "Oh well, we should see an upswing in patronage at the restaurant. Are you going to see him again?"

Blair got up from the table and helped herself to a mug from the cupboard and poured herself a coffee from the carafe her father kept constantly full. It bothered her that her father instantly thought of the advantage to Carson's. How she felt about Draco didn't enter into it.

"No. Last night was a one-time-only."

Her father turned to look her in the eye. "Really?"

"Yes, Dad. Really."

"That's a shame. You should see him again. If only because the publicity would be good for takings. Want some breakfast?"

What? Was that it? Inquisition over already? Blair could hardly believe her father had let the subject go just like that. Still, he'd equated the e-zine gossip spread with a chance to keep Carson's up there in the public eye.

"Yes, thanks. I'm starved."

Her dad laughed, the sound like wind through dry leaves in autumn. "You're always starved. About time you put some meat on that frame, young lady."

"You can talk," Blair responded with a genuine smile.

Her lean build was a direct legacy from her father. At least she assumed it was just from him. She'd never seen a picture of her mom, and her memories of her were vague—more the sensation of a brief hug here, a lingering scent of fragrance there. The trill of amused laughter. The sound of weeping late at night.

The coffee in Blair's mug left a bitter aftertaste in her mouth. What was it about Blair and her father that they couldn't find happiness in lasting love? She'd lost count of the failed relationships he'd embarked upon and then left during her childhood, let alone since her teenage years. They'd clung to one another many a time, secure in the knowledge that no matter how often others came and went they'd always have each other.

Yet, would they? Blair felt increasingly vulnerable. A heart attack had forced Blair Sr. into early retirement. In fact, it had only been her taking over his dreams and vision for Carson's that had seen him agree to withdrawing from the restaurant. He'd had to move out of Auckland as well, because he hadn't been able to stay away, or out of the kitchen, when he'd remained in town. And while he'd been happy to cover for her during her Tuscan culinary tour—a trip that was supposed to have been her honeymoon—she could see how taxing it had been for him when she'd returned.

She owed it to her dad to see his dream for Carson's—her dream as well—come true. And if she was to achieve that ever-elusive five-star ranking for the restaurant, she had to pour everything she was into making it work.

Which meant pushing last night's memories and Draco Sandrelli very firmly into her past.

Blair felt completely reenergized when she returned to her flat at midday on Wednesday. Reenergized and refocused. A call to Gustav had confirmed her father's prediction that the e-zine article would see an upswing in business. Traditionally quieter nights, Monday and Tuesday had produced far higher receipts than usual and the restaurant had operated at near capacity each night.

She hummed to herself as she skipped downstairs and checked that preparations were well underway for the evening's menu. In the tiny office off the kitchen, where she made calls to suppliers and drafted menu plans, she came to a shuddering halt. There on her seat was a dry-cleaning package. On top of it a sheet of paper with a large question mark next to the words "not yours, I presume—G."

Damn, she'd forgotten about Draco's clothes the minute she'd dispatched them to the laundry. Would he have missed them? She doubted it. What worried her most was that sending them back to him would only rouse his interest in her again.

She picked up the packet from her chair and shot back upstairs to her rooms. She'd shove it in the cupboard and deal with it another day. She wasn't up to facing Draco again.

The evening started with the usual hustle and bustle, and Blair was glad to be back in her own kitchen. As capable as she was, her father was proprietary about his space—worse so, now that his space was so limited at the beachfront bach. She swung into the ebb and flow of cooking and plating up dishes with the years of experience and pleasure she took in her work.

By the time the front door was closed to patrons and the last diner had been seen off into a taxi at the curb, Blair was ready to put her feet up. The cleanup done in the kitchen and the last of her staff off on their way home, she took a moment to sit at one of the tables and relish the silence that now reigned supreme.

A sharp hammering at the front door had her catapulting out of her chair in shock.

Who the—

She swiveled the slim-line blind that screened the glass front door to peer out into the evening gloom.

Draco. Her heart skittered in her chest.

“Let me in, Blair. We need to talk.”

“We said all we have to say, Draco. One night. Remember?”

“Vividly. Do you remember too, *cara mia?* Would you like me to repeat just which were my favorite parts—I’m sure the reporter sitting in the car just behind me would be keen for all the details.”

Reporter? Blair peered past Draco’s dark form. There was a car pulled right up to the curb. She caught a brief glimpse of the reporter’s camera through the open window. The thought of the headlines in tomorrow’s gossip pages was enough to get her to open the door and usher Draco inside immediately, not quickly enough to completely avoid the sudden flash of white light as the reporter took their picture.

“Why on earth did you bring that reporter here?” Blair demanded, her hands fisted on her hips to avoid using them for any other purpose.

“You’re mistaken. I did not bring him. He was already waiting here, much as there have been reporters stationed outside my apartment and following my driver from pillar to post since early Monday morning.”

Draco stepped closer to her and lifted his hand to trace a finger along her cheekbone.

“You’ve caught some sun. Where have you been hiding the past two days?”

Blair bristled instantly. *Hiding?*

“For your information, Draco Sandrelli, I wasn’t

hiding. I went to visit my father. I do that sometimes on my days off."

"I'm impressed that you take days off," Draco said, whistling softly. "According to your staff, that doesn't happen often. Some coincidence, don't you think, that you should slip out of my apartment without saying good-bye and then go incommunicado immediately after that? Looks like hiding to me."

"What you think isn't important to me. What do you want, anyway? The restaurant, as you can see, is closed."

"Hmm, what do I want? A leading question, no?"

He closed the remaining distance between them, his arms wrapping around Blair with the familiarity of lovers, his head bending to her ear. A shiver of anticipation danced down her spine as she felt his breath against her skin.

"I'll show you what I want," he growled, before his tongue licked out to tease her earlobe.

Her hands moved to his shoulders as her knees went weak, then common sense prevailed. They were in her restaurant with reporters outside. This was totally crazy.

"No, Draco. Stop, please."

The words wrung past her lips as Blair drew on every ounce of self-control she possessed to push him away.

"We can't," she continued. "Not with—"

She gestured toward the front of the restaurant and shook her head. When the heck had her life grown so complicated?

"Fine then, we will go somewhere more private. Your rooms, perhaps?"

"To talk," Blair asserted.

"If you wish."

A tiny smile pulled at Draco's lips, the sight of that sensuous curve sending a bolt of sheer longing through Blair's body. She pushed the sensation down, refusing to let her desire for him control her, and showed him through the kitchen to the back of the restaurant.

She felt the sheer presence of him at her back, like a wall of heat imprinting the length of her body. The hairs on the back of her neck tickled with awareness.

Blair went to unlock and open the back door, but Draco forestalled her action, his hand big and warm as it trapped hers against the doorknob.

"Wait just a moment. We will open it slowly to ensure none of those reporters have snuck around the back."

Blair did as he suggested, looking both ways before signaling to him that the way was clear. He followed her up the stairs to her flat. As she pushed open the front door she was suddenly assailed with the massive differences between their lives.

Draco came from wealth, a long, long line of money and privilege with a heritage that stretched back centuries. Even his apartment here in Auckland shrieked money, although the simple, modern lines were a far cry from the opulence of the palazzo. She smiled to herself. *Palazzo.* How many people could say a palazzo was their home?

Oh yeah, they were different all right. For some reason it hadn't seemed to matter when she was in Tuscany—she'd been wooed by the strength of their attraction and by the sheer luxury of simply indulging in one another. But even so, back then she'd known it couldn't last. Nothing ever did in her life. His life was so totally at the extreme opposite of the scale to hers, and clearly no one had ever said no to him before. At least no one had ever said no and meant it.

"Can I offer you a drink?" Blair said, as Draco stood just inside the door taking in their surroundings.

She supposed that to his eyes it would all look very temporary and not a little bit shabby. For the amount of time she spent here, it did the job.

"No. I didn't come to have a drink with you."

"Then what did you come here for?"

The look in his eyes nailed her feet to the floor where she stood. Heat suffused her body in a slow wave. He wanted her, period. And weakling that she was, she wanted him too.

"Come back to my apartment." His voice was low, slightly uneven. "Come and stay with me until I have to go home."

"I can't."

"Why not? My building's security would give you some peace from these wretched reporters. Besides, you know you want to. Just look at you. Already I can see you're aroused in the way your eyes gleam, in the way you're breathing. If I touched you, your skin would be hot beneath my fingers, and if I cupped your breast I'd feel your heartbeat against my palm."

Breath shuddered from Blair's lungs. She could almost sense his hand against her, so evocative was his tone.

"Come back to my apartment," he coaxed.

"How long?" Blair dragged the edges of her sanity around her like a deflective cloak. Somehow, she had to find the courage to resist him. If she didn't, she knew there could only be heartbreak in store.

"Two weeks, perhaps three."

The thought of continuing where they'd left off the other night rippled through her body in a cascade of longing. Draco had insinuated himself under her skin, into her very psyche. But it wouldn't be forever, she told herself. They had a finite time. They could be together and then he'd leave to reassume his life and she could go on with hers.

She looked around the apartment. Very little of her own personality resided here. Aside from packing some clothes to bring with her, there wasn't anything she'd miss. And yet, if she agreed to this temporary affair—because that's exactly what it would be—could she be certain she'd escape with her heart intact?

"Blair?"

"Yes."

He smiled and her stomach did a little flip-flop in excitement as she absorbed his pleasure in her decision.

"Let me get a few things together, it'll only take me a moment."

Her hands shook ever so slightly as she shoved clothing, underwear and toiletries into a small case. She was mad. Totally and utterly mad to be doing this. But didn't she deserve to reach out and grab some happiness too, however short-lived?

Five

The next couple of weeks saw Blair take her creativity to new heights. After their nights of lovemaking, she expected to leave work each night drained. But instead, the opposite was true. She'd never been more invigorated in her life. She still suffered from the occasional recurrence of nausea or dizzy spell, no doubt still a hangover from the niggling stomach upset she'd had a few weeks ago, but overall she'd never felt better.

Tonight the restaurant was humming, as it had for a while now. This week in particular had been crazy when Draco's friendship with newly-engaged billionaire entrepreneur Brent Colby had been at the forefront of the gossip magazines. It seemed as if every aspect of Draco's life was fodder for the papers, and by association, hers too.

Reporters still hung around outside each night, but instead of the headlines reading things like “Is Carson’s Going Italian?” or “Italian Stallion on the Menu?” they were more focused on the increasing high number of local celebrities who’d taken to wanting to be seen at what was rapidly becoming *the* place to be seen.

Blair turned to check the latest round of orders from her wait staff, only to feel the kitchen floor tilt beneath her. *Whoa,* she thought, gripping the stainless steel countertop to steady herself.

“You okay, sweetie?” Gustav hesitated in front of her, his hands and arms filled with entree plates heading out to a group of actors from New Zealand’s longest-running soap opera who were celebrating local television award nominations.

Blair swallowed back against the bitter bile that had risen in her throat as the dizziness had hit, and took a steadying breath.

“I’ll be fine. You’d better get those out.” She gestured to the plates on his arm. “Can’t keep the punters waiting, right?”

“Maybe you should get checked out. Who knows, you might have brought back something more than just a gorgeous Italian stud muffin from Tuscany.”

Gustav gave her one of his trademark cheeky smiles, but underlying his humor, she could sense he was worried about her.

Blair reached for the bottled water she always kept on hand, and took a long draw from it. That spell had been worse than most, she acknowledged. Maybe she really did need to see a doctor just to get to the root of what ailed her. It wasn't as if it was debilitating, but dizzy spells in a working kitchen were risky at the best of times. And these *were* the best of times, she smiled to herself.

Business had never been better, and at the end of each evening Draco was waiting for her to take her back to his apartment where they'd enjoy a late supper together before retiring to bed. Although there wasn't much retiring in that department.

The next afternoon, when Blair arrived at the restaurant her staff were abuzz with the news that the food critic from *Fine Dining* magazine was reported to be coming to the restaurant that night amongst a bevy of his friends. Blair's nerves shot off the Richter scale as she realized what this could mean.

Tonight could be the night that would realize her dream—or seal her fate into the "almost-ran" category forever. It was imperative that everything be perfect.

She checked and rechecked the storeroom and walk-in-fridge, ensuring that everything she'd ordered was of the highest quality and at its peak of freshness.

Draco let himself in through the back door of the restaurant and waved a quick hello to Blair's sous chef, Phil, who was busy overseeing the kitchen hands' preparations for the menu that night. He was surprised not to see Blair in the kitchen, but caught a glimpse of her in the little office off to the side.

He crossed the distance between them on silent feet. Her back was to the door and she was intent on the computer screen in front of her. The online version of *Fine Dining* magazine, he noted.

He dropped his hands on her shoulders and stroked them down her arms as he leaned forward to kiss her lightly on the back of her neck.

“Draco! This is a surprise,” she said with a jubilant smile as she spun round in her computer chair at his touch.

She reached up and pulled his face down to hers. His pulse quickened as her lips pressed against his, then parted, allowing him access to taste her. *Dio,* it seemed as if he could never get enough of her. It would make the news he had to tell her now even more difficult to impart.

“So,” she said when he finally drew back from her welcoming embrace, “what brings you here at this time of day?”

“Not so good news, I’m afraid.”

“Oh?”

She made a tiny moue with her mouth, making him want to kiss her again.

“I have to go away for a few days, to Adelaide. My Australian business manager has unfortunately been in an accident and won’t be out of the hospital for several days. I need to meet with some of our exporters.” A sudden thought occurred to him. “Come with me. Leave the restaurant in Phil’s hands and run away for a few days. It’s beautiful in the Adelaide hills this time of year. You’ll love it.”

“When do you leave?”

“In a couple of hours. I’m traveling by charter, I’ll call them and delay the flight to give you time to get ready. All you have to do is say yes.”

Suddenly he wanted her to come with him more than ever. It would be a slice out of time for them both. Granted, he'd have some business meetings and dinners to attend, but he could complete the social side of his business with Blair on his arm. A warm glow started in the pit of his belly as he started to look forward to doing just that. It would be good to get her away from Carson's. She worked as if one possessed her, and he wanted a chance to again see the woman who'd so enticed him while she was at Palazzo Sandrelli.

He studied her face, expecting to see it light up with excitement. Instead a frown pulled her eyebrows together.

"Draco, I'd love to, but I can't. I have a business to run, and tonight—well, tonight is probably going to be the most important night of all."

"Why tonight?" He asked, clamping down on the frustration at having his newly formed plans summarily discarded.

"It sounds as if Bill Alberts—you know, from *Fine Dining*?—will be coming tonight. It's my chance to lift our rating in the magazine. To be the best!"

She glowed with an inner light as she spoke, but for the life of him he couldn't understand why that meant she couldn't come with him. Surely she trusted her kitchen and waitstaff to provide the same level of service they'd give, whether she was there or not.

"So this Bill Alberts, has he made a booking?"

"Not exactly, but one of his associates has made a booking for six guests tonight. It's the way he operates. I just know tonight is going to be *the* night. I have to be here. It's important to me."

While Blair was no further away from him physically than before, he could sense she'd emotionally widened the distance between them.

She pushed her chair back a little, letting it bump against the desk, and stood up. "When do you expect to be back?"

"I'll be gone for five nights." He stepped closer, cupping his hands on her hips and pulling her into him. "Will you miss me?"

He felt the fine tremor run through her before she answered.

"You know I will. But it's okay." She laughed, the sound almost artificial. "It's not as if we have a permanent arrangement together or anything. Now, if you'll excuse me, I have a big night to prepare for."

She went to pull free from his hands, but rather than let her go he tightened his grip, cradling her between his hips. He ran his hands up the long muscles of her back until their bodies were aligned. Her breasts pressed against his chest, full, firm. Different, yet the same. A different bra, perhaps? He couldn't wait to see it, to peel it off her. But in the meantime, he'd have to settle for a kiss that could last him the five nights he'd be away.

He took her lips hungrily, determined to imprint himself indelibly on her both physically and mentally. It bothered him more than he cared to admit that she was prepared to put her work before him, but he reminded himself, it was her intensity, her focus and her drive that he'd found so compelling. The first time he'd seen her, in the kitchens of the commercial arm of the palazzo that catered to groups on culinary tours, she'd stood out from the rest. A humming, vibrant energy amongst a collection of people who only played at being artists in the kitchen.

Blood pooled in his groin and he ground his hips against her, letting his tongue slide into her mouth in a pale imitation of what he wanted to do with her body. She melted against him, her body no longer stiff and reluctant in his arms, but pliant and willing.

The sound of a throat clearing dragged his attention back to where they were.

"You guys want to get a room or something?" Gustav asked from behind him.

"We were just saying *arrivederci.*"

Draco reluctantly let Blair from his arms. The instant feeling of emptiness came as a surprise, but then again, they'd been all but making love here in this tiny cluttered room. It was no wonder that he physically missed her already.

"Gustav, you're here early," Blair said, a warm blush rising up her neck and invading her cheeks.

"Didn't want to miss the show," her headwaiter replied. "The one tonight, I mean—Bill Alberts."

"You people have no proof this man is even coming tonight. Why are you all so…so?" Words failed Draco and he gestured widely with his hands.

Blair caught his hands in hers. "Because this is everything we have worked for for months. If he doesn't show, we'll have had a great trial run."

"But isn't every night a trial run?"

"Of course. But this one could be it. It's as close as

we've gotten. Now, I'm sure you have things to do before you leave tonight, and I know I have a lot to see to."

Draco couldn't believe she was dismissing him! Usually, he was the one to make an exit. He didn't know whether to be annoyed or amused. He settled for amused. He didn't want their parting, however brief this time, to be tainted by any sour words between them. But when he came back he planned to absorb all her attention—to the extent that she wouldn't want to be without him again.

"*Ciao, bella.* Until next Wednesday."

"Take care, Draco."

Her attention was already back on her computer screen before he'd even left the room.

"It's a bugger, isn't it?" Gustav said at his side.

"What is?"

"That she's so absorbed in her work."

"A minor problem, *si.* But nothing that can't be dealt with," Draco replied confidently. With any luck she'd miss him as much as he knew he would miss her in the next few days. It would make his suggestion to her when he got back that much easier to implement.

"Well, good luck, buddy. You'll need it. She's married to this place, you know."

"We will see about that."

He would definitely see about that, Draco decided as his driver pulled away from the front of the restaurant.

Blair picked up the phone and dialed her father's number. He deserved to know that tonight could be the night they'd all been waiting for.

"Dad!" She said the second the phone was picked up, not even waiting for his gruff "hello," then gushed with the news that Bill Alberts could be reviewing them that night.

He was understandably excited for her, and apprehensive. As they finished their call he said, "Well, good luck for tonight, honey. I wish I could be there with you. What about your man, will he be there?"

"Dad, Draco's not my man, he's just—" Blair hesitated, unsure and unwilling to peg a title to exactly where Draco fit into her life right now, let alone examine her growing feelings toward him or how difficult it would be to say goodbye when he returned to his homeland.

"A friend?" Her father laughed in her ear. "Be careful, Blair. He doesn't strike me as the kind of man who takes 'friendship' lightly."

"I know," Blair sighed, "but it will be okay. He's away at the moment, and when he gets back? Well, we'll cross that bridge when we get to it."

A few minutes later, when she hung up, she wondered just how tricky that bridge would be to negotiate. He'd been so *Italian* today, expecting her to drop everything and just be there with him at his behest.

She stared at the wall calendar. Five nights he'd be gone. Five whole, lonely nights. She wouldn't bother going to his apartment, even though she had a key. She preferred the familiarity of her flat, if she was going to be alone.

It was time she changed for work, she thought, flicking a glance at the wall clock, when her eyes drifted back again to the wall calendar. Something wasn't quite right, she thought, looking back over the past two months. She was missing the annotation that marked the start of her period. It wasn't a big mark, just something she did to keep track, out of habit. But since her trip to Tuscany, nothing.

She searched her memory, had she had a period and forgotten to mark it up?

A cold chill settled on her shoulders. No. She knew she hadn't had a period since about a week before she'd gone away. But she'd faithfully taken her pill. There was no way she could be pregnant, could she? She counted two weeks forward from her last period and her finger stopped slap bang in the middle of the week she'd spent at Palazzo Sandrelli. The week that should never have happened. She'd forgone the balance of her culinary tour for the pleasure of being with Draco. Besides, she'd learned so much more from his chefs than she'd have picked up elsewhere.

So what had happened? Was her cycle so out of whack because of the travel and how busy she'd been since her return? But she had been, and still was, on the pill.

Her stomach flipped uncomfortably, reminding her of the nausea, the dizzy spells.

No. She couldn't be pregnant.

Six

"So, you're saying that because I didn't take my tablet at the exact same time every day, being the time I would take my tablet here in New Zealand, that I was unprotected?"

Blair fought back tears as she tried to simplify what her doctor had told her. She'd already left a urine sample with the nurse, but if what her doctor said was true, she had a horrible idea she knew exactly what the result of the pregnancy test would be.

"Blair, you are on a very low dose contraceptive. You were aware of that at the beginning, weren't you?"

"Yes. Yes I was."

And she'd had a reminder set in her cell phone to go off at the exact same time every day so she never forgot a tablet. But since her phone hadn't had a global roaming facility she hadn't taken it overseas with her.

Draco had used condoms when she was in Italy, but after a couple of nights, and days, Blair remembered a couple of occasions where their passion had gotten the better of them. He'd gone to great lengths to assure her of his sexual health, and she knew for herself there were no troubles in that regard. But this, this was another kind of trouble altogether.

The doctor's phone trilled on her desk and Blair jumped, her eyes locked on the doctor's face as he answered.

"Yes, yes. Thank you, nurse."

The doctor turned to face her. Blair could read nothing in expression.

"You say your last period was in the second week of February?" the doctor asked.

Blair nodded. At least that's the last time she'd marked it on her wall calendar. She sat rigid in her chair as the doctor referred to a sheet on her desk.

"Hmmm, well, Blair, that would make you about ten weeks pregnant."

At Blair's shocked gasp the doctor's face settled into sympathetic lines. "Blair, I can tell this is a shock. I take it the father isn't on the scene?"

Blair shook her head, not trusting herself to speak. Pregnant? It was her worst nightmare. How could she have failed so horribly? Risked so much—and lost.

Her mind was numb as she endured the physical examination her doctor requested, and as her appointment came to an end she numbly accepted the slip of paper to order her blood tests.

"Everything looks good so far, Blair. We'll book you in for a scan to confirm your dates, et cetera, but from the exam and your last period I think we can safely assume your baby's due date will be around mid-November."

Mid-November. It seemed so far away, and yet so close too. Blair drove herself back home and curled up on her favorite chair, trying to absorb the reality that she was pregnant—*with Draco's child.*

Oh heavens! *Draco.* He'd be back in two days. How on earth would she keep this from him? He was the kind of man for whom family was everything. She'd understood that early on, when she'd first met him. He'd never support her need to keep working and to keep running Carson's. The kind of family values that defined him had no place in her world. Her world was constantly in motion, moving from one challenge to the next in her field. Carson's itself had only been up and running for three years, the last of which being under her sole guidance.

She had so many plans for the restaurant's development, there was no time for a baby. *A baby.* It was too much to even think about right now. Her life had tilted off its axis with just one stupid mistake. She needed to take stock, find her feet again, to pour herself into something familiar. Even though it was one of her days off, she decided to go into the kitchen and work tonight. She couldn't stand to be alone with her thoughts right now.

Blair peeled off the small dressing that had been secured over her vein where the blood sample had been drawn. The last thing she needed when she went downstairs was for someone to ask her why she'd had blood tests. She would deal with her pregnancy, and Draco, when she absolutely had to.

Draco seethed silently as he listened to Blair refusing to see him. Even as tired and jet-lagged as he was, he couldn't wait to see her again, get her into bed. Unfortunately, she didn't appear to feel the same way.

It frustrated him intensely that she could be so flippant about the connection between them. Not even with Marcella had he felt such passion.

"Blair, didn't you miss me?"

"I did. But it's crazy busy here at Carson's right now. We're fully booked for weeks. We even have a waiting list for diners. Can you believe it? To be honest with you, I'm so tired at the end of each night, it's all I can do to get up the stairs and go to bed."

There was a brittle note to her voice he didn't like.

"Are you brushing me off, Blair?"

"Of course not. It's like I told you. I'm really just too busy to see you, and to be honest, Draco, I just don't have the energy to put into seeing you right now."

"So you're saving all your passion for your work?" he asked lightly, even though inside he was a tumbling roil of rage. "Your dedication is admirable, but what about you?"

"I'm fine. I'm happiest when I'm busy like this. It's what I've always wanted for Carson's, and the rumor is that Bill Alberts was very impressed with his visit here. His online review is due out later this week."

Again, there was that almost-false tone to her speech.

"Blair, is there something you're not telling me? You sound different. Please, let me pick you up tonight and take care of you."

His body hardened as he remembered the first time he'd done just that. Could it only have been just over three weeks ago? It felt longer, just as the past five days and nights in Adelaide had felt longer too. He'd missed Blair on every level, and he had planned a reunion that would satisfy all her senses, not to mention tide them both over for when he had to return soon to Italy. It was disappointing that she wasn't as keen to reunite as he was.

"Blair?" he prompted again in response to her silence.

He heard her draw in a deep breath and exhale heavily before she spoke.

"Look, it's probably better this way anyway. The restaurant is taking all of my time right now and then some. Besides, you'll be gone very soon, and we'd have to say good-bye all over again. I think we should cut our ties before things get too messy."

"Messy?" he asked.

"You know, emotional and all that."

So she thought the life, color and passion in their relationship lacked emotion? He bit against the growl that rose in his throat. More than anything, he wanted to refute her words, needed to coax from her the truth she wouldn't admit to herself.

He'd loved and lost before. When Marcella had died he'd known grief, but it had been heavily laced with guilt. Guilt that he hadn't loved her enough or understood her enough to realize that she would go so far as to risk her own life to give him what he wanted. A sharp pain lanced through him at the memory. It hadn't been just one life, but two.

Marcella should never have gotten pregnant, but she'd hidden from him the details of her congenital heart defect that made pregnancy dangerous, and in her second trimester, she'd paid the awful price for loving him. At a time when most women glowed and blossomed, Marcella had become hypertensive and frail. When her beautiful, generous heart had failed, taking her life and that of their unborn child, Draco had sworn to honor her memory and had promised he wouldn't pass on passion if it presented itself. He may not be ready to love but he certainly couldn't deny the chemistry he and Blair shared.

He cleared his throat before speaking. "And are you telling me there is nothing *emotional* in our connection?"

"There can't be. I won't be that kind of person. It takes too much from me and what I want to do."

"Can you deny that since we have been together your work, your creativity, has bloomed into something that people now stand in line to appreciate?"

"You're being ridiculous."

"Is it ridiculous when you shake with pleasure in my arms? Is it ridiculous when we share an incredible bond at that moment I enter your beautiful body?" He pressed as hard as he dared without making her hang up in his ear.

"Draco, please. Stop." Blair's voice shook.

"Stop? Blair, that sounds suspiciously like emotion in your voice. Without emotion, *cara mia,* we don't really live. Believe me, I know."

"As do I, and I know what I don't want. I'm sorry, Draco. This really has to be good-bye."

The soft click in his ear severed their connection, and for an instant Draco felt that break through his body. He gripped the phone so tight in his hand the plastic squeaked in protest. Slowly, deliberately, he replaced the handset of his phone on its cradle.

Well, as his old professor was always fond of saying, there was more than one way to skin a cat.

Blair made her way out of the lobby of the post office where she'd just picked up her mail. Absently, she flicked through the envelopes as she walked back to her car. Bills, bills—there'd been a time when that fact would have worried her, but not now. The daily receipts were through the roof and the much-coveted and long-awaited five-star review had been posted on the *Fine Dining* Web site. Life had never been better.

Except for the issue of her pregnancy. It had been a week since her confirmation. Five days since she'd severed contact with Draco. She was still in turmoil about whether she should tell him or not. Her favorite option right now was *not,* even if it was horribly wrong. He deserved to know, but she didn't want to tell him. She had no doubt he'd want to take control of her life at that point, and that was not going to happen. Not now, when she had everything else running exactly as she'd imagined when she took Carson's over from her dad.

Blair stopped in her tracks as she came across a high-quality envelope that had been hand-addressed to her. She flipped it over to see who the sender was and frowned as she identified the name as her landlord's lawyers. She'd dealt with them over the lease for

Carson's when her name had been substituted for her father's as the lessee. What on earth could they want from her now?

She unlocked her car and sat down, dropping all the suppliers' invoices on the passenger seat before hooking her finger under the seal and ripping the envelope open. Her eyes scanned the contents of the letter once quickly; then again as she read more slowly, the words sinking in with mind-numbing dread.

The lawyers had been instructed by the owners of the converted villa which housed Carson's that the property had been listed for sale.

She bashed the palm of her hand against her steering wheel in frustration.

"Damn, damn, damn!" she shouted, garnering some strange looks from passersby.

What if a new owner wanted to use the building for something else? They weren't bound by the lease she had with the current owner, an elderly widow. She scanned the letter again for any indication of who might have listed the property, but there was nothing. She'd have to call the lawyers and ask them. She had to find out how much her landlord wanted for the building. Maybe, just maybe, on the coattails of her current success and with the money she'd managed to save, she'd be able to raise a loan to buy the building herself?

The next day, despite not having been able to get ahold of the lawyer dealing with her landlord's affairs, Blair walked as confidently as she could manage into her bank manager's office. She laid out her position and showed him the financial statements for the business, supplemented by her past month's receipts. After much discussion and juggling of numbers, the bank manager leaned back in his chair and steepled his fingers together. Blair's stomach clenched in a knot of nerves.

"Well, Ms. Carson, I think we'll be able to help you out."

He named a figure that made Blair's heart swell with hope, even as her brain shrank back in horror at the requirements to meet such a loan. She couldn't even begin to think how she'd meet the repayments if she had to slow down her workload later in her pregnancy, or how she'd cope after the baby was born.

"Now, I suggest you put an offer together to your landlord's lawyer based on what we've discussed today." He stood up and offered his hand across the table. "Good luck. I look forward to hearing from you so we can get the paperwork drawn up."

"Thank you so much. You have no idea how much this means to me."

"Oh, you'd be surprised. Now you go and make that offer and call me when you hear back, okay?"

"Yes. Yes I will."

Blair almost ran back to her car, barely able to suppress her excitement. The trip back to her apartment passed in a blur. She raced up her back stairs and flung open the door, scrabbling for her phone on the side table before the door was even fully closed behind her.

She drummed her fingers on the tabletop as she was put on hold, the piped music setting her teeth on edge. She was almost on the verge of hanging up to call back and leave a message when the phone was answered at the other end.

Blair wasted no time in getting to the point.

"It's Blair Carson here, I received a letter from you regarding the possible sale of the building I lease from Mrs. Whitcomb. I'd like to put in an offer based on pre-arranged finance."

Blair named the sum she and the bank manager had agreed she could afford. He'd suggested she offer lower and then come back with another figure if the vendor counter-offered, but Blair just wanted the place so much she went in with her highest bid. She curled the cord of the phone around and around in her fingers as she waited for the lawyer on the other side to respond.

"I'm sorry, Ms. Carson. But Mrs. Whitcomb has already accepted an unconditional offer."

"I beg your pardon? But I only got your letter yesterday."

"Yes, the letter was a formality required under your tenancy agreement, however at the time of writing it, the property had already been sold."

"But—"

"As I said, Ms. Carson, I'm terribly sorry. Mrs. Whitcomb was more than happy with the offer and has signed the transfer papers."

"Who…who bought the property?" Tears spiked in Blair's eyes—hot, burning tears of anger and frustration.

"I am not at liberty to disclose the identity of the purchaser at this time."

"And their plans for the building? Have they said anything about that yet?"

"Not yet, Ms. Carson, but might I suggest, as a precaution of course, that you consider where you might relocate to, should the necessity arise."

Blair hung up the phone without saying good-bye and sank to her knees. The tears were coming thick and fast now. *Relocate?* How the heck would she do that? Suitable property in Ponsonby was in very high demand, and with her patronage now at an all-time high, to shift to another suburb could spell total ruin for Carson's.

Raw sobs tore from her throat as she allowed the devastation of the lawyer's words to take full effect. What the hell was she going to do now? Not even when Rhys and Alicia had betrayed her had she felt this distraught, this dispossessed.

It was late afternoon by the time she managed to pull herself together. Downstairs she could hear the noises of preparation in the kitchen. It would be another busy night and she needed to pull herself together and get down there.

Blair dragged herself through a quick shower and put on her double-breasted chef jacket and checkered trousers before lacing up her shoes.

A sense of inevitability settled on her shoulders. What would be would be. She'd find some way to get around whatever the new owner wanted. Besides, why automatically assume that they wouldn't want to keep her on? Carson's made an excellent tenant. Feeling slightly buoyed by the thought, she made her way downstairs.

Gustav bailed her up the minute he saw her.

"What's up, sweetie? You look like you've been through the wringer. Is it your Italian? Do I need to deal with him?"

"No…no, it's not Draco. We've stopped seeing one another anyway. It's—"

Blair's chin started to wobble and Gustav led her straight into her office, pushing her gently down on her chair. He squatted down in front of her and took both her hands in his.

"C'mon, sweetie, let it out. Tell me what's wrong."

"The building's been sold. I tried to buy it but they said it had already been sold."

"But they can't do that," Gustav protested. "Don't you have to be given notice?"

"I got that yesterday, but I thought I'd have time to put an offer forward, that as the tenant I might stand a better chance to buy the property. But it was too late."

"And what about your lease?"

"It's with the previous owner only."

"So it's simple. We renegotiate with the new owner, yes? No need for tears. They'd be mad to lose us here."

"But what if they wanted the building for something else? What if—"

"It'll be okay, just you wait and see. Now dry your eyes and get back into that kitchen. We've got an amazing night ahead."

"Hey, who's the boss here?"

"I am," Gustav answered with a cheeky smile. "I just let you think you are most of the time." He went to leave her office.

"Gus?" she called, making him stop and turn around. "Thanks. I'll see if we can set up a meeting with the new owners and negotiate a new lease in the next few days."

"That's my girl," Gus said with a wink.

The night was chaotic but satisfying. By the time Blair laid her head on her pillow she was too exhausted to even think, let alone dream up possible scenarios for Carson's.

The morning dawned bright and clear—one of those incredibly crisp autumn days that made the sky so blue you felt as if you could stare into its ceiling forever.

Blair contacted the lawyer again and requested a meeting as soon as possible with the new owners. The lawyer said he'd need some time to sort it all out, but when he rang back just before she went into the kitchen, he sounded just as surprised as she did that the new owner had agreed to meet with her the next morning.

She could barely keep her mind on her work, she was so apprehensive about the meeting. But she tried to channel Gustav's positivity, as if by hoping for a positive outcome, it could genuinely make it happen.

The night seemed endless, even after she'd done her final rounds and locked everything up—even after she'd showered and lay in bed for hours, staring at the dark painted ceiling above her.

Finally it was morning. She dressed with extra care, wanting to present the most professional impression of herself and the restaurant that she could.

They'd agreed to meet in the dining room itself at ten, and Blair was pacing back and forth between the tables, wondering for the umpteenth time whether she should have changed from her only suit—a severely cut black number with which she'd teamed sheer black stockings and low-heeled shoes, eschewing a blouse underneath for a wisteria-blue silk camisole she'd treated herself to in Italy—into something less dramatic. The waistband on her skirt was snug, the first visible indication of her pregnancy. She rested her palm against her lower belly. Her baby—Draco's baby—was growing. She wouldn't be able to ignore it for much longer.

The rap at the door made her jump and she wheeled about, taking a second to smooth her hands down over her jacket, giving it a little tug to straighten the edges, before moving across the floor to welcome her new landlord.

"You?" she gasped as she pulled the door open.

A chill ran through her body and the blood drained from her face and dropped to her feet. Draco's frame filled the doorway, his face as dark as thunder, his brows a thick, straight line, and his lips—normally bearing the slight curve of smile—were set in lines that didn't bode well for Carson's, or for Blair.

Seven

"Who else? I couldn't get you to agree to see me any other way. I'm not above using my wealth and influence when I have to. You'd do well to remember that in future, *cara mia*."

"Don't. Don't call me that. I'm not your darling, your lover. Your *anything*."

Suddenly it occurred to Blair that antagonizing Draco was probably not the best thing to have done under the circumstances. A roiling wave of nausea rose from the pit of her stomach. She spun around and flew toward the women's restroom, her hand over her mouth, tears once more streaming down her face.

In a toilet stall she fell to her knees and retched until her stomach was empty.

"Here."

A folded wet paper towel was pressed into her hand from behind her. *Oh no.* Had Draco followed her in here? Witnessed her embarrassing loss of control?

"When you're feeling okay I will be waiting for you outside."

There was a tone to his voice that left her in no doubt that he wouldn't wait long. She freshened up as quickly as she could, rinsing out her mouth before she straightened her jacket again and checked her appearance in the mirror.

Her pantyhose were laddered from the knees down. Well, there was nothing she could do about that right this minute, aside from remove them altogether, and she didn't think he'd wait while she did that. There was one thing about Draco of which she was certain: when he wanted something, or someone, he wanted them right now.

On legs that were surprisingly steady she walked back out to the restaurant. Draco leaned up against the bar, his casually elegant pose a front for the coiled tension she sensed simmering below the surface. He pushed himself upright as she approached and crossed his arms, his feet planted about shoulder width apart.

His dark hair was slicked back off his forehead today, creating a stark demarcation line, framing his face which was set in stern lines. His heavy brows drew together slightly, his green eyes narrowed as his gaze swept her body. She feared he saw everything—each of the changes in her body she'd so staunchly tried to ignore. Her stomach pitched again.

"How long were you going to wait before telling me?" he demanded, his voice like velvet over steel.

She decided to try and bluff him out, then abruptly

changed tack, choosing to attack him on his own terms. "I could ask you the same thing. How long were you going to wait before telling me you'd bought this building? Just how much did you offer Mrs. Whitcomb? I never stood a chance to buy out, did I?"

"You would have known in good time, Blair. Now, it is not like you to be unwell, and I assume it can be due to only one thing. So, I will ask you again. How long were you going to wait before telling me?"

He covered the short distance between them in the blink of an eye. One arm curved around her back, holding her captive against his body. Darn it! Her body responded instantly to his touch, his warmth. When his hand stroked inside the lapel of her jacket and across the silk of her camisole, her nipples tightened instantly, as if seeking the softness of his palm.

"Did you think I would not notice your breasts are fuller?" His hand slid down to her waist before coming to rest against her lower belly. "That your waist is even now thickening with the growth of my child?"

A shiver ran through her from head to foot. There was a note now to his voice that frightened her. A staunch sound of possession, ownership.

"This changes everything. I was prepared to let you have some space, to give you time to see the sense in our relationship. But no more. Not when this involves my child."

"And what about me? You make it sound as if my wishes have nothing to do with whatever you decide."

Draco's lips compressed in a straight line as he looked at her closely. His eyes turned the color of a storm-tossed sea and she shivered again, only this time it wasn't in fear. This time, it was in pure reaction to the intensity she saw there, and every ounce of that intensity was focused on her.

A weaker woman would crumble. Throw herself on his mercy. But then again, she reminded herself tersely, a weaker woman would probably happily accept Draco's imperious manner.

"Well?" she prompted. "Don't I have any say?"

"The baby is a Sandrelli, and he, or she, will be brought up with all that entails," Draco replied in a voice that brooked no argument.

"What are you talking about?" Blair pulled free from his hold.

"I have a responsibility to my family, to the generations of Sandrellis who have gone before me. This baby, this child of ours, has a birthright, a heritage, that stretches back centuries. It will be born where I was born, where my father was born before me and his before him."

Draco struggled to control the rising sense of sheer joy that plumed like a massive cloud of excitement from deep inside him. A baby. A child. *His* child. Finally he could bring his parents something to look forward to, some happiness in lives that had seen altogether too much sorrow. First the death of Lorenzo, his brother, ten years ago, and then more recently, Marcella and their unborn infant and his father's ill health.

No matter what Blair thought, this baby would be born right where it belonged. In the heart of Tuscany.

"You're being unreasonable," she argued. "This is exactly why I would never have told you that I was pregnant. You don't even know yet if it is your baby, and you're already riding roughshod over me and making decisions about it without any thought to how this affects me."

Draco stiffened. "You have been intimate with other men since we met?"

She couldn't hold his gaze, instead letting her eyelids flutter down over her eyes, hiding from him her deepest thoughts. It was all the answer he needed. She could no more deny the baby was his than she could stop him in what he was going to do now.

"You will appoint a new chef to take over from you immediately," he said firmly.

"I will do no such thing. Carson's is my restaurant. I'm in charge here, not you. Besides, I *am* Carson's, as was *my* father before *me!*"

She all but spat the words at him and he fought to control a smile. As if her claim to familial lineage could be compared with the generations-old traditions and responsibilities handed down through his.

"You cannot argue with me on this, Blair. It will serve no purpose."

"No purpose? How dare you. You cannot dictate to me where I live. I have a business to run here, my home is in New Zealand and my baby will be born here."

"If you want to play hardball with me, that is fine. I can match you any day of the week. If you do not agree to return to Tuscany with me and have our baby there, where it belongs, I will terminate your lease on the restaurant. The choice is yours. I will be back this time tomorrow for your answer."

He strode out the door, barely trusting himself to remain in her presence. He'd already lost one child. He would not lose another in this lifetime if he had any say in the matter.

His mind was already ticking over as his driver shot out the car to open the passenger door for him. As he settled against the buttery-soft leather of the interior of the limousine he took his mobile phone from his breast pocket and flipped it open.

His instructions to his New Zealand–based assistant were terse and to the point. "Get me the address of Blair Carson's father. I need it immediately."

Before ten minutes had passed his driver had pointed the limousine down the Southern Motorway and they were headed for an appointment he had no intention of leaving until he had exactly the answer he wanted.

Blair Carson, Sr., was not as Draco had expected. The house in which he lived could barely be called more than a casual beachfront holiday retreat. If his information was correct, the man rented on a month-by-month basis. Hardly the kind of stability that Draco took for granted in his world, and hardly the kind of family stability Draco wanted for his unborn child either.

Draco instantly noted the similarities between the elder Carson and his daughter. Similar height and build, although the man walking toward him now was slightly stooped, his black hair streaked with grey.

He extended his hand, wasting no time in getting to introductions and outlining exactly what he wanted from him.

"So you're telling me my daughter is pregnant?" Blair's dad looked incredulous.

"Yes, sir, and it would mean everything to my family if I could take Blair back to my home in Tuscany to have the baby there. But you know how she feels about Carson's. She isn't happy to leave the restaurant in just anyone's hands. I understand you oversaw the kitchen while she was on her tour in February."

"That's right. It was good to be back in charge." Blair's father nodded, a smile wreathing his face.

"Then, could I presume upon you to do the same again for me while she is in Tuscany until the birth of the child? I will certainly make it worth your while." Draco mentioned a figure that was more than competitive. "I would like you to take over as soon as possible, as I have business to attend to back home, and I would like Blair to travel with me. Obviously, I understand that your health makes it impossible for you to do all that Blair has undertaken in recent months, however, I believe I can trust you to appoint someone in the kitchen who would give her the peace of mind she needs to be able to step away."

"You seem to be prepared to go to a great deal of trouble for my daughter, Mr. Sandrelli."

"Draco, please, and believe me when I say I will do everything in my power to protect Blair through this pregnancy. The hours she's been working, the responsibility and pressure she's put upon herself. None of it can be good, long-term, especially as she gets bigger."

An image of Blair, swollen with his child, sprang into his mind and a rush of pride rose within him so strong and so deep it made his heart ache.

"No, I agree. Well, Draco," Blair's father extended his hand, "it looks as if you have yourself a deal."

"Thank you, sir. You have no idea how much this means to me."

"And Blair? I take it she isn't yet aware of your plans, because to be honest, I know exactly how stubborn she can be, and I can't see her agreeing to this in a hurry."

Draco smiled. Her father knew her well. "I will take care of Blair. You can rest assured of that."

At ten the next morning Draco pulled up outside the restaurant. Before he could rap his knuckles against the glass-paneled door it swung sharply open.

"What have you done?"

Blair looked furious.

"I warned you not to underestimate me. Did you think I said those words in jest?"

"How could you go behind my back before I'd even given you an answer?"

Draco stepped past her and waited for her to close the door before responding. "I did what was necessary."

"Necessary? Do I have to remind you this is *my* restaurant?"

"Not at all, nor do I need to remind you that I own the roof over this restaurant, the walls that surround it and the floor beneath it. You want Carson's to continue, then yes, it will. But it will be without you slaving yourself to exhaustion in the kitchen."

"My father isn't well. He can't take over my role here full-time."

"I'm well aware of your father's limitations, Blair. I'm

not inhuman, despite what you think. He has instructions to appoint a new chef in your absence. However, I think it will do him good to have his hand back in, rather than moldering away where he is now."

"Moldering? He's having a well-earned rest."

"Tell me, Blair, does your father really strike you as the kind of man who would be happy to 'rest' for the balance of his years?"

He could see he'd made his point when she ceased pacing back and forth across the floor and her hands, which had been so animated as she spoke, fluttered uselessly to her side.

Draco stepped closer to her and took her chin in one hand, forcing her to meet his eyes.

"Well? Does he?"

He felt her capitulation in the frustrated breath she let out in a rush through her delectable lips.

"No. He doesn't."

"Then we are settled. We leave at the end of next week."

"What? So soon?"

"There is no reason to linger, Blair. Everything will be under control here. Who is more eminently qualified than your own father to make sure of that?"

"Me. I'm more qualified. I'm younger, I'm fitter and this is my restaurant." Blair's voice rose, her tone becoming frantic.

"And you are also pregnant. Pregnant with my heir. That is a responsibility you must put before all others now."

Her brown eyes blazed her frustration and her fury back into his.

"Fine. I'll go back to your precious palazzo with you. I'll have your baby. But know this, I will return home to New Zealand as soon as I can after the birth."

Draco held his breath a moment, his jaw clenched as he bit back the retort that immediately sprang to mind. Instead, when he spoke, he did so with a voice that was level and which showed no indicator of how he felt inside.

"If you return, it will be without the baby."

Blair's response was vehement. "Whatever it takes to be free of you."

Eight

The next few days turned into a whirlwind of activity. Blair barely had the chance to set foot in the restaurant as Draco commandeered her every waking moment, even going so far as to accompany her to her doctor on the Monday morning before they were due to depart.

She felt odd as they entered the doctor's rooms with him at her side, the breadth of his palm nestled warmly against the small of her back. To all intents and purposes, they'd look just like a normal couple coming for a prenatal visit, but Blair knew they could never be anything so simple.

"Really, Draco. It's only two weeks since I last saw the doctor. Everything's fine. I wasn't due to see her again for another two weeks."

"Let me be the judge of what is fine and what is not," he responded grimly.

Blair rolled her eyes. “Are you a doctor now too?”

“No, I am about to become a father, and I have a responsibility to ensure that my son or daughter is well.”

“Honestly, you’re overreacting. I’m only twelve weeks pregnant, I’ve been keeping excellent health, aside from a little tiredness, which,” she held up a hand as he started to speak “is perfectly normal at this stage of a healthy pregnancy.”

“Ms. Carson? The doctor will see you now,” the receptionist summoned them, bringing to a halt any further discussion between her and Draco.

The instant Draco sat down in the doctor’s office Blair felt as if she was invisible, as he launched into a series of questions about both her health and the baby’s.

“So you can assure me that there are no underlying concerns about Blair’s health that could put her or the child at risk?” he asked.

“Certainly nothing we’ve come across, Mr. Sandrelli. Blair’s most recent physical showed her to be in excellent health, with blood pressure, cholesterol, blood sugars—basically everything—within normal ranges. There’s no cause for concern that this pregnancy will be anything but smooth sailing.”

Blair seriously doubted her blood pressure was within normal ranges at present. Draco’s interest in her physical condition bordered on obsessional. Not a side of him she’d ever seen before, and she didn’t feel comfortable with it. It was almost as if he’d reduced her to an object, rather than a woman.

“See, I told you everything is fine.”

Draco shot a look so bleak that it made her heart

skitter in her chest. "Forgive me my concern, *cara mia*, but I wish to be certain that you and our baby will be safe through this pregnancy."

Blair bristled at his obvious use of endearment to keep the doctor on his side.

"Commendable, Mr. Sandrelli, but let me assure you that I expect no complications for Blair, and I'm sure that while you're back home in Italy you will be able to arrange excellent care for her. In the meantime, here is some literature that may give you some idea of what Blair should be eating, and avoiding—I always think it's kinder on our mothers-to-be if the whole family avoid the foods she has to. Blair is already on folate, calcium and iron supplements, and she has all this information, so I'm sure you can trust her to look after herself equally as well as you." The doctor gave Blair a reassuring smile, clearly well used to dealing with anxious first-time fathers.

"Thank you, doctor. I am much assured."

"Good. Now I'm sure Blair is becoming quite uncomfortable waiting for her scan, so let's take her through to our radiology rooms."

Blair could have hugged the doctor. Let Draco try and sit still with a straining bladder while someone asked inane questions. As they walked through to the radiology rooms, which formed part of the medical center, the doctor continued to talk to Draco.

"I'll receive the scan report and can either have a copy ready for you before you leave for Italy or, alternatively, I can forward a copy to your doctor over there, once you have chosen someone."

"We'd like to take it with us," Draco said before Blair could utter a word. He flipped out a business card. "Please send it through to this address. We leave at the end of the week, I trust that will provide you with sufficient time to get the report to me?"

"Yes, definitely."

The doctor introduced Blair and Draco to the radiographer conducting the scan. Draco sat to one side, now uncharacteristically silent as the radiographer prepared her for the scan by squeezing some gel onto her stomach. The woman described each step in the process of what she was doing as she did it, for which Blair was grateful. This was terrifying territory. Only two weeks ago she hadn't even considered pregnancy, in fact, had purposely avoided any thought of the possibility, now it was very much a reality. Even more so as the grainy image appeared on the screen.

"Here we are," the radiographer said with a smile. "It's time to meet your baby."

Blair's eyes fixed on the screen as the radiographer pointed out the baby's—*her* baby's—legs and arms and its head and body. It was hard to believe this tiny human being was growing and moving within her body, when externally, there was little sign of its existence.

"Oh boy, it's busy, isn't—" Blair turned her head to Draco but never got to finish her sentence as she was suddenly struck by the look on his face.

There was wonder there in his eyes, but at the same time an expression of raw grief that took her breath away. Their current animosity temporarily forgotten, she reached out her hand to him, needing to connect with him, to rid him of the anguish he'd exposed.

At her touch his expression changed and he turned his face, his eyes locking with hers. She was shocked to identify tears in his eyes, and suddenly the reality of the baby and what it meant to him began to hit home.

Already he loved this baby. Already it was a part of him. Yet for her, the pregnancy still felt so foreign. Even the visual evidence on the screen beside her didn't seem real.

The sense of division and separation between herself and Draco yawned like a chasm between them. As if he sensed her thoughts, he gently squeezed her fingers then let her hand go.

"May I have a print-out of the screen?" he asked, his voice surprising Blair with how level it was.

"Sure you can, here I'll print you one each."

Blair wanted nothing more than to curl herself up into a ball in the darkest corner of her bedroom and weep. But even that was lost to her, since her father had moved back into the tiny accommodation in preparation for taking over the management of the restaurant. Now she was back in Draco's apartment, and if the sense of dispossession she felt was any indicator, going to the palazzo in a few days' time was going to be even worse.

Draco settled back into the deep, comfortable leather seat of the charter jet that was taking them home. The week had been a blur of activity, tying off any loose ends to do with his business both in New Zealand and across the Tasman in Australia. He'd barely spent any time with Blair, although he doubted she minded that much at all.

All week he hadn't been able to stop thinking about

the sonogram he kept in his pocket. He'd never attended any of Marcella's checkups with her, he'd always been too busy with work, and she'd understood that—never demanding his company. Now he began to realize all he'd missed out on. It didn't alter the measure of his grief for her or their baby, but he silently vowed he would not be so distant this time.

By the time they reached the private airfield on the outskirts of the Sandrelli land near San Gimignano, they were both weary of travel. The stopovers en route had done little to break the tension between them, and despite the fact that Blair had rested in the private sleeping quarters for several hours, he could tell she was near to dropping with exhaustion. He made a mental note to ensure the obstetrician he'd engaged for her and the baby's care would come to the palazzo.

He wondered how she would find things there now. It would be totally different for her. A temporary home instead of a holiday venue.

The customs officers who met them at the airfield were polite and efficient, welcoming Draco back to his homeland in voluble Italian. Inch by inch, he began to feel his body ease into the rhythms of his land, into the undeniable sense of rightness and belonging he experienced every time he came home. His heart swelled with the thought that, in time, his child would know this feeling too. Would embrace the wide world with all its glories, but would eternally want to return to its roots.

It had been just over six weeks since he'd left, and the land had awakened from the lingering chill of winter that had extended into March. Around them, fields were ablaze with the fire of poppies and the golden glow of wild mustard.

Yes, it was good to be back.

Once the official requirements had been met, Draco ushered Blair into the waiting limousine. As they neared the palazzo, Draco looked around him with great eagerness, observing the various plantings that sustained part of the business enterprises of the Sandrelli Corporation. Olive groves, in the peak of health, marched like a giant green army over the gently rolling hills, while on the rise of land leading up to the palazzo lay row upon row of grape vines. At the top of the hill, inured against marauding invaders by a 16th century stone wall, stood the palazzo. Home.

It was good to return to what were essentially the grass roots of his heritage.

He flicked a glance at Blair. She sat pale and rigid on the seat, her eyes fixed out her window. She had barely said a dozen words on this final leg of the journey. He hoped she would be able to relax, once settled back into the palazzo. For both her sake and the baby's.

Once inside the palazzo, Draco led Blair to her room.

"This is different from where I stayed before, isn't it?" Blair noted as they went up a wide staircase to the next floor.

"Yes, this leads to my private quarters. Where you stayed before was the wing we have reserved for guests, both corporate- and tourism-related."

"I had no idea the accommodation was so extensive here. I really only saw such a small part of it, didn't I?"

Draco nodded, his mouth pulling into a wry smile.

If you counted the commercial kitchen, where the culinary tour classes were given, and her sleeping quarters of the time, the part she saw was indeed small.

"I will give you a full tour of the palazzo when you're rested. Perhaps tomorrow, hmmm?"

"I'd like that."

Was that an overture of friendship? He realized she must feel completely displaced. Not even the room she'd be sleeping in now was familiar to her. He swung open the heavy, paneled door that led into her room. In the warm glow of the evening, the deep rose-pink drapes, edged in gold braid and tied back from the mullioned windows, looked friendly and inviting, as did the canopied 19th century bed that dominated the room.

"Oh my God, it's like a museum. Are you sure I can sleep here?" Blair said with a nervous laugh.

"These pieces have been in my family—well—since they were new. We use them. That's what they were designed for."

Draco gestured to one of his staff to put Blair's cases through another door on one side of the room.

"A maid will be along shortly to unpack for you."

"Oh, that won't be necessary. I can do that for myself." Blair protested.

"It is very necessary. You look shattered. Why don't you turn in early and in the morning we can start anew? What do you say?"

There was something in Draco's eyes that went straight to Blair's heart. *Start anew.* It was so appealing. If only she could start anew back to February when she was last here. Where would they be now? She certainly wouldn't be here. She'd be back at Carson's doing what she loved.

Well, she decided she could make herself miserable for the whole time she was here, or she could make the most of it.

"Thank you, I'd like that," she replied softly.

Draco lifted a hand and traced one finger along the line of her jaw. Instantly her nerve endings went crazy. He hadn't touched her since that brief moment when they'd clasped hands in the radiography room. Suddenly she realized just how much she missed his touch. Missed him. Tears sprang to her eyes. Stupid, helpless tears that did nothing to reflect the jumble of emotions that cascaded through her.

"I'll let you rest then." Draco turned to leave the room.

"Draco, wait. Where will you be?" To her horror a note of panic slipped into her voice.

"I will call in briefly to see my parents and then I will return. I'll be just two doors further down the corridor, in my suite. Do not worry, Blair. I will not let you go far from my sight."

Blair nodded, barely trusting herself to speak.

"*Buona sera,* Blair. Sleep well. And don't worry about the maid when she comes, she will use the door that leads straight to your dressing room, so as not to disturb you."

"D-dressing room? I barely have enough clothes to fit in a chest of drawers, and now I have an entire dressing room?"

"Perhaps we can fly to Livorno, on the coast, for the day, and do some shopping. Or even north to Firenze.

Clearly, you will need a new wardrobe, especially as the baby grows."

The excitement that began to bubble inside her fell immediately flat as she was reminded that the true purpose behind her being here was the baby, and the baby alone.

"As you wish," she managed to say, because all of a sudden it was quite clear to her that despite the exquisite furnishings and the plush elegance of her new temporary home, she was here only at his bidding.

"Blair? It is not just as I wish. I would like to think you're looking forward to this baby too. I know we said some harsh things to one another last week, but I meant what I said when I suggested we start over. Think about it, hmm? And I'll see you in the morning."

When Draco was gone Blair took a minute to familiarize herself with her room. The large en suite bathroom was as luxuriously fitted as the bedroom—although a great deal more modern, she noted with relief. She grabbed her toiletries and a night shirt from her case and prepared for bed.

Draco's parting words still rang in her ears. *Start over.* It would be so lovely to do so. But what of her dreams? She'd finally taken Carson's to five-star splendor, only to have to leave it in another's hands. Granted, that person was her father, but still she felt cheated.

She slid between the fine cotton sheets, laundered with a hint of lavender, and rested her head onto the pillow. She'd thought she had it all under control, but where was that control now? Firmly in Draco's hands, and there was nothing she could do about it. Absolutely nothing.

Nine

Blair was awakened the next morning by the clink of crockery on a tray.

"*Buon giorno,* Ms. Carson. I trust you rested well." A uniformed maid bustled into the room and placed a tray on a nearby table. "I have brought you breakfast and a request from the *Signore* to be ready in an hour for a tour of the property. And Ms. Carson, the coffee is de-caffeinated as per your doctor's instructions."

"Thank you," Blair shoved herself upright in the bed and sniffed the air as the aroma of freshly brewed coffee tantalized her nostrils. Her eyes spied pastries in a small basket on the tray. "Are those *cornetti?*"

"Yes, raspberry. Your favorite, *si?* Cristiano, our cook, he remembered, and Ms. Carson? There is a small gift here for you also. A welcome to the palazzo from the *Signore.*"

Both curious and ravenous, Blair pushed the bedcovers from her legs and rose from the bed. With a cheerful smile, the maid left the room.

A narrow, long blue-velvet jeweler's box nestled on a starched, white serviette, next to the plate of *cornetti.* Curiosity won the tug of war and she lifted the case and gently opened it. Inside, laid upon shining white satin, was an exquisite silver charm bracelet. Blair lifted it from the case and held it up, exclaiming over the delicate charms evenly spaced along its length.

She didn't usually wear any jewelry. It just got in the way in the kitchen, but for now, she couldn't wait to put this piece on. She struggled a little with the parrot clasp before managing to secure it round her wrist. She turned her arm this way and that, admiring the reflection of light on the silver and the faint jangle of the charms as they bumped together. How thoughtful of Draco to give this to her. But then her cynical, insecure side wondered if he kept a cabinet filled with such things for his female guests. She knew for a fact that he was highly sought after in international circles. Just about every article about them back home in New Zealand had put pictures of his past companions side-by-side with whichever one they'd managed to snap of her and Draco together. Whatever the case, she loved the bracelet and she'd enjoy wearing it.

Her stomach rumbled, reminding her of the sweet delights waiting for her. Blair's mouth watered as she tore off a piece of the fresh pastry and popped it in her mouth. For a moment, even her critical chef's brain disengaged as it melted on her tongue. By the time she'd picked up the last crumb and enjoyed the delicious nutty-flavored coffee, she was ready to face the day. She took a quick shower in the bathroom and dressed in a loose-fitting, raspberry-colored sundress, as the day promised to be warm. The button-down style was easy to wear, and then, just for something different, she grabbed a long, multicolored scarf and tied it across her head from above her fringe and twisted it into a knot at the nape of her neck. The tails dropped over her shoulder. She studied the effect in the mirror. It was kind of retro sixties, but with her coloring, it looked good and gave her a dose of much-needed confidence. She looked at the time. She was ready early.

She paced the floor of her bedroom for a few minutes, finally settling in front of the tall windows that gave a stunning view out across the valley. In the distance, the darker shadows of the hills loomed over the verdant countryside. How different the landscape was from the blanket of winter she'd seen last time she was here. She wondered if she was to wait here for Draco, or if she should see if he was in his room. Waiting didn't sit comfortably with her. Already she was itching to get out in the sunshine of what promised to be a beautiful spring morning. Her decision made, she spun around and opened the door.

He'd said last night he was a couple of doors down the corridor from her. Her shoes made no sound on the petit point carpet of the hallway. It almost felt sacrilegious to walk on the fine craftsmanship. A couple of doors down he'd said; a rueful smile twisted her lips. He neglected to mention just how far down the hallway a couple of doors actually was.

Blair hesitated when she reached the cream-and-gold paneled door, a twin to her own. She drew her fisted hand up and rapped gently on the wood. It opened almost immediately.

"*Buon giorno,* Blair. You look much better this morning."

"Thank you. I had a wonderful sleep. And thank you too for this." She held up her wrist.

"Ah, you're most welcome. Here, come in, I'll be ready in a moment."

Draco stepped aside and Blair walked into a comfortable sitting room. While the chairs were heavily upholstered in rich floral fabrics, there was nothing feminine about the room. The wood-paneled walls and hunting paintings took care of that little detail, Blair noted.

She felt Draco as he drew up behind her. "You look and smell wonderful today."

A small shiver ran through her body as he dipped his head to the curve of her neck and felt his hand run down her arm. His long fingers wrapped around her wrist and he lifted her arm.

"Each charm has a special significance to our land here and our place in it." He fingered the small wine bottle nearest the clasp. "This is for the vineyard, where we produce our own Vernaccia."

"That's the white wine I had when I was here before, isn't it? I tried to get it in for Carson's, but our wine merchant was unable to secure any for me."

"We'll have to see what we can do about that, for your father."

Blair bristled slightly at the assumption that she would not be equally interested in getting the wine to New Zealand, but she was distracted by the soft stroke of Draco's index finger on the pulse point at her wrist.

He continued to hold her wrist loosely as he detailed each of the other charms on the chain, and she found herself mesmerized by the cadence of his voice. When he was finished she realized she'd allowed herself to sink back against his body, his chest a warm imprint through her dress and along her back.

She straightened, pulling loose from his clasp, feeling unsettled that she'd fallen under his spell again so easily. Last night he'd suggested they start over, but now in the light of day, she wasn't so convinced it was such a good idea. He was very much the lord and master of all the land she could see from the windows of the palazzo. So where did that leave her? And where did that leave her responsibility to Carson's?

"Draco, could I use a phone to let Dad know we arrived safely and that I'm okay? I saw one in my room but I wasn't sure if I could use it for an international call."

"No matter, I have already called him. He was happy to hear you were settled and that the journey was behind you. He said when you arrived back in New Zealand in February the trip had taken a lot out of you and that it took you a few days to recover from jet lag. Hopefully, you won't be so affected this time."

"After the luxury of that plane trip? I doubt it."

Blair smiled, hiding the flair of irritation that Draco

had spoken to her father without her knowledge. She'd have liked to have touched base with him, heard how he was managing back in the restaurant without her there.

"You are worrying about your precious restaurant, aren't you?"

Was she so easy to read? "Yes, I am. And about Dad too. When we left he'd done nothing about employing a new chef. I'm concerned he'll push himself too hard."

"Blair, your father is a grown man, quite capable of making his own decisions."

"That's exactly what I'm worried about. It was the decisions that he made that made him ill the last time."

"But he is on medication, *si?*"

"Yes, but he's stubborn." *Like you,* she added silently.

"Why don't you call him tonight around ten? It'll be eight o'clock Sunday morning there."

"Damn, I forgot about the time difference," Blair muttered, remembering it was the time difference that had gotten her into this position in the first place. "What about now? It'll be evening there now, right? About seven?"

"But won't the restaurant be busy? He'll hardly have time to talk to you, and he already knows you are safe and well."

What Draco said made perfect sense. "All right. Tonight it is."

"Good. Now we have that settled, let's start on our tour. Which do you prefer first—the palazzo or the grounds?"

"Oh, the grounds, please. It's such a beautiful day."

"Your wish is my command," Draco responded with a smile that sent a bolt straight to her heart.

He offered her his arm and she rested her hand in the

crook of his elbow. As they made their way back down the corridor toward the stairs, Draco told her of the history of some of the pieces of furniture and ornaments.

"Doesn't it worry you that some of these things will get broken? Shouldn't they be in a museum?"

Draco laughed. "They are a part of my family. If they break, they break. Of course, we take every step to ensure that doesn't happen on a regular basis, and some of the more valuable pieces are locked away in glass-fronted cabinets, like the ones you would have seen in the salon used for tour guests."

Blair envied him his casual acceptance of his world. As welcoming and comfortable as the palazzo was, she doubted she could ever fit in here. Her upbringing had been so transient, she didn't even have school photos to look back on. Whereas Draco—she looked around at the portraits interspersed with deep windows along the corridor—he could trace back his ancestors to near-medieval times.

Draco led her outside the palazzo to a courtyard where a gleaming convertible sat awaiting them.

"We're going to drive?" Blair asked, surprised. She'd expected they'd be walking around the grounds.

"I thought I'd take you to the furthest point of our land and then work our way back. Would you prefer we stay closer to home?"

Home. His home perhaps, Blair thought, looking back at the size of the palazzo as he helped her into the car.

"No, that's fine. It'll be lovely, I'm sure."

Draco slid into the driver's seat, his strong, capable hands settling on the steering wheel. It occurred to Blair that this was the first time she'd seen him drive.

"You don't drive when you're in New Zealand. Why is that?"

"Parking in and around the city is at such a premium, I prefer not to be bothered with such things when I'm there on business. Generally, I keep a car there for my own use, but for pleasure, I prefer to use my motorbike when I'm in Auckland."

"You ride a bike?"

Blair was surprised. Draco had always struck her as so smooth and urbane. Imagining him in black leathers, astride a powerful bike, did strange things to her equilibrium.

"Sure. My friends, Brent and Adam, and I each have the same model Moto Guzzi. When we're all in town together we try to make a few road trips, get away from it all. This time it didn't happen, but there's always the next."

By Brent and Adam, Blair knew he meant multimillionaire entrepreneur Brent Colby and Adam Palmer. Both men featured frequently in the papers, both in the business section and the social reports. And judging by the media storm about Brent Colby and heiress Amira Forsythe, just before she and Draco had left Auckland, that popularity wasn't about to die down terribly soon.

"How did you three meet? You were all at the memorial service, weren't you? Did you go to school at Ashurst?" she asked.

"Yes. My parents felt it was important that both my older brother and I experienced education in another country. He went to Australia, I went to New Zealand."

"Your brother?"

"Yes, Lorenzo. He died ten years ago. A stupid

accident. One of those totally avoidable things. He was waterskiing with friends off the Amalfi Coast. Unfortunately, the driver of the other boat had been drinking and thought it humorous to play 'chicken' with the boat towing Lorenzo. His neck was broken in the impact. He died immediately."

Tears filled Blair's eyes. "Oh, Draco, I'm so sorry. That must have been awful for your family."

He turned to face her, lifting a hand to gently wipe away the tears that spilled over her lashes and down her cheeks.

"It was terrible, but we've learned that life must go on. And now we have a new life to look forward to, our baby. My parents—you have no idea what this will mean to them."

"You haven't told them yet?"

Blair knew Draco's mother and father lived in a more modern home on the Sandrelli land, and she half-expected Draco to introduce her to them today.

"No, when I saw them last night I didn't feel the time was right. My father was tired and my mother distracted by his health. I will let them know soon, though. Now, shall we begin our adventure for today?"

Blair nodded her agreement and he shifted the car into gear, the wheels spitting up a little gravel as they drove out the massive gated entrance to the palazzo grounds.

She was amazed at the diversity of the land here, and the way it was used. As they passed each different business unit she was reminded of the charm bracelet Draco had given her this morning. Each charm truly was representative of the expanse of the Sandrelli family's endeavors. She began to feel a new respect for him and for the responsibility that sat so well on his shoulders.

Draco felt the familiar swell of pride as he showed Blair over the land that was as much a part of him as the blood running in his veins. It was always a pleasure to see the property through another's eyes, but this time it was even more important that Blair fully understand what it meant to be a Sandrelli. What it would mean to their son or daughter.

They were about halfway back toward the palazzo when Draco pulled off the road and drew the car up a private road leading through a massive olive grove.

"Would you like to stop for some lunch?" he asked, and was surprised to catch her stifling a yawn.

"Oh," she laughed, embarrassed, if the flush on her cheeks was anything to go by. "Yes, that would be lovely."

Draco took a right turn down a barely visible lane and drew the car to a halt under the trees.

"Cristiano packed a lunch for us when I told him we'd be out for the day. Just give me a minute and I will have it ready for you."

"Anything I can do to help?" Blair asked, swiveling her long legs out of the car and standing.

She slowly stretched out her back and lifted her arms above her head. Instantly a shock of desire pummeled through him like a bolt of electricity. Even with the new fullness her body now began to display, she sent every particle in his body into overdrive. She went still as she realized he was watching her.

"Is there something wrong?"

"No. Nothing is wrong. You look beautiful today. The setting suits you."

"Flatterer," she said, smiling, then and came across to him, taking the rubber-backed rug from his hands and shaking it out onto the ground in the sunshine.

"It's the truth," Draco replied. "I do not waste my time on lies."

"Yeah," Blair said, softly. "I had noticed that about you."

A tight smile pulled at his lips. *What else had she noticed about him,* he wondered.

He lifted the cooler from the trunk of the convertible and put it beside the rug. Blair was already sitting cross-legged on the blanket and had eagerly lifted the lid off the cooler and started to put the plates of food and containers of drink onto the rug, using the lid as a small table. Draco grabbed the small loaves of fresh bread Cristiano had baked early this morning and dropped down next to her.

They began to eat, Draco making the most of the setting to explain a little about the olive oil process in Tuscany. Blair had missed the harvest, which had taken place late autumn, the cooler valleys in the region demanding the harvest occur earlier than in other parts of the Mediterranean, and she was fascinated by his description. But before long she was yawning once more.

"I'm sorry, Blair, I didn't mean to exhaust you on your first day back here."

"It's not that. I've really enjoyed everything you've shown me today. Perhaps it is just a little jet lag still."

"So sleep."

"Here?" Blair waved her hand.

"Why not? We won't be disturbed. The sun is warm. Lie back and relax."

"I can't," she protested. "I don't sleep during the day. It's just so…"

"Decadent?" he asked, smiling. Yes, he'd bet she never let up during the day. But if she was going to do the best thing by his baby she would learn to slow down. "So be decadent for a change. Lie down and relax."

Blair did as he suggested.

"I bet I won't sleep."

"We will see. Just listen to the land. Let the sun caress your skin. And relax. Simple, really."

He watched as her eyelids fluttered closed and smiled again as he saw the tension in her body, as if she was coiled, ready to spring to the next activity. Eventually though, her breathing began to deepen, the muscles in her body slacken. He gave a small nod as she finally slept.

Draco stretched out beside her, taking care not to touch her, but instead watched her. Lying on her back as she was, it was easier to see the subtle changes the pregnancy had wrought on her body so far. The ever-so-slight fullness of her breasts, the tiny rounding of her lower belly, the new roundness to her cheeks which had always been so angular.

He liked the changes, liked what they did for her. Made her appear less untouchable. And just like that, he ached to touch her. To see her naked. To rediscover the intimacy they had shared. And, by the time Blair woke forty minutes later he knew exactly how their afternoon would progress.

Ten

As her eyes opened and she became aware of their surroundings, he leaned over and slanted his mouth across her. A teasing touch, but one that had the power to immediately wring a tiny moan of want from her. Her eyes darkened even more, until her pupils almost consumed the rich chocolate of her irises. A sigh drew past her lips and he breathed it in.

He bent his head to her again, this time taking his time to make love to her lips with his own, drawing her lower lip between his, sucking gently on the tender skin, stroking along its fullness with his tongue.

A shudder ran through him as Blair traced her tongue against his upper lip, in a mirror of what he was doing to her. He let go of her lip and deepened their kiss, hungry for more of her. He positioned himself over her body, holding himself up and away, but feeling her heat imprint through the layer of his clothing and against his skin.

Blair ran her hands up the cords of his arms and he reveled in her touch, in her enthusiasm as her lips met his again and again, as their tongues dueled and tangled together. This thing between them he could understand. It was as elemental and as vital as the energy of the land beneath them.

He supported his weight on one arm and with his other hand flicked open the top buttons of her dress, following the path of his fingers with his mouth. The fabric fell away, exposing the sheer white lace bra that cupped her breasts…breasts topped with hardened rosy peaks that begged for his caress. He lined the edge of her bra with his tongue, following the scalloped pattern with his utmost attention, then swooped against the tight bud pressing against the fine lace. He covered her nipple, still encased in material, with the heat and wetness of his mouth, and drew her into him.

Blair let out a low-pitched scream, her lower body arching to meet his as he grazed his teeth against the sensitive nub, over and over, before doing the same to its twin. Her hands fisted on his shoulders, squeezing tight. He'd bear the marks of her fingernails, he was certain, and the thought brought a smile to his lips.

Draco continued to unbutton her dress, finally baring her skimpy lace panties to view. He cupped her, pressing his palm against her, discovering her wetness, her heat. She squirmed against him and suddenly he could play with her no longer.

His plan to make slow, leisurely love to her would

have to wait until another time. A time, perhaps, when the very essence of her didn't drive him crazy with need. He ripped his shirt open sending buttons flying, desperate to feel the texture of her skin against his, then lowered his chest to contact hers. But there was still the barrier of her bra. He gently coaxed her up, sliding the straps of her sundress off her shoulders, and with deft fingers reached behind her to unsnap her bra.

Tiny goose bumps raised on her skin as he peeled it away.

"Are you certain you want this?" Draco asked, his voice as coarse as gravel. She could refuse him now, and he'd manage to hold back.

"I want this. I want...*you*."

Her words were his undoing. Blair knotted her fingers in his hair and dragged his face down to hers, and he groaned into her mouth as their skin touched, as her nipples pressed against his skin, as their warmth commingled and combined to ignite into a need for more.

Her hands slid down his back, squeezing and kneading his muscles, as if she couldn't get quite enough of him. Then they were at the waistband of his pants, unbuckling his belt with a dexterity he doubted he was still capable of, and sliding the zipper open, pushing the fabric down over his buttocks.

He flexed against her then. He could no longer hold himself back. To his eternal frustration, they each still bore a layer preventing him from reaching his goal. Draco drew up onto his knees and eased her panties off her. God, she was so beautiful, dappled with sunlight and shadows. A knot built up in his chest. He hesitated a moment longer, drinking in the sheer joy of her glory, then his desire asserted itself once more. Dispensing with his footwear and clothes took but a second.

Blair's legs fell apart as he knelt between them and positioned himself at her entrance.

"Tell me again that you're certain."

"Draco, please. I want this. I want this so much."

"Then I shall give you what you want," he growled.

He reached beneath her buttocks, angling her hips to meet his, then slowly—ever so slowly—allowed his length to penetrate her heat. As he did so, his eyes met hers and held them, the intimacy of their look lending a new poignancy to his possession of her body. Her eyes widened as he slid deeper, still taking his time, until he was buried within her.

Sweat beaded on his upper body as he fought to control the urge to plunder her. But he forced himself to hold back, to make this last as long as humanly possible.

Blair wrapped her legs around his hips, holding him to her, and rocking her pelvis gently against him. He shook with the effort of staying still, of concentrating on the sensation of her movements, of the clench and release of her inner muscles. Over and over, until he was nearly mindless with passion.

His hands gripped her hips and he surged back, before sliding home again. He'd never felt this way with another woman. Never experienced this sense of vulnerability or level of need before in his life. Instinct overtook reason, as he set up a rhythm calculated to drive them both to shattering completion.

His climax ripped through him just as he began to feel her body tighten and bow beneath his, and he gave himself over to the waves of pleasure that pulsed between them. His whole body shook as he lay down beside Blair, pulling her body up and over his so they could remain joined for just that moment longer. She sagged against him, her heart beating furiously against his chest, her breathing as ragged as his own.

This is life, he thought, as he smoothed his hand down her back and cupped her buttocks, pulling her tight against his body, as if they could stay like this forever. *This is living.* Anything else he'd done before today, before this moment, had merely been a rehearsal.

They dozed together in the sunshine, oblivious to all but the slowing of their breath, the even rhythm of their heartbeats, the languorous warmth enveloping them. But even so, a darkness hovered on the periphery of Draco's thoughts. It was Blair's determination to return to New Zealand once the baby was born.

No matter how perfect their physical union, she had no intention of staying, of creating a family with him. He'd had to threaten her precious restaurant before she would agree to come home with him. The reminder was sobering and took an edge off the pleasure that had saturated his senses.

Draco stirred, as uncomfortable now with his thoughts as he was with the hard ground beneath his back. He needed some distance from Blair, time to regroup his thoughts, remind himself what they had was lost.

"Come," he said softly, stroking her short, black hair with a steady hand. "We should think about heading back."

Blair groaned in protest but disentangled her limbs from his and slid off his body in a sensuous glide. She slipped her underwear back on and watched from under her lashes as Draco did the same. Her body hummed with satisfaction but her mind whirled with confusion.

Where did this leave them? Continuing their affair while he'd been staying in Auckland was one thing, but what had happened today changed things again. When Draco practically forced her here she would never have believed that within twenty-four hours of their arrival they'd be making love. And it had been lovemaking. He'd been so reverent, so tender with her. She knew at any time she could have called a halt to his attention, but she hadn't wanted to.

She wanted to make love with him again. The heightened sensitivity of her skin, her breasts—nearly every molecule in her body—had made the entire experience one she ached to repeat.

She dragged her creased sundress back on and found her head scarf, which had slipped off her hair at some stage during their lovemaking. Only when she was fully clothed could she meet Draco's eyes.

He had packed away the cooler and its contents into the back of the car, and now stood, tall and straight and endearingly handsome, looking into the distance. He turned and caught her eye. A small smile briefly twisted his lips, sending a jolt of desire through her again.

Blair scrambled to her feet and thrust them into her

sandals, then picked up the blanket to give it a shake and fold it back up again. Draco took the blanket from her, his fingers lingering a moment as they grazed hers.

"We will have to do this again, before it grows too warm."

"I'd like that," Blair answered, holding eye contact. Trying silently to tell Draco that she'd like that and more.

He'd tucked the tails of his shirt in at the waistband of his black trousers, but the absence of buttons meant closing the edges of the fabric was impossible. Her gaze was drawn to the smooth, golden planes of his chest. Without thinking, her tongue swept her lips.

"If you keep looking at me like that, we may not get home before dark," he said, with a note of humor in his voice.

But beneath the humor there was something else that Blair couldn't quite put her finger on. It was almost as if he'd created some mental distance between them. She felt the distance widen as he opened the car door for her and gestured for her to get in. Once she was seated he closed the door and walked around to his side of the vehicle.

Draco barely spoke on the journey home, and as they re-entered the palazzo he made his apologies, saying he had work to attend to. Blair watched him go.

"Draco?"

He hesitated and turned to face her, his face inscrutable. *"Si?"*

"Is something wrong?"

"Nothing is wrong. I will see you at dinner at eight. If

you need me for anything before then, you'll find my office extension on the list next to the phone in your room."

Blair nodded, but her mind latched on to his expectation that she'd spend the rest of her time in her room. Banished perhaps?

She certainly needed to shower and freshen up, but she'd be darned if she was going to spend the next few hours hemmed up in her room, no matter how beautiful it was. There was plenty she could explore before meeting Draco for dinner.

After Blair had showered and changed, she went back to the ground-floor level of the palazzo and headed in what she hoped would be the direction to the kitchen. If Cristiano was there preparing for their evening meal, she wanted to see if she could lend a hand. And if she couldn't help, maybe she could learn something that she could take back home with her.

Large glass-and-wooden doors led off a gallery and onto a wide, tiled patio, and the shine of late afternoon sun on water distracted her from her intentions to find the kitchen and instead led her outside. Topiaried orange trees and low box hedging defined a beautiful formal garden. A few yards away a large stone building squatted—an old stable by the look of it—its golden brick bathed in sunshine. Blair meandered along the pathways, intrigued by the building ahead.

As she got closer she could see inside the deep, arched windows. State-of-the-art gym equipment took possession of the carpeted floor. Here was something else she could fill her time with, she thought. She wondered if the large outdoor pool, further off to her right, was heated. Between the two, the gymnasium and the pool, at least she could keep her fitness up.

At home, being constantly on the run with the restaurant, she'd never had to worry about her fitness, but now—being virtually on holiday until the birth of the baby—she would have to keep "in shape" or she'd struggle to keep up her pace when she returned to work.

Eventually, Blair began to make her way back toward the palazzo, and with a soft exclamation of delight realized the herb garden she'd come through had led her to her original destination—the palazzo kitchen. A wide door stood open, and beyond it she identified hanging copper pots and a large black coal range.

"Hello?" she called from the door.

"Ms. Carson! It is a pleasure to see you again!"

Cristiano bustled across the terra cotta-tiled floor and clasped Blair exuberantly to his rotund figure.

"Cristiano, lovely to see you too. Please, call me Blair. I was wondering if I could help you with anything for tonight, I'll go mad if I don't have something to do."

The cook made a rude noise and flapped his hands toward the long wooden table that dominated the center of the kitchen.

"Sit down, sit down. You're not here to work. You can watch and learn instead," he answered with a wink.

Blair did as she was told and sank into one of the cane-bottomed wooden chairs at the table. Time passed quickly as Cristiano peppered Blair with questions about what she'd been doing since she left the palazzo back in February. She found it hard to believe that it had been less than three months since she was here, even harder to believe she was back.

She smiled at Cristiano's voluble sighs and laughter, as she told him about Carson's latest achievement and how the restaurant had grown from seventy-percent capacity to over a hundred-percent bookings, weeks in advance. But she itched to throw on an apron and work alongside him.

An idea sprang to mind and before she could think it through further Blair found the words spouting from her mouth.

"Cristiano, if I don't cook while I'm here I think I'll go crazy. Besides which, when I go back home I will need to bring something new again to the restaurant. Could I take some lessons from you? I know you often conduct demonstrations when tours come through to the palazzo. Would it be too much of an imposition if you coached me privately?"

Before the chef could reply, his eyes flew to one of the internal doorways.

"Blair, you aren't here to work."

Blair stood rapidly at the sound of Draco's voice. Small black spots swam before her eyes and she put a hand out to the back of her chair to steady herself a moment. When the spots receded Draco was at her side.

"Are you all right?" he asked.

"I'm fine, just got up a little too quickly, that's all," she brushed aside his concern. "And for what it's worth, I wouldn't think it work to have the chance to learn some new dishes from Cristiano."

Draco shot a glare at Cristiano before the other man

could speak. "We will discuss this later. For now we have other, more important matters to discuss. Can you come with me now or would you like to sit a while?"

"Draco, I'm not an invalid. I told you, I'm okay."

Where had the man who'd been such a tender lover this afternoon disappeared to? she wondered. The Draco she saw now was more like the overpowering man who'd bought her restaurant building out from under her so he could control where she lived and where she bore his child.

He said something in rapid Italian to Cristiano, who answered in kind before turning back to his work.

"Come with me," Draco said, offering Blair his arm.

Irritated by his high-handed attitude, she fell in step beside him, but refused to touch him. He led her to a salon that looked out over the formal garden she'd found near the gymnasium. Ripples of light from the swimming pool reflected through the deep-arched wood-and-glass doorways onto the high ornate ceiling. Blair felt as if, in many ways, she'd stepped into another world. Certainly she was out of her world.

She sat on the edge of a richly upholstered sofa and gestured to the gymnasium across the garden.

"I was thinking I could use the gym, would that be okay?"

"The gym?" He frowned a little.

"Yes, and the pool too, if it's warm enough. If I'm not doing anything else, I'd like to at least have some regular exercise."

"The pool is heated, but we will wait and see what

the doctor has to say first. I have made an appointment for you to see a specialist tomorrow."

"A specialist?" Blair shot to her feet. *How dare he go ahead making appointments without discussing things with her first?* "Whatever for? I'm fit as a horse. I've barely even been sick. Besides, I spent some time checking on the Internet before we left Auckland, and there's an extremely well-appointed birthing center not far from here," she protested.

"A birthing center?"

"Yes, run by midwives. It's a perfectly safe and professional environment for me to have the baby."

"Safe." Draco's jaw tightened, a sign she was rapidly identifying as a precursor to his controlled temper. He pushed a hand through his hair and drew in a deep breath before continuing. "And you know yourself to be in perfect health? You're absolutely certain there is nothing you do not know about that could happen to you or the baby?"

He was almost shouting. Blair looked at him in surprise. *Where the heck had that come from?* Whatever, she was less than impressed. Before she could say a word, though, he reached for her hand, turning it over and stroking his thumb across the soft skin at the indentation of her palm.

"I'm sorry, I didn't mean to shout. But I do insist that you see a specialist. This baby—you—deserve the very best of care. I do not want to take any risks or have any last-minute emergencies that could have been avoided."

Blair felt the tingle under her skin at his touch, heard the depth of feeling in his words. For whatever reason, Draco was privately terrified. While she had to admit to some fears of her own, it came as a surprise to realize that he too felt vulnerable.

Draco continued to stroke Blair's palm. Her expression left him in no doubt that she was surprised by his outburst. Perhaps he'd gone over the top just now, but she hadn't been through what he'd been through. And he had every intention of making certain she didn't. Whether she agreed or not.

Eleven

Her emotions played across her face—irritation followed by surprise, then something else. He didn't have to wait long to discover what that something else was.

"Fine. I'll agree to see your specialist, if, and only if, you agree to let me take lessons from Cristiano while I'm here. I won't get in his way or impede his work, but I need to keep fresh and learning new dishes to take back to Carson's when I leave."

He forced himself to stifle the surge of anger that rose as she talked about when she would leave. She'd been here just over a day, and it was as if she had begun the count down to her return to New Zealand. Still, what would it cost him to let her dabble in the kitchen? It would keep her exactly where he wanted her, and once her pregnancy was common knowledge among all the staff, not just the maid he'd assigned to her, she would be cosseted and prevented from overdoing things.

Draco found himself nodding in acquiescence.

"And the gym too. I want unrestricted access to the equipment. Restaurant work is more physically demanding than many people realize. I can't afford to get soft."

"If the specialist is in agreement, then yes, you can use the gym too. I will hire a trainer for you so we can ensure you and the baby work out safely."

He was rewarded with a sudden smile.

"There, that didn't hurt too much, did it?" she teased him. "Letting me have what I want?"

A pain settled in the region of his chest. Why could she not want what he wanted? Why did she persist in holding on to her ambitions for Carson's? Certainly it was easy to agree to her terms, provided she saw the specialist for the duration of the pregnancy. Her health, and that of the baby's, was paramount. But while a child could cope easily with one parent, two would be infinitely better. Was it selfish to want his son or daughter to know the love of a mother and father as he and Lorenzo had known love as they'd grown up? He did not think so.

Somewhere deep inside he'd hoped that in the next few months he could convince Blair to let go of Carson's, but if she insisted on continuing to train in her field, what chance did he have?

The remainder of the week fell into a gentle pattern. Blair and Draco would have breakfast together before he'd head away for business for the day, sometimes returning at lunchtime to show her around parts of the palazzo or further afield. She'd thoroughly enjoyed their trip to San Gimignano and had marveled over the remaining towers there and the variety of shops and vendors in the narrow streets.

Blair's mornings, with her specialist's blessing, were spent in the gymnasium. Gabbi, the trainer Draco had hired to oversee her fitness regime, spoke excellent English, and the two women enjoyed one another's company for the two hours they spent together each day. Her workout, if it could be called that, was neither taxing nor exhausting, and Blair felt better and stronger each day.

Her afternoons were spent with Cristiano—time she cherished, as the kitchen was probably the only place in the palazzo where she truly felt at home. She was slowly building up a new collection of recipes and techniques to show off at the restaurant, although with each day, her return to Auckland seemed further and further away.

As Draco spent most of the afternoon and into early evening in his office, or visiting the various business units on the property, Blair had taken to having a leisurely swim in the heated pool in the hour or two before their evening meal. The rhythm of her life was so different from what she was used to, and day by day she could feel herself winding down.

She and Draco had not made love again since that time in the olive grove. She wasn't sure whether she should be bothered by that or not. She did feel a sense of loss each night, however, when after dinner he saw her to her room before continuing farther down the hall to his own suite.

One morning Blair noticed Draco appeared to be uncharacteristically distracted at breakfast.

"I may have to go away in the next few days," he announced. "There are matters in our London office that require my urgent attention, and I cannot deal with them from here."

"When will you know?" Blair asked, fidgeting with her linen serviette. As strange as it felt spending time with Draco this past week or so, it would feel a whole lot worse being here on her own. "We'll have to postpone our trip to Livorno, I suppose."

"Yes, I'm sorry. I wish it could be different. I had hoped not to have to travel again during the months you are here."

There it was, a reminder that she wouldn't be here for long. Confusion bubbled through her mind. Why did it bother her so much? She wanted to leave. As idyllic as her time here was, as stunning as the surroundings were, she ached to be home and back at Carson's. But she'd agreed to stay here, to have her baby here. Then, and only then, could she return home.

Her baby? When had she started thinking of it in those terms? Blair laid a hand gently on the small swell of her belly, still barely noticeable through her clothing but making its presence known in the number of jeans and shorts she was now incapable of fastening. So far, she'd managed to keep her mind pretty much off the baby, to keep any thoughts purely based on the fact that it was Draco's child. But something had happened along the way. Suddenly it was her baby as well.

Could she do it when the time came? *Leave her child? Leave the man she loved?*

Blair's eyes shot up to the man seated across the table. *Loved? Oh, my God,* she thought, a faint tremor rippling through her body. *She did love him.*

Every cell in her body was attuned to him. Her days became better, brighter, when he was with her. Life before him compared to life now, was like the difference between tinned spaghetti and the deliciously delicate flavors of porcini mushrooms and date shell mussels in the Spaghetti Allo Scoglio Cristiano had shown her the day before.

And that in itself was a perfect example of how she felt. On the outside looking in on perfection, yet not permitted inside.

She ached to see him each morning and missed him each night when they parted. Somehow, sometime in their tumultuous relationship, attraction had deepened, had turned into something more. Or perhaps, she realized, she had loved him all along but had fought tooth and nail to deny her own feelings. After all, her experience with Rhys had led to disaster, both emotional and financial, and her father's views on life and love had long tainted her own—making her distrustful, careful not to commit to anyone fully. In hindsight, that had probably been what had driven Rhys into Alicia's arms, Blair realized. Could she dare to hope that with Draco things could be different?

It would mean taking a chance, the biggest risk she'd ever taken in her life. Was she capable of such a thing?

"Is something wrong?" Draco asked, bringing his cup of coffee to his lips.

Blair shook her head, she barely trusted herself to

speak. Since the day they'd made love, Draco had been withdrawn from her. Sure, he remained friendly, a perfect host in fact. But he'd withdrawn from her emotionally. Different from the man she'd spent time with here, and again back in Auckland. One throwaway remark, cast by her in anger and shock when he'd discovered the pregnancy, had hardened him and created a gulf between them she had to decide to bridge or forever leave as a yawning chasm. The afternoon after they'd arrived here he'd let down his guard around her, and for the space of a few hours they'd recreated the bond they had between them.

But then she'd somehow damaged that closeness and he'd withdrawn back behind the demands of his work. Granted, they were many and spanned the globe—but they'd lost something she hadn't even known they'd shared, until it was gone. The loss—now she acknowledged it—had a left a gaping darkness deep inside her.

"I'll see you this evening then," he said, settling the fine china of his cup back on its saucer and rising from his seat.

"You won't be back at lunchtime?"

"Unfortunately not. I have business in Firenze today, but I'll be back in time for dinner."

"Florence? Could I come with you? It wouldn't take me a moment to get ready." She'd love the opportunity to find herself some new clothes and to poke around the culinary shops.

"Perhaps next time. I'll be tied up in meetings all day and I have no wish for you to get lost on your own."

"Draco, I'm a big girl. I can look after myself for the day."

"I'd rather show you the city when we have time to really enjoy it, and I'd like to see it through your eyes when I take you there for your first time."

Blair's heart somersaulted in her chest when he smiled at her. She swallowed back the disappointment that flooded her as he left the room, the disappointment and the ridiculous sense of abandonment she suddenly felt. Today was no different than any other, she scolded herself. She'd get ready now for her session with Gabbi and then enjoy the rest of the day as she'd enjoyed every other so far. So what if she had to amuse herself for lunch before her lesson with Cristiano? As she'd said to Draco, she was a big girl now, and besides, she had an awful lot she needed to think about before she saw him again.

Blair completed another lap of the pool, relishing the smooth glide of the water along her skin. She was no further ahead in her ponderings than she'd been this morning, in fact her concentration had been so off all day that even Cristiano had begun to lose a little patience with her in the kitchen this afternoon. In the end, she'd withdrawn from his domain pleading tiredness, and had enjoyed an unaccustomed afternoon nap in the shade here by the pool. She'd woken feeling fuzzy in the head. A fuzziness that was dissipating with each stroke of her arms as she turned and swam another length.

Blair's hands bumped against the edge of the pool and she stood ready to pull herself up and onto the edge. Suddenly she realized she wasn't alone.

On a lounger at the poolside sat an impeccably groomed woman. Blair didn't have to look hard to reognize a family resemblance. If she wasn't mistaken, this was Draco's mother. The woman rose and walked with a graceful stride toward her, offering a hand to Blair to help her out of the pool.

"Here, my dear. Let me assist you."

"Thank you." Blair took her hand, wishing like crazy that she'd opted today to wear her full-piece swimsuit. The bikini she'd slipped on did little to hide the thickening of her waist, and the new fullness to her breasts made her old bikini top almost indecent.

She accepted the thick, white towel the woman handed to her and wrapped it protectively around her, but the assessing look in the other woman's eye proved she had missed nothing.

"You must be Blair," she said, with a gentle smile. "I am Sabina Sandrelli, Draco's mother."

"I'm sorry, I wasn't expecting anyone," Blair started.

"I should have called first, I know. But I grow tired of waiting for Draco to introduce us. It is as I expected. You are pregnant, are you not?"

Blair felt color rush to her face. "I…"

"Don't worry, I am happy for the news, although it would have been nicer to have been told by my son than to have confirmed it myself." Sabina leaned forward and gave Blair a pat on her arm. "Umberto, Draco's father, will also be pleased. He tried to talk me out of bringing us both here today, but Draco has had long enough to keep you to himself. It was past time for you to meet the family, such as we are left."

"Draco's father is here also?" Blair asked, her eyes darting around to see if he was here at the poolside.

Sabina smiled. "He's in the kitchen, no doubt driving Cristiano crazy picking from his pots and pans to see what's for dinner. I heard the company helicopter come in a short while ago. Why don't you run along and get dressed and we can welcome Draco home together."

Without waiting for a response Sabina walked away, her elegant cream trousers and matching jacket fluttering gently in the light breeze that chased around the poolside patio. Blair slowly sank into the lounger Sabina had been sitting on. Draco's mother—*wow, that was an experience.* Clearly the woman was used to taking charge—*like mother, like son,* she thought ruefully, and reached for the sarong-style wrap she'd brought down to the pool with her. She wrapped it around her and wished that for once she'd had the presence of mind to grab a robe or something that would cover her more efficiently.

By the time she'd quickly showered and dried herself off, she started to worry about what on earth she could wear tonight that still fit. From the quality of Sabina Sandrelli's clothing and the way she carried herself, Blair had no doubt that she would expect her to dress for dinner. She'd decided on a pair of wide-legged elastic-waist pants and a loose-fitting top, but when she went through to her room there were two boxes sitting on her bed, with a brief handwritten note from Draco.

"I thought of you when I saw these."

She lifted the top off the first box and parted the tissue wrapped around its contents. A sigh gushed past her lips as she lifted out an exquisite mint-green nightgown, so sheer as to almost be indecent. He'd thought of her when he'd seen this? Perhaps there was hope for her after all. The next layer revealed a matching peignoir. Blair held the gossamer-fine garments against her skin. She couldn't wait to wear them, but somehow she doubted that this would be the kind of thing that the elegant Sabina had been expecting.

Blair removed the top off the second box and pulled out a cobalt-blue gown. She held it against her and swirled in front of the mirror. The color did amazing things for her skin, she decided, and the design—a full skirt dropping from the wide Empire-style waistband—would be perfect not only now, but in the coming summer months too. She dressed quickly and slid her feet into high-heeled black pumps.

A knock at the door dragged her from the mirror where she'd been standing, admiring the fall of the gown.

"Ah, it looks even better on you than on the model," Draco said, coming into her room and closing the door.

Her eyes feasted on him. Dressed in a tailored, charcoal-gray suit, he was both formidable and undeniably sexy. Suddenly Blair felt self-conscious. She plucked at the fabric of dress.

"Thank you, it's beautiful," she said softly. "It's all lovely."

"I'm glad. I notice you haven't worn earrings since you've been here, yet your ears are pierced. I hope you don't mind, but I bought you these."

Draco withdrew a small jeweler's box from his jacket pocket and opened it. All the breath in Blair's lungs froze when she saw the platinum-set diamond ear studs there.

"May I?" Draco asked.

He put the box down on the table next to him, then

gently slipped one earring from its nest and removed the butterfly clasp off the back. His fingers brushed against Blair's neck, his touch setting a flame across her skin as he put first one earring in one lobe, then the other. He turned her to face the mirror.

Blair lifted a trembling hand to touch an earring. She'd never owned anything so valuable before. As she reviewed her reflection, she almost didn't recognize the woman who'd returned to the palazzo just over a week ago. There was a bloom to her skin that spoke of her increasing health, and the skin under her eyes was clear of the usual shadow of tiredness. In the gown and with these earrings she could almost fool herself into believing she belonged here amongst the sumptuous furnishings, at the side of the impeccably attired man reflected beside her. But she knew that was little more than a futile dream.

"Thank you, Draco, they're beautiful. But I can't accept such an expensive gift. Really."

Regret sliced through her as she spoke from her heart. No matter what her trappings, she'd still be Blair Carson, chef and restaurateur. That title, and Carson's, were what defined her. It was what she was, pure and simple.

"They are yours to do with what you wish, it makes no difference to me." The warm light that had been in his eyes dimmed a little. "Now, shall we join my parents downstairs?"

Blair had almost forgotten. Almost, but not quite. Butterflies danced nervously in her stomach.

"She knows, Draco. Your mother, she knows I'm pregnant. She guessed."

"I expected as much. Don't worry. It is not a problem."

Blair fervently hoped it wouldn't be, and that she wouldn't be put on the spot by Draco's parents over their relationship. Tonight promised to be awkward. Already, she was looking forward to its end.

Downstairs they joined Sabina and Umberto in the formal salon Blair had only glimpsed from the doorway in the past week.

"Ah, don't you look lovely," Draco's mother said, rising from her chair and crossing the room to take Blair by the hand. "Umberto, come meet Blair."

Draco's father was clearly a shadow of the man he'd once been, one side of his body clearly difficult to move and control. Once the introductions were completed, Sabina drew Blair to one side of the room, seating her by one of the tall, arched windows and taking the chair opposite.

"We can leave the men to their business. If they get it out of the way now, they won't disturb us with it over our meal," she said conspiratorially.

Blair just smiled. There was something about Sabina that made her feel inadequate. Nothing obvious, just a sensation. She was probably being ridiculous, but as Sabina gently prompted Blair for information about herself and her family, she felt as if she was sinking deeper and deeper in the other woman's estimation.

Technically, she supposed she should be the hostess in this situation, but she knew that Sabina had spent most of her married life here in the palazzo, only moving to a smaller villa on the property a couple of years ago. Her general air of command put Blair very much on the defensive—a position she didn't enjoy.

"Tell me, when is the baby due?" Sabina asked once she'd plumbed the depths of Blair's family tree. Something that hadn't taken very long.

"Not until the middle of November," Blair managed to say through stiff lips.

"Ah, a winter baby. The nursery here is well-insulated, so you will not have to concern yourself that he will be cold."

"There is a nursery?" Blair blurted out before she could think.

Of course there'd be a nursery here. Generations of Sandrellis had been born here so it made perfect sense the children would have had their own accommodation. A pang of concern struck her. Despite her agreement with Draco, she didn't want to leave her baby. The very thought now filled her with dread.

"Men!" Sabina rolled her eyes. "I cannot believe that Draco has not shown you the nursery. After dinner I will show it to you. Now, tell me more about yourself. How did you and my son meet?"

Sabina was a great listener, and before long Blair had told her not only about how they'd met but how Draco had come back into her life in New Zealand. The older woman was nodding with a smile on her face.

"That's my son. Never one to stand back and wait when he can just take what he wants. But despite that, he's a good boy."

Blair fought back a grin, it was hard to imagine that anyone could refer to Draco as a "boy." As far as she was concerned he was all man—and it made the current distance between them all the harder to bear. She missed the closeness they'd shared before he discovered the pregnancy. As Sabina waxed lyrical about her son's achievements, Blair gained a new insight into the complexities of the man she loved. It was clear he would do anything for his parents, and that despite the fact his father was no longer capable of being active in the Sandrelli's business affairs, he regularly consulted with him about business decisions.

"Of course, when Marcella died we were all devastated. Umberto and I are very happy he's found another so special."

Sabina's words made Blair sit upright. "Marcella?"

"Ah, I see Draco hasn't told you about her yet." Sabina's lips formed a moue of irritation and she sighed. "Well, now, since I've mentioned her name, I should probably put your curiosity to rest."

"I'm not—"

"My dear, don't worry. Curiosity is a good thing, and if you and my son are to be married, then you should know about his late fiancée."

Married? Before Blair could disabuse Draco's mother of the idea another word sank into her head. *Fiancée?*

"It was terribly sad, of course. Marcella was such a darling girl. No one knew about her heart defect."

"Had they…had they known each other long?"

Blair both wanted to know about this other woman and didn't. She knew she'd be found wanting if she was to be compared side-by-side with the woman he had loved enough to offer marriage.

"Oh yes, she was the daughter of old friends. We'd always hoped for a family alliance, but sadly, it wasn't meant to be." Sabina lapsed into silence for a moment before continuing. "It's why I wanted to see you for myself, you know. I suspected, when Draco told me you were living here, that you were more than just one of his passing flings. Then when I saw you, I knew you must be pregnant. I'm so glad he now has the chance to have the child he lost when Marcella passed away."

"She was pregnant?" A cold chill ran down Blair's back.

"Yes, she knew how important family was to Draco, especially after Lorenzo's accident. She didn't want to wait until after they were married to start their family. Of course her parents were horrified when she announced to us all that she was having Draco's baby, but they soon came to look forward to it as much as we did."

"You mentioned a heart problem. Did Marcella know?"

"Apparently so. She'd been warned not to have children, but I think she was scared she'd lose Draco if she didn't. She risked her life to have his baby. Sadly, the risk was too great. We lost them both. I thought Draco would go mad with grief."

Again Sabina lapsed into silence, but then drew in a deep breath and straightened her shoulders.

"But that's in the past, and now we have a new baby to look forward to. And a wedding!" She clapped her hands together. "Have you two set a date yet?"

"No, Mamma, we have not."

Both women wheeled around in their seats as Draco's voice interrupted them. He handed his mother a glass of white wine and Blair a fruit juice. Blair couldn't tell from his expression whether he'd overheard his mother's conversation. Draco speared her with a searching glance. Did he imagine for one minute that she'd told his mother they were engaged? Blair knew she had to put Sabina right.

"Actually, we're not engaged," she said, slightly breathless.

"Not engaged?" Sabina's perfect eyebrows shot toward her hairline and she directed a stern look at her son.

"No, Mamma," Draco confirmed in a voice that did not encourage further discussion on the topic.

His father shuffled over to join them and conversation turned to more general topics, but all evening and all through their meal Blair was plagued with questions racing around in her mind about his dead fiancée.

Suddenly, Draco's heavy-handed approach to her pregnancy began to make sense now. She had a deeper understanding of what this pregnancy meant to him, why his reaction had been so sudden and so severe when he'd found out about it, and why he was so determined she have the best care that money could buy. Not that it had saved poor Marcella, she thought grimly. She wondered what had driven the other woman to deliberately enter into a pregnancy, knowing it could take her life—take her from the very man she loved enough to want to spend the rest of her life with him.

For a moment, Blair allowed herself the luxury of envy of Marcella—of the fact that she had loved Draco and been loved in return. But then she felt ashamed. Jealous of a dead woman? That was taking herself to a new low indeed.

That Draco already loved their unborn baby Blair had no doubt; but she knew that love couldn't extend to her as well. It was ironic. The last time she'd believed herself in love with a man, her best friend had come between them. This time it was a baby and the memory of Marcella. How could she ever hope to compete with that?

At least she had Carson's. It was the one constant in her life and would be waiting for her when all this was over. She had to hold onto that thought. It was the only thing that would get her through all of this.

She wanted more than that, though. She wanted Draco. She wanted what he'd shared with Marcella, together with all the hopes and dreams for the future. The idea terrified her and exhilarated her at the same time. She fingered the charm bracelet she'd worn since the day he'd given it to her, and considered the earrings he'd put in her ears himself this evening. He wasn't totally uncaring of her. Maybe, just maybe, they could make it work.

It was late when Umberto and Sabina left to return to their villa and Blair let herself into her bedroom. During the tour of the nursery with Sabina, Blair had expressed surprise that, with the size of the palazzo, Draco's parents didn't keep a suite of rooms here. But Sabina had explained that all her married life she'd done what had been expected of her in the Sandrelli name. Now that Draco had taken over the reins from his father, it was time for them to truly be a couple and have their own home and their own dreams together. And besides, with his disabilities from a series of small strokes, Umberto was far more comfortable in their single-level dwelling.

Sabina's comments had struck a chord with Blair. Despite Sabina's hopes that the men would confine their business discussions to their predinner drinks, the dinner table had been dominated by Sandrelli affairs. She could understand why the other woman would have wanted some distance between work and home life, but it was her compassion and obvious love for her husband that struck a deeper chord.

It was clear to her that Sabina was very much still the lady of the palazzo. She'd given up all of this so her husband wouldn't need to struggle or rely on others for what independence he still held.

Again it occurred to Blair that Draco would have very little time for their baby, once it was born. She had to find some way to heal the rift between them and span their differences. She couldn't bear the idea that their child would be raised by a succession of nannies if she failed to convince Draco of her need to now be a part in their baby's life.

Blair may not have had her mother's love growing up, and her father had been focused on his work a lot of the time, but he'd been there for her one way or another. And she wanted to be there for the baby too.

Blair had to talk to Draco. Tonight, before her courage deserted her. She had to convince him to consider a future between them.

Carefully, she took off the blue dress Draco had bought her and placed it on a hanger, then she removed her underwear and slid the nearly translucent nightgown and peignoir on over skin that had suddenly become hypersensitive to the silky-soft texture of the garment. She tangled her fingers through her hair and pinched at cheeks that had suddenly paled.

That would have to do, she thought, and before she could change her mind, she let herself out the room and padded on bare feet down the hall to Draco's suite. Without hesitating, she rapped her knuckles on his door and, not even waiting for his reply, opened it and stepped inside.

Twelve

"Is there something wrong?"

Draco turned from the desk where he'd been standing, reading a sheet of paper. He placed the paper and the cut crystal tumbler he'd held in his hand on the glossy wooden surface of the desk and crossed the distance between them, concern pulling his eyebrows into a frown.

"No, I'm fine, I just wanted to talk to you a while. That's all."

Now that she was here, she suddenly felt nervous. She shouldn't have changed into the nightgown that was for sure. While it had seemed a good idea at the time, right now she felt as if she'd put herself on display, when what she wanted was Draco's total attention—and not in *that* way.

"The night wear looks lovely on you."

Appreciation gleamed in Draco's eyes, and Blair felt her body warm and stir under his gaze.

"Thank you," she said, her words a little breathless.

She averted her eyes and sat down on one of the comfortable, overstuffed couches in his sitting room and cleared her throat.

"Your mother spoke to me about a few things today," she started.

"I can imagine," Draco said with a smile. "My mother generally has much to say on every topic."

"She told me about Marcella." There, she'd said it. The other woman's name had slid off her tongue without so much as a hint of the envy she unrealistically bore his dead fiancée.

Draco's eyes narrowed into cold, emerald chips. "What, exactly, did my mother tell you?"

Maybe this was a mistake. Blair smoothed an imaginary wrinkle from her sleeve and drew in another breath before speaking.

"She told me you were engaged and that Marcella died while she was pregnant, before you could be married."

"And?"

Blair shot him a look. His expression gave nothing away. If he still bore any love for Marcella it wasn't evident on his features.

"I…I wondered if you could tell me about her. It might help me to understand a bit better."

"Understand?" Draco paced the floor in front of her. "What is to understand? My life with Marcella has nothing to do with you and me. Marcella loved me, we were engaged to be married, and yes, she was pregnant with my child when she died of a heart defect she'd neglected to inform me of. Had I known—"

Draco broke off and swore volubly in Italian. He stopped his pacing and came to a halt in front of Blair.

"Had you known?" she prompted, wishing she hadn't embarked on this conversation. To hear him talk of Marcella—to talk of love—could only flay her fragile heart. What the heck had she been thinking?

Draco sighed, a violent huff of air from his lungs that spoke volumes about his emotional frustration.

"Had I known, I would have been more careful. She would not have become pregnant. We would have married and grown old together. It would have been enough."

"Perhaps she didn't believe that. Perhaps she knew how important your family was to you. And with your brother gone, she felt she had no choice."

"Choice? She gave me no choice. She knew her weak heart would never sustain a pregnancy, yet she never shared that information with me at any time."

"I'm sorry, Draco. Losing her must have been hell for you."

"Hell for me and for my parents. They had been looking forward to the baby so much. After Lorenzo's death, a piece of them died too. Knowing Marcella was pregnant brought so much joy and anticipation to their lives. But that was destroyed when she died. Tell me, Blair, how is a man supposed to go on when the woman he loves holds such a truth from him, and by doing so takes not only her life but the life of his child?"

Words stuck in Blair's throat at the raw grief so evident in Draco's question.

"I was everything to Marcella. She was devoted to me, and it cost her life. Is that what you wanted to know? She would never have put work ahead of me and the baby, especially not the baby."

Blair's back stiffened. "Is that some sort of criticism of me?"

"Take it however you want to," Draco responded wearily. "But at least be honest with yourself. I know you could never love another person as much as Marcella loved me, or be as self-sacrificing, because you only have one priority in your life—your precious restaurant. But that doesn't matter. At least you are honest about it and you and I both know exactly where we stand. Besides, we both know that you have no intention of being a real mother to the child."

Blair jerked as if he'd slapped her.

"And tell me, Draco. Just when in your business schedule do you think you'll have time to be a *real* father? I barely see you. So, what kind of parent will you be? You're so quick to criticize my desire to have a successful career, but maybe you should look at yourself first."

She was shaking with reaction, as first fury, then something else coursed through her body. She didn't want to think about how she felt right now, but all that ran through her mind was the truth that he would never consider a long-term future with her. Her thoughts were backed up by his next words.

"My duty will always lie first and foremost with my family. Don't ever doubt that. I will be there for this baby—far more than you—so before you start flinging rocks at me you should check you are not standing in a glass house. You've made it clear that your career is worth more to you than a relationship with your child or with me. Even now, every day, you work toward your goal of returning to your kitchen."

Blair couldn't deny it. Every day she took lessons with Cristiano, but the past couple of days her enthusiasm for translating the recipes into the menu at Carson's had waned a little. In her nightly calls to her father, he'd gone to great lengths to say how he was coping brilliantly with the workload. In fact, she hadn't heard him sound as happy and fulfilled in a long time. It still concerned her that he hadn't yet appointed a new chef, but she consoled herself that it was only a matter of time.

"At least I have a goal," she responded staunchly, grasping at straws to bolster her flagging self-esteem. "I'm not solely allowing myself to be defined by the man I'm with or by our children."

Draco grew still, and Blair knew she'd gone too far.

"I pity you," Draco said through gritted teeth. "I pity you that you can lower yourself to insult a woman who was a saint in comparison to you. A woman who gave her life for what she thought *I* wanted. Remember yourself, Blair. You chose this course of events. You chose to be no more than the vessel that will bring security to the Sandrelli name and happiness to my family, rather than be a part of it. And when you have delivered on that promise you will go back to your restaurant and our lives will continue as they have for centuries."

Ice poured through Blair's veins. He couldn't have put it more bluntly. He and his family belonged here in a way she never could. They were a part of the land, a part of the people, a part of each other in a way she'd never known and never would. At least her baby would have that, be part of that.

She blinked back the tears that burned like embers against the back of her eyes. She'd been a fool to think she could come here and talk to Draco about a future together. It would never have worked anyway. She was probably just mushy-brained because of this pregnancy—wooed into the lifestyle and surroundings and dreams of what she could never have or be.

Summoning all the dignity she could muster, Blair rose from her seat. The soft folds of fabric of her nightgown and peignoir settled around her body like a lover's caress, and she shuddered to think that, if things could have been different between herself and Draco, he would no doubt have been removing the garments by now.

But instead of making plans for a new future she clung to every last shred of what she had left. She lifted her chin and met Draco's glittering gaze head on.

"Thank you for the reminder. You're right. Of course. To be honest, I can't wait for all this," she gestured to her belly "to be over so I can get back to my life."

She saw Draco's jaw clench, noticed the muscle working on the side of his face. She'd struck him a blow, but she'd struck one equally as deep to her own heart.

She'd fallen in love with a man who would always put others—their child, his family—ahead of her. Just for once in her life, she'd ached to be first in a man's life; but she could never hope to be that person with Draco.

She forced one foot in front of the other until she reached the door, then gripped the handle and turned it sharply. Every cell in her body urged her to stop, to turn and look back at Draco. To see if he showed one hint of softening toward her, one chance to change his mind about her and the baby. But men like Draco took their responsibilities too seriously to ever be that yielding.

With her back still to him she said bitterly, "I feel sorry for you, Draco. At least I'm moving on with my life. You? You're still locked in the past…"

She pulled the door closed behind her and staggered to her bedroom, and once inside, she ripped off the peignoir and nightgown, hearing the fabric shred as she sought to rid herself of its softness, its sensuality—its reminder of all it was and all she wasn't. With shaking hands she removed the diamond ear studs Draco had given her, and unsnapped the clasp on the charm bracelet. She needed none of it. They were trappings of someone else. Someone she could never be. She was Blair Carson, chef and restaurateur, and damned proud of it.

And that's what she kept reminding herself as she tugged on an old T-shirt and slid beneath the covers of her bed. She and her baby didn't need anyone or anything else. Ever. And certainly not Draco Sandrelli.

The next few days dragged out interminably for Blair. Draco was cool and distant, and on those rare occasions they crossed paths, it was painfully clear that every last vestige of the camaraderie they'd tentatively shared was wiped from their existence.

Blair threw herself into her lessons with new enthusiasm; she needed something—anything—to keep her focused on her future. The time she spent in the kitchen and scouring the markets with Cristiano became a salve to her wounded soul, so much so that, when she sensed a tiny flutter of movement in the pit of her stomach one morning, it took her completely by surprise. At only fifteen weeks pregnant, she knew it was early by most standards to sense any movement of the baby, and initially she shrugged the bubbling sensation off as something else. But when it happened again she couldn't be so sure.

She pressed a hand to her belly and waited for the sensation again, yet nothing happened. But later that night, as she settled into bed, she became aware of the sensation again. Tears pricked at her eyes as she stroked her hand against her belly again—suddenly, irrevocably, connecting with her baby in a way she'd never thought she'd experience. *How different things could have been if only she could share this with Draco,* she thought, as she let hot tears glide down her cheeks.

The next morning, she was surprised to see Draco in the kitchen waiting for her. They'd barely spoken more than a half dozen words to one another since the night his parents had come to dinner.

"I will be leaving for London as soon as the jet is ready," he informed her. "But I will be back in time to take you to the doctor for your sixteen-week checkup."

"It doesn't matter if you're not back yet. I can go on my own," Blair stated baldly. In fact, she'd prefer it if he didn't come, so strained had they been around one another lately.

"I said I will be back in time, and I will. I keep to my word, Blair. You'd do well to remember that."

Blair flung a look at Cristiano, who had his back to

them as he sprinkled sage into the omelet he was preparing for her breakfast, and blushed. She hated that Draco felt he could speak to her like this in front of one of his staff.

"Whatever." She shrugged. "It doesn't matter to me either way."

It was petty and childish, she knew, to have answered him back like that, but his stiff, overbearing manner with her made her feel like a child. She sat at the table and pushed her eggs around on her plate, tension drawing a tight line across the back of her shoulders until she felt him move away and out the room.

She heard the revving engine of his car as he sped away from the palazzo and down the private road that led to the airfield, and deep inside of her a part of her wept that they had come to this.

By the end of the week, Blair was becoming used to the occasional tiny flutter that signaled the baby's movement. Granted, the sensations were still slight, but for the first time in ages she didn't feel so alone. She'd heard nothing from Draco in the time he'd been gone. Given her parting comment to him, it was no great surprise. She'd expected to feel more relaxed at the palazzo without him here, but instead she felt like an intruder. As if she didn't belong. And she didn't, not really. As he'd so succinctly put it that awful night, she was here to deliver. And once she did, she'd be heading back home.

Blair had been in the kitchen garden, picking a little flat-leaf parsley to add to the potato croquettes she was experimenting with, when she heard the distant peal of the telephone. Since Draco had left, the phone had hardly rung at all, and for a moment she felt her heart leap with anticipation that he might be calling her. As she entered the kitchen, she eschewed the idea. He was no more likely to call her than he was about to drop on bended knee and ask her to stay.

She shook her head slightly, castigating herself for being a fool. But to be honest with herself, she was missing him terribly. It was hard to admit that she wanted him here, with her. She, who needed no one, apparently needed him a whole lot more than she'd ever realized.

"*Signorina!* The telephone. It is for you," one of the maids came rushing through to the kitchen, gesturing to the wall phone.

"Thank you." Blair smiled.

Butterflies took flight in her stomach. Was she wrong? Could it be Draco?

The voice at the other end of the phone soon put that thought out of her head.

"Ms. Carson, my name is Doctor Featherstone, from Auckland City Hospital. Your father has been admitted with a heart attack. He's stable at present, and we will need to operate. But he appears to be more concerned about his restaurant than his health. He refuses to consent to the surgery. Quite frankly, if we don't operate he won't be so lucky the next time around."

Blair's head swam. *A heart attack? Oh God, no!* She should never have left. She should have known he'd take on all the responsibility of the restaurant and refuse to hire another chef, or even share more of the workload with the sous chef. This was all her fault—and Draco's.

"Can I speak with him?" she managed through lips that felt numb.

"He's sedated at present, but I can pass a message on."

"Please, tell him not to worry about Carson's. I'll be on the next plane home. Tell him I'll take care of things. All he needs to do is get well again."

She took a few details from the doctor, then hung up the phone and sank against the wall. A heart attack. She closed her eyes and drew in a shuddering breath. She could have lost her father, and all because Draco insisted on her having his baby here in his beloved Tuscany. Well, as far as Blair was concerned, where the baby was born was neither here nor there anymore. Her father needed her, and, as Draco was so fond of pointing out to her, family came first.

Her duty to her father was no less than his to his family, celebrated history or not.

She pulled her ragged thoughts together and picked up the telephone to dial Information. She had to get home as quickly as possible. Her father's health, even his life, depended on it.

Thirteen

By the time Blair staggered up the stairs to the flat above the restaurant she was shattered. The irony of flying from Rome to London and then making a connecting flight via Hong Kong to Auckland wasn't lost on her. Briefly, she'd been in the same city as Draco and he hadn't even known it. With the number of time zones she'd been through, she felt as if she'd been traveling for days, even if it had only been something over thirty hours. But she was here. Home. Where she was needed and wanted.

It was nearing lunchtime, but all she wanted was to fall into bed and sleep. She made a quick call to the hospital and asked to be put through to her dad, but her call was intercepted by a nurse who told her he was resting comfortably. Blair left a brief message with the nurse for her father, disappointed she couldn't speak to him. She'd only be able to manage a few hours' sleep before she'd need to be on deck downstairs. Calling him again would have to wait until morning. But still, he'd know she was here and taking care of things, and now he could consent to the surgery that would keep him with her longer.

Aside from the weariness of her first day back, Blair fell back into the rhythm and routine of Carson's with a comfort and familiarity she'd always taken for granted. Her father had been scheduled for surgery later in the week and, all going well, he could expect a strong recovery—although he'd never be up to the strain of working at the pace required to keep Carson's at the peak of its popularity.

Two days later, at the end of her shift, Blair made her way upstairs and gratefully sank into the sagging sofa bed she didn't quite have the energy to pull out and climb into properly. She kicked off her shoes and wiggled her toes.

Despite some swelling in her feet and legs at the end of her shift, she was managing just fine with being back in a busy working kitchen. Although she was coping, it still felt as though something was missing for her. The thrill and excitement of the restaurant's hectic pace didn't fire her up and motivate her as much as it had done in the past.

She'd grown soft at the palazzo, she decided. But that didn't explain the ache in her heart, or the sense that something far more important in her world was missing. She told herself it was only to be expected. She was in love with a man who only saw her as some sort of broodmare, even if that situation was pretty much of her own making. It was no wonder she was a little deflated—okay, maybe a lot deflated. With the travel, followed by immersing herself straight back into work and the worry about her father's health, she was entitled to feel a little down.

She wondered if Draco had returned to the palazzo yet. She had no doubt he'd be livid when he discovered her gone. Maybe he'd even sell the restaurant building out from under her. Right now though, she couldn't care less. Her first priority was to her dad, and in making sure he got through his surgery with flying colors, and the only way to do that was to keep the restaurant humming.

Carson's maintained its five-star rating on the *Fine Dining* magazine site, but somehow the accolade seemed hollow. It was, after all, one person's opinion. Why had it been so important to her, when now it barely mattered at all? In all the years her father had run Carson's he'd strived for that rating, and during the time they worked together it had become their joint dream. Then, when her father had retired, Blair had assumed the goal as her own—pushing herself and her staff to greater heights to reach that ever-elusive award.

And what for? For something her father had wanted? For something that had ruled his life, determined his creativity? Measured the man and the chef he was? Even though their earlier years had been transient, he'd always been sought after. Was she so driven to be just like him that she'd lost sight of what she was—what she wanted?

All her years growing up, she'd craved the stability of a secure home and a steady income and she had that here with Carson's. Or did she? Blair had dared to hope for love, had dared to believe that she could blend her career with marriage, and maybe one day, a family.

Or maybe, she thought as she compared herself to her father's single state, she'd allowed her father's dreams and goals to set the course for her life at the expense of her own. She bent down and massaged her aching feet, wishing, not for the first time, that she had a partner to do this for her. No, someone more than a partner. More than she'd ever allowed Rhys to be. She wanted a soul mate. Someone without whom life was empty, someone with whom the stars shone that much brighter in the sky at night and the world was a brighter and happier place.

Blair shook her head at her fanciful thoughts and changed feet. The closest thing she'd have to a partner right now was her relationship with a foot spa that she was invariably too tired to lug out of the cupboard and set up to soothe her tired feet.

She wondered how she was going to cope as she grew bigger, especially with her father unable to return to work. The doctor, this morning, had been adamant. If, after his surgery, he couldn't pace himself to a few hours a day, then he had to stay away from the restaurant completely. Blair made a mental note to advertise in the national newspaper for someone to share her role at the restaurant. She'd hoped Phil would be up to speed by now to take the promotion, but he had a wife and a toddler, with another baby on the way, and he'd made it clear when she'd broached the subject with him that he was happy where he was while his family was still so young.

She'd envied his wife in that moment more than she'd

ever believed possible. She tried not to think about it, but right now it pressed heavily on the back of her mind. What would happen to her after the baby was born? She had no doubt that Draco would insist on full custody, and, to be totally honest, she couldn't maintain her work pace and be a parent as well. She was between a rock and a hard place, and neither of them were where she really wanted to be.

"What do you mean she is gone?" Draco thundered, striding through the salon at the palazzo. "Why did no one tell me of this?"

"Ms. Carson said not to concern you, *signore.*"

The poor maid who'd informed him of Blair's defection looked as if she was on the verge of tears.

Concern? She didn't want him to be concerned? How ironic when she had been on his mind every second of every day, and he'd been in a fool's paradise, imagining her here at the palazzo. Safe. Secure.

"When did she leave?" he asked, pitching his voice lower, softer.

"Last Friday, *signore.*"

"Thank you, Maria, and I'm sorry for shouting at you."

His apology earned him a watery smile and another liberal dose of guilt. It went a long way toward showing how upset he was that he'd lost control with one of his staff. Draco looked at his watch—it was midday. The time in New Zealand would be around ten in the evening. Hopefully a good time to get hold of Blair at the restaurant—because he knew without a single doubt that was where she'd be.

Two hours later Draco snapped his phone off for what felt like the hundredth time. So, Blair was too busy to come to the phone and talk to him, was she? He'd see about that. He'd been shocked to hear that her father was in the hospital awaiting bypass surgery, but he didn't see why both Carsons needed to work themselves into early graves. His instructions to Blair's father had been explicit. That the man had ignored them and that Blair was now putting herself and their baby's health in jeopardy was enough to make Draco see a violent shade of red.

Draco swiftly punched in the phone number of Blair's apartment and left a message on the answering machine that would leave her with no doubt of his intentions.

"We had an agreement, Blair. I will do whatever it takes to make sure you stop working until my baby is born. Be sure of it, and expect to see me very soon."

The next morning Draco readied himself for the long flight back to New Zealand. For the number of times he'd used the charter jet recently, he may as well invest in one for himself, he decided, as one of his staff zipped his suitcase closed and took it down to the waiting car.

He stopped in Blair's room on his way back downstairs. He hadn't set foot in here since the day he'd returned from Firenze—when he'd given her the earrings and the clothes. A trace of her fragrance lingered in the air and he inhaled it deeply.

He hadn't wanted to admit it, or even to believe it, but he'd missed Blair terribly during his time in London. It had been a physical ache, permeating his body and his mind. Not calling her had been difficult to deal with, but they'd left on such awkward terms—what could he have said on the phone that shouldn't be said face-to-face? Yes, he'd missed her all right. Enough to realize how wrongly he'd treated her the night she'd asked about Marcella.

Wrongly? Hell. He'd been cruel. Deliberately deflecting his pain, his loss—his shortcomings—onto Blair.

But talking about Marcella had been like ripping the scab off a wound. And through it all he'd still been forced to beat back the desire that raged through him every time Blair was in his orbit. She'd sat there in that delicious concoction of night wear, her skin glowing translucent through the sheer folds of material, looking nothing like the woman he'd promised to marry, yet everything like the woman he loved.

The realization had been as painful as it had been eye-opening.

He had never loved Marcella as much as he knew he now loved Blair. What he'd felt for her was a pale comparison to the emotions that ripped through him now. And that made him feel even more guilty, if that was humanly possible—even more responsible for Marcella's death. She'd been prepared to do anything for him, even risk her life for what he wanted, and how had he repaid her? By working all the hours that God sent him, by being a fleeting fiancé at the best of times. And yet, she'd stuck by him, loved him when he hadn't deserved so much as an ounce of the measure of her love.

He hadn't been the man Marcella deserved, and he hadn't protected her as he ought to have, but one thing was certain. He would protect Blair and their unborn child with every last breath in his body, and that began with getting her back here, back home under his roof—and this time within the secure circle of his arms and his love.

Convincing Blair her place was at his side was going to take some doing. Carson's was in her blood, of that he was now convinced. Yes, he could understand her needing to return home to be at her father's side after his heart attack, but from what he'd understood from his brief conversations with her staff at the restaurant, she was busy in the kitchen for nearly all the hours available to her. A brief visit to her father each morning on her way home from the markets hardly counted, in Draco's mind. She was there for the restaurant. She measured everything she was by that place, and somehow it was more daunting for Draco to know he was fighting for her against some*thing*, rather than someone.

He spied the jewelry she'd left behind on the dresser. That small gesture as telling as if she'd graffiti-sprayed it on the wall. She wanted no part of him. Well, it was time for her to reconsider.

It was nearly two in the morning when Draco's jet touched down at Auckland International Airport. As the plane taxied to the private air terminal he itched to disembark, chafing at the delay created by the requirements to go through customs and immigration, however efficiently it was conducted. His driver waited for him in the terminal building and stepped forward to take Draco's bag and lead him to the waiting limousine.

Draco drummed his fingers on his leg as they seemed to get every red light on George Bolt Memorial Drive, on their way to the motorway link that would lead them into the city. It was far too late to show up at the apartment and talk to Blair right now, but he had every intention of being there first thing in the morning—before she headed to the hospital to see her father, and before he was taken into surgery.

He rested his head briefly on the leather headrest, but started as his cell phone chirped in his breast pocket. He identified the number as that of his second in command here in New Zealand and flipped open the phone.

"Sandrelli." His voice was clipped and cool in the confines of the luxury vehicle, but what he heard next struck fear into his heart and changed the tone and pitch of his voice in a split second.

"A fire? At Carson's. When? Has anyone been hurt?"

As his questions were answered in succession, Draco felt as if a giant hand had reached out and squeezed his heart. If the fire started in the kitchen, would Blair have had warning as she slept upstairs in her tiny apartment? Then he heard the news he'd been dreading.

Casualties.

Fire fighters struggling to contain the blaze.

The bad news came in a succession of blows, but none of it told him the information he most dreaded.

"Blair Carson. Where is she?" he demanded, his voice cracking on her name.

"I don't have any news of her yet, I'm sorry."

Draco closed his phone with a shaking hand and redirected his driver to Ponsonby. He had to get there and see for himself if Blair was all right. He wouldn't allow himself to think of anything but seeing her safe and well, because right now the alternative was, quite frankly, too terrifying to even consider.

Access to the road where Carson's sat was closed by snaking fire hoses across the bitumen and the organized chaos of emergency vehicles and personnel. Two ambulances stood at the head of the road, one closing its doors and racing away from the scene, siren screaming. Before the limousine had even rolled to a halt, Draco was out the door and racing toward the restaurant.

His eyes were drawn in horrified fascination to the beast of fire that, even with the hoses trained upon it, continued to consume the restaurant with unequalled appetite. A police officer approached him.

"Excuse me, sir, you'll have to stand back."

"Blair Carson. Do you know where Blair Carson is?"

A loud boom suddenly shook the air and a ball of fire shot skyward. Firefighters continued to train their hoses on the fire, but Draco could see already it was only a matter of confining the flames to Carson's and protecting the neighboring buildings. For the restaurant itself there was no hope.

He caught the look of pity that swept across the officer's face, and Draco felt as if the bottom had just dropped out of his world.

"Please," he demanded, "tell me where she is. Tell me she's not still in there."

"I'll see what I can find out for you, sir, but please, you must stand back."

The officer gave Draco a gentle shove and he took a couple of steps back, silently praying as he'd never prayed before.

Fourteen

How long he stood there on the side of the road he didn't know, but a sudden movement near the back of the remaining ambulance caught his eye.

Blair! She was all right.

He covered the distance between them in a matter of seconds, reaching to take her into his arms and to confirm for himself that she was okay. Her face was smudged with soot, her clothes also, and the indentation of an oxygen mask on her face left him in no doubt she'd been in terrible danger not so very long ago.

Blair batted away at his hands as he sought to touch her. Shoving hard at him when he tried again to hold her.

"How could you?" she rasped, her voice raw and tears tracking pale lines down her face. "Was this what you meant when you said you'd make me stop working? Was it?"

She was hysterical with grief.

"Blair, no. How could you think such a thing? I would never do something like this to you. Never," he answered vehemently.

She started to cough, and a burly paramedic came up beside her to gently urge her back, to sit on the back step of the ambulance. He placed the oxygen mask once again over her nose and mouth and spoke quietly to her for a moment. When he straightened up again Draco stepped forward.

"Why is she still here? Surely, she should be in hospital. She's sixteen weeks pregnant. Shouldn't she be checked out?"

"Ms. Carson has refused to go to hospital for assessment. I'm keeping her on oxygen for now."

"Is it true, Blair? Have you refused to go to the hospital?"

Tears continued to streak down her cheeks. Draco squatted down in front of her, taking her hands.

"*Cara mia,* you must see a doctor."

"I can't," her voice was muffled by the mask. "I can't go until it's over."

Her eyes were riveted on the conflagration that had been her pride, her home and her very life. Draco understood her need to be here, even though his every instinct screamed at him to bundle her into the back of the ambulance and direct the crew to take her to the hospital immediately. It was some consolation that they would have done that very thing, had her life or that of the baby been in danger.

He sat down beside her on the wide step of the ambulance, hooking an arm around her shoulders and pulling her against his body. And he watched and waited.

As dawn broke across the water-washed street, Draco stirred. Satisfied with her breath sounds, the ambulance officers had left some time earlier and Draco had managed to coerce Blair into waiting in the limousine for the fire department to finish.

Under the cold, spreading light of sunrise, the true devastation of the building became clear. Charred beams hung at drunken angles from the ceiling, roofing iron in scorched twisted ribbons falling to what remained of the restaurant floor. The air was still thick with the stench of destruction, rancid with the fight of the flames against the firefighters' defense.

There would be an investigation, Draco had been told, and even though the building was insured and Blair had insurance to cover loss of business, the stark impact of the smoldering, sodden, charcoaled ruin that had been her livelihood rammed home with a finality that no one could deny.

Blair got out of the car as the fire department cordoned off the remnant of what had been her home and her life. Deep shudders rocked through her body. There was nothing left. Absolutely nothing. Her legs began to buckle beneath her, but strong arms closed around her, lifting her off her feet and carrying her back to the limousine.

She didn't even have the energy left to protest. What

was the point? Every last thing that had mattered to her was irrevocably burned to the ground.

Draco took her back to his apartment and she dragged in a breath of the sea air as they got out of the car. But still the scent of burning dreams remained lodged in her nostrils. She made no protest as he guided her to the elevator that sped them upstairs to his penthouse suite, and was docile as a baby as he stepped into the shower with her, both of them fully dressed, and began to peel away her clothes under the warm flow of water.

He tossed their wet clothes out of the shower door and they fell in a sooty, sodden mess she was too tired and broken to care about. With tender hands Draco shampooed her hair and rinsed it out before repeating the action, then with a soft cloth and liquid gel soap he gently washed her whole body until the water pooling around her feet ran clear.

Once she was clean, he switched off the water, dried her and dressed her in one of his oversize T-shirts, then slid her between the cool cotton sheets of his bed. Then and only then did Blair allow her mind to let go of the horrors of the night, and let sleep claim her.

Blair woke hours later to the drone of male voices from the other room. Her throat still felt raspy, and she gratefully reached for the bottle of water that Draco had no doubt placed at her bedside while she slept. As she let the deliciously clear liquid slide down her throat she heard Draco's voice.

"And the baby? The baby will be all right?"

He must have called a doctor. She listened as the

voices grew more distant, and then heard the faint sound of the front door being opened and closed.

She sank back against the sheets, feeling more lost and alone than she ever had in her entire life. The baby was still his primary concern. Yes, she knew it should be hers too, but just for once, the little girl buried deep inside her cried, why couldn't it be her?

She cast a blurry gaze over at the bedside alarm clock and sat upright when she saw how late it was. Her father's surgery would be over by now. She was supposed to have been with him before he went in, and then later when he was moved from recovery.

Blair swung her legs over the bed and put her feet on the floor, but before she could stand Draco was there at her side.

"Can I help you? Do you need the bathroom?"

She shook her head; she didn't need his solicitous behavior. It wasn't as if he truly cared about her, anyway.

"No," she said, her voice rougher than usual, "I need to get to the hospital to see my father. He'll be worried."

Draco gently pushed her back down onto the bed.

"Your father has come through his surgery with flying colors, you don't need to worry. And the surgeon explained to him why you couldn't be there. He's sleeping now, and I have one of my people there to let us know the minute he wakes. If you're up to it, I'll take you to see him myself."

Blair allowed him to lift her legs and tuck them back under the covers. Then, to her surprise, he sat down on the bed next to her.

"We can rebuild, you know," he said softly.

"Rebuild? The restaurant?"

An image flashed in her mind of the carnage the fire had wrought. It would take a hell of a lot to rebuild. A lot of money and time, neither of which she had at her disposal. But then again, she didn't own the building, did she? Draco did.

She remembered what she'd said to him as he'd arrived at the scene and had the grace to blush. She'd been overwrought. Why on earth would he do something as destructive as set fire to his own building? She wanted to apologize, but the words stuck in her throat.

"Yes, the restaurant. There are many photos of the exterior. We could rebuild, using recycled timbers wherever possible, and remain true to the original building. It will be better than before. We can ensure that it has all the charm of the old restaurant, but with all the convenience and functionality of a new one. What do you say?"

"Is that what you want to do?" she asked tentatively.

"How can it not be what I want, Blair, when it is so important to you?"

He took both her hands in his and lifted them to his mouth, the softness of his kisses to her knuckles making her feel cherished. The sensation was foreign to her. All her life she'd had to be responsible. To look out for herself. But this, this felt surprisingly like being looked after. Warmth bloomed deep inside her.

"Blair, I cannot explain to you how I felt when I arrived back in Auckland and heard of the fire. They said there were casualties, but I had no way of knowing if it was you they were talking about. That journey from the airport was the longest of my life. And then, when I got to the restaurant, I couldn't see you anywhere. To be honest, it was a relief to see you come at me with all your accusations."

"I'm sorry. I was upset, crazy. I should never have said those things to you."

Of course he'd been relieved to see her. After losing Marcella and their unborn babe, he would have been frantic about this child. Her heart ached with wanting even a fraction of that care to have been about her—just for herself.

"Don't apologize," Draco said, letting go of her hands and getting up to pace the room. "It is I who should apologize. I treated you as if I were some feudal overlord and you nothing more than one of my serfs. I saw you. I wanted you. It was that simple. And when I discovered you were pregnant with my baby, Blair, I was prepared to do anything and everything to keep you."

A glimmer of hope kindled to life in Blair's shadowed soul. Could he have feelings for her that went beyond the physical attraction that drew them together, that even now simmered beneath the surface?

"I was unfair to you when you asked about Marcella. To be honest, it pained me to talk about her. Not for the reasons I imagine you're thinking. Yes, I loved her. Who could not? But was I in love with her? Did my sun rise and set with her? Did I spend every waking moment of every day after I met her looking forward to when we could be together again?" He shook his head disparagingly, his face drawn into sharp lines of self-contempt. "No, I did not. And she deserved that. She deserved someone who would love her every second of every day. But instead, she loved me. And because she loved me she destroyed her life to give me what she believed would tie me to her in a way she never could. She allowed herself to become pregnant, knowing how dangerous that was, to make me love her more.

"I have lived with the guilt of knowing that for too long, Blair. I didn't believe I deserved to love or to be loved. Not after being so cavalier with Marcella's feelings, with her love for me.

"But then I met you, and instantly you brought light into my life. Suddenly I found reasons to work from home. You remember, *si?* When you first arrived at the palazzo with your tour, I was on my way out the building, but I saw you get off the tour bus and it was as if I was hit by lightning. I wanted you in that instant, and I still want you—even more than I did back then."

"How could I forget?" Blair answered in a whisper.

Listening to Draco talk about their first meeting was like reliving the exquisite sensation of being instantly desired all over again.

"I thought that I was being given another chance," Draco said, his voice so low she could barely hear him. "But you were only supposed to be with us that day. When you agreed to stay, I couldn't believe my luck. My world began to spin on a new axis, up until you left again. You were so focused on your work, on Carson's, that I couldn't begin to see how I could tempt you into staying with me forever. Instead, all I could see again was what my life could be like. It was as if fate was playing a cruel joke on me by giving me what I so justly deserved. I'd taken Marcella's love for me for granted and poured myself into my work, and suddenly, even though I didn't realize yet that what I felt for you was love, you did exactly the same to me."

Blair pressed her hand to her heart. If for one moment she'd known the depth of his feelings, could she believe she might have acted any differently? She had probably been so damaged by her father's slant on love and his own obsession with his work, not to mention her own painfully failed relationship with Rhys, that she would not have been open to a permanent overture from Draco. Not then.

"Draco, I think you're being too hard on yourself. How could Marcella not have loved you? You're strong, successful and so handsome it makes me ache deep inside whenever I see you. And your heart, your passion for all that you love, is like a drug that makes those around you want to be part of that love—part of you.

"You terrified me and drew me like a magnet at the same time. But because of you, I've learned an awful lot about myself that I wasn't prepared to see before. And I've learned to identify exactly what my greatest hopes and dreams are—"

"Carson's," Draco interrupted her sitting back down on the bed beside her. "I will rebuild it for you. I promise you Blair. If that's what it takes, I will do it for you."

Blair reached out and pressed her fingers to his lips. "No. That's not what I want. Sure, I thought Carson's was my be-all and end-all. What else did I have to dream and strive for in my life? No, I've learned that Carson's was my father's dream and his alone. I absorbed his hopes and dreams as my own when I had nothing else, exactly as he did when my mother left him. It was easier to pour all those feelings into work than into setting himself up for failure again with other relationships, and believe me—he failed often.

"I think seeing that example in my life showed me that you can have control of something in your life. What you do, if not what you feel. By default, his dreams became my own. But you know, deep down inside, I always wanted what he never had—a partner to stand by me, through anything and everything. Someone to love me and be loved by me in return. But it was so much easier not to take the risk. Loving hurts. It leaves you open and vulnerable and requires the utmost trust to commit to."

She leaned forward and pressed her lips against his.

"I don't want to be like my father and drive myself so hard for something that it eventually destroys my life, and I don't care if you don't rebuild Carson's. It doesn't matter to me, not anymore."

"What *does* matter to you?" Draco asked, as he tilted her chin so she looked him straight in the eye.

"You. You and our baby and the life we can have together, if you'll have me. Draco, I love you. I've fought it tooth and nail, but I can't deny it any longer."

"*Cara mia,* never doubt it. I love you more than I ever believed a man could love a woman. I don't ever want to lose you. You and only you are the love of my life—my reason for being—and, if you'll let me, I want to spend the rest of my life with you. Growing old with you. Loving you."

Blair wrapped her arms around Draco's neck and drew him closer to her. "Then start now," she said softly against his lips. "Show me."

Draco pushed aside the covers of the bed and gently coaxed her against the pillows. His fingers skimmed her arms, her legs, before gently lifting the hem of the T-shirt up and over, until she was exposed before him—naked, but for the cloak of love that swathed around them both.

Her body thrummed with desire, but this time it felt different, as if they were finally in perfect tune with one another. And when he removed his clothing and settled his body over hers she knew what made that difference. It was the absolute security of knowing she was safe with him, that she had offered him her heart and that she knew at a level that went soul-deep, that he would cherish and protect that gift for all of his days.

And as their bodies slowly began to move in unison, Blair knew that she would do the same for him.

Forever.

* * * * *